# HUNTING LUCILLE

## A Trials and Temptations Novel

### Dakotah Gumm

Mom

The original dedication said, "When you can't be in Europe, I'll bring Europe to you. Please skip the sex scenes."

Then you started pestering me about dedicating a book to you. And then you said you weren't reading this one. It's too late now, so you'll just have to settle for this dedication.

Sorry about your cow.

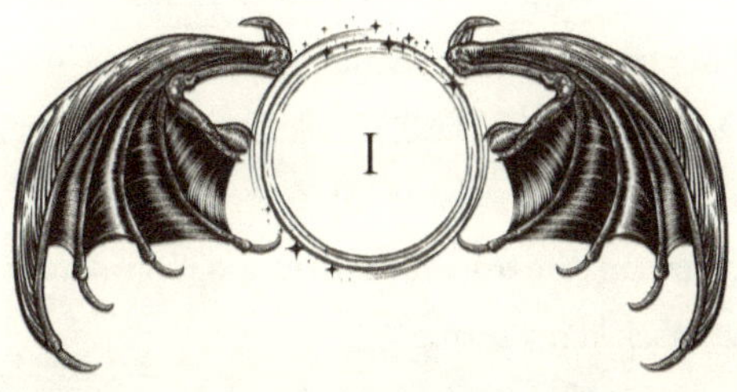



The bells of Notre Dame chimed midnight, drowning out the pounding of my feet on the cobblestones and the rush of blood in my ears. Henri stuck close behind me as we gained on the creature we hunted.

She raced toward the river, desperation on her face when she glanced back. If she thought the Seine would protect her from Les Gardiens, she was wrong. She was on our land now, and nothing could save her.

"Go left, Anne!" Henri shouted when we reached the river. We flanked her, backing her up against the riverbank. Her only options were to dive into the freezing water or fly away. The cold wouldn't bother her, but the water would slow her movement. Flying would be faster, but a wooden bolt through her wings would bring her down.

I drew my crossbow pistol and loaded a bolt. Across from me, Henri did the same. The vampire looked between us, fear written on her beautiful face. No matter which escape she chose, we had the upper hand.

Her eyes landed on something behind Henri, and the fear flickered out, replaced by a wicked smile. My blood ran cold. I turned to look, opening my mouth to cry out a warning—

The newcomer grabbed Henri's dark head in both his hands and snapped his neck.

A guttural scream tore from my throat, and I let my arrow fly at the vampire that attacked my partner.

My shot went wide past a target no longer there. He snarled as he dropped Henri's lifeless body to the ground and turned to me.

I reached for another bolt, but a splash in the river drew my attention. I glanced toward the first creature, the female. She was gone, disappeared into the depths of the Seine.

The second vampire still stood over Henri. Our eyes locked before he vanished into the night.

I rushed to my partner, collapsing to my knees.

"Please don't be dead," I whispered, though I knew it was foolish to hope. My fingers searched for a pulse on his neck. His skin was already cold, either from death or the frigid winter air. The bristles of his beard scratched my hand as I searched, praying to all the saints above that he's not dead.

My prayers went unanswered. Choking on the lump in my throat, I closed his eyes for him. He was dead, and his murderer had gotten away.

The rage in me burned cold. The beasts who had done this would pay, but it was too late to go after them now. They were gone, and it would take hours to pick up the trail again. By then it would be close to dawn, and they'd be holed up in whatever nest they'd claimed in our city.

Besides, I couldn't leave Henri lying here in the snow.

I couldn't carry him back to headquarters, either. He was too heavy, and we were too far out.

Bile rose in my throat. This was all wrong. Henri was the logical one. The planner. He'd know what to do. *Do I leave him and go for help? Stay and wait for someone to come looking?*

Closing my eyes, I counted to ten. The familiar action did little to calm me—nothing could make this situation better—but it cleared my mind enough that I could think. I dragged Henri's body into the shadows, then took off running for headquarters.

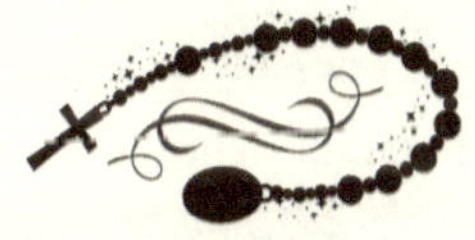

It was well past dawn when I finished debriefing. My eyes burning with unshed tears and exhaustion, I stared into the black depths of my coffee searching for answers.

"Go home," Captain Rodin said. I looked up to see her long red braid swinging as she cocked her head at me. "It's been a long night. If you want to take the next few days off—"

"No." The word came out harsher than I intended, but the captain didn't flinch. "No. I have to..." My throat tightened, and I swallowed. "Not until it's over."

She nodded briskly. She'd been one of Les Gardiens for twenty years, ever since she lost her husband to a vampire, and she'd been captain for half that time. In those years, she'd lost enough people to understand what I meant.

Justice first. Grief later.

I gave a weary salute and turned to leave, but she stopped me with a hand on my shoulder.

"I'm sorry," she said. "Henri was a good man."

He was the best, but I couldn't think about that. Couldn't think about his grin after telling an obnoxious joke, or about how he'd always buy us a bottle of brandy to share at the end of a case. Couldn't think about the woman he was courting and what she'd think when she learned he was dead. He'd planned to marry her; he'd told me just last week. He was just waiting for the right time to ask her.

I should have been the one to tell her he was dead, but that was against protocol. The identity of Les Gardiens was a closely-guarded secret. I couldn't even tell Lucy, my little sister and only remaining family, who Henri was to me. She knew Les Gardiens existed—there were some things I couldn't keep from her—but she didn't know where we headquartered or who I worked with.

I shrugged off the captain's hand. "I'll be back at sundown."

Back at home, the house was silent. Lucy was still asleep, and Emile, our father's cousin and our guardian, hadn't left his apartment behind the house yet.

I made myself a cup of coffee and sat down at the dining table. The warm silver cup soothed me, as did the rich, dark aroma of the drink.

How long would they wait to assign me a new partner? It had been years since a Gardien died—before I joined—so I didn't know the protocol. Would they expect me to adjust to someone new by the end of the week? The month? The thought set my teeth on edge. I trusted the other Gardiens, but no one could replace Henri. He was my other half. Not in a romantic sense, but the understanding between us was far more than friendship. More than family, even. I trusted him with my life.

Unfortunately, he'd also trusted me with his. And I'd failed him.

"Good morning." Lucy's cheerful greeting broke through the grim downward spiral of my thoughts. She took a seat across from me. "Long night?"

I blinked, turning my attention from my cup of coffee to my sister. "Very."

"Anything you want to talk about?"

I didn't want to talk about it with anyone, least of all with my innocent, sheltered sister. I'd done my best to keep the grim nature of my work from her. She knew what stalked the streets at night, the vampires and witches that lurked in the darkness. She knew that vampires killed our parents a decade ago, when she was still a child. But aside from Maman and Papa's deaths, none of that darkness touched Lucy. I planned to keep it that way.

"I'm fine," I said, taking a sip of my coffee.

"Hey." She reached across the table to take my hand. "I can handle it."

"I said I'm fine, Lucy!" Anger rose up, hot and fast. I snatched my hand away from hers and rose, shoving the chair backward.

"Okay!"

What happened last night wasn't Lucy's fault. I couldn't take my anger out on her. I closed my eyes and let out a long breath, counting silently to ten. Once my emotions were more under control, I opened my eyes again. "I need to get some sleep. I'll be working double shifts until this nest is eradicated. Just—" I shook my head. "Stay out of trouble."

Without waiting for her response, I headed upstairs. Exhaustion and grief reached down into my bones, but my mind buzzed with energy. *I should be out there hunting the monsters that killed my best friend.* But I'd be no use to anyone without a couple hours of sleep.

In my room, I stopped in front of the altar on my dresser and lit a candle, illuminating the small portraits of Maman and Papa, my silver crucifix, and the image of St. Joan of Arc.

I removed my coat and belt, hung them over the chair, and drew a lock of Henri's hair from my pocket. I'd cut the brown curl off at the station and tied it with a bit of string, a memento of my partner. I placed it on the altar, then opened the vial of holy water and dabbed a little onto my hand to cross to myself.

I went to my knees on the bedroom floor, taking the rosary from around my neck, and lost myself in prayer.

Nearly a half hour later, I'd finished the rosary, leaving my soul fractionally lighter. I looked up at the relief of Joan d'Arc, my patron saint. "Pray for him," I whispered. The only words I could think of, the only prayer I could pray. But she heard me anyway. She was a soldier, too. She understood what I couldn't say.

With a sigh, I doused the candle and collapsed in bed.

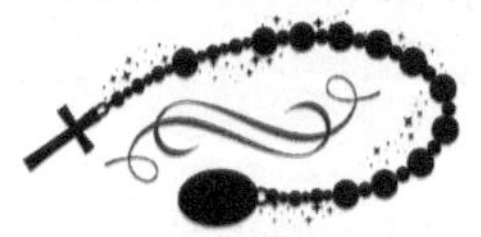

I woke after a few short hours of restless sleep. My wrinkled clothes reeked of dried sweat. Henri had always teased me about my lack of care for my appearance, just as I'd teased him for putting more effort into his than a woman.

A pang tightened my chest. He'd been meticulous about how he looked. Where I would gladly spend all day in trousers, Henri only wore casual clothes for work. If we went to breakfast after our shift, he took care to comb his hair and beard, wax his mustache, and put on a suit before we left. I rarely did more than wipe the sweat from my neck. Our odd pairing had attracted stares from everyone—though that could have been my appearance in general. The white patches on my gold-colored skin drew attention no matter who I was with. Henri had called them beauty marks. The doctors called them vitiligo. Whatever they were, coupled with my clothing, they drew far more attention than I was comfortable with.

I scrubbed my face, then brushed out my sand-colored hair and braided it. Dressed in a slightly fresher set of clothes, I hurried downstairs. It was already late afternoon, and I wanted to be at headquarters early.

Lucy was painting in the drawing room when I came in. A mess of green and white paint spotted her smooth skin as a bouquet of chrysanthemums took shape on the canvas in front of her.

"I'm sleeping at headquarters for the next few days," I said, buckling my belt around my waist. Checking to make sure all my weapons were in order, I slung my black wool coat around my shoulders. "I doubt I'll be home. You'll be okay?"

She nodded distractedly as she dipped her brush back into the paint. "Be safe."

"Love you."

Outside, a brisk wind had blown the clouds from the sky, and the cold muted the ever-present stench of the city. I stopped at the bakery on the corner and purchased a pain aux raisins, then hailed a cab. I didn't want to waste my energy on walking across the city. Not when there were monsters to catch tonight.

Captain Rodin met me at the door of the inconspicuous building that served as Les Gardiens' headquarters. "There was no need to rush in, Allard. They won't leave without you. You should rest."

"With all due respect, captain, I could say the same to you." *Has she slept at all?* Judging by the rings around her eyes, I doubted it.

She waved a hand in dismissal. "I won't be on the street tonight."

She wanted to be, though. I could see the light in her eyes, the need for vengeance that matched my own. One of her men was killed, and she wanted to be part of the team to take down the creatures responsible.

Which is why she wouldn't deny me that opportunity, even though protocol advised against it. Her rank prevented her from taking an active role in raids, but she'd do everything in her power to give us justice for Henri.

"How did the family take it?" I asked as we walked into the kitchen, where I put a pot of coffee on the stove and took two silver mugs from the cabinet. Henri's mug, a small, well-polished thing, stared down at me, the letter F he etched in the handle, for "Fontaine," marking his claim. My eyes burned at the sight.

*Don't cry,* I scolded myself. I didn't have time to sink into the well of grief. Henri deserved more than my tears.

"As well as you can expect." She took a seat at the table, propping her foot up on the opposite chair. "The official story is a robbery gone wrong. I sent Heroux and Dupont to notify them."

I nodded, my gaze fixed on the stove.

Her chair shifted behind me, legs squeaking against the floor. "How are you doing?"

"I'm—"

"The truth."

I turned to look at her. Her red hair had come loose from its braid, and the slight wrinkles around her brown eyes crinkled in concern.

The burning in my own eyes intensified as a lump formed in my throat. "I should have seen him coming."

"And Fontaine shouldn't have?" She leaned forward, hands clasped and brow knit together. "Even Les Gardiens can't see every eventuality, Allard. The only ones guilty for this are the fangs that killed him."

The whistling of the coffee pot cut into the tension between us, and I welcomed the distraction of pouring us each a steaming mug. Even if it wasn't my fault, Henri was gone, and I was here. Nothing the captain said could change that.

"I lost my first partner, too," she said.

My head jerked up. I hadn't known that.

She walked over and took her cup from me, dropping a lump of sugar into it. "She recruited me after my husband died. Trained me. About six months after I joined, we were sent as part of a team out to Versailles to track a nest that had settled near the palace."

I waited as she gathered her thoughts. Les Gardiens rarely took assignments out of the city; we just didn't have the manpower for it. In the ten years since I joined, I'd never been sent out.

When the captain spoke again, her voice was little more than a whisper. "There were twice as many fangs as we expected. They killed three of us before we could retreat—including my partner."

I sucked in a breath. "Did you get them?"

Closing her eyes, she leaned against the table. "We got them...but it didn't bring her back."

Getting the monsters that killed Henri wouldn't bring him back, either. "I'm not looking to resurrect him." The best thing for Henri now was a burial on sacred ground. I'd seen what happened when the dead rose, and it wasn't what I wanted for him. "Just to enact justice on the creatures that killed him."

She clapped me on the back. "So long as you remember who's really at fault, Allard."

As if I could forget, with Henri's death replaying in my mind every moment I closed my eyes. "I will."

"Grab a cot." She picked up her coffee and headed for the door. "Get another hour of rest before sunset. That's an order."

"Yes, Captain."

After an hour of restless tossing and turning on one of the rock-solid army cots we used for sleeping at headquarters, I rose and strapped on my belt. *Stake sharpened. Vial of holy water filled. Saint-Etienne freshly loaded with silver bullets. Full quiver of crossbow bolts.* I went through my pre-hunt checklist in my mind. Ready as I could be, despite the emptiness at my side. Henri and I always got ready together. Always went out together.

I grabbed my rosary and kissed the crucifix. *St. Joan, protect us.*

The captain's briefing began just before sunset. Over a hundred men and women—the entire force of Les Gardiens—crammed shoulder to shoulder in the room. No one made a sound as we waited for the captain to speak. Standing next to her, I clutched my rosary, the beads digging into my skin.

At last, she began. "As you know, we lost one of our own last night." Her voice came out clear and strong, filling the room. "Henri Fontaine was a good man, a devoted Gardien, serving with us for nearly a decade. He was killed in the line of duty, and he will be rewarded by God and the saints for his dedication to the destruction of the demons that plague our world."

The pain in her voice was evident; she felt the loss as deeply as anyone. I couldn't bear to look at her. I fixed my gaze on the wooden floor, tracing the cracks in the boards with my eyes.

"Fontaine has been released from duty, but we remain to take up his mantle. The fangs who did this will be held accountable." Her voice rose, causing my chest to swell, and I swallowed down the tears that threatened to blur my vision. "His death will not go unpunished, and we will not rest until every last demon has been turned to dust." She raised her fist in the air. *"Mors certa!"*

*"Hora incerta!"* we shouted in reply. *Death is certain. The hour is uncertain.*

Our rallying cry had never felt so poignant. Henri didn't know that last night would be the hour of his death, but it came for him anyway. He knew that risk, and still he took it.

I brought the rosary to my lips and kissed it again. *May we all be prepared for our deaths.*

Speech concluded, Captain Rodin turned to more pragmatic matters. "I want open communication tonight. We'll work in teams of four, with a heavy presence around Montmartre and around the entrances to the ossuaries."

She passed around a sketch of the fang Henri and I were chasing last night, along with a sketch of the one who killed him. I'd spent the early hours of the morning working with one of my fellow Gardiens to create the images, describing the fangs' faces to him until they looked back at me from the paper. The woman had sable hair, her lips scarlet with blood from the kill we'd interrupted. The other vampire, an olive-skinned man who looked to be near my twenty-seven years—though undoubtedly he was centuries older—had dark eyes that sparkled as if he knew some secret.

Looking at the images made my stomach turn.

Captain Rodin assigned everyone patrol routes. A few would stay at headquarters with her, ready to provide backup if needed. Gradually, the room emptied, leaving me alone with the captain.

"You can choose your patrol team," she said, tucking the remaining sketches into a file before fixing me with a stern gaze. "Don't go off half-cocked, Allard. We have protocols for a reason. I'm bending it for you by letting you go out tonight, but if you endanger yourself or another Gardien in this search, I'll bench you."

I had no intention of endangering anyone. I saluted. "I won't."

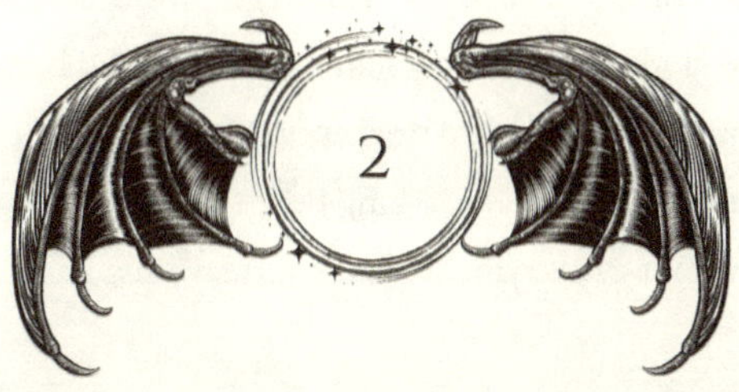

I joined the team patrolling the river where Henri was killed. They allowed me to take the lead, giving me deference and distance—almost too much deference. *If I have to hear one more person tell me how sorry they are, or use that infuriating voice intended for children or fragile people...*

Still. At least they followed my lead. Not that it did any good.

The fangs must have known we would be out in full force, because everything was quiet. Even the usual human-on-human crime was limited. It was as if the entire city knew a Gardien was dead, and they'd settled into tense silence, awaiting our response.

Without an outlet for my bloodlust, I led my team through the sludge of mud and snow along the river's edge, more from a need to move than from any actual hope of finding the fangs' trail. As expected, we found nothing but a few half-frozen vagrants huddled around an insufficient fire. We managed to convince a couple to abandon the fire in favor of a safer, warmer space to stay, and one of the team took them to a shelter where they could rent a bench for the night.

Finally, as the gray fingers of dawn crept across the sky, we trudged back toward headquarters. My breath fogged in the cold air, and my sweat-soaked clothes clung to my skin. I looked like I'd been rolling in the street, though the night had been entirely uneventful. If Henri saw me, he'd laugh and elbow me, asking how I could make such a mess of myself without even trying. He, of course, would still be perfectly coiffed.

If he was here.

As soon as I stepped inside the unobtrusive gray building that housed our headquarters, I knew none of the other teams had any success, either. The atmosphere was grim, muted. The smell of coffee and sweat suffused the air, along with the sound of quiet chatter. Some of my fellows made their way out of the building, eager to head home and find their own beds. Others sipped coffee as they talked, preparing for a long, tiring day of work at their regular jobs. A few, like me, would be staying at headquarters, snatching a few uncomfortable hours of sleep on a cot before heading out for another night on patrol.

I didn't bother joining any of the conversations. I made my way through the crowd and found the dark dormitory where cots lined the walls. Unlike the day before, I wasn't the only one in the room, and the sound of soft snores filled the room from the Gardiens who'd already found their beds.

I shucked off my coat and belt, shoved the belt beneath the bed, and slumped down. The thin blanket did little to warm me—one of the reasons Henri loathed sleeping at headquarters and did it as rarely as possible—so I used my coat for additional warmth. Exhaustion gripped me tight, the fruitless night of patrolling leaving me drained, and I drifted almost immediately into a dreamless sleep.

The smell of coffee woke me a few hours later, and after a quick visit to the toilet, where I wiped off the worst of yesterday's sweat and mud, I stumbled to the kitchen.

A few of the Gardiens who stayed at headquarters were already sitting around the table. Their conversation stalled when I entered the room, and though they tried to hide it, pity filled their expressions.

I ignored them, going straight to the pot of coffee on the stove. A plate of bread rested on the counter, and someone had cooked a pan of runny eggs. I filled a bowl, took a seat at the table, and started shoveling food into my mouth. The eggs were cool, but I barely tasted them, too focused on filling my rumbling stomach.

"How are you doing, Allard?"

I looked up to see Heroux, one of the more senior members of our order, watching me with sympathy and concern written across his face. His bulbous nose and large mustache twitched involuntarily, and I shoved a bite of bread into my mouth to keep from laughing. Henri did—used to do—the best impression of Heroux, scrunching up his nose and imitating the man's throaty voice.

"I'm fine," I said when I could speak without fear of laughing. The other two men at the table watched me, their expressions as concerned as Heroux's.

"I'm sorry to hear about Fontaine," he said.

Henri's voice filled my head. *I'm sorry to hear about Fontaine,* he mimicked, his nose twitching in time with the words.

"Thanks."

"If there's anything I can do, don't hesitate to ask."

*If there's anything I can do, don't hesitate to ask,* Henri twitched in my head.

If I didn't leave, I was going to spew my breakfast all over Heroux's mustached face. I shoveled the last of my eggs into my mouth, then grabbed my plate. Tossing it into the sink, I took my bread and coffee and muttered something about needing to see the captain before tonight's briefing.

Finally away from the sympathetic faces of Heroux and his companions, I found a quiet corner to sit with my coffee, still mercifully hot. I dunked my bread into it, took a bite, and closed my eyes.

*You're going to get me in trouble,* I thought to Henri. I imagined him sitting next to me, his laughter ringing in my ears at my narrow escape from the kitchen. His favorite thing to do was get me in trouble. He'd told me on more than one occasion that I had a stick up my ass and needed to remove it, and he'd done everything he could to force me to relax. Thanks to him, I'd spent many late mornings scrubbing toilets after a shift.

*Someone has to,* my imagined partner replied. *Otherwise you'll be stuck a dull, intractable bore for the rest of your life.*

*And what a tragedy that would be,* I deadpanned.

His laughter echoed through my head as the image of his face melted away. I leaned back against the wall and sighed. *Henri's right. I'm dull, intractable, boring. And what does following the rules get me? The death of my partner.*

Without Henri, I was useless. He'd been the better half of our partnership, the one who made things work when I was sure everything was lost. With him, everything had been an adventure. He'd always had a solution, some unique way of looking at things when I was stuck. He was the only reason I was any good at my job.

"Allard!"

The captain's voice cut through my morose reflections. I jerked upright, nearly dropping my coffee.

"Yes, captain?"

"Briefing starts in five." She jerked her head in the direction of the meeting room.

"I'll be there."

She raised a quizzical brow but walked away, leaving me alone with my coffee and my thoughts.

I couldn't trade places with Henri—and he'd be furious with me even if I could manage it—but I could still avenge him. And I would.

I switched teams tonight, joining one of the groups patrolling the tunnels beneath the city. This area was usually a hotbed for supernatural activity. Skeletons make up most of the walls, and the grim atmosphere drew the undead like moths to a flame.

Forneau, a stout man, walked on my right. He was new, untested against fangs, but I'd seen him train with the silver chains he carried. He was lethal, his size all from muscle. On my left walked Lavaud, Forneau's partner and polar opposite in every way. Lavaud was tall and slender, chatty where Forneau was silent. Not that anyone was talking tonight.

Behind us walked Bechard, a small, fashionable upper-class woman from. If Lucy and I had remained active in our parents' social circles after they died, we would have crossed paths with Bechard regularly. When not patrolling, she was the life of every party, hosting balls and salons, glittering at the opera, attending to her court of suitors.

I'd teased Henri endlessly that they were the perfect match, but he'd always insisted he couldn't be with a woman who spent more time on her appearance than he did on his own.

Bechard was no less deadly than the rest of us, though. Perhaps more so, because people tended to underestimate her. Next to her partner, the stern, mustached Heroux, she seemed like no threat. Next to most of us, she seemed like no threat. She looked completely out of place in her regulation black pants, ill at ease in anything but a dress. It was all an act.

The four of them—Lavaud, Bechard, Heroux, and Forneau—made a good team, but my chest ached as we descended into the ossuaries below the city. Henri was the team player, not me. He'd have broken the night's tension with a well-timed witty remark. He'd have made me laugh with a twitch of his nose as Heroux passed us, or flirted with Bechard and joked with the men until we all forgot our worries.

*Everything about this is wrong.*

Silence filled the tunnels. Even the ever-present scuffle of rats was missing. I shivered, holding tight to my lantern and pistol. Our footsteps echoed too loudly against the stones and bones that made up the walls. The frigid air soaked into our clothes, more a product of the grim surroundings than of the winter night.

We walked deeper into the ossuary, and my skin prickled. Something was nearby.

I gestured for my companions to be alert. Holding the lantern high, I looked around, waiting for some sign of the fang that had to be nearby. The lantern left us exposed, a beacon in the night. Anything approaching us would see us from a distance, but we had no other choice. Unlike the fangs, whose eyes adjusted to darkness with ease, we were dependent on the light.

We entered the main chamber of the ossuary. A sloped ceiling of human skulls stretched above us. I waved to the others to spread out around the enormous room.

A flash of movement caught my eye. I whirled around, pointing my pistol toward it, and came face to face with the fang who killed Henri.

"What a surprise," he murmured in a smooth voice. The faint accent hinted at an Italian heritage, as did the dark hair and olive skin.

He wasn't even trying to hide. It was too easy. "Stay back!" I barked at my companions. "Keep an eye out for his nest. There's at least one more." I wouldn't make the same mistake I did with Henri.

The fang smiled, tilting his head as he looked at me. "My children won't be joining us this evening. They're otherwise occupied."

Warning bells clanged in the back of my mind. *It's a trap.* He was there to draw our attention from something else.

There wasn't time to warn the other teams. I just had to pray St. Joan guided them to the other fangs and not to more diversions.

"Where are they?" I circled him, drawing his attention as my four companions closed in. He didn't hold a weapon, but that didn't matter. As I'd seen with Henri, his body was weapon enough. It would take all of us to take him down.

"Where are who?" He took a step backward, placing his back to the column in the center of the room so he could keep us all within his field of vision.

I crouched to set the lamp on the floor, not daring to turn my gaze from him. I'd need both hands free for this fight. "You know who. Where is the rest of your nest?"

The smile on his face grew even more predatory. Then he lunged for me.

I dodged left, coat whirling behind me as I spun away. Forneau jumped in, dual silver chains whipping through the air. They weren't lethal, but used properly, they'd do the job we needed. Until we knew how many there were, our orders were to capture, not kill.

One of the chains caught the fang around his wrist. He hissed as the silver blistered his skin, but he shook it off, surveying us for signs of weakness. His eyes fixed on Bechard.

Wrong choice.

He moved toward her in a blur, but she was almost as fast as a fang herself. She ducked under his arm and slashed at his belly with her dagger. He let out a vicious howl as blood oozed from the wound.

Forenau's chains wrapped around the fang's neck, forcing him to his knees. The vampire let out a deafening shriek, but the fight wasn't over. He tore the chains off and jumped to his feet as he lashed out at the nearest arm, Lavaud's.

A cracking sound set my teeth on edge. Lavaud's arm hung at an odd angle. He stumbled back, clutching it, and the fang turned his attention to the rest of us.

Heroux bowed his head and charged toward the fang. He grabbed him by the legs, and they tumbled to the ground in a tangle of limbs.

"Get in there!" I shouted at Forneau, but my words went unheard amid the growls and the snarls. Forneau stood dumbstruck as Heroux and the fang wrestled on the ground. Why had the captain sent an amateur out with us? Forneau was a liability. Bechard circled, waiting for an opening, but the fang gnashed his teeth dangerously near Heroux's neck.

*I won't risk another Gardien.*

I snatched the chains from Forneau and landed on my knees behind the fang's head. Grabbing his hair in one hand, I wrapped one chain around his neck and twisted it, pulling hard until he was forced to release Heroux.

Finally, the rest of them jumped into action. Heroux, breathing hard enough to make his mustache tremble, held tight to the fang's legs. Bechard and Forneau grabbed the arms and forced them behind the creature's back.

We bound his hands with Forneau's silver chains, then gagged him with rope soaked in holy water. He hissed as red welts formed where the rope and chains met his skin, but he couldn't break free.

Our orders were to take him in, not kill him, but the captain hadn't said anything about the condition he had to be in when he got there. I took my dagger from my belt and dragged it down his cheek, leaving a deep gouge in the skin. "That was for my partner."

He grinned through the rope as half-clotted blood oozed down his face.

I moved behind him and held my dagger against his back, near his kidney. "Move."

We marched through the city, me behind him, my comrades flanking him. I kept a wary eye out for the rest of his nest as we slowly made our way down back alleys and unoccupied streets, but no one stopped us. Finally, we reached headquarters.

Captain Rodin met us at the door. Her mouth formed a line, nostrils flaring, as she saw the fang chained between us.

"This is him?" She looked over his shoulder to me for confirmation.

I nodded. "The female wasn't there."

"We'll get her location out of him." She looked him over, fury written in her eyes. "And anyone else he might be hiding. Take him to the interrogation room."

As Heroux and Bechard dragged the fang off, the captain looked over the rest of us. "Lavaud, get that arm treated. Any other injuries?"

"None."

Relief painted her face. "Let the fang rot for the night. We'll deal with him in the morning."

The need to tear the fang apart burned up my insides, but the captain was right. He'd be more inclined to talk after a night wrapped in silver.

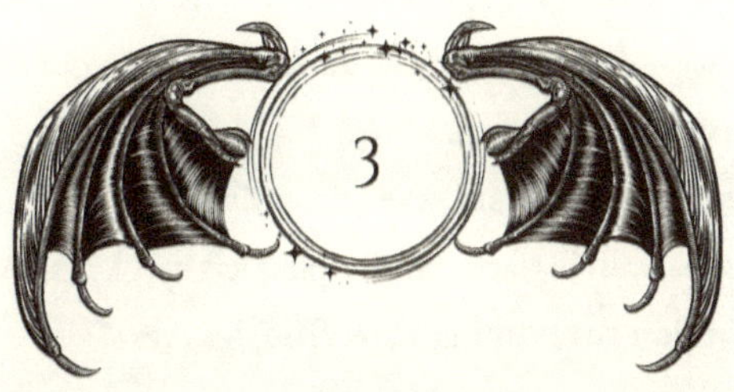

"Where are they staying?" The captain's voice cut through the stone room like a whip.

It had been five nights since we found the fang, but he still hadn't given us much. He'd told us the names of his offspring—two of them, a male and a female. Jakob and Leda. That was all the information we'd managed to pry from him.

Too absorbed in the interrogation even to leave headquarters, I'd spent all week there, snatching a few hours of sleep in between sessions. My whole life boiled down to wringing vengeance from the fang's body. The captain was keeping me at arm's length, not allowing me to touch the fang, but I'd stayed in the room for every session, watching as she beat and questioned him.

Bruises, cuts, and welts lined every inch of bare skin, but despite his injuries, I couldn't help feel that he was playing us. He'd fed us just enough to keep us interested, enough to tell us that he was holding things back. I hated him.

Captain Rodin's patience matched his own. She circled him, waiting for him to answer the question. One hand held a spritzer filled with holy water—hardly the most deadly weapon in our arsenal, but sufficient to cause discomfort.

When he remained silent, eyes drooping with exhaustion, she sprayed holy water in his face. The droplets left his olive skin pink, and he blinked to clear the burning water from his eyes.

"I'm losing patience, fang." Her voice remained steady through the lie. Her composure was endless. "Tell me where your nest is."

"I don't have a nest." He tilted his head, looking between us. I stood behind the captain, coffee forgotten in my hands. "Am I a bird?"

"He's playing us." I stalked forward, a few drops of my now-cold coffee sloshing out onto the filthy floor. "He needs more incentive."

Captain Rodin considered me. Dark circles ringed her eyes. Her red hair formed a cloud of frizz above her pale face. She looked as exhausted as I felt.

"Fine. Your turn." She sank into a chair and rested her elbows on her knees. "Just don't kill him."

Finally.

I took the dagger from my belt. No more playing around.

"Where are they?"

"Is the foreplay finally finished?" He smirked at me, the split in his lip cracking from the movement. "It's about—"

I drove the dagger into his stomach. Behind me, Captain Rodin dragged a breath in through her teeth.

His immortality meant the wound wouldn't kill him—the ways to kill a vampire were limited—but it still had to hurt like hell. He coughed, the sound almost like laughter. "You don't hold back, do you?"

I held my dagger, now coated in viscous blood, beneath his chin. "Where were your offspring staying?"

"In a hotel, obviously. We're not savages, unlike some." He grinned again, mouth bloodied as if he had just fed.

"Which one?" I snarled the words, sounding half-fang myself.

It was like he'd been waiting for me to ask. He told me everything I wanted to know. The name of the hotel, the cabarets and clubs they'd frequented while in the city. I didn't even have to touch him a second time.

When his well of words finally dried up, I wiped my blade clean on his shoulder. The captain and I stepped out into the hall.

"Well done." She clapped me on the shoulder. "I should have let you try him sooner."

I frowned, something niggling in the back of my mind. "I don't like it. There's something missing. It could be a trap."

"He held out for longer than I expected."

"But he gave in as soon as I touched him." Crossing my arms, I paced the hall. Why would he hold out for the captain and give in immediately to me? "It's like he was waiting for me."

Exhaustion dragged down her features as she considered it. "Maybe you should stay behind."

I opened my mouth to argue, but she held up a hand. "If you're right, if this fang has something on you, then sending you into the field is playing right into his hands. I'm not risking you."

"I have to go. This is personal."

"And that's exactly why you're not going. You're too close to this. If it's a trap, you won't be objective enough." She sighed, running a hand over her face. "You've barely slept since Fontaine died. You can take this one night off. Go home. Rest. If they're still in the city, we'll find them, and I'll send someone for you."

I turned, gritting my teeth. Orders were orders. A few hours of sleep, and then I could come back. I needed a fresh change of clothes, anyway. Henri would have dunked me in the Seine for the way I smelled.

"Oh, and Allard?"

I glanced back at her over my shoulder.

"You should go through Fontaine's effects before you head home. They're in the kitchen. Take what you want; we'll distribute the rest."

I ground my teeth so hard I could almost feel them cracking. Henri's belongings shouldn't be *distributed* among Les Gardiens. Nodding sharply, I left her alone in the hall.

The wooden crate of Henri's effects sat on the kitchen table, filled to the brim. His stakes, his revolver, his silver bullets. His crossbow pistol. The rosary and vial of holy water he carried. Even his coffee cup.

I could see it all from the doorway, but I couldn't bring myself to approach. *I'm not ready.*

*Man up, Allard.* I heard his voice in my head. *It's not going to bite you. It's just a bunch of weapons.*

*Weapons and hair pomade,* I thought back at him. Taking a deep breath, I sat down at the table and started pulling objects from the crate.

He'd left a scarf here. I pulled it out and wrapped it around my neck. The soft brown cashmere still smelled like him, pipe tobacco and fine cologne. The woman he'd been courting hated the smell of tobacco, he'd told me. Not that he'd planned to give it up for her. He'd just smoked at night, when she wasn't around.

*And how were you planning on keeping your habit once you were married?* I wondered as I pulled his pipe and case of tobacco from the crate.

Moving the wooden box of tobacco leaves revealed a small tin can, and I laughed out loud as I picked it up.

*Hair pomade? Really?*

The Henri in my head smoothed his already-perfect dark brown hair. *A gentleman should always be prepared.*

I shook my head, a melancholy amusement filling my chest. He really was more invested in his appearance than a woman. Tucking most of his belongings back into the crate, I kept the scarf around my neck and pocketed his pipe.

*The pipe? Really?* I heard him say.

*A reminder that even you had vices.*

*A habit hardly counts as a vice, but I take your point.* He gave me a cheeky grin. *Take care, Allard.*

My heart felt a tad lighter as I headed home. It was late, already midday, when I finally reached the house. Staggering upstairs in search of my bed, I didn't see Lucy anywhere. *She's probably at the library, or maybe studying paintings at the Louvre.* Neither would have been unusual. She spent all her time reading about exotic places or studying art. She'd covered half of the house in her own paintings and sketches, usually of foreign sights she'd read about.

I collapsed into bed, too exhausted to dwell on Lucy or the events of the past week. I was asleep before my head even hit the pillow.

When I woke, the house was dark. Strange. Lucy usually preferred to keep the house illuminated like daylight. It helped her see whatever her latest fascination was, whether that was painting the pyramids or reading about the Great Wall of China. She'd been begging me to have all the lights replaced with electric lighting so she didn't have to go through the trouble of finding matches all the time, but I didn't like the idea of inviting so many strangers into the house. Even the few servants we had made me uncomfortable. Inviting strangers into the house was what got our parents killed. I wouldn't make that same mistake.

*Lucy must be asleep,* I decided as I went downstairs to the kitchen. It was an odd time for her to sleep—usually she kept the same hours I did—but maybe with my absence, she'd been taking advantage of the daylight to enjoy the city.

I fumbled around the kitchen cupboards for the matches, not wanting to wake her. The gas lamp illuminated the large room, wasted on us now that Maman and Papa were gone. I never let the servants stay in the house long enough to use the kitchen properly, and Lucy and I could barely cook.

I might not have been able to cook, but I could make a cup of coffee. I put one on the stove and rummaged through the pantry in search of something to eat. A piece of crusty bread paired with dried fruits and a hunk of hard cheese; I placed it all on a silver plate—after I discovered the existence of vampires, I'd replaced all of our dishes with silver—poured myself a cup of fresh coffee, and went into the dining room.

The lamp I lit revealed a small white envelope in the center of the table. It was addressed to me, written in Lucy's chaotic handwriting.

Frowning, I picked it up and tore it open.

*Dearest Anne,*

*I hope you won't be angry with me when you find this letter. I wanted to tell you in person, but so much has happened in these past few weeks, I didn't know where to begin. I hardly know now, but he's waiting for me, so I suppose I just have to write it all out quickly.*

*I'm getting married.*

I stared at the paper, reading those three words again. Married? To whom? She'd never even had a suitor. I couldn't even recall hearing about someone who might *become* a suitor. Her social circle was limited to me, Emile, and...I thought for a moment, trying to remember anyone she'd mentioned meeting, but there wasn't anyone else. And surely Emile would have mentioned if Lucy met someone while out with him. Emile forgot things at times, but he wasn't *that* forgetful.

I read on.

*His name is Jakob Peller, and he rescued me from a robbery when I was late coming home one night.*

My heart stopped. Jakob. The fang told us one of his offspring was named Jakob.

No. It couldn't be the same. Lucy was smarter than that.

*I know what you're going to say. "You shouldn't have been out at night at all, Lucy! Then you wouldn't have needed rescuing." But I simply <u>had</u> to see the Villiers play. Anyway, I was walking home after the show, and I realized I was being followed. I ran into Jakob, who scared off whoever was following me. We talked for a while, and it was like fate. Like we were made for each other.*

*He walked me home after that. (Don't worry. I didn't invite him into the house that night.) We spent the next few weeks getting to know each other, and our love only grew from that first meeting. Last night he told me he has to leave the city suddenly, and he won't be able to return for many years.*

It had to be one of the fangs. One of the fangs had my sister. After the sire killed Henri, the whole nest would have planned to flee the city. They knew we'd be coming for them.

I sped through the rest of the letter, desperately searching for some hint of where Lucy was.

*Anne, I know you'll be hurt that I didn't tell you what was happening, but truly, I can't live without Jakob. I have to leave with him. Our wedding is tonight, and by the time you find this letter, I'll be on my way to my new home with my husband.*

*I must go now, but I'll write as soon as we arrive. I hope you can understand. Once you meet him, I know you'll love Jakob as I do.*

*All my love,*

*Lucille*

My stomach turned to lead. I flipped the paper over, searching for more, but there was no mention of where they were going. Not even so much as a date. How long had it been since they left? *They could be clear across the continent by now.*

*Lucy could be* dead *by now.*

This explained everything. The fang's interest in me, his confidence that his children left the city. *They took my sister.*

I didn't even bother to grab my coat in my rush out the door.

Captain Rodin looked up from her desk with raised brows when I burst into her office. "I thought I told you to take the night off, Allard."

"They have her. They have Lucy." I gasped the words out, barely able to breathe after running clear to headquarters.

She frowned. "Your sister? Who has her?"

I thrust the letter under her nose. "The nest that killed Henri. Now they're coming for me."

She scanned Lucy's words before looking up at me with pity written across her face. "I understand this is a shock after losing your partner, but—"

Snatching the letter back, I shoved it into my pocket. "She said his name was Jakob. That's the name the fang gave us. And this isn't like Lucy. She's a good girl. She wouldn't just *leave.*"

Her lips formed a line, disbelief evident in her eyes.

Lucy had always followed the restrictions I put in place to protect her from the fangs, even when she didn't agree with them. When I checked in at midnight every night, she was at home painting or reading a book. I knew she hated the smell of the purple garlic flowers that adorned all our windows, but she kept them watered anyway.

But if she followed the rules, why would she have been out the night she met this man?

I paced the office. "She's young. Impressionable. She went to see this play because she doesn't understand the dangers out there."

"Paris is a big city. Jakob isn't an unusual name. It could have been anybody." The captain set aside her work, giving me her full attention, despite the pile of papers on the desk in front of her. "It's easy to forget, in our line of work, that not all dangers are supernatural. I understand it's concerning that she's eloped with someone, but isn't it possible that he's just a normal human, taking advantage of a young girl? Or, to be optimistic, maybe they're both just young and naive."

"It's not just a coincidence," I insisted. "He has the same name. She met him weeks ago, right around the time we got word of the new nest in the city. And he had to leave now, just after Henri was killed?" I stopped in front of the desk and put both hands on it, leaning toward her. "I know my sister, captain. This isn't like her." Fanciful she might have been, but Lucy wouldn't disappear like this.

The captain let out a long, tired breath. "I'll question him. Go home and start the search there. Maybe one of her friends will know where she's gone." She turned back to her papers, a clear dismissal.

Lucy didn't have any friends. Since Maman and Papa died, she hadn't had anyone but me and our guardian Emile. And Emile's memory was too frail to be a reliable source on Lucy's whereabouts.

The only one with any information was trapped in our interrogation room, and I wasn't going to let the captain stand in my way.

With the door to the captain's office closed behind me, I looked up and down the hall. The building was silent. Almost everyone was out on patrol. The few that weren't hunting were trying to catch a brief bit of sleep.

Silently, I made my way to the interrogation room. The door opened at my touch, and I slipped inside. The fang sat in the middle of the room, bound hand and foot to the chair. He looked better than he did when I left. The captain must have given him a reprieve after the information he offered last night. Some of his cuts and bruises had healed with supernatural speed, and he looked almost rested.

"Where is she?" Rage shook my voice, but he just smiled at me.

"I'm sure I don't know what you're talking about."

"Don't lie to me." I placed the point of my dagger beneath his chin. *"Where is my sister?"*

He looked me over, unperturbed by the sharp point digging into his skin. "I've seen a lot of women since I arrived in Paris. You'll have to be more specific."

I drove the dagger in, just enough to draw blood. The foul substance oozed down my blade, reeking of sulfur.

"Her name is Lucy Allard. She has golden hair and a constant smile, and she doesn't know how to spot *demons.*" I spit the last word, forcing his chin up higher.

He bared his teeth at me. "Ah, dear Lucille. I remember her."

My blood ran cold.

"So young. So trusting." His voice took on a lilting tone. "She's lucky Jakob got to her first. Such a tempting little morsel. I wouldn't have been able to restrain myself."

"What happened?" I demanded.

He leaned back in the chair as much as the chains allowed, completely at ease. "I couldn't say. We went our separate ways after the wedding."

*She's still alive. She has to be.* "Where would he take her?"

"Allard!" The captain's voice, sharp and cold, interrupted my interrogation.

"Captain!" I turned to her, dropping my blood-coated knife to my side. "He knows where Lucy is. He knows they took her."

"I told you to leave him to us." She circled around, coming to a stop between me and the fang. "You're too close to this case."

"Of course I'm close to it!" I threw my hands in the air, narrowly missing her with the tip of my blade. "They killed my partner and took my sister."

She sighed, taking me by the arm and leading me out of the room. I followed reluctantly with a glance back at the fang. He sat comfortably in his chair, wearing a smug grin.

"I understand how you're feeling," she said once we left the interrogation room. "What you've been through is more than anyone should have to face. But too much emotion breeds sloppiness."

"And too little breeds sloth." I tossed my knife onto a small corner table and crossed my arms. "We don't have time to waste. That monster could be killing Lucy at this very moment."

"I won't risk more of my soldiers on a half-formed rescue attempt, Allard. We've been through too much this week already."

"I'm not asking you for that. Just let me get the answers I need. I'll go myself." I didn't need backup for this. I'd fight the legions of hell barehanded if it meant I could save my sister.

"No."

"But I—"

She cut me off. "You'll stay in Paris until you're given leave, and you'll stay away from the prisoner." Her expression brooked no refusal. "Go home, Allard. That's an order. I'll send someone for you once we get answers."

Fuming, I watched her walk back down the hall toward the interrogation room. Lucy didn't have that much time. I couldn't risk losing her just because the captain was too afraid to act.

*She won't leave the fang alone for the rest of the night, though.* Henri's voice appeared in my head. *What are you going to do?*

*I'm going to get my sister back. Whatever it takes.* I'd have to wait until midday, when the captain would be sleeping and headquarters nearly empty. Then I could get my answers from the fang.

Henri's face materializes in my mind. *This is more than casual flaunting of the rules, Allard. This will mean the end of your career with Les Gardiens.*

*I won't lose another family member to those brutes,* I told him. I'd joined to protect Lucy. If I couldn't do that anymore, there was no point in me staying.

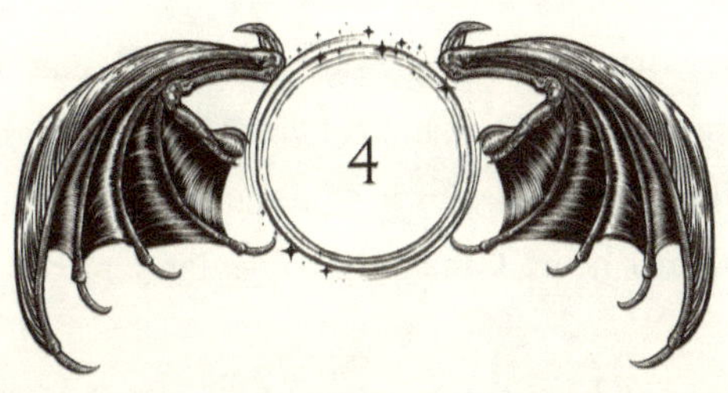

4

I returned to headquarters late the next morning. The building was as empty as I'd ever seen it; even the captain seemed to have gone home for the day.

I found Forneau, the sole occupant, sitting outside the interrogation room. A book laid open on his lap, but he wasn't reading. His nostrils flared with gentle snores, head tilted back .

He jerked upright as I approached.

"Morning, Forneau."

Rubbing the sleep from his eyes, he stood. *"Mademoiselle* Allard. Is there something I can do for you?"

"The captain sent me to be your replacement." I shrugged, tucking my hands into my pockets. "She figured you'd need the rest after a night out on patrol."

He shifted his feet, not meeting my eye. "Meaning no offense, but Captain Rodin specifically said you weren't to have access to the prisoner."

*Merde.* I'd hoped she'd overlooked that. I offered him a sheepish grin. "Sorry. I just need a few minutes with him."

"I can't do that. Orders." Genuine sympathy filled his face.

"No. I understand. Thanks anyway." Luckily, I'd come prepared. I made a show of turning away and sighing. As I started to walk down the hall, I paused and turned back. "I'm going to have a cup of coffee before I head back home. Can I get you one? I'm sure it's been a long morning."

He furrowed his brow for a moment, then nodded. "I'd like that."

In the kitchen, I brewed a strong pot, then arranged a tray with two cups, pouring liberal amounts of milk and sugar into Forneau's. Once it was finished, I added a few drops of chloral hydrate, a drug Emile took to help him sleep. I'd snatched the bottle from his apartment while he was out at the market. I was hoping the strong, over-sugared coffee would mask the taste of the bitter liquid.

Forneau accepted the cup without suspicion, and I tried my best not to watch him as we sat in silence in the hall, drinking our coffee.

I finished mine before the drug in Forneau's took effect, so I stood, glancing at the door to the interrogation room. "You're sure I can't talk to the fang for just a minute? You can be in there the whole time."

"I'm sorry." He looked sorry, too.

Guilt bubbled up in my chest, but I pushed it down. *It's him or Lucy.* No contest.

The smile I gave him didn't reach my eyes, but he didn't seem to notice. He turned back to his book, eyes already growing droopy. I walked at an unhurried pace out of the hallway and waited outside for him to fall asleep.

Twenty minutes later, I made my way back down the hall and found him unconscious. He'd slumped out of his chair onto the floor, and the tilt of his neck was going to leave him sore for days. I cringed, but I didn't stop to move him. I didn't know how long the drug would last or how deep he would sleep, and someone else could come at any time. I needed to get my answers and get out.

Electric light filled the interrogation room. They were a torture in themselves, meant to drive the fang insane from overstimulation.

It didn't seem to be working.

"I wondered when you'd be back. We were having such a pleasant time together, and then you left. What happened? Was your captain afraid I was getting to you?"

I didn't answer him. He was trying to get a reaction out of me, and I didn't have time for that.

I opened the giant wooden cabinet in the corner and pulled out a few things, placing them on the table in front of the fang with deliberate slowness. Torture was an art, one Captain Rodin didn't seem to know. She could inflict pain, but the real torment came from within the recipient's own mind.

"I'm sure you'll recognize some of these." I trailed my finger along the table. "Holy water. Garlic. Sacramental wine." The captain had used all of them on him during the past week. I picked up one she hadn't tried yet, a brown glass bottle, and twisted open the top. "Others might be less familiar. Have you heard of colloidal silver?"

"I'm afraid I haven't had the pleasure."

I took some of the liquid out with a dropper. "You're familiar with the effects of silver on a fang's body, but have you ever consumed it? Felt it burning you from the inside out?"

His face settled into a mocking grin. "An intriguing concept, but I'm more of a traditionalist myself. A silver bullet does the same work more efficiently."

Efficiency wasn't my goal, and he knew it. I didn't have to kill him to make the rest of his existence miserable, and I didn't intend to give him the mercy of a swift death. I needed answers. However I could drag them out of him, I would.

"Tell me what I want to know, and I'll give you that bullet. Where did he take my sister?"

He was silent, so I reached for a contraption on the table, a metal ring attached to leather straps.

He fought me when I approached, jerking his head back and forth and gnashing his teeth. Normally, this would have been a two person job, but I didn't have that luxury.

A drop of the colloidal silver on his lips caused him to open his mouth enough for me to slip the gag between his teeth. I buckled it before he could react.

He glared at me, nostrils flaring, but the ring held his mouth open wide. "Tap your foot when you're ready to answer my questions," I said. Then I poured several drops of the liquid silver down his throat.

Horrific gurgling sounds emanated from him as he thrashed against his bindings. What little silver spilled out over his chin left a trail of blistered red skin in its wake. He refused to swallow, the liquid settling in the back of his throat, but I forced his head back by his fine black hair and held it there until he coughed, spewing drops into the air.

"Where is my sister?" I demanded.

The flames in his eyes were hot enough to melt the chains binding him, but he didn't move, didn't make a sound beyond the coughs trying to expel silver from his throat and lungs.

I'd expected resistance, so his response didn't surprise me. I dribbled some more silver down his throat, waiting for him to choke on it again before repeating my query.

After several unsuccessful rounds of colloidal silver, I switched tactics. Too much of the same form of torture could desensitize him, which would do me no good.

Stoppering the bottle, I set it aside, then dragged the fang's chair toward a low trough of holy water in the corner. He recognized it; it was one of the tactics the captain had used when he first came in. A hint of fear lurked behind his eyes as he looked at the water.

Special bolts near the base of the trough locked the chair in place. I tilted his chair backward until he was almost upside down, his head just inches above the water.

"Where did he take her?"

I gave him a moment to consider the question, to make a sound through the gag or tap his foot to indicate his surrender. When he didn't reply, I turned a crank next to the chair. His head lowered into the trough, a hiss of steam going up as the holy water hit his skin.

He thrashed, splashing water over the sides. When I felt he'd been submerged long enough, I turned the crank back, drawing him out of the water. Droplets clung to his skin, which swelled red from the contact with something sanctified.

"Where did they go?"

His nostrils flared, eyes wild with rage, but he didn't even attempt to answer me. I dunked him again, and again, and again, until my arm ached from twisting the crank.

My desperation grew with each passing minute. I was getting nowhere. Forneau could wake. The captain could return, or one of the other Gardiens. *And how far could the monster have taken her by now?* He'd had plenty of time to kill her.

No. She wasn't dead. He wouldn't have spent so much time grooming her—right under my nose!—if he'd meant to kill her as soon as they left the city.

Unless he'd planned to transform her.

The thought stopped my heart. I'd thought Lucy's death would be the worst thing that could happen to her, but I hadn't even considered that he might condemn her to the damnation of a living death.

Every fiber in my body screamed to beat the fang senseless, to drag the answers from him. But I couldn't allow my emotions to rule right now. The fang was too old for brute force to motivate him. I had to take something from him. I had to think logically.

Amid the sounds of his raspy coughs, I walked to the cabinet in the corner and flung it open. Devices, both ancient and modern, filled it, all designed for killing and torturing fangs. It had to hold something of worth. But what?

My eyes landed on a small black object with a series of movable lenses. A light-catcher. Designed to focus light on small areas, it could create burn marks on the fang's skin. Just minor damage, meant as a precursor to the real torture.

But focused on the right spots, it could cause just the kind of pain I needed.

His face held trepidation, mouth still held wide open by the metal gag, as I removed his chair from the drowning mechanism and moved it to the center of the room.

Next to the switches for the electric lights, a cord on the wall connected to a shutter on the ceiling. I flipped off all the lights and pulled the cords, releasing a sunbeam that stopped just before the fang's feet.

He raised a brow as if to say, "That's it?"

I allowed myself a brief, sadistic smile. "You've felt sunlight before, I'm sure. Painful, but nothing you can't handle.." Setting the light-catcher on a table directly beneath the sunbeam, I rotated the lenses. A speck of light appeared on the wall behind the fang. "But have you ever felt it drilled into your eyes like needles?"

A flicker of fear crossed his face. He shut his eyes tight as I directed the light-catcher toward him. A path of red formed across his cheek where the light moved.

I stopped the light on his eye, and he gnashed against the gag, eyelid swelling beneath the sunlight. Moving to stand behind him, I held his head in place, forcing his eye open with my fingers. He tried to jerk away, but bound as he was and weakened from days of torture, he was no match for me. I held him steady until the sunlight burned a hole through his eye.

"Where is my sister?" I hissed the words into his ear. "Answer me, and I'll give you a quick death."

Garbled noises came from his throat, and I unbuckled the gag.

"Alsace," he gasped. "There's a town there named for him. Blaubart. He lives in the castle there."

The castle in Blaubart. It wasn't a lot of detail, but it would be sufficient to find Lucy. It wasn't far, only a few hours by train, and the day was still young enough that I'd be able to get there before nightfall.

Hopefully, I'd find Lucy still alive and well.

I turned the fang to face me. The torture had left both eyes bloodshot, a hole in the right one. Pitiful.

I put a hand on the stake at my belt, and he sagged against the chains, disgustingly relieved at the coming release.

"You don't deserve the mercy of a quick death," I said. I kicked the chair backwards, into the sunbeam, and turned away. His screams followed me from the room.

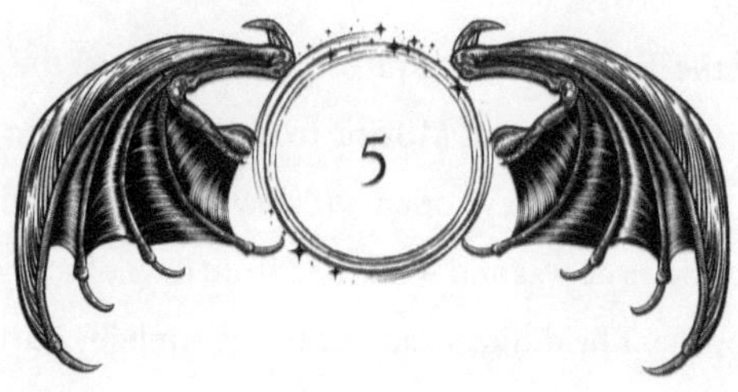

5

As the train chugged through the countryside, I could hardly breathe. We pulled past snow-covered hills, tiny villages dotting them. A young boy carrying a pail along the path saw the train coming and waved excitedly, his rose-colored cheeks turned up with a bright grin.

Folding into myself further, I clutched my rosary. I couldn't focus enough to say the prayers, but God and the saints knew what I needed. What Lucy needed.

*How could I have missed the signs?* Thinking back over the past few weeks, I didn't remember anything different about Lucy, but there had to have been something. She'd been painting more, but she'd spent so many years on her art, I hadn't paid any attention to the recent subjects. The last time I'd seen her, she'd been painting chrysanthemums. Had he bought them for her?

He had to have manipulated her, possibly even hypnotized her. And I'd been so absorbed in hunting this nest, I hadn't even noticed the fangs striking within my own home.

It wasn't the first time fangs had tried to take something from me. I could still see Maman and Papa's bodies on the parlor floor, their necks bent at odd angles, blood staining their evening wear.

I wouldn't let Lucy join them.

The train finally pulled to a stop in Colmar. Snow dusted the gothic architecture of the beautiful city. It was the sort of place Lucy would love to see, but I didn't stop to admire the view. As soon as I disembarked, I found a carriage to take me to the quaint, snow-covered village of Blaubart.

I peered out of the carriage window, ignoring the wary looks of the other passengers at my nontraditional clothing, as we pulled into the village. Brown-and-cream buildings lined the streets.

The carriage stopped in the village square. Off in the distance, illuminated by the late afternoon sun, there was a castle, its dark towers foreboding. The fang's home. I took off toward it at a run, saying a silent prayer for speed to whichever saints were listening.

By the time I arrived, I was gasping for breath. Two wrought iron knockers decorated the door, designed to look like wolves. I banged on them until a servant answered.

"I need to see Jakob Peller." I gasped out the words. "Or whoever owns this house." *Let her still be alive.*

"Baron von Peller is away." He looked at my filthy coat and pants with poorly disguised disgust. "But I'll ask the mistress if she will see you." He let me inside and told me to wait in the foyer.

Peller wasn't there. Was the "mistress" he spoke of Lucy, or was it another fang? If Lucy was there alone, we could escape without fear of being pursued. We'd have to hurry, but if we could make it back to Colmar, we could hide out in one of the churches or convents until dawn.

I paced by the front door until footsteps approached.

Lucy entered the room, looking wan and tired in a tea gown I'd never seen.

"Anne!"

I ran to her as she ran to me. When we met in the middle of the hall, I clung to her. My crucifix dug into her chest, but she didn't flinch. *She's still human.*

"Lucy, thank God. You're alive." I looked her over, searching for any injuries. She'd been fed on recently, evidenced by her pale skin and the dark circles below her eyes, but besides that, she seemed unharmed.

She laughed out loud, the sound like tinkling glass. "Of course I'm alive." She took my hands in hers. "I'm sorry I left without talking to you, but it was all so sudden. We met weeks ago. I wanted to tell you—" She cut herself off, looking away. "But he had to leave Paris, and I couldn't be without him. We're in love. We're married now. We're happy! I want you to be happy for me."

I scowled, irritation finally finding its way through my worry. Even after coming to his lair, suffering through his feedings, she still didn't see what he was. He'd ensnared her more thoroughly than I thought.

I had to make her understand. "You barely know him, Lucy. He's not who you think he is."

"What do you mean?" Her smile faded slightly. "You've never even met him."

"I don't have to. I know his type. I've hunted them for years. I know it's hard to hear, but your *husband* isn't human."

The laugh she gave this time was sharp, disbelieving, and she pulled away from my touch. "What? Of course he is. I understand you want to protect me, Anne, but Jakob isn't—"

I cut her off with a wave of my hand. "Have you ever seen him in the daylight? Ever seen his reflection? Ever seen the bed he sleeps in?"

"I—" Doubt crossed her face.

Good. She was starting to see reason. "You've been unusually tired lately, haven't you? Dizzy? Cold?"

She frowned, not answering me. I pressed on.

"He's a vampire, Lucy. And judging by the way you look, he's been feeding on you. The nest I was tracking before you left? It was his. We caught one of them. He told us everything, all about the rest of his nest." I left out the part that my unauthorized interrogation of the fang probably cost me my position with Les Gardiens. "About his spawn, Jakob, who left the city just before we closed in on them." I held her gaze, desperate to make her understand. "About you, the golden-haired bride his 'son' was taking with him."

She didn't respond for several long moments, thinking deeply about my words. Her hand went to a small bronze key on a chain around her neck.

Finally she shook her head, taking a step back. "I can't believe it. Not without proof."

I threw my hands up in the air. "What more proof do you need? Is my word not enough?" I didn't want to drag her to safety, but I would if I had to.

She twisted the key between her fingers. "Come with me."

She led me through dark, crowded halls. The place felt more like a museum than a home, artwork decorating every surface. My skin prickled. What if the fang was still there, watching us?

I kept my hand on the stake at my belt as we went up a narrow set of stairs onto a cold tower landing. The faint smell of rot hung in the air, masked by dust and incense. My stomach turned as Lucy looked at me, holding up the key in her hand.

"Jakob gave me this," she said. "He told me whatever is behind this door can destroy him. If he's…" She trailed off, swallowed, and started again. "If he is what you say he is, there's proof inside this room."

It had to be near sunset, but if I wanted her to go with me willingly, I had to let her process this at her own pace. I nodded, taking a step back so she had room to open the door.

With trembling hands, she turned the key. As she stepped inside, she stopped in the doorway.

I stepped up behind her and pressed a hand to my mouth, horrified. The room was full of corpses of his past victims.

Dozens of women lined the walls, all mummified husks. Many wore headdresses; the bareheaded ones had long, golden hair, just like Lucy's. Their dresses were ancient, perfectly preserved. "Are these his…" His wives. All the wives he took before my sister.

She married a serial killer. Worse than a fang. He wasn't killing for necessity, but for sport. And Lucy was the latest in a long line of victims.

"I've never seen anything like this," I said. "Some of the creatures keep trophies, but I've never found a room full of mummified victims before. This is sickening."

The women seemed to be arranged in chronological order in a semicircle around the room. The one to the left of the door—his first wife, I assumed—wore a tall, cone-shaped hat and sleeves that reached past her wrists, a style from the fourteenth or fifteenth century. The latest wife, to the right of the door, wore a green dress that I might have seen on the streets of Paris during my childhood.

I glanced at Lucy. She stared wide-eyed at the bodies, but her expression didn't hold the horror mine did. Instead, she looked almost...admiring. But what could she consider admirable about this? I opened my mouth to ask her, but a voice behind me made my heart stop.

"You couldn't resist, could you?"

The man—no, the fang—standing in the doorway had dark hair, so black it was almost blue. He tilted his head, brows furrowed in disappointment as he looked at my sister.

"I'm sorry," she breathed, taking a step toward him.

I grabbed her arm to stop her from surrendering to his demonic draw. "Don't apologize. You have nothing to apologize for. He's a monster."

The fang ignored me completely, looking around the room. "They never can help themselves. No matter how I warn them, they always come into the room." He looked back at Lucy. "I thought you were different, Lucille. Hoped you were different."

From the look on her face, learning her husband's true nature didn't free her from her infatuation. I stepped between them, drawing my stake. I didn't want to make things harder for Lucy than they had to be, but if I had to kill the creature before she accepted it, I would. I wouldn't risk letting him take her from me again. Better to let her hate me forever.

"She knows what you are now," I told him. "You don't hold any power over her." I knew it wasn't true, but if I could rile him into attacking me, she'd see the monster he truly was.

It was as if I wasn't even there. Lucy's voice wavered as she asked him, "What if I had been different, Jakob? What if I'd stayed out? Would you have kept your secret forever?"

"Stop engaging with him, Lucy. You can't reason with these creatures. You're nothing but a meal to them." I said a silent prayer that she'd see sense.

"Was that all this was to you?" she cried. "Did you marry me just so I would be here for you to feed on?"

*Tell her. Tell her the truth,* I urged him silently. *Let her see the monster you are.*

He stepped closer, but I held my stake out between us. "Don't touch her!"

He stopped just out of reach, still ignoring me. "I meant what I said, Lucille. I have desired a companion for longer than you can imagine. Someone to share my eternity with. Someone with my same taste for beauty, the same outlook on the world. Aeron and Leda, they have no finesse. Aeron may have sired me, but I cannot spend the rest of my existence in his nest. I need someone who understands me."

He circled us, a predator closing in on his prey. I turned, holding the sharpened wood at the ready. He'd drop his guard eventually, and I'd be prepared for it.

Waving a hand at the macabre scene surrounding us, he went on. "For centuries I've claimed brides like you. Innocent, trusting women with no one to protect them. I gave them the key and left them alone in my house. At the first opportunity, they opened the door, and their affection turned to fear.

"But you... You were different. I warned you away from me, and you kept coming back. When I left you alone with the key, I thought you might leave the room untouched. I began to think you could be my companion. My *true* companion. My equal."

I couldn't believe anyone would be drawn in by his ridiculous speech, but a glance at Lucy showed tears trickling down her cheeks. He'd completely bewitched her, and I didn't know how to break it.

A hearty sigh passed his lips as he stopped to run a hand through the hair of one of his grisly trophies. "But I return to find you here."

"I trust you!" Lucy burst out. "I trusted you. I didn't want to come in."

"And yet you did," he said. "I wanted to make you like me. Instead I must add you and your sister to my collection."

I wouldn't let him get that chance. "You can try, demon." I lunged for him, but he dodged with a sidestep.

Lucy grabbed my arm. "Don't!"

This had gone on far too long. I didn't remove my gaze from the fang as I spoke to my sister. "He's not real! Whatever you thought you had with him is imagined, Lucy. He wants to *kill you.*"

"Then let him! Better death than a life without him."

If I couldn't reason with her, maybe the death of her captor would make her see sense. I shook her off, and she fell to the ground with a sob.

"You've destroyed her mind!" I shrieked at the fang. He stared at Lucy, momentarily distracted. I dove at him, my stake aimed at his heart. This time, he wouldn't be able to dodge.

Wood separated flesh, and warm blood gushed over my hands. I jerked the stake back with a gasp as Lucy looked up at me.

The crease between her neck and shoulder poured blood. Fatal. I'd seen enough death to know she wouldn't survive it.

I stumbled back into the wall. *What have I done?*

She swayed, then fell to the ground. The fang caught her in his arms.

"What have you done, my Lucille?" he asked, his tone soft. He brushed the hair from her face as I watched, too stunned to move.

So much blood. She had minutes to live, maybe less. I yearned to go to her, but my legs wouldn't move.

I could barely hear her weak reply. "I couldn't let her kill you, Jakob. I promised you eternity. I can't imagine living without you."

"Living?" he said. "Our servants will do that for us." He tore into his wrist with his teeth and shoved his own wound into her mouth.

My stomach threatened to revolt as she lapped up his blood. He lowered his face to her bleeding neck, lifting her in his arms as he stood.

*I've already killed my sister. Must I watch while this demon damns her?* But I remained frozen in place, an unwilling spectator to the destruction of everything I held dear.

The fang pulled the curtain back and opened the window, revealing the night sky. Then he looked into Lucy's dying eyes.

I had to strain to hear him. "Come, my love," he said. "Let us begin our eternity."

With my sister in his arms, he leapt from the window.

Whatever had been holding me in place finally broke, and I rushed to the window in time to see wings burst from the demon's back. They soared into the air, silhouettes rising in the night sky.

Lucy's blood spattered my hands. Cold. Sticky.

*I killed her. I killed my sister.*

Her body still moved—I could see it in the distance, cradled in the arms of her inhuman husband—but it wasn't *her* anymore. That thing living inside her was a demon. Lucy's soul, my sister's soul, was dead and gone.

*It's not your fault,* Henri's voice whispered in my ear. *She went with him willingly.*

*But I hold the blame for her eagerness to leave.* I'd sheltered her too much. I'd thought I was keeping her safe, but I was keeping her naive. Too naive, too trusting to see the danger when it came for her.

I stood in silent vigil as the last gray hints of daylight faded to black and the stars came out. When I finally turned away from the window, my eyes were as dry as the blood flaking off my fingers.

I was too late to save Lucy, but I could still fix things. The blue-bearded monster and his undead bride had to be destroyed.

I had to warn the inhabitants of the castle and village. They didn't know the evil they'd been harboring. It was time they learned the danger they were in.

Next, I had to officially resign from Les Gardiens. Even if they still wanted me, I couldn't be a protector of Paris. Not if I couldn't protect my own sister.

Once I was free, the hunt could begin.

I descended the tower steps, shocking screams from the maid passing by. Her cries woke the house, and in a few moments, servants in various states of dress surrounded me. The butler, a grim-faced man wearing slippers and a nightcap, looked at my blood-stained hands, and the sleep in his features transformed into rage.

"She came out of nowhere!" the maid babbled, clinging to a footman. "All covered in blood, the baroness nowhere to be seen!"

"Where is the baroness?" the butler demanded.

"She's dead." The words sounded flat to my ears. "Your undead master drank her blood, and he jumped out the window with her." I knew he wouldn't believe me. Vampires were experts in deception; doubtless he'd convinced his servants and the entire town that he was nothing more than an eccentric nobleman.

"Did you kill her?"

I ignored the question. Guilt for Lucy's death wasn't the most pressing matter. "Look in the tower. Peller has been killing women for centuries. The bodies of his wives are all up there."

"What tower?" He looked up and down the hall as though searching for it.

I frowned, waving up the narrow staircase I'd just descended. "Up there, at the top of these steps. All your proof is right there."

His eyes glazed over. He shook his head, blinking several times. "I don't know what you've done with the baroness, *fraui*, but you can plead your case before a judge." He grabbed my arm, and another servant grabbed the other.

I didn't fight as they dragged me through the castle and to the front door, grip tight enough to bruise. I could have broken free; I'd been trained to fight supernaturally strong vampires, not humans, but fighting wouldn't do me any good.

Besides, they weren't wrong. Lucy's blood coated my hands. And while I had no intention of rotting in a cell while the demon paraded around the countryside wearing her face, I deserved justice for my crimes.

They tied my hands together behind my back before relieving me of the weapons on my belt—completely missing the dagger in my boot and the sharp pin tucked into my braid. Then they shoved me into a carriage.

Sitting in the darkness, I twisted my wrists, testing the knot. It was loose, easily undone, but I didn't take advantage of their carelessness or the sudden solitude to escape. Let them underestimate me. I'd bide my time.

The carriage jostled me back and forth as they drove toward the town. Why hadn't they acknowledged the tower? Their reaction baffled me. They hadn't shown any fear at the mention of it, so the fang couldn't have terrified them into obedience. I had to assume he'd hypnotized them into believing the tower didn't exist. It was an efficient way to keep his trophies hidden.

Hopefully, he hadn't taken the same precaution with the local law enforcement.

When we pulled to a stop, they left me alone for so long, I began to think they'd forgotten me. What felt like hours later—but couldn't have been longer than a half hour—someone threw the door open. I blinked in the bright light of early morning. A young police officer looked in at me, brown eyes peering up from under a mop of untidy black curls. He was attractive, in a romance-hero sort of way. He grinned.

"I hear you killed our new baroness," he said, his voice dripping with irony.

Did he think this was some sort of joke? I fixed him with a glare but didn't respond as he helped me out of the carriage and onto the street. Before me was a small police station, just two stories tall, indistinguishable from the rest of the buildings in town but for the sign above the door that read *Polizei.*

"I'll send someone over if we need more from you," the officer told the two servants who brought me. They both gave me looks of loathing before they climbed up onto the seat of the carriage.

*Excuse me for trying to save your lives.*

As they drove off, the officer looked me over. "Can I get you a coffee? Something to eat?"

After the last twenty-four hours, the offer of food and hot coffee made my mouth water, but I shook my head. He was a cop, and I was covered in blood. Anything he offered me would come with strings attached.

My stomach didn't agree with my logic as it rumbled loudly. He flashed another grin as he said, "Suit yourself. I'm Officer DuMont, by the way."

I didn't offer him my name, and after a beat of silence, he led me into the station.

Inside, one electric lamp lit up a solitary desk. Apparently he was working alone this morning. He directed me to a chair in front of the desk, taking his own seat opposite me.

"I'd offer to untie you, but it doesn't look like you need much assistance with that."

The rope was nearly falling off my wrists. I shook it off, letting it fall to the floor, and stretched my arms. Officer DuMont watched me, resting his chin on his hands.

"The men who brought you in said you came to the castle yesterday evening to meet with the baroness, and they found you this morning covered in blood and ranting and raving about some nonexistent tower. Why don't you tell me your side of the story, Legs? Where's the baroness?"

I crossed my arms. "She's dead." My eyes didn't burn as I said it. I didn't deserve to cry.

He opened a drawer and began to set my belongings on the desk one by one. "A stake. A revolver. A cartridge full of silver bullets. A crossbow pistol and wooden bolts. A vial of what I can only assume is holy water. A dagger...and another one tucked into your boot." He gestured at me. "And you're wearing men's clothing and a crucifix. Clearly you didn't come here to kill a regular human. So what happened? Was the baroness a witch?"

He hadn't yet accused me of insanity for dressing like a man or carrying a veritable arsenal of weapons. He was more open-minded than I expected a cop to be. Did he believe in the supernatural, or was he humoring me to try to get the answers he wanted?

Regardless of his intentions, I had to tell him the truth. "I came here to kill a fang. She got in the way."

"I see. And a fang is...?"

Yes, he was definitely humoring me. "A vampire."

"So the baroness was not the vampire in question?" His expression was neutral, but I knew he was laughing at me inside.

"No, my sister was not a vampire." *Was not. She is now.* He didn't have to know that, though.

"Ah, you are the sister of our new baroness." He inclined his head to me. "My apologies."

I wasn't imagining the upward twitch of his lips. I scowled, retreating further into my chair.

"Why don't you talk me through what happened? Beginning with what brought you to town." He settled back into his seat and watched me expectantly.

I sighed. His condescending attitude was insufferable, but if I wanted to warn the town about the fang they'd been harboring, I had to start here.

"I found out a couple days ago that my sister had eloped with a fang—a vampire. She didn't know what he was. As soon as I found out where he'd taken her, I followed them. I got here late yesterday afternoon and went straight to the castle. My sister was there alone, and when I told her what her husband was, she took me up to a tower, where we found—" I cut myself off, assailed by the image of that awful room. The floor would be bloodstained now, Lucy's lifeblood saturating the wooden boards.

"Where you found...?" he prompted.

Shaking myself, I went on. "The room was full of the mummified corpses of his previous wives."

He flinched, narrowing his eyes at me before he slipped back on his previous expression of casual interest.

Maybe he'd believe me after all. I pressed on.

"As we were looking at the room, the fang, my sister's 'husband,' found us. I drew my stake to kill him. My sister stepped between us, and I stabbed her by accident instead."

His brow wrinkled in contemplation. "And what happened then?"

"The fang took my sister's body and jumped out the window." I didn't mention the fact that he transformed her before fleeing. One crisis at a time.

"The baron jumped out the window?"

"He grew wings," I added, well aware of how stupid it sounded. "To fly away."

He shook his head, sighing. "You should consider it a blessing I was the one on the overnight shift, Legs. My fellow officers wouldn't be so patient with your story."

"My name is Anne," I spat. "Not Legs. And it's not a story. It's true."

"Our beloved baron, Jakob von Peller, is a vampire, and when you accidentally killed his wife, he grew wings and jumped out the window?"

"He jumped out the window first."

"I see." He nodded sagely. "So Baron von Peller jumped out a window, grew wings, and soared off into the night, intent on terrorizing the countryside with his blood-sucking ways?"

I just stared at him.

"And the bodies you found, can you show me? The men who brought you in deny that such a tower exists."

"If you can get me back into the castle, I can show you. It's obvious you won't believe me without proof."

"Who said I don't believe you?"

The look I gave him told him exactly what I thought of that statement. This was a waste of time. I needed to be making a plan to hunt down Lucy and her new husband, not arguing with this idiot.

He stood. "It would be imprudent of me to believe the word of everyone who comes into this station with their hands covered in blood and an arsenal of weapons on their belt. But I need to see that room."

"You don't need me to lead you to it. I'm sure if you go to the castle and tell them you're investigating, the servants will let you see whatever you want. Even if they are enamored of their master." *Ensorcelled, more like.*

"Yes, but why explore every inch of the place looking for a room the servants don't believe exists, when you can lead me right to it?" He walked around the desk to offer me his hand.

I didn't take it. "Even if I do show you the room, you'll still arrest me for murder. Blood on my hands, a missing baroness, and a confession. What more do you need?" I was more likely to be locked in an asylum than imprisoned or executed, but neither option was pleasant. And while I knew I needed to show him the bodies, I wasn't feeling particularly inclined to cooperate with someone who wanted to lock me up. The night had been taxing enough already.

"Why would I arrest a Gardien for murder?"

My head snapped up so hard I heard an audible crack.

Les Gardiens were a secret organization. Few knew we existed, and of those few, most of them were the creatures we hunted. So how did a police officer so far from Paris know what I was?

"A what?"

"Don't play coy." He pushed my belongings toward me. "You came here from Paris, armed to the teeth with knowledge and demon-hunting weapons, in search of a vampire. Either you're one of *Les Gardiens*, or you've read that Stoker novel too many times."

I didn't know what novel he was talking about, but I stood and put on my belt. "How do you know about *Les Gardiens*?"

He looked around the room as though ensuring we were alone, then lowered his voice to answer. "I've been here for months trying to get information on Peller. You were here for one day and found his trophies."

"You're a hunter?" I stepped back, looking him over. He didn't look like he spent his spare time hunting demons. He had that self-assured swagger all cops had. I wouldn't have assumed he was anything but what his uniform proclaimed.

"Of a sort." He didn't explain further. "You should probably wash up before we leave. I doubt Peller's servants will take kindly to me bringing you back still covered in their mistress's blood."

My gaze went to my hands. I'd almost forgotten, but once he mentioned it, the dried blood was all I could think about. My skin itched, and I scratched at it, watching flakes fall to the ground.

Lucy was dead, and it was my fault. The words pounded through my head. *My fault. My fault. My fault.*

"Sorry," he muttered. "That was insensitive."

I shook my head. "I'm fine. Washing up would be good." I couldn't allow myself to grieve yet. Not until I'd righted my wrongs.

Officer DuMont led me to a washroom and stood outside the door while I scrubbed my hands clean and used the toilet. Glancing at my reflection in the mirror, I could hear Henri's voice in my ear.

*Saints, Allard, when was the last time you bathed? I can't even see your beauty marks beneath all that filth.*

I hadn't exactly had time for luxuries like baths since the fang had killed him, but I frowned at my reflection. He wasn't wrong. I was filthy, specks of dried blood mingling with dirt and sweat on my face and neck. A fresh change of clothes would have been nice, but I hadn't thought to pack any when I was preparing to chase after Lucy.

I splashed water over my face, scrubbing off the worst of the week's grime.

A knock at the door reminded me of the officer waiting outside. "I'd like to have this done before dinner," he called.

Rolling my eyes, I dried my face and stepped out of the washroom. "I'm ready."

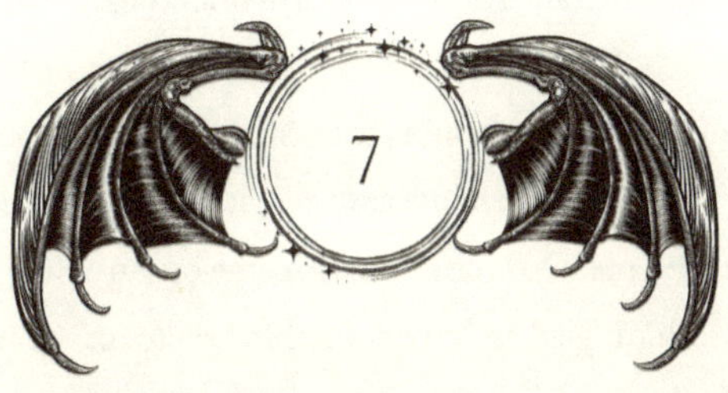

The servants allowed us into the castle without complaint, though I didn't miss the fear and anger in their eyes as they looked at me. Lucy had only been here a few days, but apparently she'd already managed to worm her way into their hearts. It wasn't surprising. Lucy could charm anyone.

"We'll need to be alone," Officer DuMont told the footman who showed us into the house. "Clear the upper floors to ensure we're not disturbed."

He gave us a curious look but did as DuMont requested. After a few minutes, the officer and I were the only ones left in the gloomy halls. My skin prickled as I led him toward the tower, the sound of our footsteps dampened by the tapestries and paintings lining the walls. I knew the fang was gone, but it still felt as though he could be around any corner.

My anxiety grew, churning in my gut, as we ascended the steps into the tower. The door on the landing remained ajar from when I left, and mingling odors filled the air—the must of old clothes, the tang of blood, the sweet fragrance of incense, and underneath it all, the faint smell of rot.

I steeled myself before stepping into the room, but I couldn't help the shudder that ran through me at the sight of Lucy's blood staining the floor. Behind me, DuMont's breath came out in a hiss.

I turned to him, glad to have something to focus on besides my sister's death. He surveyed the room, face screwed up in revulsion. "This is..." He trailed off, unable to find the words.

"Appalling," I finished for him. "He needs to be stopped."

"I had no idea he was this bad," he muttered, seemingly to himself, as he reached out to touch the faded red dress of one of the corpses in the middle.

"You said you've been tracking him for months," I said. "Why?"

He looked up at me, blinking as though he just remembered I existed. The pause dragged on, until I had decided he wasn't going to answer me, before he finally said, "He took someone from me."

The fang killed someone he loved. "I'm sorry," I said. "Is she..." Swallowing hard, I glanced around the room.

"No." He shook his head. "She's not here. But I didn't expect to find her here."

She hadn't been one of the fang's brides, then. Unless he'd had more that weren't displayed here. Maybe she'd been a hunter as well, or maybe she'd just been a meal for the blue-bearded demon. I couldn't bring myself to ask. DuMont's face was drawn, his expression somber for the first time since I'd walked into the station, and I felt a connection between us. We'd both lost loved ones to fangs—*this* fang.

"The town has to be warned. They don't know what they've been harboring." I gestured at the bodies. "Who knows how many other victims he's had in the past? The townspeople need to be prepared in case he returns."

He gave me a sharp look, sadness fading in an instant. "And you expect them to believe you? I'll admit, small towns breed superstition, but Blaubart is modern. They won't believe their highly respected baron is a demon. The town was named for his family. They've been a stronghold in this area for generations."

"You mean *he* has been. He's centuries old. He's been faking his death, coming back as the next generation, probably since the inception of the town. We have the proof here!" I waved around the room. "How could they doubt it?"

"All we have here is proof of a murderer, albeit a truly vile one. And who's to say the bodies are as old as the dresses seem to indicate? Why does it have to be the baron who put them here?"

"Who else would it be?"

"A servant. One of the baron's ancestors." He shrugged. "Maybe you set it all up as an elaborate hoax after your sister ran away with him."

*How dare he?* I opened my mouth to tell him exactly what I thought of his theories, but he held up his hands.

"I believe you! But the townspeople won't. At best, you'd be wasting your time, and at worst, you'd be putting yourself in the line of fire."

I glared at him. Wasn't it his job to protect the people? He seemed more interested in making excuses than anything. I'd expected that, as someone who'd faced loss at the hands of these demons, he'd be more sympathetic. "So what do you recommend?"

He motioned toward the door, and I stepped out onto the landing. He followed, closing the door to the vile room.

"Since you asked so nicely for my opinion…" DuMont grinned, leaning against the wall. His presence overpowered the small space, taking up all the air. He smelled of gunpowder and coffee, and his dark brown eyes seemed to bore into my soul. "We hunt him down together and end him ourselves."

I took a step back to put some distance between us. I'd already planned on killing the demons. I didn't need his approval to do it. "And why do I need your help?"

"You're a Gardien, so maybe you don't. But isn't it better to have a partner?"

The memory of Henri rose up, sharp and painful. This man was a poor replacement—arrogant, domineering, stubborn. And he shouldn't have even known about Les Gardiens. "You never told me how you know Les Gardiens exist. Why should I trust you?"

His expression went from casual to guarded in a heartbeat. "I've had my encounters with the supernatural."

It wasn't an answer, and his caginess made me even more hesitant. "And if I refuse to work with you? Will you throw me in a cell?"

"You're not the trusting type, are you, Legs?" He smirked, going on the offensive. "Of course I won't lock you up. Not unless you ask me to."

I ignored the wink he threw my way. "So I'm free to go?"

The sigh he let out dragged on far too long, grating on my nerves. "I need you to sign some paperwork back at the station, but if you truly don't wish to work together, yes. You can go. I'll hunt them down myself."

It took me a moment to process what he said. "Them?"

He chuckled. "You don't think I missed the secret you were trying to hide, did you? Or am I wrong in assuming that your sister is now undead?"

"She won't be for long," I vowed. "Stay out of my way."

"Of course, *mademoiselle.* I wouldn't dream of interfering with the work of a Gardien."

I wasn't a Gardien anymore—or I wouldn't be for long. As soon as I finished with him, I was going to write my official resignation letter. Next I would need to make a list of all the places the fangs might have gone, and then the hunt could begin.

"Are we done here?"

When he nodded, I turned on my heel. The walls were threatening to close in on me, and I had places to go.

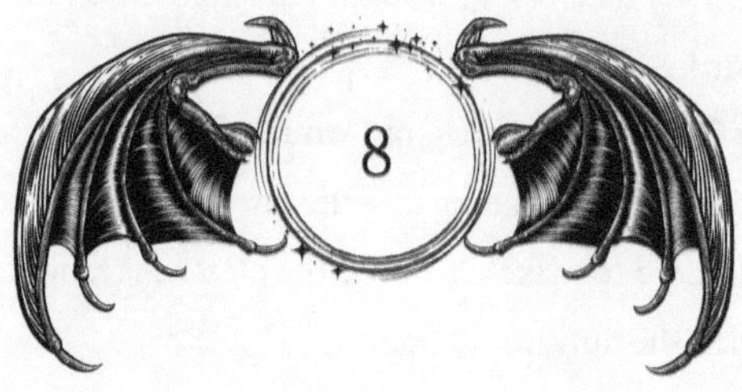

I took a deep breath and scanned the horizon. It had been almost three months since the demon left Alsace with Lucy's body, and I hadn't had a single hint as to their whereabouts. I was growing desperate. What if they'd left Europe entirely? It could take years to find them on another continent.

At least Lisbon made a pleasant backdrop for my crisis of mood. I'd been here for a fortnight, and while it was nothing compared to Paris, it was still a beautiful city. The smell of the sea filled the air, invigorating and restorative. Painted tiles decorated most of the buildings, giving the streets a bright, cheerful air, and the streetcars that ran through the city made travel easy.

Staring out at the ocean wouldn't do anything to fix my problems. I'd searched all the ship registers I could for any indication of Lucy and the fang. Still no sign of them. I forced myself to turn away from the water and head back to the *Avenida* where I'd rented a room.

DuMont's luck didn't seem to be much better than my own. He wrote weekly, pestering me to reconsider his offer to team up together. I was beginning to regret leaving him my forwarding address. I'd ignored every letter, but still he wrote. The man was tenacious, if nothing else.

On my way to the *Avenida,* I detoured to the Cathedral of Santa Maria Maior. Its twin towers, casting a shadow over the courtyard below, left an ache in my heart. I missed Notre Dame more than words could say. Still, it was a comfort to have a church to pray in. Even if it wasn't the cathedral of Our Lady.

The sanctuary was dark and quiet when I entered. I dipped my hand into the frigid bowl of holy water, knelt, and crossed myself. The sweet scent of incense lingered in the air from the matins service, and I let it fill my lungs, washing away the troubles of the day.

As I walked up the aisle, my footsteps echoed back to me from the arched ceiling. Tallow candles surrounded each altar with a golden glow and a haze of smoke. It wasn't home, but my heart still belonged to this holy ground.

I found the altar to the Virgin and knelt in the pew. Crossing myself again, I reached for my rosary, the worn wooden beads slipping over my fingers. As I began to pray, the familiar words soothed my soul, and by the time I finished, my mind was less cluttered.

"Holy Mary, help me to find her," I whispered as I rose.

I lit a candle by the altar for Henri, wishing I had him here to guide me. Lighting another candle for Lucy's soul, I dropped my offering into the box and headed back outside, slightly more at peace.

Back on the *Avenida,* my mood lightened further. The street was designed with Paris in mind, and though they didn't manage to capture my home city perfectly, it had a familiar feel.

The apartment I'd rented wasn't far from the new Avenida Palace. Sra. Cruz, the old woman leasing the house, spoke no French and disapproved of everything about me but my money. When I stepped inside the pink house, she met me at the door, a scowl creasing her already lined face.

*"Boa tarde,"* I said. My Portuguese was limited, though improving. I'd had to make do with my skills in English and Spanish.

She didn't seem impressed with my progress in her mother tongue. Mumbling under her breath, she shuffled into the sitting room before calling over her shoulder, *"Tem uma carta."*

*You have a letter.* Presumably from DuMont, filled with pointless ramblings and requests to join him. Or from Emile, telling me how I was neglecting my responsibilities at home.

I found the thick white envelope, crumpled and worn, on the table by the door. The from bore Emile's refined handwriting. I tore it open.

The first page was full of scolding about my prolonged absence. He needed me at home to look over the affairs of the household. With Maman and Papa gone and Lucy off traveling with her new husband—the excuse I'd given him because I couldn't bear to tell him she was dead—the responsibilities fell to me.

I rolled my eyes and skimmed the page, looking for anything more relevant. My heart skipped a beat when I saw Lucy's name.

*Lucille addressed the enclosed letter to you. I did not open it, but you ought to give her your forwarding address when you reply. I am your caretaker, not your postmaster, and it should not be my duty to share key details about your life with your sister.*

Hardly breathing, I reached into the envelope and found a second, folded letter I hadn't noticed before. I opened it and read the contents.

*Dear Anne,*

*I'm sorry I haven't written sooner, only I've been so busy adjusting to my new life. Oh, I wish you could see the sights I'm seeing right now! Jakob has taken me all over the continent—not just France, but Germany, Spain, Luxembourg, and even Portugal! He insists that I not tell you where we are going next, because he fears you might be hunting us. He doesn't know you as I do, though. I know we left on a sour note the last time we saw one another, but now that you've had some time to think on it, I'm certain you understand that things had to happen the way they did. Truly, they could not have ended differently.*

*But I won't go against my husband's express wishes, so if you want to know where I am, you'll have to guess. I'll give you a hint: Jakob has promised to dance with me in a tulip field under the light of a full moon (isn't that the most romantic thing you've ever heard?) and to take me on a boat ride through the canals.*

*There's no time to write more. Our train leaves soon, and I want to post this before we leave. Once you have the chance, promise you'll come visit? I long to see you, and I know you'll love Jakob once you know him as I do.*

*Must go now. I'll write soon.*

*All my love,*

*Lucille.*

My throat ached with suppressed emotion. Every word sounded so like my sister, I could almost hear her voice. Whether the demon had access to Lucy's memories to mimic her, or whether it actually believed it was Lucy, I didn't know.

But I did know she'd given me enough information here to find her. Tulips and canals. They had to be traveling to Holland. My best guess was Amsterdam. Lucy had talked about Amsterdam before. About the artists there, the tulips and canals and museums.

She'd talked about lots of places she wanted to visit. I wished I'd taken her to all of them. Maybe things would have turned out differently, and maybe they wouldn't have. Either way, she would have gotten to see the world before she died.

I shook off the grim thoughts. It was too late for regrets now. It was time to focus on avenging her.

Sra. Cruz's ever-present scowl deepened when she finally understood that I was leaving. I paid her for my room through the end of the month, and her expression softened—not enough to be considered a smile, but at least it didn't seem like she was ready to throw me out on the street.

It only took me a few minutes to put all my belongings into the green carpetbag that served as my suitcase. When I reached the front door, Sra. Cruz waited with a brown paper pouch. She shoved it into my hands.

*"Pegue,"* she said. "Take."

I accepted the offering with a slight frown. *"Obrigada,"* I replied, thanking her. At least, I hoped I was thanking her. From her expression, one would have thought I'd called her ancestors thieves and whores.

She shooed me out the door. Standing on the *Avenida* outside her small salmon-colored building, I opened the package she gave me. It was full of filhós—sweet fried dough. I took a bite of one, and the taste of cinnamon and sugar burst on my tongue.

Glancing back at the window, I saw her watching me. I gave her a big smile and waved, and she jerked the curtains shut.

Strange woman.

The train station wasn't far, only a block from the house. I hurried to it, anxious to get back on the trail. Lucy hadn't dated her letter, and I didn't know how long they'd be in Holland. The sooner I got there, the better.

At the window, I told the clerk I needed a one-way ticket on the next train to Amsterdam.

"There's one leaving this afternoon." He rifled through some papers. "Oh, but unfortunately it's fully booked. I'm sorry."

I couldn't miss them. This was the first clear lead I'd had since Lucy died. "When does the next one available leave?"

Consulting his papers again, he said, "Not until next Thursday."

"That's too late." I slammed my hand on the counter. "I *have* to be on this one."

He didn't so much as flinch at my outburst. "I cannot make room where there is none, *senhora*. You'll just have to wait."

*I'm going to be late. If I'm not already.* Huffing in frustration, I grabbed my bag and strode off toward another ticket desk. Maybe another clerk would have a better answer.

Someone tall stepped in my way, and I nearly collided with him.

"Watch where you're—"

"My apologies, *mademoiselle*." He doffed his hat, brown eyes twinkling with mischief. "It's entirely my fault."

"Officer DuMont." Lisbon was the last place I expected to find him, but here he was, as cocky and attractive as the last time we met.

"Just El," he said. "I'm no longer with the force in Blaubart. I hear you're having some difficulty getting a ticket. Maybe I can be of some assistance?"

I scowled, shifting my bag to my other hand. "Unless you can create space on a full train, I doubt it."

His grin widened as he pulled something from his coat pocket. "As it happens, I seem to have booked a double room by mistake. I'd be happy to give you the other ticket, if you like."

He'd planned this. He had to have. It was no coincidence that he had the only remaining ticket. "What do you want for it?"

"Just your assistance. Work with me."

I didn't trust him. Glaring at the outstretched ticket, I asked, "What's in it for you?" I was usually an excellent judge of character, but El DuMont confounded me. Did he really come all this way just to get me to work with him? People didn't do things like this for free.

"Maybe I just want a pretty face to look at while I hunt."

When I didn't respond, he held up his hands in surrender. "Okay, fine. You caught me. I've been hunting Peller for a long time with no success. You showed up and in a single night managed to drive him from his home. You're a Gardien. You have skills, training, and resources I don't have access to. With your help, I might actually be able to catch the bastard."

"To avenge your...loved one." Who was she? His sister? His lover? It didn't matter. For the time being, our interests aligned. "And what can you offer me?"

He held up the papers again and winked. "A ticket."

*Take the ticket, work with him, and make it to Amsterdam in time. Or refuse and risk missing them.*

I had no choice. I snatched the ticket from his hand. "Fine. I'll work with you. In Amsterdam only. If we miss them there, you're on your own."

"Naturally." He bowed. "It's a pleasure to do business with you, *Mademoiselle* Allard. Might I take your bag?"

"I can carry it just fine myself." I stalked off toward the train.

DuMont's long strides caught up to me in a moment. "I'm looking forward to learning from you. I've never had the opportunity to observe the prowess of Les Gardiens firsthand."

Holy Mother, did the man ever stop smiling? He already grated on my nerves, and we'd barely spent any time together. Two days stuck in a tiny train car with him would be torment. He was far too assured of his own attractiveness. He was right, of course—he had one of the most beautiful bodies I'd ever seen—but that didn't give him the right to act like it.

"Enjoying the view?" he asked, and I realized I'd been staring.

I smiled sweetly. "I was wondering where someone like you finds the audacity."

"The same place I found my good looks and sense of humor." He winked at me.

"In the pockets of someone else more deserving?"

He laughed, the sound deep and rich. "I'm going to enjoy sparring with you, Allard."

"I wish I could say the same, DuMont."

We'd reached the train. DuMont took our tickets and gave them to the conductor, who guided us to our room. It was small, decorated with dark wood. The flimsy lock wouldn't keep anything out, and the bunks were the size of my cot back at headquarters. The washroom, shared with the room to our right, held only a small sink and toilet.

Lovely. No privacy, and no security.

"Top or bottom?"

I narrowed my eyes at him. "Excuse me?"

"Berth." He indicated the beds. "Do you want top or bottom?"

Heat coursed through me. Of course he meant the beds. "Top. Thank you."

"Noted." His eyes twinkled with a light that made me think he knew exactly where my mind went with his question, but he didn't comment further. Instead, he tossed his bag on the bottom bunk. "I'll leave you to freshen up. I'm going to find the dining car."

My glare followed him out the door, which I closed and locked behind him.

How had I ended up stuck on a train with him for two days straight? I should have found another way to get there. Arrogant, insufferable man. Maybe it wasn't too late to get off.

No, I'd made the choice I had to. If I'd missed this train, I would have missed Lucy entirely, and it would have taken months to catch up with them again. I couldn't risk it. Even if my choice meant spending two days in close quarters with the swaggering peacock El DuMont.

I took advantage of his absence to use the toilet and wash up. I'd planned on bathing this evening, but my hasty departure had taken precedence. The last thing I wanted was for DuMont to comment on my smell.

A quick rub of the cloth over my body had me feeling fresher, as did a change of clothes. I even took the time to rinse my hair. I dried it with the hand towel I found beneath the sink and braided it into a tight coil around my head. Then I washed my clothes in the sink and hung them over the bunk to dry.

And if they dripped a bit onto his bunk, it couldn't be helped. Tight quarters made things difficult for everyone. He'd survive a damp mattress.

By the time I finished, the train was moving. The steady chug of the wheels on the track comforted me as I headed down the corridor in search of the dining car. One way or another, I'd catch up to the demon using Lucy's body as a marionette.

It was early afternoon, so the dining car was full of people. I looked around for DuMont and found him sitting at the bar. A beautiful woman with perfectly coiffed brown curls sat next to him, sipping a glass of champagne and fluttering her eyes. Her hand rested on his arm as he laughed at something she'd said.

Incredible. We'd been on the train for less than an hour, and he'd already found someone to distract him from our work. No wonder he hadn't been making any progress in hunting Peller.

If he was looking for a dalliance, he'd have to find it *after* he finished with me.

I walked up to him and slipped my arm around his waist. "Darling, where have you been? I was waiting for you."

The woman sat upright, frowning. "I'm sorry, am I—"

Mouth open in an 'o' of feigned surprise, I looked over at her. "My apologies. I didn't realize I was interrupting. Why don't you introduce me, darling?" I gave DuMont my most simpering smile.

He looked more amused than vexed. "I didn't realize you were waiting for me, *ma jolie*. I was making friends." To the woman, he said, "Might I introduce my wife, Anne?"

Wife? Rather than rolling my eyes like I wanted to, I held out my hand. "A pleasure to meet you."

She looked me up and down, taking in my worn brown travel coat and trousers, and wrinkled her nose. "Please excuse me." Leaving her glass on the bar, she hurried off.

As I moved to pull away from DuMont, he grabbed me by the waist and leaned in as though to kiss my cheek. "If you're jealous of my attention, Allard, all you have to do is say so. There's no need to go to all this trouble." His breath tickled my ear, sending a rush of unwelcome warmth through me.

"Jealous?" My laugh sounded strangely forced. "I'm not jealous, but if we're going to be working together, the least you can do is give me the courtesy of staying on task."

"My apologies." He pulled back, a heat in his eyes that caused my stomach to flip. "You have my undivided attention."

Shifting from his touch, I took a seat at the bar and signaled to the bartender. I was going to need a drink for this. Or several. "You never mentioned how you knew they were in Amsterdam."

"I have my sources." He cocked his head. "I could ask you the same question."

"Likewise." If he didn't want to share, neither would I. I didn't need him prying into my personal correspondence.

The bartender, an older Spanish man with salt-and-pepper hair, stopped in front of us. "How can I help you, *señora?*"

"A gin and tonic, *por favor.*"

He nodded, reaching for a glass. *"Y su casado?"*

I opened my mouth to say he wasn't my husband, but DuMont cut me off. "Whiskey. *Gracias.*"

Did he expect me to continue to go along with the ruse of being married? I had no intention of playing a meek and obedient wife. I narrowed my eyes, frowning at him.

DuMont met the challenge in my gaze, smirking, when the bartender returned with our drinks, I took a swig, grateful for the distraction.

"What are your plans in Amsterdam?" I asked.

He sipped from his own glass. "Find the...what did you call them? Fangs?"

"And how, exactly, did you plan to do that?"

"I was hoping you might have some insight. She's your sister, after all."

"She was," I clarified. "Not anymore."

Raising a brow in question, he waited for me to continue.

I glanced around, ensuring that no one was listening to our conversation. My appearance made me stand out enough; the last thing I needed was to be placed in an asylum for believing in vampires.

The chatter in the car masked our voices, but I lowered mine anyway. "My sister is dead. That *thing* is not my sister." A lump formed in my throat, and I picked up the sprig of juniper from my drink to distract myself.

DuMont watched as I slowly stripped the leaves and berries from their stem. "Even so," he said slowly, "the transformation doesn't cause a drastic change in personality. Where would your sister have wanted to go, if she had the chance?"

Everywhere. Anywhere. Tears threatened at the corner of my eyes. I blinked them back before DuMont could see.

"She's always loved art," I said finally. "Theaters, museums, libraries. She would have lived at the opera if I let her."

He gave me an encouraging nod. "We can ask around at the museums and theaters. Someone might have seen them."

"And tulip fields," I added, remembering her letter. "She wanted to dance in the tulip fields."

"That's a good start." He picked up his drink and drained it. "I'm going to get some rest before they serve dinner. If you think of anything else, let me know."

I stared down at the stripped sprig of juniper. "I will."

# THE CURATOR

She glides through the hall of the museum, trailing her fingers along the wall. The building is dimly lit, the curator having only illuminated what was necessary. He stands in the corner watching them, transfixed, through beady eyes. He's been handsomely compensated for keeping the museum open so late, though he would have let them in without payment, if only for a chance to spend more time in the presence of the golden woman.

A man with a beard so black it's almost blue wraps his arm around the woman's waist. "What do you want to see first, my sweet Lucille?"

Lucille ponders the question for a moment. "Rembrandt."

He smiles fondly at her. *"De Nachtwacht?"* A strand of her golden hair has come loose from her ornate French hairstyle, and he tucks it back behind her ear. "Then see it we shall."

The curator, a middle-aged man with a prominent chin, flinches when the blue-haired man turns to him. *"De Nachtwacht? Ja, meneer. Right this way, meneer."*

He leads them to a dark room and takes a moment to light the lamps. As orange light illuminates the painting, the golden woman gasps.

*The Night Watch* fills most of the wall, the subjects life-sized. Lucille walks toward it, pulled by an invisible thread. She reaches a long, graceful arm toward the woman in the center of the painting.

"Ah—" the curator starts to speak, but a warning look from the man silences him.

"It's incredible, Jakob," Lucille breathes. "The way he uses light and shadow, how he highlights the key elements…"

Jakob steps up beside her. "How he obscures others. Yes. You see what I see." He smiles down at her. "I am grateful to have found you as a companion, my love."

The golden woman has an innocent face, but the look she gives the blue-haired man is anything but. The curator shudders as light glints off her teeth. They seem sharper than any teeth he's seen before…but that must be a trick of the light.

"Do you have the time?"

The curator flinches when Jakob addresses him. There's nothing in the man's tone to frighten him, but he's terrified anyway, like some ancient instinct warns him of danger. He can't focus enough to read his pocketwatch; with trembling hands, he passes it to the man.

"Yes, we still have plenty of time." Jakob closes the watch and hands it back. The curator tucks it into his pocket, swallowing down his fear. These people have done nothing to him; what does he have to be afraid of?

"I didn't know we were on a schedule," Lucille says, running a hand down her husband's arm. "What are we doing next?"

"A man must have his secrets, my sweet Lucille." He smiles fondly at her. "Be patient. All will be revealed."

The curator does his best not to shake as he leads them through the museum. Normally, he would tell people about the artwork as they walk, but he can't bring himself to speak to these two. They don't seem to mind his silence, too absorbed in each other and in the art to even glance his way.

They follow him from room to room, making comments about the art and sharing stories about different experiences they've had. Strange stories. There's something uncanny about these two people. The man, especially. He speaks about history as though he was there, and the woman clings to his every word.

At first, the curator was drawn to the woman, but the more time he spends in her presence, the more frightened he becomes. It could be the late hour, or it could be her unnatural smile. Whatever it is, he's unnerved. He doesn't dare suggest that he needs to close the museum before they've finished, but he desperately wants to.

Their last stop is the library, and the curator breathes a sigh of relief. They're almost finished.

Lucille turns to her husband with fluttering eyes and pink cheeks. "You took me to another library once, Jakob. Do you remember?"

He draws her into a passionate kiss, one that lasts long enough to make the curator turn his face away. When they break apart, Jakob says, "How could I forget, my sweet Lucille? It was a night I'll treasure for all eternity. I got to experience the taste of salvation."

She whispers something into his ear, and her husband gives her a smile that promises seduction and danger.

"But of course," he says. He turns to the curator. "I believe the tour is at an end. Thank you for your service to us."

9

T he lack of security on the train left me tense, and I spent a restless night tossing and turning. When I finally woke late the next morning, DuMont was gone, his blankets tangled and dirty clothes strewn all over the lower bunk. I shook my head as I made my own bed, tightening the sheets until they were wrinkle-free.

Dressed for the day and with my hair braided out of my face, I made my way to the dining car, where I saw DuMont sitting at a table with an old bearded man. The language they spoke was unfamiliar, but they were deep in conversation, cups of coffee in hand.

DuMont saw me approach and rose to his feet. *"Ma jolie!"* He offered me his hand, and I took it with a wary look at his face, which revealed nothing.

"This gentleman was just telling me the best places to take my wife in Amsterdam," he said. His eyes twinkled as he guided me into a seat. "How would you like to take a moonlight stroll through Vondelpark this week?"

*Blessed Virgin, it's too early for this.* The old man watched us with an expectant grin. I pasted a smile on my own face, gritting my teeth behind it. "That sounds lovely. But if you'll excuse me, I need to find some breakfast."

"But of course, *ma jolie.*" DuMont leaned in as though he was going to kiss me, but he must have seen the threat of murder in my eyes, because he took my hand and pressed a kiss to it instead. "Actually, I was going back to the room. I'll see you soon." Bidding farewell to his breakfast companion, he hurried out of the train car.

Coffee obtained, I found a seat in the corner and slowly drank my liquid breakfast. Outside, the spring countryside rolled past. Where were we? Spain? Sunlight painted the fields green and gold, highlighting the purple flowers and white sheep dotting the landscape.

There wasn't much to do on a train beyond staring out the window, so when I finished my coffee, I got up with a sigh. Cleaning my weapons would be a productive use of my time, but I assumed that would be frowned upon in the dining car.

I headed down the corridor to the room DuMont and I shared. When I opened the door, I froze.

He was shirtless. Suds covered his face, and he dragged the straight edge of a razor down his cheek, but that wasn't what caught my eye. Tattoos covered his body.

His back bore an enormous black cross that rippled with movement as he continued shaving. The center was a Trinity knot, and intricate braids made up the arms of the cross. His right arm bore what looked like orange feathers or flames, wrapped tight around a firm bicep, trailing down past his elbow. The artwork was beautiful, made breathtaking by the body it adorned. My mouth watered thinking about the power of those muscles, the strength he must have.

"Something catch your eye?"

His eyes fixed on mine in the mirror, and flames of humiliation burned from my head to my toes.

"I was just—" I couldn't think of anything to say.

He set the razor down and turned to face me. Too close; the room was too small, and he was close enough that I could hardly breathe. Or maybe it wasn't the distance that had me struggling to get enough air. Maybe it was the fact that he was very nearly naked, his pants low around his hips. I forced myself not to look at the v-shape of muscles that descended below his waist.

"You were just...?" he prompted.

"I—I left something in my bag." It wasn't true, but I couldn't remember why I'd come back to the room.

He took another step closer, and the rest of the air vanished. "If you see something you like, all you have to do is ask." He looked me up and down. "Because I see a lot that I like, Legs."

*Legs.* The demeaning nickname threw a bucket of cold water over my hyperactive libido. I looked at him through my lashes. "I was just wondering how big it is."

My answer stunned him into silence—a rare occurrence. I turned to leave, laughing internally at his wide-eyed stare, but he grabbed me by the waist, shocking the breath from my lungs.

"How big what is?" His eyes bored into mine, hazy with lust.

I smirked. "Your ego. I can't imagine how it can possibly fit in such a small room."

"It can fit in much smaller places." He lowered his voice. "I'd be happy to show you. All you have to do is ask."

The image filled my mind. DuMont, lying naked before me, that signature smirk traded for a look of unabashed desire as I straddled him.

The momentary pleasure would be far outweighed by the humiliation of surrendering to his needless flirtation, though. I pulled back from his touch. "I can think of far better uses of my time."

He laughed out loud. "Shame." Turning back to the mirror, he picked up his razor again. "I'll be finished in a few minutes, if you need the room to yourself."

A quick glance at his face revealed just what he thought I might *need the room to myself* for. I grabbed my bag and stalked out of the room, slamming the door behind me. His laughter followed me down the hall.

I did my best to avoid him the rest of the journey, and finally we made it to Amsterdam.

I hated it.

We hadn't even left Amsterdam Centraal yet, and I was already miserable. The crowd jostled us to and fro as we made our way through the train station, the towering ceiling echoing the sound of voices all around us. DuMont kept a tight grip on my arm, and for once, I didn't object to his touch. He seemed to know where he was going.

Tucked back away from the platform, a man stood with a sign bearing DuMont's name. He wore the black coat and hat of a police officer, and sandy brown hair dusted his brow. We made a beeline for him.

"Braam?" DuMont released me to shake the man's hand. "I'm El DuMont."

"Good to finally meet you," he said, tossing a questioning glance my way.

"This is my—" DuMont broke off mid-sentence when I pinched his arm in warning against any more ludicrous stories about me being his wife. "My partner, Anne Allard. Allard, this is Jan Braam. He's a detective."

The detective's eyes held questions, but he was tactful enough not to ask what a woman was doing partnering with DuMont. "You were right," he said. "He's been here."

My heart caught in my throat. They'd found something.

"Someone was killed?" DuMont asked.

"Just found him this afternoon." Detective Braam jerked his head in the direction of the exit. "I convinced them to leave the body undisturbed, but we'll have to hurry. I'll give you the details on the way."

Outside, the colorful streets reeked of fish. Bikes and streetcars zoomed past as the detective led us to a waiting carriage. We climbed inside, and Detective Braam knocked on the wall to tell the driver we were ready to leave. We set off with a jolt. I watched the city through the window; it was brightly colored and bustling, thoroughly modern. Not remotely the type of city I'd expect Lucy to appreciate.

But it wasn't Lucy I was chasing.

It was easy to forget my sister was dead. No matter how much I might have wanted to believe I could save her, she wasn't coming back. The only salvation I could give her was the peace of eternal rest. I could exorcize the demon inside her and bury her on holy ground.

DuMont settled back into his seat, leg brushing against mine. "Where are we headed?"

"The Rijksmuseum. The curator didn't make it into work today. When one of the workers took a shortcut on his way home, he found the body in the woods."

DuMont and I exchanged a look. A museum, just as I'd suggested.

"What makes you think it was our man?" he asked.

"We got a matching description from last night. A man with bluish-black hair and a fair-haired woman came up to the museum near closing time. They weren't locals. And the state of the body." The detective shivered. "You'll have to see it for yourself. This wasn't a mugging gone wrong. This was murder for sport."

My mouth went dry. It was one thing to know, abstractly, that a demon was killing using my sister's body as a puppet. But to be faced with that reality?

DuMont's leg pressed into mine, and when I looked over, he was watching me, his face inscrutable.

I cleared my throat, looking away from DuMont's piercing eyes. "What time was he killed?"

"Some time after midnight. No one saw him after the museum closed, and when they went to open it this morning, it hadn't been locked properly."

"Was anything taken?"

"Theft wasn't the motive." The detective shook his head. "You'll see."

When we arrived, he led us behind the museum. Dozens of police milled around in the warm afternoon sun, and onlookers stared, trying to find the source of the excitement. Detective Braam pushed through the crowd with us on his heels.

We reached a small copse of trees that shielded the crime scene from the view of bystanders. "You may want to prepare yourselves," the detective said.

A clean white sheet covered the body. DuMont knelt and removed it, and my stomach turned.

The man's arms reached upwards as though fighting off invisible attackers. His head, nearly severed, hung at an odd angle, and his legs, rigid in death, seemed to flail. His eyes stared off into the distance, wide with horror. White sheets and a red blanket covered his nudity; his clothes lay in a pile nearby.

The scene, gruesome as it was, sparked something in my memory. A book filled with art made by women. Lucy had carried it with her for months. One of the paintings had been a horrifying depiction of two women cutting off the head of a naked man.

*"Judith Slaying Holofernes."* That had been the name of it. An old Italian painting.

El frowned up at me from his position next to the body. "The Gentileschi?"

"That's how he's positioned. Like Holofernes in the painting." I waved at the scene. "It's like they were trying to recreate it." I could picture it, the two vampires standing over him, Lucy severing his head from his body as her husband held him down. The contents of my stomach threatened to reappear, and I turned away from the scene.

"I see it." DuMont leaned back to take it in. "With Judith here, and her servant next to her."

"They're recreating paintings?" Detective Braam's face contorted in disgust. "With murder?"

"It's possible." DuMont opened the pouch he carried and took out an inkpad, a small jar of black powder, a fine brush, and a notebook.

"What are you doing?" I asked.

"Taking fingerprints." He pressed the man's lifeless fingers into the inkpad, then pressed them onto a clean page in the notebook. Once he finished all ten fingers, he wrote something at the top of the page, then set it aside.

The detective and I shared a look of bewilderment as DuMont took the powder and brushed some of it onto the man's pocketwatch.

"Perfect," he muttered under his breath. He blew the powder gently, then took the watch and pressed it against another page of the notebook. When he lifted it again, a faint oval outline remained on the paper.

He took the victim's leather shoes next, brushing the dust onto those and making sounds of delight when he found another mark to press into his notebook. Detective Braam and I watched his strange ritual in silence.

At last, he stood. "There aren't many surfaces to take a print from, but I got a couple good ones." He opened the notebook back to the victim's fingerprints and held it out for us to see. "See these ridges and grooves in the ink? Each print is different from person to person. If you can find fingerprints on something at a crime scene, you can match it to the perpetrator and prove they were there."

Frowning, I leaned in, peering at the prints. Now that I looked closely, I could see the details. I examined my own fingers, looking for differences.

"Huh." Detective Braam tucked his hands into his pocket and whistled. "That's clever."

DuMont grinned. "Afraid I can't take credit for it. I like keeping up with the latest scientific discoveries. I read a book on it."

"You'll have to leave me the title so I can look into it."

"And what's the conclusion?" I asked, still looking at my hands. "Was it him?"

Flipping through the pages, DuMont compared the prints he took from the man's shoes and watch to other fingerprints throughout the notebook, each labeled "Bluebeard" at the top.

"Bluebeard?"

He rubbed his neck, looking almost sheepish. "I had to call him something."

Because his name hadn't been an option. Obviously.

"Got him." DuMont stopped, holding the notebook open to two pages at once. "He left a print on the watch."

I looked over his shoulder, comparing the two pages, as Braam asked, "Why wouldn't he have taken it with him?"

"He's not interested in trophies," I told him. Not trophies like watches, at least. The memory of the room full of his wives assailed me, and from the tension in DuMont's shoulders, I knew he was thinking of the same thing. "His kills—they don't mean anything to him." Unless they were his wife. "They're just a means to an end."

Braam's sandy brow knit together. "What end?"

DuMont closed his notebook. "Power? Lust for blood? The beauty of the kill? It could be anything." Tucking his supplies back into the bag, he shouldered it. "I think we have all we need here."

"I booked you a room near the Basilica of St. Nicholas," Braam said as we walked back out of the copse of trees and into the crowd. "The hotel should be able to call the precinct if you need us. You'll pass on anything you find?"

"Of course," DuMont lied smoothly. We could hardly tell them their perpetrator was a vampire. "I'm sure you'll do the same."

"Naturally. I appreciate your insight."

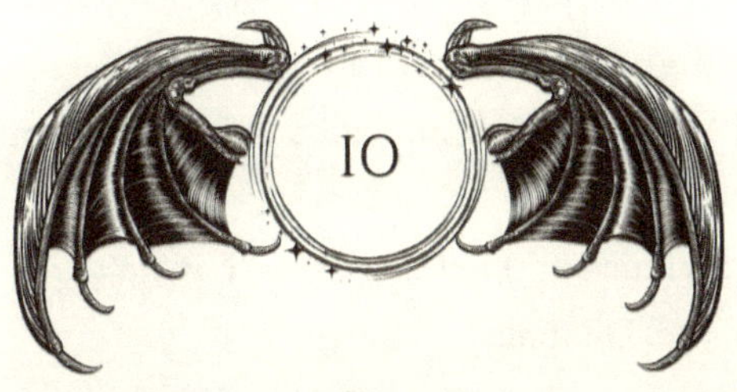

# 10

A room.

Detective Braam hadn't been speaking metaphorically. He'd booked us a single room. I stared at the solitary bed.

"There wasn't time to let him know I was bringing a partner," DuMont said. "You don't mind sharing, do you?" He brushed past me, tossed his bag into the chair in the corner, and took a seat on the bed.

"I'd rather not have to try to squeeze in next to your enormous ego." I turned to the door. "I'll get my own."

"You won't be able to," he called after me.

Whirling back around, I scowled at him. "Why not?"

*"Eerste paasdag."*

Any goodwill I might have felt toward him after observing his investigative skills was quickly evaporating. "Which is?"

"Easter." He leaned back and folded his hands behind his head, kicking his feet up on the bedcovers. "The whole hotel is booked. The whole city is. We were lucky Braam could get us this much."

In the chaos of the past few days, I'd forgotten it was Holy Week. I dropped my bag to the floor with a groan.

He smirked. "Afraid I'll compromise your virtue if you stay here with me?"

"Not even a little bit." I rolled my eyes. "But I'm not interested in sharing your bed, DuMont."

His grin widened as he lowered his voice. "The bed isn't a requirement, Legs."

How could one man be so infuriating and so attractive at the same time? I didn't deign to respond to his innuendo.

"If you're so desperate to be away from me," he said, "you might be able to find an unoccupied room somewhere else in the city. I wish you luck with it. In the meantime, I'll spend tonight hunting."

Scouring Amsterdam for a hotel room wasn't the most productive use of my time, not when I should be looking for the fangs. Nor did sleeping on a park bench sound appealing.

"Fine." I picked up my bag and placed it on the dresser. "I'll stay—but if you touch me, I'll cut your balls off." Not that I wouldn't have enjoyed tangling with him, if only to wipe that ridiculous grin off his face. I didn't need the distraction.

Wicked delight spread across his face. "So violent, Legs. Never fear. I won't touch you until you ask for it."

*Until.* Not *if.* I didn't dignify his comment with a response. "So we know they're here, or at least they were last night. How do we find them? We can't search every museum and theater in the city."

"We'll have to ask around at the more upscale hotels for anyone matching their descriptions." He went to his suitcase, a large leather trunk, and rummaged through it. The contents were a mess; he had no sense of organization. "I've got a list of previous murders they might have committed. It's in here somewhere..." He pulled out a wrinkled paper. "Here it is!"

I took a seat at the desk and began the process of disassembling my revolver to clean it. "You didn't think to mention that in your letters?"

"It wasn't anything substantial."

"So it's like everything else you wrote me. A waste of my time." My Saint-Étienne didn't need cleaning—I kept it in perfect condition at all times—but the familiar process was a welcome diversion from DuMont's oh-so-punchable face.

"One of these days you'll have to admit you actually like me, Legs." He took a seat on the desk and winked, handing me the paper. "All the deaths showed classic signs of vampire attack: exsanguination, no indication of resistance. They were all in cultural centers. Florence, Berlin, Salzburg. But there wasn't anything else to tie Bluebeard to them. Until today."

I skimmed the page, reading the limited descriptions of the bodies. "What changed?"

"See the one in Berlin?"

*Naked young man in a laurel crown laid out on a park bench, draped in a brown blanket.* "The crown?"

"I didn't make the connection until you mentioned the Gentileschi painting. The body in Berlin seemed to be laid out deliberately. It reminded me of the painting, *Andromache Mourning Hector*." He shrugged. "One crime scene staged like a painting isn't a pattern, but two could be."

In Lucy's letter, she'd mentioned being in Germany at one point. Was it possible they were killing people and arranging them to look like artwork? The thought left a bitter taste in the back of my throat. I'd been so focused on protecting my sister from the world, I'd never thought I'd have to protect the world from her.

"What do you think?" DuMont prompted.

"It could be them." This corruption of Lucy's passion for art...it was appalling. "If it's the start of a pattern, we have to stop them before it goes further."

He stood, taking the paper from me. "It's getting late. I thought we could split up tonight."

"After all that effort to convince me to work with you, now you want to split up?"

"Afraid you'll miss me?" he teased.

"Just trying to understand why you bothered if you were just going to run off as soon as we got here."

"We'll cover twice as much ground this way. You can patrol the area around the Rijksmuseum and Vondelpark, and I'll see what I can find in the center of town."

Vondelpark. He'd mentioned that on the train.

From the amused look on his face when I glanced up at him, he'd followed my thoughts to the same place.

"So you *did* have a motive for that conversation. Other than irritating me, I mean."

"I'm hurt that you would think otherwise." He held a hand to his heart. "I asked the gentleman on the train about the most romantic places in Amsterdam. Bluebeard is on his honeymoon, after all. It's not my fault if the man thought I was asking for places to take my wife."

"Hm." I'd finished cleaning my revolver. As I reassembled it, I looked over to find DuMont watching me.

"You seem to know your weapon well," he said, nodding at the gun. "Do you make your own bullets?"

"Sort of. I buy the bullets, then replace the heads with my own silver ones. You?" I'd not seen his gun, but if he hunted fangs, he had to have one. Or at least a crossbow pistol. Stakes only worked in close proximity, and while I wouldn't have given up the sharp wood at my belt for anything, I also wouldn't have surrendered my Saint-Étienne.

He chuckled at the question. "I don't carry one."

"Really? I thought you were a cop."

"For a brief time, yes. I'd rather work with a knife, though. It's more personal."

"Strange choice for hunting fangs," I said, packing my things neatly and methodically back into my bag. "I've always found a stake to be more effective."

"I haven't exactly made a career out of hunting vampires."

The wry note in his voice caused me to look up, frowning. "I assumed..." I shook my head. "Sorry. I thought you'd been doing this for a while. How long has it been since—well, since you lost her?"

He looked out the window. "It's almost sunset. We should head out."

I bit the inside of my cheek to keep from pressing for answers. Lucy had always told me I was tactless. I shouldn't have expected an answer to such a personal question.

As I tucked my revolver into the black leather holster at my waist, DuMont pulled a crumpled paper from his pocket and handed it to me. "A map," he said at my querying look. "Stick south of the Rijksmuseum for tonight. I'll handle the north."

"And if I find them?" I'd spent the past few months alone. I wasn't concerned about facing the fangs by myself, but it was a little unusual that he'd spent so much time trying to get me to join him, only to separate at the first opportunity.

"Don't get bit." He grinned, slipping out the door before I could respond.

I opened the map and considered it. At some point during the day, he had drawn a circle around the area he wanted me patrolling.

Something felt wrong about this. Going to the window, I worried my lip as I watched him exit the building and hurry down the street.

Where was he going, and why didn't he want me with him?

It was dark outside now. The streetlights illuminated the few passersby, men returning home from work or heading out in search of entertainment. It was the right time for hunting fangs, but I had the feeling that wasn't DuMont's goal.

*Follow your instincts, Allard,* Henri's voice whispered in my head.

I never liked secrets between partners, and if DuMont was going to insist on being my partner, I would have to find out his secrets. Whether he liked it or not.

The ever-present smell of fish permeated the air as I stepped outside and turned in the direction I'd seen DuMont walk. He wasn't in a hurry; I caught up to him easily, keeping several buildings' distance between us to keep from being spotted. The few people I passed ignored me, too focused on their destination to spare a moment of attention to the woman dressed in men's clothing.

We followed the curve of the river, passing homes and churches and countless places of sin. I was far from puritanical, but when I passed a half-naked woman copulating with a man against an alley wall, I clutched my rosary, keeping my eyes fixed firmly ahead.

*I hate Amsterdam.*

At last, he stopped and entered one of the buildings. My stomach twisted when I caught sight of the red-tinted light above the door. He'd gone into a brothel.

Was this what he'd been so desperate to get out alone for? I hadn't immediately fallen into his bed, so he'd had to seek out companionship elsewhere?

My blood boiled, and I paced the street. We weren't really partners. He wasn't Henri. But he'd insisted that we work together, and now I found him, rather than chasing leads like he'd implied he would be doing, carousing in a place like this. The least he could have done was keep his dick in his pants long enough for us to find Lucy and her husband. Then he would be welcome to go off and whore all he liked.

Maybe he didn't care about hunting fangs. Maybe he'd made up the story about losing someone to Peller as a way to get my sympathy in hopes that I would sleep with him. And when that hadn't worked, he'd tried to talk me into working with him, and then he'd chased me halfway across the continent to strong-arm me into it.

No, that was ridiculous. DuMont had an insane ego, but even he wouldn't go that far.

*But what do I do now?* I wondered. *Do I go in and confront him? Wait until he leaves? Pretend it never happened and go off on my own?*

No answers came, and the longer I waited for DuMont to come back out, the more furious I became. A man stumbled out of the brothel, nearly knocking into me as he staggered down the street. I glared after him. Such reckless hedonism.

I had to go inside.

From the street, it looked like a normal house, and the foyer didn't do much to dispel that impression. Up the stairs, I heard the sounds of pleasure, moans and slapping flesh filling the air. I suppressed a shudder, looking around. Laughter and conversation poured out of the parlor to my left, along with a smoky haze and the smell of liquor and cigars. I stepped toward it, hoping that DuMont hadn't found a girl yet. I needed to smack his perfect face before he went off to fornicate with one of the whores.

The occupants of the large parlor were all in various states of dress. Loud chatter filled the air, drowning out the sounds of sex from upstairs. In the center of the room, men sat around a table playing cards, several of them with women on their laps. I spotted DuMont in the middle of the group, laughing heartily. He didn't have a woman, but the glass of amber liquid in front of him was only half full.

The man sitting next to him saw me and grinned. He leaned over and said something to DuMont, who glanced toward the door. When his gaze landed on me, DuMont froze, eyes wide with something akin to fear.

*Good. He should be afraid of me.*

The expression disappeared in an instant, and he sauntered over to me. "Miss me already?"

I lifted my hand to smack him, but he grabbed my face in his hands and pressed his lips to mine.

I couldn't even breathe, let alone hit him. His kiss overwhelmed me, tasting of whiskey. He backed me into the wall, hard body pressed into mine.

How much had he drunk?

When he finally released my lips, our breath came in pants. He rested his head against mine and whispered, "What the hell are you thinking, Allard?"

"What am I—" I started, but he dropped his hand to my butt and squeezed it.

"Quieter," he whispered, the sharp edge to his voice at odds with the lust-filled haze on his face. "I need you to look like you're passionate about me. Hard though it might be for you to imagine."

I couldn't decide between kneeing him in the balls and kissing him again. I settled for trailing a finger down his arm. "And why, exactly, do I need to look like your doxy?" I asked, looking at him through my lashes.

His smirk didn't quite meet his eyes. "Because you thought you could walk into a vampire den looking like that, and I'm doing my best to keep you from being the center of attention. Are you trying to get yourself killed?"

A hole formed in the bottom of my stomach. "A what?" This was so much worse than I'd thought. We weren't just in a brothel; it was a *fang* brothel. What was he doing here?

"We need to get you out of here." He brushed his lips over my neck, sending a shiver down my spine. "They might not be able to hear us over the rest of the noise, but I don't trust them to miss the crucifix around your neck or the stake at your waist."

Much as I hated to admit it, he was right. An unknown number of fangs surrounded us—at least some of the occupants of the room had to be human, but I didn't know how many. A fight would be suicide.

I gave him a lustful smile, raising my voice to a normal speaking volume. "Why don't we get out of here, then?"

"Is that an invitation to your bed, Legs?" His hands wrapped around my waist, and I felt him pluck the stake from my belt. A moment later, it was hidden in his pocket.

"If I say yes, will you stop asking?" I tilted my head to give him better access to my neck, and he trailed his lips downward. He caressed my cheek, then lower. When he reached my breasts, I felt the wooden beads of my rosary in his hand as he tucked it beneath my shirt. He lingered, and though I knew it was just for show, I couldn't stop the warmth spreading outward from his touch.

"Whatever you want," he said. Removing his hand from beneath my shirt, he turned toward the door.

A call from behind stopped us. "Where are you off to, DuMont?"

He pivoted, and I glanced back at the man at the card table. No, not a man. A fang. I could see the sharpness of his canine teeth. He had shoulder-length blond hair, and piercing blue eyes looked at us from beneath a heavy brow. He held a busty woman in his lap, her corset slipping down enough to reveal the pink of her areolae.

"She's so desperate for me, she followed me halfway across town." I pinched his rib at that, but he ignored me. "How could I say no? We'll have to finish our game tomorrow."

"Surely she can wait another half hour." The fang raised a brow at me. "We're almost done here, love. You can have him back as soon as I'm finished. DuMont could use a good luck charm, anyway."

I looped my arms around El's neck. We couldn't risk arousing more suspicion than I already had. "I suppose I can wait a little longer, darling. But hurry." I pressed a kiss to his cheek, praying silently to St. Michael for protection.

He slid back into his seat. "Okay, but this is the last game. You wouldn't believe the cockstand I have right now," he confided in a conspiratorial whisper to the fang.

As he settled me firmly onto his lap, something hard pressed into my buttocks, and I blinked at him. He wasn't lying. It wasn't the stake I felt—I could feel that, too, in his pocket.

My core turned molten. What would he feel like in my hand? Inside me?

"Pretty little thing you've got there, DuMont." One of the other men at the table eyed me as he picked up his cards again. "Where'd you find her?"

"Alsace." He ran a possessive hand up my stomach, coming to a stop just below my breast. My breath hitched, and it was all I could do not to lean into his touch. Something about the danger of the moment, the heat of his skin, and the knowledge that he was as affected by me as I was by him, all combined to send an exhilarating rush through me. "She was looking for her sister, and I thought I'd help her out a bit. In exchange for a price, of course.

"Of course." The man leered at me, and I leaned back against Du-Mont, running my hand through his hair.

Conversation lulled as they played their next two hands. I lounged on DuMont's lap, tracing the collar of his coat. Every so often, he took my hand and pressed a kiss to it or squeezed my waist. It was all for show, but with every passing moment, it became harder to see the line between truth and fiction.

Finally, he shifted in his seat, the movement drawing me from the haze of my thoughts. "You hear about the death at the Rijksmuseum?" he asked, considering his cards.

The fang's face darkened. "Yes. The idiot who did it is endangering us all."

"You know who it was, Koen?" one of the other men asked.

I tensed as we waited for his response, and DuMont put his lips on my neck, brushing them over my pulse. The silent warning grounded me, even as it traced a line of need straight to my core.

"I have my suspicions," Koen, the fang, replied. "There's a new nest in town, and while he's old enough to know better than drawing the attention of local authorities, I can't speak for his bride."

*Lucy.* I forced myself to stay relaxed in DuMont's arms as he said, "Friends of yours?"

Koen snorted. "Not remotely. Jakob von Peller is a pretentious ass. I'd give him a wide berth, if I were you."

El squeezed my waist. "Hopefully they'll move on soon."

"I doubt it. But one can always hope."

He sighed, then threw down his cards. "That's your win." Shifting me to his other leg, he took a stack of money from his jacket pocket and tossed it onto the table. "Thanks for the game."

"Thank *you,*" Koen said, gathering up his winnings and counting them.

The other man at the table leaned back in his chair. "Come back again. And bring your pretty pet with you."

The attention made me want to shudder, but I pasted a flattered smile on my face as DuMont set me on my feet. We made our way out without incident, but I didn't breathe a sigh of relief until the door to our hotel room closed behind us.

I pulled away from DuMont and crossed my arms. "Why didn't you tell me where you were going?" I backed against the wall. His nearness clouded my thoughts.

He tucked his thumbs into his pockets. "I thought you'd want to come with me, and I didn't want to risk my cover being blown. You're a better actor than I expected." He trailed his eyes down my body. "Unless you really are that attracted to me."

I forced a laugh. "You could only dream of being so lucky, Du-Mont."

"I think we're a tad too intimate for 'DuMont' now, aren't we, Anne?" He lowered his voice, and the sound of my name on his lips sent a shiver through me. He chuckled.

"How did you even know that place existed?" I asked, hoping the question would distract him from my unwelcome arousal.

"Did you catch the name of the street?" When I shook my head, he said, *"Bloedstraat."*

"Blood Street?"

He nodded. "The humans have different theories about where the name originated, but let's just say it isn't the safest part of the city to be in after dark."

I gripped my crucifix through the fabric of my shirt, looking out the window at the city. "You think that's where they are?"

"Bluebeard isn't exactly sociable with his own kind, as you heard tonight. He prefers to settle in among the humans. I doubt he's staying on Bloedstraat, unless his bride convinced him otherwise."

Not if she was anything like the sister I'd known. "Lucy would want to be in the center of the culture, nearest the art museums and dance halls and whatever else they have in this godforsaken city."

He grinned. "Not impressed with Amsterdam?"

"There are more brothels here than *churches!*" I hissed, waving a hand at the window. "There's a whole street dedicated to fangs. And everything smells like fish!"

"Paris isn't exactly the fairest-smelling city in the world," he laughed.

I glared at him. He wasn't wrong, but I didn't appreciate the criticism of my beloved city. "How did you find that place, anyway?" I asked, sinking into a chair. A chilling thought occurred to me, and I froze, staring up at him with wide eyes. "You are human, aren't you?"

"Would you like to test me to see if I'm a vampire?" He walked toward me, stopping inches away, and trailed his fingers down my neck. My breath caught when he stopped at my cleavage. "I'm happy to oblige."

For a moment, I thought he was going to pick up where we'd left off in the brothel, but when his hand dipped between my breasts, it was only to draw out my rosary. Holding it in his bare palm, he raised a brow. "Sufficient?"

His touch left me off balance, unable to think of an immediate response, and he took my silence as discontent.

"No?" Grabbing the vial of holy water from my waist, he popped the top off and took a swig. "Proof enough yet?"

I held up my hand. "I believe you! You're not a fang. But how did you know about that place?"

"I did some digging. If you know where to look, they're not hard to find."

If someone had asked me that same question in Paris, I'd have answered similarly. I knew what to look for when I was tracking a nest—signs of a recent feed, likely victims, common gathering places.

Which made it all the worse that I hadn't seen the warning signs with Lucy. An isolated young woman out at night alone...

"Hey." DuMont put a finger under my chin. "You look stuck inside your head. What's wrong?"

I shrugged him off and wiped my face of all emotion. "It's nothing."

He considered me for a moment before saying, "You know, I was wrong earlier."

"About what?" I wished he would step back. I couldn't think with him so close.

"You're a terrible actor. Your every thought is written on your face." His eyes twinkled with mischief. "Which means you weren't acting in the brothel."

My cheeks flooded with heat. So did my core.

I shoved him backwards, knocking him to the ground. He laughed loudly as he landed on his ass.

"You're insufferable, *El.* Did you know that?" I grabbed his coat from where he'd thrown it on the bed and pulled my stake from his pocket. Not to threaten him—though the hint of fear that crept into his eyes was an added bonus—but because I needed something to focus on besides him.

I tucked the stake into its sheath as El climbed to his feet, still laughing.

"I'm going back out to hunt," I said, turning to the door. "Whenever you're able to focus, you're welcome to join me."

He stopped just inches behind me, breath hot on my ear. "I can focus on the chase just fine. But you know what I'm going to dream about when I go to bed?"

I swallowed hard. I refused to answer him, but I couldn't bring myself to tell him off again. Not when rejecting his advances already took all my willpower.

"You. Naked beneath me, screaming my name."

Lewd, filthy images filled my mind as he stepped away, giving me space. I tucked my coat tighter around my body, as though it could protect me from my own weak will. Getting involved with him would only draw my attention from where it needed to be: on catching the fangs we were hunting.

"I'll see you at sunrise," I said, and I slipped out the door before I could go back on my resolve.

I spent the rest of the night patrolling Vondelpark. Moonlight reflected off the waterways, and the perfume of flowers and greenery provided a welcome reprieve from the stench of fish, but I saw no sign of the vampires.

The bed was undisturbed when I returned to the hotel near dawn. I hoped El's search had proven more fruitful than my own. I took my hair down from its braid and dressed for bed, trying not to let my thoughts dwell on him.

A soft knock sounded at the door as I knotted the belt on my dressing gown. El walked in carrying a tray of food and coffee.

"Oh, good. You're still awake." He turned his charming grin on me, setting the plate on the desk. "I wasn't sure what you liked to eat in the morning, so I brought you a *uitsmijter*. It's my favorite Dutch breakfast." He handed me toasted white bread topped with cheese, fried eggs, and ham. My stomach rumbled at the savory smells of the food mingling with the perfume of fresh coffee.

"Thank you," I said, settling onto the bed. I cut into the food and took a bite. The egg yolk ran over the plate, soaking the crunchy piece of toast, as El poured us both a cup of coffee and set mine on the table next to the bed.

I'd expected something...different. Not of the food—it was good—but of him. He was acting as though last night hadn't happened. Unless I'd imagined everything between us.

No, I hadn't imagined his response in the brothel or the lust in his eyes before we left for our patrols. But if he wanted to act unphased, so could I.

"How was your night?" I asked.

"Nothing to report," he said around a bite of *uitsmijter*. "They weren't taking a midnight ride through the canals, and none of the staff at the theaters I went to had seen them. You?"

"The same. I searched all of Vondelpark and didn't see a single sign of them."

We lapsed into silence as we ate. The past day and night were starting to wear on me, and the combination of food and hot coffee lulled me into a contented state of relaxation. El seemed the same; his eyes drooped as he sipped from his cup.

"You should get some rest," he said at last. "It's been a long night."

"What about you?" The bed was big enough for both of us, but I didn't relish the thought of trying to fall asleep with his body pressed against mine. Not after the brothel.

"I'm not tired," he lied. "I'll probably go for a run, then come back and bathe."

The image of him in the bath filled my head, but I pushed it away. "Wake me up when you're ready to go to bed. I don't need more than a couple hours, and that way you can have the bed to yourself."

I didn't miss the way his throat bobbed, but he nodded. "Sleep well." Before I could say anything else, he was gone.

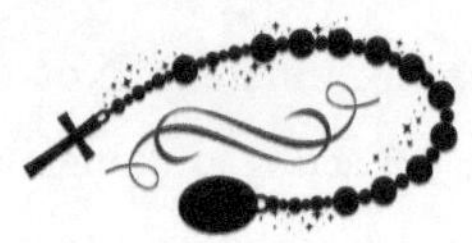

I woke up alone that afternoon. Rubbing my eyes, I looked around. The bathroom door was closed, and I could hear faint splashing sounds behind it. I'd slept for hours, far longer than I'd expected to.

The knock that had woken me sounded again. I stood, tightened the belt on my robe, and went to open the door. A young boy stood in the hall, holding out a paper.

"A message for El DuMont," he said.

I took it, then fumbled in my bag for a coin. Prize obtained, he ran off.

The bathroom door opened behind me. I turned to see El coming out, shirtless and freshly shaved, hair glistening from his bath.

"You have a message." I passed him the note, trying not to notice how the droplets of water clung to the lion etched into his chest, or the way the feathers of the phoenix on his right arm rippled with movement.

He read the note and cursed under his breath.

"What is it?"

"They left town." He handed the paper to me. Detective Braam had called the hotel to let El know they'd found the hotel where Bluebeard and his bride were staying. They had checked out unexpectedly late last night.

"We have to go. We have to catch them." I reached for my pack. Thankfully, I hadn't unpacked; as I had been every night since Lucy died, I was ready to leave at a moment's notice.

"Go where?" El reached for his shirt, unperturbed. "They're vampires. If they left last night, who knows how far they could be by now? Rushing off half-cocked won't do any good."

He was right, and it only infuriated me further. If he hadn't diverted my attention last night, I might have been focused enough to find Lucy and Bluebeard as they fled the city. This could have all been over by now.

I closed my eyes, counting silently to ten. When I opened them again, my frustration had ebbed slightly. El watched me with a question written on his face.

It wasn't him I was angry with; it was myself. I'd lost sight of my goal for one brief night. I wouldn't make the same mistake again.

He reached for his jacket. "The trail's not cold yet; we can't just run after them, but we can still question the hotel staff. Someone might have overheard mention of their next destination."

I grabbed my own coat and slung it around my shoulders. Maybe we could still catch them. This was the closest I'd been since Alsace, and I had no intention of losing the trail now.

The hotel Lucy and her husband had been staying at was new, only eight years old. Situated near the Centraal station, it was enormous and thoroughly modern, illuminated with electric lighting. While I didn't understand the appeal of such a place, I could picture Lucy being fascinated with it. She'd always adored novelty, and the views of the canals and churches would have thrilled her.

The worker at the desk wore a bored expression, eyes half-glazed. He stirred as El and I approached.

"We don't have any vacancies," he said, angling his body away from us. "You'll have to try somewhere else."

El tucked his hands into his pockets, grinning. "That's not strictly true, is it, *meneer?* You had a couple check out late last night. Or have you already booked that room?"

He scowled as he turned back to us. "I already told the police everything I know. And you don't look like officers." He gave me a disparaging look, clearly unimpressed with my unconventional attire.

El pulled a badge from his coat and showed it to the clerk. "Detective El DuMont. This is my partner, Anne Allard. We're tracking a criminal who passed through here recently. I believe you might have come across him. Tall man, bluish beard, traveling with his young wife?"

The clerk squinted suspiciously at the badge and then at me. "The French will allow anyone to join the police force, I see. *Ja,* I saw him. As I said, I told the police everything I know."

"Our investigation is separate from the local police," El said, all smiles and charm. "I'm sure you don't mind answering some questions from me and my *fully qualified* partner."

"What do you need to know?" From the set of the man's jaw, it was clear that he *did* mind, but he'd decided to cooperate for the moment. I resolved to remain quiet and let El ask the questions. We needed his cooperation, and it was clear that he wouldn't respond well to me.

"Did they mention where they were going?" El asked.

"South. She said something about beaches. As I told the police a few hours ago."

El glanced at me, and I nodded. It wasn't a lot to go on, but it did give us a start. Spain, Portugal, Italy, Greece...Lucy would have loved to visit any of those places.

"Did they socialize with anyone while they were here?"

"No." He pursed his lips. "They stayed in their room all day, refused all service, and went out every night."

"How long were they here?"

"Almost a month." He glanced at the clock. "If that's all, I have duties to attend to."

There were plenty more questions we could have asked, but the most pressing one had been answered, and it was clear that the clerk had reached the end of his patience with us. "Thank you for your cooperation," El said. "If you think of anything else, please don't hesitate to reach out. We're staying at the—"

He was already walking away. El shook his head, turning to me.

"Where to next?"

I made a face at him. "Pardon?"

"She's your sister. Where would she want to go? Somewhere south, with beaches."

As we left the hotel, I thought back on all the places Lucy had talked about. "I think it's safe to assume the Mediterranean. We can eliminate France, probably." After spending her whole life in France, she wouldn't be likely to wish to return so soon. Her letter had mentioned that she'd already been to Spain and Portugal, and knowing Lucy's penchant for novelty, she wouldn't want to revisit those countries already. "Italy would be my best guess."

"Half the country is holy ground. Would they really risk it?"

The Lucy I'd known was never daunted by a challenge. "Bluebeard is old enough to know how to avoid holy ground. Everyone who's seen them together says he's smitten with her. If she wanted to go somewhere, do you think he'd deny her?"

"If she's half the beauty her sister is, he wouldn't dare." He winked at me, and I rolled my eyes. The man was shameless.

The despair that I'd felt at the arrival of Detective Braam's letter had abated slightly. Maybe we would catch them.

El stopped, leaning against the railing over the canal. "We should see what Braam has to say about the case, and then we can catch the next train headed south. What do you think—Rome? Naples? Palermo?"

The answer was out before I had time to think about it. "Rome." When we were younger, Lucy had gone through a period of fascination with the Roman Empire. She'd spent hours reading books about emperors whose names I could never remember, painting pictures of the Colosseum and the Pantheon.All that had been before Maman and Papa died, but her love for the culture hadn't faded. She wouldn't be able to see the Sistine Chapel or the other sights in Vatican City, but of all the cities in Italy, Rome would be her first choice. "If I'm wrong, we'll be that much closer to the sea."

"If they spent a month here, I think it's safe to assume they'll spend just as long wherever they go next. We'll have time to catch them." He glanced at me, brown eyes twinkling. "Though perhaps I'm being presumptuous. I seem to recall you stating that our agreement was for the duration of our time in Amsterdam."

I had said that. I hated being proven wrong, but working with him had been to my benefit. He had more resources, more hunting skills than I did. He excelled at detective work; I was little more than a weapon in need of a target to aim at.

"What do you think, Legs? I thought we made a pretty good team."

I wasn't sure there had been much *teamwork* happening. He'd done everything. I'd just watched. But I couldn't admit that to him. "I suppose you didn't slow me down too much," I said, keeping my voice casual.

His wicked grin turned my pulse erratic. "So you'll stay."

"We can extend our arrangement a bit longer."

"Excellent." He pushed off the railing. "Why don't you get our train tickets, and I'll check in with Detective Braam. We can meet at the hotel in an hour."

The train left early the next morning. Unlike the train into Amsterdam, it was far less busy, and I'd managed to book us adjoining rooms. From the smirk on El's face, I could tell that he had considered the possibility of being forced to share a room again—and that he hadn't been as concerned by that thought as I had been.

We spent the first day on the train planning our stay in Rome, making lists of places to search and people to speak to. When he was younger, El told me, he had lived in Rome for a year, and he still had friends on the police force in the city.

I slept restfully that night alone in my room, and the following morning, the train pulled to a stop alongside a crystalline lake. The conductor, passing through the cars, announced that we'd reached the Swiss city of Interlaken.

As passengers disembarked and new ones boarded, I took the opportunity to stretch my legs outside on the platform. Brisk air blew down from the craggy, snow-capped mountains and across the lake.

I breathed it in, glad to be free from the fishy smell of Amsterdam. The sunshine sparkled on the azure water below us, and above us, mountains brushed the bottom of the clouds.

It almost made me wish I was a painter, just so I could capture the beauty of the scene.

El stopped beside me, shoving his hands in his pockets and looking out at the water. "You've never been to Interlaken?"

"I'd never left France until a few months ago," I said. I looked out at the city, the picturesque hotels and churches dotting the base of the mountains.

"I'm glad you've finally stepped outside of your bounds." His voice held a strange note, but when I glanced at him, he looked away.

*"Herr* DuMont?" A rosy-cheeked boy approached us.

"That's me."

The boy held out a paper. "A telegram for you."

He opened it and read, sucking in a breath. "Saints above. It looks like your instincts were right." He passed me the telegram.

It came from Detective Braam in Amsterdam, alerting El of a murder that had occurred overnight in Rome. The body had been laid out deliberately, just like the bodies at the Rijksmuseum and in Berlin.

"How did he hear about it?" I asked, passing the telegram back to him. "He's further from Italy than we are."

"My contacts in Rome knew where to find me. They must have sent word to the station in Amsterdam as soon as they found the body."

"And Braam sent the telegram here, knowing we'd have to stop to let off passengers." How far did DuMont's network of influence extend? Contacts in Lisbon, Amsterdam, Rome. Did he even need me on this hunt?

The boy who delivered the telegram looked back and forth between us, rubbing a spot on his red nose as he frowned in confusion. "Shall I send a reply?"

El dug in his pocket for a pencil. When he didn't find one, I sighed loudly and pulled one from my bag—even on a first-class train, I wasn't leaving my belongings unattended in the room. El wrote a quick answer on the back of the telegram, pressing it into the boy's hand with payment.

As the boy ran off into the city, the conductor began calling for us to board again. I groaned at the thought of being stuck on the train for the rest of the day.

"Not enjoying the journey?" El asked as we walked back toward the train.

"It's not that." I hefted my bag back onto my shoulder. "I was just hoping for more time to stretch my legs."

He glanced sideways at me. "I'm sure I could find something to do that would stretch you out."

I rolled my eyes, ignoring the thrill that ran through me at the thought. The man was incorrigible and entirely insincere. "I thought I said I wasn't sleeping with you, DuMont."

"I live with the hope that you'll change your mind." He offered his hand to help me board. "Come on. I'll buy you a drink."

I ignored his hand and stepped up. "Not even if you get me drunk."

"I meant coffee, but I like the way your mind works, Legs." He stepped onto the train close behind me, and his body heat seeped into mine. "I'll keep that in mind for next time."

The rock he kicked thunks against the wall of the stone theater. It's dark enough that he can barely see what he's kicking, late enough that he should be home, but he doesn't want to go home. Not yet. He'll wait until Papà is asleep in his chair. Until the house is dark and quiet and it's safe enough to slip through the front door, past his sleeping father and down the hall to his bedroom.

It's more fun to wander the streets at night, anyway. With school in the morning and work at the docks until well after sunset, he doesn't have time for fun during the day. At night, when the streets are empty, Rome is his to explore. As long as he avoids the few people who prowl the city, he can kick rocks or splash in Trevi Fountain or sneak into the Colosseum and play gladiator in the ruins. Papà won't come looking for him. No one will.

Ambling down the street, he spots something small and round hiding in a corner. Fruit! Someone must have dropped it. His stomach rumbles at the thought. He didn't eat supper tonight, too afraid of what Papà might be like if he went home.

He grabs the orange, glancing furtively around for anyone who might dare to steal his treasure. Finding no one, he tears into the rind, releasing the tangy smell of citrus into the night. It's still fresh, not yet spoiled by the warm, springtime air. He bites into the sweet fruit, and juice bursts on his tongue, trickling down to fill his aching belly.

"Are you lost, dear boy?"

A woman's voice interrupts his feasting, and he flinches, shoving his hands behind his back so she doesn't take his prize.

He doesn't see her, but he swallows the mouthful of orange and says, "No, *signora.*"

"Sweet things shouldn't be out so late." The voice is nearer now, though there's still no one in sight. "They ought to be tucked up in bed."

"I don't want to go home," he admits. His skin prickles as he looks around for her.

"Little boys should be home after dark." The voice comes from a different direction now.

Where is she? He backs into the corner, scanning the empty street. He's held his orange too tight; juice drips from his fists. "I was going to go home soon."

The shuffle of feet nears, and his heart races. He should have gone home tonight. Facing Papà and his nightly anger would have been better than being out here with whatever ghost is haunting him

Something unseen grabs him, and he screams.

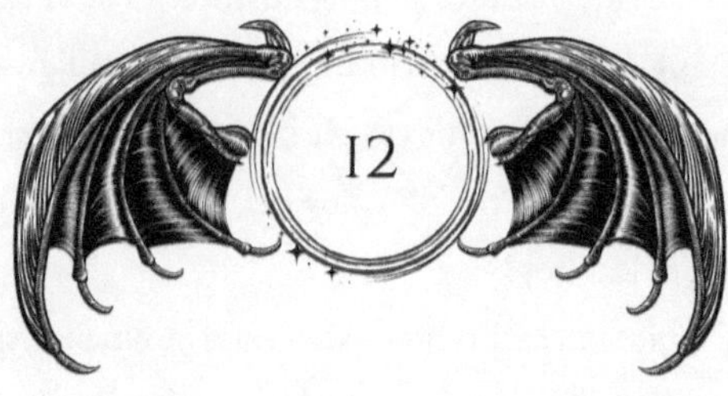



Salt-kissed air washed over me as we walked through the city. Modern buildings sprung up like vines between ancient ruins, and each step was like walking through time. The sounds of the boisterous Italian tongue filled my ears as the orange sunset lit everything on fire.

Unlike Amsterdam, no one had met us at the train station. El seemed to know where he was going, though, weaving seamlessly through the busy street without pausing to look around. I kept close behind him, not wanting to get lost in the bustling city.

A hand reached out to grab me. *"Bellissima,"* the old man said, running his fingers over my braid. He said something too fast for me to catch, but judging by the leer on his face, it wasn't complimentary.

I reached for the weapon at my waist, but El was there before I could react. "Leave her alone," he said, stepping between us. The man held his hands up, backing away as he muttered a response.

"Oh, *vaffanculo!*" El shouted as the man melted back into the crowd. He turned back to me, looking me over to ensure I was unharmed. "Are you okay?"

"I'm fine. Thank you." I hadn't been in any danger—I would have been able to overpower the man if it had come to a fight—but I appreciated his interference anyway.

He scanned the crowd, but everyone gave us a wide berth. "We're almost there. Stay close." Keeping a firm grip on my arm, he guided me down the street to a white stone building marked *Polizia*.

Inside the busy station, El waved to a bearded detective frowning at paperwork on his desk. "*Dottore* Bianchi!"

The man's face lit up when he saw DuMont. "*Signore* DuMont! *Salve!*" He strode over to us, arms out wide, and shook El's hand, clapping him on the back. "*Como stai?*"

"*Bene, bene.*" El turned to me. "Bianchi, this is my partner, Anne Allard. Allard, Detective Alonzo Bianchi."

"Such a *bella,*" he said, smiling broadly at me. "How did you end up with this *vecchio, signora?*"

I hardly thought El counted as an *old man*, but I laughed. "It was a matter of shared interests, I suppose." I held out my hand to him.

He shook it, keeping it in his grasp when he looked back at El. "You are here quickly, DuMont. You cannot have received my telegram?" He raised a dark, bushy brow in question. "I sent it only last night."

"We were on the train here already. Amsterdam forwarded it to our stop in Interlaken. Do you have time to talk us through the case?"

"I can spare the time for an espresso and conversation with an old friend." He tucked my hand into his arm. "You will permit me to buy you a true Italian *caffè, signora?*"

"I think you'll find *Signora* Allard is more resistant to your charms than the women you're used to, Bianchi." El winked at him. "After all, she hasn't fallen for me yet."

"Or maybe I just prefer to be wooed with fine Italian espresso," I retorted.

Detective Bianchi laughed as he led me toward the door. "Yes, perhaps you should work on your technique, *amico.*"

The hour was still early for dinner, not quite eight, so the cafe he took us to, labeled "Antico Caffè Greco" by the weathered metal sign above the door, was nearly empty. We stood at the bar while the barista made three tiny *caffès* and placed them in front of us.

El reached for the sugar as Detective Bianchi and I picked up our cups and drained them. When I gave him a judgmental look, he shrugged. "Coffee should be savored." He stirred a generous spoonful into the thick black liquid before taking a sip.

"*Dai, amico.* Still so uncultured. You have not changed." Bianchi shook his head. "In more ways than one. I do not believe you have aged a day since the last time I saw you."

"I could say the same of you," El said, taking another sip of his drink. "Though I think you've gotten fatter."

"You would be fat, too, if you had a wife who could cook like mine." He patted his belly and let out a booming laugh. "Perhaps one day you will be so lucky."

I fiddled with my empty cup, determined not to show any reaction to that statement. There wasn't anything between me and DuMont. We were partners. Just partners.

*Ah, but then why do you find it so hard to keep your eyes off him?* I heard Henri's voice say in my head. I scowled at the remaining drips of espresso in my cup.

Luckily, El took the opportunity to change the subject. "Your telegram said you had a case for us?"

"Yes, yes." He nodded vigorously. "It was not the sort of crime that would draw attention. Tragic, yes, but hardly newsworthy. A young boy, perhaps a beggar, found in an alley near the Colosseum. He was filthy with blood and dirt, wrapped up in a blanket. He looked as though a wild animal had attacked him, and someone came along and staged the body afterwards."

Strange. I wouldn't have expected Lucy to choose someone covered in dirt for her victim. One year, when we were children, we'd gone to visit Maman's cousin in the countryside. Lucy had seen the pigs wallowing in the mud, and after that, she'd refused to eat pork for months. She had an aversion to all things dirty.

But Lucy was dead, I reminded myself for the millionth time. I was chasing a demon wearing her skin, not my sister. The craving for blood would overwhelm any human sensibilities that remained in her.

"Is that not newsworthy?" I asked, returning to the issue at hand. "A child murdered in the shadows of a historical monument?"

"Unfortunately not, *signora.*" The detective gave me an apologetic shrug. "This is a large city. Without someone to claim the boy, his death, macabre as it is, will likely go unnoticed by all but a select few."

Anger at the injustice pounded against my skull. It wasn't fair that this child's murder should go overlooked just because he had no one to look for him. I'd been infuriated by the same thing when working for Les Gardiens. We'd been required to investigate certain crimes and leave others alone. And while the reasoning for that had made sense—the police existed to deal with *normal* crime, while we dealt with the supernatural—it had never sat right with me.

I knew I couldn't help everyone, but I never could understand overlooking something just because it didn't fit the parameters I'd been given.

El gave me a curious look, and I shook myself, turning my attention back to the conversation. "What made you think of me?" he asked.

"You said you were looking for neck wounds, bodies drained of blood and laid out with care, *sì*? So when I saw it I knew I must send word to you."

"I'm glad you did. We had a suspicion he was traveling this way, though we didn't expect him to move so fast." Draining his coffee, he set the cup back on the bar. "Where is the body now?"

"A small abbey took it to prepare for burial." He glanced at his watch. "They won't be accepting visitors now, but perhaps tomorrow after *Pasqua* services they will permit you to view the body."

*Pasqua.* Easter. I was entirely unprepared for the holiest day of the year. It had been months since I'd gone to Confession, let alone Mass, and I didn't have a single dress with me. While I didn't care what most people thought of my attire, I tried to dress appropriately when entering a cathedral, at least.

"We'll do that." Pulling a map of the city from his pocket, El said, "If you'll give us the address, we'll go tomorrow. Unless you have any objections, Allard?"

Dragging myself from my guilt-filled reverie, I shook my head. "That's fine."

"*Bene.* Here is where the body was found." Bianchi marked it on the map. "The abbey is here. You might find a spare room at one of the hotels nearby. And perhaps I will see you soon, *sì?*"

Waving goodbye, he headed out the door, and El turned to me.

"We should find a place to stay," he said. "We can patrol the area where the body was found tonight, and rest up in the morning while the abbey holds their Mass."

"And miss Easter Mass?" I shook my head, heading toward the door. "I may not be a good Catholic, but the only way I'm missing that is if they bar me from the cathedral."

El kept pace with me as we walked down the street. "Do you expect to be locked out of Mass?" he laughed.

I gestured at my brown coat and black pants, which were drawing stares from passersby again. "I didn't exactly pack cathedral-appropriate clothing for a hunting trip."

He stopped, and when I realized he wasn't walking with me, I turned around. His gaze bored into me.

"What?" I shifted my bag so I held it in both arms, a shield against the intensity in his eyes. "Do I have something on my face?"

He shook his head, seeming to come back to himself. "Nothing. It's nothing. I'm just having difficulty picturing you in a dress."

"Well, you'll have to keep picturing it. Unless you happen to have a woman's Sunday dress in your case," I nodded at the large leather trunk he carried, "I'll have to remain in my pants." I cringed internally at that, knowing I'd given him the perfect opportunity to make a comment about helping me out of my pants.

He didn't take advantage of my slip of the tongue, hefting his trunk again and continuing down the street. "I'll see to it that you make it to Mass in the morning, Legs. Dress or no dress."

Easter festivities left the city packed with people, and we were lucky to find a tiny room available for double what it was worth. I stared at the bed, trying not to dwell on the idea of spending hours pressed up against him. At least in Amsterdam, I'd been able to scoot against the wall and pretend he wasn't there. In this miniscule bed, that would be impossible.

After depositing our things in the room, we headed back out to streets filled with people heading to and from dinner. We made a quick stop at the police station, where El slipped inside to tell Detective Bianchi where we were staying. Then we blended back in with the crowd as best as we could. My appearance, as ever, drew stares, but unlike earlier in the day, no one made any unwanted comments as we kept an eye out for unusual activity.

As the crowds began to disperse, El bought us each a small dinner of *filetto di baccala,* crispy fried fish, and we ate it against the ancient walls of the Colosseum.

"Do you think they'll visit the same place a second night in a row?" I asked, looking out over the garden below us.

"I should be asking you that same question." Crumbling the paper cone his fish came in, he tucked it into his pocket and brushed the crumbs from his coat. "They shouldn't need to feed again so soon, not after two kills in a week, but would your sister consider a single night hunting outside the Colosseum sufficient time to explore it?"

"No." I crumpled my own paper cone and tucked it into my pocket. My fingers were greasy, the salty taste of the fish lingered on my lips, and my stomach was filled. "She'd probably spend nights upon nights perched on a wall outside, sketching it from every angle."

We began to circle the amphitheater again. "Does she like to draw?"

"She did." I let my mind wander through the halls of our home, remembering all the art she'd decorated it with. "And paint. She sculpted, on occasion, too, but she preferred to paint and sketch."

He fell silent for a moment. Then he asked, in a voice so low I almost missed it, "You loved her a lot, didn't you?"

My throat swelled. "She was my everything." And then I'd killed her.

I pushed back the unwanted feelings. "It doesn't matter anymore. She's gone. But the demon could still be here."

He didn't respond, and I looked up at the clear night sky. The waning moon cast bright light on us. These past few months I'd felt out of touch with my faith, disconnected from the Church. Absent from both Mass and Confession, I'd been punishing myself for the sins I'd committed against God and my sister.

Tonight, the cool spring wind wrapped around me, reminding me of the Easter Vigil. The moon served as my candle, and the Lumen Christi echoed through my mind. *Deo Gratias. Thanks be to God.* I hadn't found much to thank God for lately, but shouldn't I have? Despite all I'd done, the damnation I should have earned by murdering my sister and allowing her to become a demon, He'd lain in the tomb on this Holy Saturday for me.

I took a deep breath, drawing my rosary from beneath my shirt. I would spend centuries, perhaps millennia in purgatory, but at least one day I would see paradise.

El seemed wrapped up in thoughts of his own, staring off into the sky, so I took advantage of the silence of the night to pray the Sorrowful Mysteries, reflecting on Christ's sacrifice for me.

The night remained uneventful, peaceful. As the sky turned gray in the east, we headed back into the hotel.

"If you expect to find a Mass to attend, we ought to leave soon," El said. "Or else we'll end up standing for the whole service. Go get ready. I'll find us some breakfast."

I reached for my bag, but he nudged it out of reach with his foot. "You won't need that." He jerked his head toward the bathroom. "In there."

Frowning, I slipped into the bathroom, and my heart stuttered. Hanging above the bathtub was a high-collared lavender dress. The long sleeves gathered at the shoulder, loosening at the wrists. Brass buttons lined the front of the fitted waist down to the fuller skirt.

I rarely felt comfortable in anything but pants, but this was perfect for me. Simple and loose enough to allow for freedom of movement, it didn't look—unlike so many popular dresses—like a ribbon shop had vomited on top of it. Even the hat next to it, a few shades darker than the dress, was small and unpretentious, adorned with a single white lily.

When I emerged from the bathroom clean and fully dressed, El sat on the bed finishing a pastry, cappuccino in hand. His eyes widened as he looked me over.

"Where did you get this?" I asked.

His cheeks pinkened. "I thought you might like something to wear to Mass. Something that wouldn't get you expelled from the cathedral," he added with a wink. "I asked Bianchi to find something and have it delivered to the hotel. And he outdid himself."

"Thank you, El. It's perfect."

He shook himself and waved toward the desk, where a second cappuccino and pastry waited. "You should eat. I won't be long."

The room was too small—he had to squeeze past me to get to the bathroom, and my stomach did a little flip at the proximity. When the door closed behind him, I heard the sound of fabric hitting the floor, followed a moment later by water running. He was naked just on the other side of that door...

No. I didn't need to think about that. I already had too much to confess. I picked up my cappuccino and took a giant gulp of the foamy drink. I could still hear the water splashing.

I reached for my revolver, hoping to lose myself in the familiar process of cleaning it, but I had already cleaned it thoroughly on the train to Rome. The same went for my crossbow pistol. Everything from my Saint-Étienne to my dagger was polished, waxed, and sharpened to perfection.

When DuMont emerged from the bathroom twenty minutes later, I'd arranged all my weapons in a line across the desk, and I was inspecting them for nonexistent blemishes.

"I thought we were going to church, not battle," he said.

I turned to him, and a hot rush of need went straight to my core. The dark olive tweed of his suit hugged his body. The crisp white shirt beneath his vest sent butterflies through me as I imagined the tattoos it hid. I followed the fabric up to where his brown eyes twinkled at me.

"If you keep looking at me like that, Legs, I can't promise you'll make it to church." He pulled a folded paper from his breast pocket. "Which would be a shame after I went to the trouble of securing tickets for the Papal Mass."

It took a moment for the words to sink in. "The Papal Mass?" I couldn't tear my eyes from the paper he held. "At St. Peter's Basilica?"

"Unless you know of another one." He took the hat from under his arm and put it on. "Come along. We don't want to be late."

By ten that morning, St. Peter's Basilica was packed with people, but the pounding in my chest had nothing to do with the crowds pressing in on every side, or even with the man holding tightly to my arm. As the bells called us to Mass, I wanted to look everywhere at once. The towering cathedral with its white stone columns rivaled even Notre Dame in beauty. I drank it all in, from the tall domed ceiling to the rich artwork adorning every surface.

When the procession passed by, I had to stand on my toes to catch a glimpse of the white-haired Pope Leo XIII carried on his red-and-gold throne. The sweet incense smoke wafted over the crowd, accompanied by the sound of trumpets. It was like being inside the gates of heaven.

Tears threatened, blurring my vision throughout the chanting of prayers and Scripture. When His Holiness received Communion, they spilled over onto my cheeks and streamed downward. I closed my eyes, listening to the chants echo around me. It was as though I could actually see paradise before me. I wanted to collapse to the ground in worship, but the press of people and El's steadying hand kept me on my feet.

As the service ended and worshipers trickled out of the sanctuary, I remained awestruck, caught up in the glory of the Mass. El didn't pressure me to move, and by the time I finally shook myself back to my senses, the crowd had dwindled significantly.

"*Pardon,*" I muttered, wiping the already-dried tears from my face. El watched me with a strange look, as though he'd never seen me before.

He gestured down the aisle. "Would you like to see more of the cathedral?"

It was an opportunity I couldn't refuse. Crossing myself with the near-empty bowl of holy water near the entrance, I breathed in deep, smelling the lingering tendrils of incense and the stench of sweat from thousands of worshipers. Other churchgoers crowded around the Altar of St. Peter in hopes of a chance to touch the papal throne. His

Holiness had already left, and I felt too reflective to battle the crowds about St. Peter's tomb, so I looked around.

My gaze landed on the altar for St. Michael, and I moved toward it, pulled like a magnet. Compared to St. Peter's altar, it was nothing, but I dropped my offering into the box and lit a candle, kneeling before it. As the leader of the army of God, St. Michael seemed fitting. I was fighting a battle of my own, small though it was.

I heard the clink of another coin as El dropped his own offering and knelt next to me.

I'd never pictured him as a particularly religious man, and the act set me off balance. I peeked at him out of the corner of my eye. His head bowed in reverence, no hint of mockery on his face. He was more sincere than I'd expected he could be.

When he remained silent, eyes closed and head down, I turned my attention to my own prayer.

*Saint Michael the Archangel, defend us in battle.* How many times had I prayed that prayer before a hunt? It took on a new meaning now that the demon I hunted was my sister.

*Be our protection against the wickedness and snares of the devil.* I could feel it within me, an insidious vulnerability to the devil's snares. I knew the demon we hunted wasn't my sister, but even after all these months, I still found myself caring for her. If I saw her, if she spoke to me, I didn't know that I'd have the strength to kill her a second time.

*May God rebuke him, we humbly pray; and do thou, O Prince of the Heavenly Host, by the power of God, thrust into hell Satan and all evil spirits who wander the world for the ruin of souls.* All evil spirits. Lucy was one of those evil spirits. Was I really asking St. Michael to cast her into hell? Did she deserve that? Tears stung my eyes, and I blinked them away.

Lucy, my Lucy, was dead. I wasn't petitioning the archangel to damn her. I was asking him to grant peace to her body, impossible though it might have felt. And like all the saints and angels, he would hear my prayer and answer it.

I just hoped he didn't judge me as damned along with the demons I hunted.

"Amen," I murmured, crossing myself. Next to me, El did the same. He rose and offered me a hand.

I let him pull me to my feet. Turning my head, I dabbed at my eyes, and he tactfully didn't mention the tears that I failed to hide.

"Did you want to see anything else?" he asked.

Glancing at the altar to St. Peter, I saw that the crowd hadn't abated. I'd have been happy to spend all day in the basilica, hiding from the demons that plagued me, but I couldn't hide forever.

If—*when*—we finished this hunt, I would come back here and pay my respects to St. Peter. I clutched my rosary, making my silent vow. I'd return and see the whole basilica. I'd light a candle for my sister's soul at every altar.

"No," I said, shaking my head. "I've seen enough."

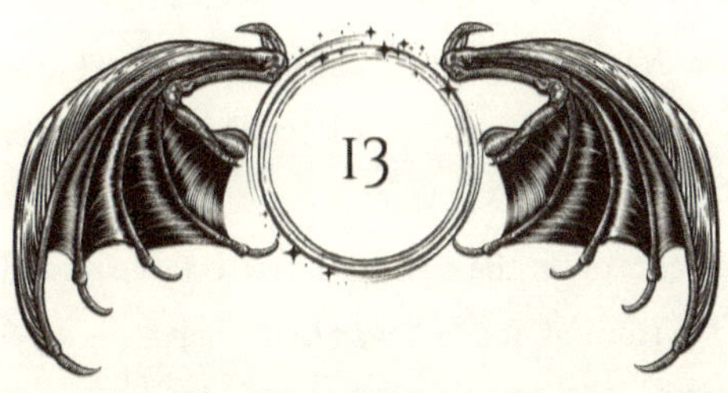

13

The small abbey sat tucked into an easily overlooked back street. El rang the bell, and after a long moment, the rusted iron grate swung open with a creak. A nun appeared, the black veil over her head casting a severe shadow over her features.

"Good afternoon, *signora,*" El said, sweeping the hat off of his head and bowing. We hadn't changed clothes after service, so I still wore the elegant lavender dress he'd had his friend obtain for me. The sister didn't look twice at me—a novel sensation. "*Dottore* Bianchi sent us. I'm El DuMont, and this is my partner, Anne Allard. We're here to examine the body you received the other day." He produced a paper from inside his coat and handed it to her with a flourish.

She read it over, then gave me a curious look. Even dressed properly, a woman was an odd addition to a murder investigation.

"Follow me," she said finally.

The sound of chanting echoed from the stone walls, evidence that the abbey's occupants were conducting their midafternoon *none* service, as she led us down a long hall. The sound faded the further we went from the sanctuary, leaving in its wake the echo of our footsteps on the polished floor. The sister directed us to a small, white-washed room, where a child's body lay on a cot, covered in a white linen sheet.

"Thank you, sister," El said. "We'll let you know if we need anything else."

She raised her brow at the clear dismissal, but she bowed her head, hands folded in front of her. "I'll wait in the hall."

Despite the dead body lying in the cool, clean room, no flies had found their way to it. As the door closed behind the sister, El folded the cloth down to reveal the head and bare chest of a young boy, no older than ten. His mangled skin—a sun-kissed brown, as though he spent most of his time outdoors—bore jagged bite marks. There was no doubt he'd been killed by a fang, though if the papers mentioned him at all, they'd call it a wild animal.

El set down his bag and knelt next to it, rifling through to find a tape measure. He measured the width of each bite mark and made notes. He frowned and muttered to himself as he worked, too quiet for me to hear. I looked on in bemusement, unsure what else to do.

Finally he stood. "It looks like there's just one attacker."

Disappointment flooded me. I'd been so sure this was where Lucy would go. "So it's not Bluebeard—Peller." *Bluebeard.* It seemed El's ridiculous nickname for the fang was wearing off on me.

"I can't say for sure." He handed me his notebook, flipping to a page filled with numbers. "Here's his marks on the women in the tower, but with the desiccation, they won't be precise enough for comparison. I have some older measurements from some of his presumed victims, but all I can say for sure is that all the wounds were made by the same creature."

"A fang."

He nodded. "There's nothing to confirm the attacker's identity, unless you have other suggestions."

I laughed. "I was a Gardien, not an investigator. My job was to wait for orders and attack. I'm no good at the rest of this."

"That's not true." He nudged me with his elbow. "You made the connection about the last body and the painting, and you led us to Rome."

"Only after *you* found out they were heading south."

"You're smarter than you think you are, Legs. You have to trust yourself." Opening the door, he waved to the sister waiting in the hall. "Did he have any effects?"

"Just his clothes. They're with the police."

"Then I think we're finished here." El turned to me. "Unless you have any questions."

I shook my head.

He gave her a slip of paper. "If you think of anything else that might be helpful in our investigation, please reach out."

She led us back through the long halls of the abbey. Once the gate closed behind us, I asked, "What now?"

The grin lighting up his face told me I wouldn't like what he had to say. "How do you feel about another round of acting?"

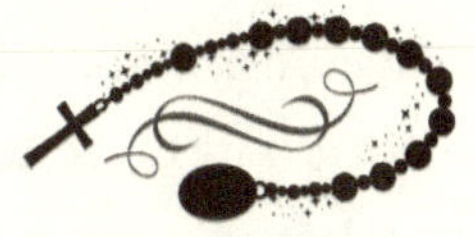

When I woke late that afternoon in the hotel bed, the smell of coffee and gunpowder filled my nose. My cheek pressed up against something comfortingly warm and solid.

I opened my eyes, and my heart stuttered to a stop. I was resting on El's chest, his breathing deep and even. Caught between him and the wall, I had nowhere to go.

As carefully as I could, I inched toward the foot of the bed.

His arm snaked out to wrap around my waist, stopping me in my tracks. "If you wanted to get up," he said, not opening his eyes, "you could have just asked."

Irrational mortification burned through me. I'd done nothing wrong; why should I feel embarrassed? I'd been alone when I fell asleep. He'd gone out in search of "appropriate attire," in his words, leaving me to rest in the room. If he'd come in and curled up with me while I slept, that wasn't my fault.

He opened his eyes, the characteristic twinkle already in them. "I'd planned to sleep in the chair, but when I came in, you said my name and rolled over to make room for me. And when I laid down, you cuddled up against me with the sweetest little sigh. Honestly, how could I resist?"

He was lying. He had to be. I jerked out of his touch with a huff, tightening my dressing robe around my waist. "You're insufferable." And I desperately needed a cold bath to cool my overheated body.

His laughter chased me to the bathroom.

The deep blue dress waiting for me was scandalous, a far cry from the one I'd worn to Mass. It clung to my skin like water, with a mere two petticoats beneath. The neckline would have been unsuitable for public wear if not for the inch of black lace at the top. If I breathed too hard, I'd spill out of it. More lace peeked out below the bottom hemline, revealing my bare feet and ankles. I pursed my lips and wiggled my toes. I wouldn't be able to wear my boots. Hopefully El—or whatever source he got the dress from—had taken that into consideration. My shoulders were bare, the tiniest scrap of a sleeve dangling over each arm. Glancing in the mirror, I wasn't sure if I should be horrified or impressed. I looked like a harlot...but I'd never felt so desirable.

El was already dressed when I left the bathroom. At the sound of the door, he stopped in the middle of rifling through his bag to glance up at me. He froze.

The silence stretched too long between us. I smoothed my skirt, searching it for flaws. "Is there something wrong?"

He swallowed hard and shook his head. "It's a good thing you're wearing blue tonight, Legs, because if another man tried to touch you looking like that, I'd kill him on the spot."

My blush spread from my head to my toes. He'd explained earlier that the fang hideout we would be visiting had a strict dress code. Fangs wore all white. Humans who wanted to be fed from—for experiencing the aphrodisiac qualities of the venom, presumably—wore red. Humans not interested in becoming a meal wore blue.

The red silk waistcoat molded to his body would be a beacon for every fang there. My skin crawled at the thought, and we hadn't even left the room yet. How was I supposed to do this?

"Relax, Legs." He stepped toward me, running a comforting hand down my arm as though he had read my thoughts. "I have a Gardien with me. No one's going to push me too far."

A single taste would be too far, but he was right. It would look strange if neither of us were participating in the night's "festivities." But I couldn't tell if my discomfort had to do with the thought of watching fangs feed...or with the thought of someone else touching him. All this close proximity was making it hard to think straight.

Our eyes met, and his warm touch was suddenly scorching. My breath came short. His brown curls were tousled, his suit—minus the jacket draped over the chair in the corner—tailored to fit him perfectly. If I'd thought he was attractive before, he was irresistible now.

He skimmed his hands down my side, barely touching the fabric of the dress. "Beautiful," he murmured. Our breath mingled, our faces inches apart, though I didn't know when he'd moved closer. Or maybe I'd been the one to move.

"Do you often buy dresses for women you know?" I meant the words to put a barrier between us, but the needy, breathless tone of my voice failed to have the effect I wanted.

The corner of his mouth quirked up. "No, but when I saw this, I knew you had to have it." He took a fold of my skirt, running it through his fingers. "Shantung silk. Almost as soft as your skin."

I definitely couldn't breathe now. The room was too small, and he was too close—or too far away. I couldn't decide which.

He put his lips to my ear, and my heart stopped.

"Sit down," he whispered.

My body obeyed, settling on the bed before my mind could register the words. He sank to his knees before me, and I didn't dare speak. Whatever he was doing, whatever was happening, I didn't want him to stop.

He reached for a long, slender box at the foot of the bed. Opening it, he drew out two pieces of black silk. Stockings. He took my foot in his hand and gently slid one on, tying it at the top with a blue ribbon garter that matched the dress. When he tied the second, his hands lingered on my thighs, our eyes locked.

"If it wasn't sunset already," he said, his voice choked, "I'd lay you down on this bed and do everything I've wanted to since we first met."

A whimper escaped me, but I couldn't bother to be ashamed of it. He trailed his hands back down my leg, then picked up a black silk shoe I hadn't noticed yet. Cradling my calf with one hand, he slipped the shoe onto my foot with the other, never removing his eyes from mine. Then he repeated the process with my other foot.

Finally he released me, rising with a guttural groan. "If you keep looking at me like that, Legs, I can't be held responsible for what happens next."

As tempting as it was to give in to this heat between us, now wasn't the time. We had a job to do.

I stood, looking everywhere but at him. "We should go," I muttered. I tugged at my dress to smooth the wrinkles. The revealing ensemble left no room to hide a weapon, and I felt naked without a means to defend myself.

"Wait."

He reached for me, and I tensed. Had he changed his mind?

"Don't worry. I'm not trying to compromise your virtue." He grinned. "Yet." He took my hair down from its braid, and I did everything in my power not to surrender to the intoxicating sensation of his fingers combing through my hair.

Once it was loose, he took a portion and twisted it up on top of my head, then slid two long wooden pins into it to keep it up. "There. If you're cornered, you'll have a weapon."

"Was there anything you didn't think of?" I marveled, feeling for the pins.

"Is that a compliment, Legs?" His mask of amusement was firmly back in place. With deft fingers, he slipped the crucifix from my neck and dropped it onto the table by the bed. "Let's go."

A cab dropped us off at an unobtrusive little cafe a couple blocks from the Colosseum. My heart pounded in my throat as we approached the door, the building indistinguishable from the others on the street but for the tiny pair of wings carved into the top of the doorframe. We were about to enter a nest of fangs, and I was armed with nothing but a pair of sticks.

"Relax." I jumped when El's lips brushed my ear, his arms wrapping around my waist to pull me in close. "All you have to do is pretend you're desperate for my touch. No one will even notice you're here." He kissed my neck, and a shiver ran through me. I tilted my head back to give him access. "Just like that," he said, amusement lacing his words.

Inside the cafe, the sole occupant, a woman in a lacy white dress greeted us. *"Buona sera.* Can I help you?"

*"Mortui vivos docent,"* El said. *The dead teach the living.* A dark sentiment, but it was the key to getting in.

The woman smiled, revealing sharp white teeth. She pulled back a curtain on the wall behind her to open a gaping hole. "Enjoy your evening."

My feet stuck in place, but El held me tighter. "Come, darling. Let's have some fun."

I trusted him. We'd be fine. Steeling myself, I let him guide me into the darkness.

We didn't have long to walk before the sounds of music and conversation reached our ears. Cool air and trepidation combined to send a shiver down my spine, and I slowed to a stop.

"I'm sorry, Legs. I should have thought about the weather." El shrugged off his coat and draped it over my shoulders.

The sharp smell of him surrounded me. I took a deep breath, and the warmth filled me with confidence. "I'm ready."

We rounded a corner, and the tunnel widened into a room. Skylights lined the ceiling, leaving pools of moonlight on the floor. It was clearly ancient. The faded frescoes around the room portrayed images of chariot races and gladiator battles. A bar lined one wall, while on the other, booths and tables held people in various states of decency. A few lone dancers in the middle of the floor moved their bodies to the music of the band, but dancing wasn't the purpose of this place. No, the true purpose was evident in the combinations of white and red scattered throughout the room.

At one booth, a man with a red scarf lolled his head back, ecstasy written on his face as two fang women in scraps of white lace drank greedily from his wrists. At another, a woman in a scarlet dress straddled a white-clad man and bared her chest to him, while a second man in a cobalt waistcoat watched them with greedy eyes.

The decadence and sin sickened me. I reached for my crucifix, remembering too late that it wasn't around my neck.

El spun me, pinning me to the wall with his body. "You're still tense." He skimmed his nose along my neck. "No one's going to touch you."

*No. They're just going to touch him. I can't do this. Can't watch a fang sink their teeth into someone else I care about.*

"Say the word, and we'll leave." His breath kissed my skin. "I'll take you back to the hotel, and we can create our own kind of decadence."

I didn't know if he was testing me or genuine, but I was allowing my emotions to cloud my judgment. That was how I'd killed Lucy. I couldn't allow that sort of mistake again.

I slid a hand between us and rested it on his chest. "We just arrived," I said, my voice sultry. "I'd like to stay."

He leaned back far enough to look into my eyes, and his grin turned wicked. "Then stay we shall."

The club provided more than blood to drink. El ordered himself a whiskey, neat, and I sipped a gin and tonic. I wouldn't normally drink while hunting, but I wouldn't walk into a vampire's lair with no weapons, either. Nothing about tonight was normal.

We found a booth with a clear view of the room. I rested a hand on El's thigh and cast a lazy glance around us. The air reeked of blood and sex, the pungent scent of liquor lingering underneath it all.

I saw no sign of Lucy nor her demonic husband, but we hadn't expected to see them here. Tonight was about gathering information. The supernatural world was small; if they were in Rome, someone here would know about it.

It didn't take long before a fang noticed us sitting alone. The ivory ballgown she wore gave her the appearance of an angel, an impression helped along by her small stature and the way her brown hair framed her head like a halo. She gave us both a deceptively sweet smile.

"Ye look lonely." A lilting accent—Irish, I thought—added music to her words.

El looked her over, allowing his seductive smirk to slip over his face. "We might be persuaded to invite a guest."

Her teeth flashed as she laughed. "And what might the cost be for such an honor?"

He leaned in close as if confiding a secret. "My wife is a bit nervous about sharing."

"I see." She considered me for a moment, her eyes taking in everything my dress revealed. "We wouldn't want that." Reaching for my hand, she pressed a kiss to the center of my palm. I suppressed a shudder as her cold lips touched my skin. "Maybe another drink would help?"

"It might," I said, looking up at her through my lashes and praying she mistook my revulsion for apprehension.

She flagged down a server, a man—human or vampire, I couldn't tell—wearing all black. "My friends need another drink. And a glass of champagne for me. Put it all on my tab."

When the server disappeared, she turned back to me. "I'm Erin." She drew out the 'e,' her accent making it long. "What's your name, love?"

We hadn't decided on aliases. Should we have? I flicked my gaze at El, but his expression revealed nothing.

"I'm Anne," I said finally.

"A beautiful name for a beautiful woman." She brushed her fingers against my arm. "It's a shame you're not wearing red. I'd love to play with you, too."

El draped his arm around me, pulling me tight into his chest. "You'll have to settle for me, I'm afraid. You see, she might be nervous about letting others enjoy me, but I would go absolutely *feral* if someone else got their hands on her."

The words reminded me of what he'd said earlier in the hotel. *If another man tried to touch you looking like that, I'd kill him on the spot.* Heat coursed through me.

"Oh, that blush." She sucked in a breath, eyes darkening. "A real shame."

"Another time, perhaps." El took her hand and pressed a kiss to the knuckles. "I'm El, by the way."

The server returned with our drinks, interrupting the conversation. I took a large swallow of mine to mask my discomfort.

Erin raised her glass to us before taking a sip. "What brings ye to Rome?"

"We were hoping to surprise Anne's sister," El said. "She was recently turned, and she's touring Europe on her honeymoon." He sighed heavily. "Since we were here anyway, we decided to take in some of the entertainment Rome has to offer."

She swirled her champagne. "A recent convert? What's her name? Maybe I've heard of her."

"Lucille. Lucille Allard." My heart pounded in my throat, and I leaned toward her. Was this the lead we'd been waiting for? "She's young. Golden hair, blue eyes."

El gave me a warning squeeze—*too eager*—as she considered. After a moment, she shook her head.

"Sorry, I don't believe we've come across each other. Ye're sure she's in Rome?"

"This is where they were traveling next." El shrugged. "But as I said, it's possible we've missed them. You might know her husband, though. Jakob von Peller?"

Erin snorted. "I know him. He finally started a nest of his own, now? I hadn't heard he was in the area. I'm not sorry to have missed him."

"You don't like him?" I fiddled with my glass, watching the clear liquid swirl around.

"Sorry, love! I didn't mean that." She reached out and took my hand, a comforting smile on her face. "He's just a bit of a gobshite. He'll treat your sister right, sure."

*I'm sure he will. He'd only planned to murder her and place her mummified remains on display in his tower.*

"Thank you, Erin. That's a comfort." El stood, reaching out his hand and giving her a lust-filled smile that turned my stomach. "Would you like to dance?"

*It's just a game,* I reminded myself as he helped her to her feet. We'd come here for this. No matter that we hadn't gotten the information we wanted. I wouldn't allow my emotions to get in the way.

El leaned down and put his hand on the back of my neck. "Say the word, and we'll leave," he whispered. Erin graciously turned her head away as though she couldn't hear him. "I won't do anything you're uncomfortable with."

Sincerity flowed from him. If I asked him to, he'd walk out right now, no matter how little we'd learned.

But we were playing a part, and I wouldn't be the one to break that. I reached up to run my hand over his cheek. "Have fun," I said. "I'll be watching."

His throat bobbed, and he held my gaze for a moment. Then he leaned in and captured my lips with a kiss that took my breath away.

As he led the fang onto the dance floor and placed his hand on her waist, my chest grew tight with a sensation strikingly similar to jealousy. But why would I be jealous? We were attracted to each other, yes, but I didn't have any claim on him. My focus right now was—should be—on catching Lucy. And he wasn't actually attracted to Erin. He was acting out a role. Just like I was.

So I remained still when she leaned in to whisper something in his ear. And when she twined her arms around his neck, I didn't react, though I wanted to drive the slender wooden stakes in my hair through her heart.

When she sank her teeth into his neck, I almost managed not to care.

The venom worked on him instantly. His eyes, locked on mine, glazed over with lust. He groaned, and though they were halfway across the room, I heard it as though he stood next to me. The fang pulled him closer, drinking deep. A trickle of blood escaped. Dropped onto her sleeve. Stained the white fabric red.

*I can't do this. It's just like Lucy.*

I blinked, and the room around me became Bluebeard's tower. My sister's blood stained my hands, and I heard the rasp of her dying breaths. My own breath caught in my chest. I reached for my crucifix, my pistol, anything to ground me.

Strong arms gathered me close. "It's me." El's voice brought me back to the moment. "I'm here." I opened my eyes—when had I closed them?—and looked into his face. His brow knit together with concern.

"Is she well herself?" Erin asked from somewhere behind him.

"She'll be fine." He brushed my cheek. "You're with me, *ma guerrière.* You're safe."

I blinked away the stinging in my eyes. He wasn't Lucy, and she wasn't Bluebeard. This was different, and I was ruining everything. Taking in air in deep gulps, I straightened.

"I'm sorry," I said. "I didn't mean to interrupt."

Erin took the seat across from me again. "It's no bother, love. I've had my fill."

The thought turned my stomach, but I didn't have time to dwell on it. El slipped his arm under my legs and lifted me into the air.

"I think she needs to rest," he said to the fang. "Thank you for a...pleasant evening."

She smiled. "I hope we'll see each other again."

If I saw her again, I intended to put a stake through her heart. El's mouth twitched at her pleasantry, but he said, "Me, too."

He wove seamlessly through the crowd, and I clung to his neck, trying to avoid the wound from her bite. "I can walk," I said. With the blood loss, carrying me was the last thing he should do.

"I'm not letting you down until we're out of here." His voice, almost a growl, vibrated through me.

We left the gathering behind. The smell of sex and blood and the sound of music faded into the distance as he carried me through the darkness.

"There's no one else here, and you're hurt." I squirmed, trying to get him to set me down, but he tightened his grip.

"Have you ever been bit?" When I didn't respond, he huffed a humorless laugh. "It's only painful for a second. I'm fine. But after your reaction in there, I'd say you're not."

"I just—"

"I know." He glanced down at me. Shadows obscured half his face, but the other half softened. "I promise I'll let you go when we're safe in a carriage."

I should have been offended at his insistence that I couldn't care for myself, but it tugged at something deep inside me. Relaxing into him, I sighed. "Fine. But only if you'll let me look at that bite."

His laughter rumbled against my cheek. "When we're alone, you can look at any part of me you want."

14

I took a deep breath of the fresh springtime air, filled with the smell of gunpowder, coffee, and whiskey—El's unique scent, mingled with what he'd been drinking. By the time he bundled me into a cab, my heartbeat had finally slowed to what resembled a normal pace.

"Are you feeling better?" he asked, taking a seat across from me as the carriage started moving.

"I'm...fine." A lie. My emotions were in turmoil. The lines between us had never felt more blurred. I'd panicked over him getting bitten; he'd carried me out of there like a bride. I couldn't keep doing this.

Silence, filled with a tension thick enough to cut, surrounded us. I could hear his every breath, smell him on my heated skin. I took his jacket off and set it on the seat next to me. "I'm sorry—"

He cut me off. "It wasn't your fault."

"We should have stayed longer. Talked to someone else. She might not have seen them, but that doesn't mean they're not here." I dug my fingers into my thighs, bunching up the water-like silk. "If I hadn't overreacted, we'd still be back there."

"This doesn't have to mean the end. If you want me to go back later—"

"No!" I couldn't hide the panic in my voice. I'd already lost one partner to a fang. I wouldn't lose another.

Was that what El was? My partner? He felt like less, and yet so much more. My partnership with Henri had been nothing like this.

What would he have thought of all this?

*I'd tell you you're acting like an idiot. Stop denying yourself. Let yourself be happy.*

I never could keep anything from Henri. He'd have teased me endlessly, but if he were here—really here, not just a figment of my imagination—that's exactly what he'd say. He'd tell me to accept the feelings and let myself be happy.

"Why not?" El moved to the seat next to me. His eyes dropped to my lips, and I had a feeling he wasn't asking why I didn't want him to return to the vampire den.

"I don't know." Every reason this was a bad idea had vanished from my mind.

"Do you know what I was thinking of on that dance floor?" He reached up and pulled the sticks from my hair, letting it fall over my shoulders. With his fingers, he combed out the kinks. "What was going through my mind with her venom pulsing straight to my cock?"

I couldn't look away from him. His brown eyes, black as night in the darkness, seemed to see straight into my soul. "What?"

His hand brushed my knee, the fabric of my dress doing nothing to block the heat of his touch. "You. Naked in my bed, begging for me."

I didn't beg. I wanted to tell him that, but when I opened my mouth, I couldn't find the words.

"And if you won't beg for me, I'll have to go on my knees and beg for you." He crooked his finger under my chin. "Do you know how difficult it's been, sharing a room with you night after night and not touching you?"

Probably as difficult as it had been lying to myself that I didn't want him.

"Tell me you want me," he said. "Please, *ma guerrière.*"

*My warrior.* He'd called me that earlier, when I was lost in the memory of Lucy's death. It felt too intimate, too serious to be another one of his jokes.

"I'm afraid." The words slipped out before I could take them back.

"Afraid of what?"

Afraid to lose him, like I'd lost everyone else I'd ever cared for. My parents. Henri. Lucy. Les Gardiens.

Afraid this was all a mistake, and I was endangering us both by giving in.

Afraid it was all a game to him.

"To give up control," I said at last.

We pulled to a stop, and he took my hand. "With me, you're always in control."

He helped me out of the carriage, the consummate gentleman, and paid the driver. As the cab left, he turned back to me, desire blazing in his eyes.

"Stop denying this," he whispered. "For both our sake."

My lips parted, and my eyes fluttered shut as he drew closer. I couldn't resist him anymore. Couldn't go on like this.

His hands tightened on my hips, but when he didn't kiss me, I opened my eyes. His gaze was fixed on something behind me.

I whipped around. "What is it?" The streets were empty but for a stray gray cat sitting atop a wall. At my attention, it hopped down with a loud meow and disappeared into the darkness.

Taking one of my hair sticks in each hand, I scanned for signs of danger. *What I wouldn't give for my pistol right now.* The tiny sticks I held would be precious little defense against any attacker, but they would have to suffice.

"Nothing. It's nothing." He stepped back, releasing me. "I thought I saw something. I was mistaken."

"Are you sure?" I looked down the street again before considering him. His face was unreadable, any emotion hidden firmly behind a mask of nonchalance.

"Yes. Just my imagination." He shrugged, tucking his hands into his pockets and giving me a blinding smile. He was breathtakingly beautiful, his clothes mussed from holding me and his curls windswept. But something had changed. Something was wrong, and he was hiding it from me.

The sensitive part of me wanted to assume it was my fault, because I'd admitted weakness in the cab. But the Gardien in me knew better. He was hiding something. Whatever he saw, it wasn't *nothing*.

I wanted to push until he told me everything, but I bit my tongue. He'd earned my trust. If there was something I needed to know, he'd tell me when he was ready.

"You should head inside," he said. "I'm sure you want to change out of that dress."

"Aren't you coming?" The lingering vulnerability told me this was a rejection. A few minutes ago, he'd been desperate for me. Had it been the venom making him act that way?

He waved a hand. "I need some air. I'll be up soon."

"Okay." I turned to go, then stopped. "If there's anything you need, El, you can tell me."

His mask didn't crack. "Thanks, Legs. I appreciate it."

My chest was heavy as I made my way up to our room. The dress, which had made me feel so desirable earlier, suffocated me. I stripped it off and tossed it haphazardly onto the overstuffed chair in the corner. After shoving my legs back into the familiar comfort of my trousers, I replaced the corset and petticoats with jumps and a loose black shirt.

*I'm such an idiot.*

I should have known better than to open up. To let myself get distracted by these emotions. First, I'd cut short our reconnaissance mission, and then I'd been too caught up in what was happening between us to notice whatever he'd seen outside.

Closing my eyes, I counted silently to ten. Now wasn't the time to focus on what I'd done wrong. Dwelling on my mistakes wouldn't fix them. Instead, I grabbed my belt, strapped on my weapons, and headed for the door. I wouldn't follow El—I'd made that mistake once already, and I had to trust him—but I could search the area for any threats.

Or at least I could get out of this room so I didn't have to be alone with my thoughts.

My footsteps led me to a corner near the Trevi Fountain. A show had just finished at the theater, and people filled the streets, all dressed for an evening out. I clung to the shadows, observing the crowd but not mingling with it. This sort of environment had always been where Lucy thrived, not me.

Slipping away from the mass of people, I headed toward the bubbling sound of water.

Despite the crowds leaving the theater, the square around Trevi Fountain was empty. I stopped at the edge and peered into the silver water. Coins littered the bottom, sparkling with the moonlight.

Movement nearby drew my attention, and I looked up. On the other side of the fountain, a young woman waded in the water, her white dress floating around her knees as she ran a hand along the rough white stones below the hippocampi.

Lucy.

My breath vanished, and I froze in place. After all that hunting, was it really her standing across from me?

I opened my mouth to say something—I didn't know what—but before I could, she spotted me. Her face lit up with an angelic smile, and she waded through the water toward me.

"Anne! Is it really you?"

She still looked like my sister, this monster wearing her face. A tad more graceful than Lucy had been, and a bit plumper, but to anyone else, there would have been no difference.

"What are you doing in Rome?" she asked.

"Looking for you." It wasn't Lucy. Not my sister. I had to remember that. No matter how much my heart ached.

"Jakob said you would be." She smiled wryly. "It's why he wouldn't let me tell you where we were going. He was afraid you were hunting us."

"I was. I am."

She giggled, the sound like windchimes. "You can't be serious, Anne. You wouldn't hurt me."

"I've killed plenty of fangs in my life." Never one wearing my sister's face, but I couldn't let that stop me. I'd been waiting months for this opportunity.

So why hadn't I reached for a weapon?

"It's beautiful, isn't it?" She ignored my last statement and took a seat on the edge of the fountain, trailing her fingers through the water. "Why didn't we travel? Before I left. We should have traveled."

I clenched my jaw. I'd asked myself that same question countless times since she died. "Would it have made a difference?"

She frowned up at me. "You mean would I still have left with Jakob?" She paused for a moment, considering the question. The glow of the moonlight shone around her in a halo, making her look like a saint. I knew better than to be fooled; beauty could hide the darkest rot beneath. But I'd always had a soft spot for my sister. It was hard not to be drawn in by this monster's facade.

"Jakob is my destiny," she said finally. "He always has been—even before I knew him. But if we'd traveled more, seen more of the world, I might have resisted him for a time. Not given in so easily."

The words struck my heart like a silver bullet. If I hadn't sheltered her so much, she might have held out against him, at least long enough for me to stop him.

"I'm sorry." I breathed the words, but she heard them anyway.

"There's nothing to be sorry for. As I said, this was inevitable. Jakob and I were meant to be."

Still the same romantic fool she'd always been. I could almost imagine nothing had changed. "You know what's worst about all of this?" I tucked my hands into my pockets. "It's not that you ran away. It's not the lies. It's not even your death, as awful as that is. What breaks my heart, Lucy, is that this is it for you." I glanced up at the moon, bright and white above us, and swallowed down my tears. "No matter how many prayers I pray, you'll never see heaven. Not even purgatory." My eyes burned. "You're damned, and there's nothing I can do for you."

She flicked the water, watching the ripples spread outward. "Who told you that? Les Gardiens? I don't deny that they have good intentions, but not everything walking the streets at night is evil."

"'Have respect unto the covenant, for the dark places of the earth are full of the habitations of cruelty,'" I quoted. "You can't expect me to believe that creatures who are banned from sunlight and survive on the lifeblood of others can be good." Why was I entertaining this conversation? I should have been killing the creature, not debating with it. Its existence damned my sister.

"'He that saith he is in the light, and hateth his brother, is in darkness even until now.'" She pursed her lips at me. "You aren't the only one who can quote the Bible, Anne."

How dare she? How could this demon dare to quote Scripture at me, accusing me of sin? "Even if your cursed nature didn't damn you, your deeds would," I spat. "Or is murder no longer a sin?"

She smiled, flashing her fangs. The expression changed her appearance, giving a glimpse at the monster lurking beneath the skin. "Only murder of the innocent."

That took me aback, and I stared at her for a long moment. Was she implying she'd never killed an innocent person? Did she believe that boy she'd killed the other night was guilty of some mortal sin? "Who gave you the right to determine someone's guilt?"

"Who gave *you?*" She fixed me with a piercing stare, more depth behind her eyes than I'd ever seen before. "You don't have a patent on the truth, Anne."

"No, but the Church does."

"Do they? Is the pope not human? Can priests not make mistakes like anyone else?" She sighed heavily. "I don't want to fight with you."

And I didn't want to fight with her. "But I have to kill you."

"Why?"

The look on her face was pure bafflement. It almost made me laugh, but nothing about this situation was funny. It would have been better if Bluebeard had killed us both. Better dead than damned. Then I wouldn't have to kill my sister twice.

When I didn't speak, she threw up her hands. "You never listen to me, do you? I haven't killed anyone, and even if I did, I wouldn't choose someone innocent. Just because you've been brainwashed to think all vampires are evil—"

"They are!" The words came out louder than I intended, echoing against the stone walls of the fountain. "*You* are. You don't get a pass just because you were my sister."

She flinched at the *were,* and I had to tamp down a rising wave of guilt. No matter how much she looked like Lucy, she wasn't. My sister was dead.

She stood, turning away from me as though she couldn't stand to see my face. When she spoke again, her voice was quiet and even. "We're not killing anyone, Anne. And if you think you need to kill me just because you don't approve of my lifestyle, you must not be the sister I thought you were."

It would be so easy to end it. She was defenseless, her back bare, revealed by fabric that plunged down to her hips, exposed to whatever weapon I might choose. And what a blessing it would be to kill the fang without watching the look of betrayal on my sister's face.

"If you're not killing them, then who is?" The words came from my mouth, but it wasn't me who asked. If I'd been controlling my body, I would have staked the demon through the heart by now, rather than carrying on this farce of a conversation.

She laughed humorlessly. "We're hardly the only monsters roaming the streets. You taught me that."

I had to stop this. The longer this conversation went on, the harder it would be for me to kill her.

My hand went to my stake, but before I could pull it out, a shadow blotted the moon. I tensed, searching the sky.

Perched at the very top of the fountain, far above Neptune, three angels stared down at us.

No, not three. Two. Two angel statues and one blue-bearded demon.

Bluebeard's wings flared, and he leapt off the roof, landing in the center of the fountain with a splash.

He straightened to his full height as his wings folded back into his skin. He was tall—taller than El, though he had broad shoulders just like my partner. He was shirtless, his black pants clinging to his legs with the water of the fountain. The threat of violence lurked in his stormy gray eyes.

The hairs on my neck prickled as I sensed the predator before me. The vampire that had been Lucy was no threat, but this creature was every bit the demon I'd been taught to hunt. His eyes narrowed on the hand hovering over my stake.

Lucy put a hand on his arm, and his expression softened when he glanced at her, though the warning in his face didn't disappear entirely.

"I never got the chance to introduce you properly," she said. Her own face was guarded; she sensed the simmering tension between me and her demonic husband. "Anne, this is my husband, Jakob von Peller. Jakob, my sister, Anne Allard."

"A pleasure to meet you, sister." His words held a mocking tone, an underlying irony. He, at least, understood that vampires and Les Gardiens were natural enemies.

I didn't return the pleasantry.

"Come, my sweet Lucille." Bluebeard tucked Lucy's arm into his. "We should go, before your sister does something we regret."

I didn't miss the flash of pain in her eyes as she looked at me. "I didn't want it to be like this, Anne," she said. "I hope someday you'll understand."

As they turned to go, my fingers brushed the cool wood of my stake. Now was my last chance to kill them both and end this months-long chase.

Wings burst from their backs in unison—the plunging back of Lucy's dress obviously designed for this purpose. I still didn't move. Not even as the wind from their ascent rushed against my face and water splashed over the edge of the fountain. My gaze followed them into the sky, watching until they were mere specks in the distance.

Once they were out of sight, I dragged myself back to the hotel room. El, luckily, wasn't back when I stumbled inside and collapsed onto the bed. I wasn't ready to talk to him about my failure tonight.

*Do I even tell him I saw Lucy?* There was no way I could justify being steps from her and not killing her.

I reached for my pack and dug inside it until I found Henri's old pipe. It never ceased to calm me, the scent of old tobacco and the smooth feel of the wooden bowl and amber stem.

*Even you had vices,* I thought.

In my mind, Henri appeared on the bed, filling the room with the smell of tobacco and hair pomade. *It's not a vice to be unable to kill your sister.*

*She swore she hasn't killed anyone.* It could be a lie; the logical part of me knew that. If they were willing to murder, why would they hesitate to lie as well?

*But what if it isn't?* Henri asked. *What if they're not the ones doing the killing?*

No. I'd seen the look on Bluebeard's face tonight. Lucy might not have been the monster I thought, but he was. He wouldn't hesitate to kill for any reason.

I sank onto the bed with a groan. *I'm an idiot.* Twice now, I'd let that monster fly off with my sister and done nothing to stop it.

The door opened, and El walked in, interrupting my musings. He still wore his clothes from earlier, and the memory of the way I'd acted at the vampire club filled me with hot shame. I couldn't keep giving in to my emotions. I had to have some self-control.

He loosened his tie. "Sorry I disappeared, Legs. Between the whiskey and the venom..." He grinned, showing no indication of the heat between us. "I just needed to clear my head."

"Same," I muttered.

"What did you do while I was gone?" He spotted my dress in a pile on the chair. "Couldn't wait to get out of that dress, huh? That's a shame. I liked it."

Liked it so much that he could disappear when I'd been finally ready to sleep with him. Annoyance bubbled up in my chest. Arrogant, obnoxious man. It was a good thing he'd run off before I could do anything I regretted. Now I remembered all the reasons I'd been resisting the attraction I felt.

And what had been so urgent that it drew him away? Lucy had been wading in Trevi Fountain, and though I hadn't noticed Bluebeard when I arrived, I doubted the fang would have left her alone for long. Not now that I'd seen the possessive look on his face. So whatever El had been chasing, it hadn't been them.

He walked across the room and stopped in front of me, waiting until I looked up into his face. His gaze was vulnerable, brows knit together. "I really am sorry. I should have told you where I was going. I just..." He sighed and glanced away. "I can't tell you what I was doing.

I know I haven't given you a reason to trust me, but I swear, if I could tell you, I would."

I shifted uncomfortably at that. I was angry with him for keeping secrets while I was hiding my own. "It's fine," I muttered.

"No, it's not." He sat down on the bed next to me. "You opened up to me, and I ran off. You deserve better, Anne. I need you to know that it had nothing to do with you."

"You're entitled to your secrets," I said. "I have my own things I'm not ready to share."

His smile this time was genuine, his eyes crinkling at the corners. He took my hand and squeezed it. "I think we can leave some space for secrets between us. As long as we don't tell each other lies. I want this partnership to work."

This partnership was unlike any I'd had before, but I wanted it to work, too. Whatever that would look like. "I think I can handle that."

# THE MERCHANT

He stumbles down the street, the night of debauchery taking its toll on his balance. He made the right choice leaving his wife behind in London. Prague is far more enjoyable without her hanging on his arm.

"You don't seem ready for the night to be over." A woman with golden hair melts from the shadows. She circles him, a seductive smile playing on her face.

It's only been an hour since he left the brothel, but the woman's small figure stirs him. She isn't dressed like a whore, the collar of her blue evening gown respectably high. But no respectable woman approaches a man like this.

"I wouldn't mind having some more fun." He reaches out and takes one of her golden curls in his hand. "What would it cost me?"

Her smile widens. "Just the use of your body."

Warning bells clang in the back of his mind—no whore offers her services for free—but they're heavily muted by drink and arousal. "Then perhaps you would like to come back to my room for a drink?"

She places a hand on his chest. "Why bother finding a room?" Slipping into a narrow alley between two houses, she hikes her skirt up to her knees.

The alarm bells lingering in his head vanish at the sight of her legs. Her stockings have slipped down to her ankles, revealing the bare white skin beneath.

"I would never wish to disappoint a lady," he sys. He follows her into the darkness, fumbling with his belt.

Despite the warm spring night, her skin is cold as she wraps her arms around him and kisses his neck. He finally loosens his pants and yanks them down, then pulls her skirt up higher. Her body is soft, pliable beneath his hands as he lifts her up against the wall and lines himself with her entrance.

Sharp teeth sink into his neck. He jerks away, but the pain vanishes in an instant, pleasure coursing through him. He puts a hand to his neck, and it comes away wet and warm.

"What—?" He stares at the woman as his blood drips down her chin.

"I told you," she says, "all I require is the use of your body."

His screams cut off as she tears out his throat.

Mists rolled over the green hills, tinged golden by the sunset. I rested my head against the glass of my window, feeling the cool pane against my skin. It was mid-May, but the late spring warmth hadn't reached County Kerry yet.

A knock sounded at my hotel door, and I crossed the room to open it.

"I have good news," El said.

I let him into the room. "You found coffee?" Seeing his empty hands, I knew it was a fruitless hope.

He laughed. "Unfortunately, no. But I have something even better." He drew a newspaper clipping from his pocket and handed it to me.

A drawing of an Egyptian mummy accompanied the text, but I didn't recognize the language of the article. I scanned it for familiar words; it was incomprehensible. "What does it say?"

"Oh, I forgot." He flopped onto the bed, kicking his boots off. "You don't speak Czech."

"And you do?"

"Of course."

*Is there a language he can't speak?* His skills had come in handy as we'd chased fruitless leads over the past few weeks, trying to determine where Lucy and Bluebeard had disappeared to. We'd ended up in Ireland after we caught wind of an Abhartach—the Irish legend about vampires—roaming the countryside. It had turned out to be nothing but superstition, but we weren't traveling further until we got another lead.

Passing the clip back to him, I crossed my arms and waited for him to translate.

"'Third bloody death this month,'" he read. "'Early this morning, the body of Benjamin Ford, a merchant on holiday from his home in London, was found outside his abode near the city center. The body was wrapped in linen in the style of Egyptian mummies, but when police removed the wrappings, they found him to be drained of blood and covered in bite marks. He was dressed in his evening clothes, leading police to assume he was killed while returning from a night out. The death follows two similar cases from earlier this month, where a young man and a new mother were found exsanguinated and their bodies arranged on park benches a week apart. Police urge everyone to use caution while traveling at night and to remain in well-lighted, public areas whenever possible.'" He folded it up. "It's from the paper in Prague."

"*Merde,*" I swore. "You think it's them?"

"Could be. Between the two of them, three bodies in a month would be more than reasonable."

I frowned at the paper he held. Something about it felt wrong, but I didn't know what. Prague was a center of culture and art, exactly the sort of place Lucy would love to visit. And the details made sense. Two fangs, three bodies. Deliberate, artistic rituals in the placing of the bodies.

"She did talk about Prague once or twice," I admitted. I was letting my emotions cloud my judgment again. After my conversation with Lucy in Rome, it was hard to remember she was still a monster. That no matter how many lies she'd told me, she'd still been murdering rampantly across the continent. "The year after Maman and Papa died, she gave me a painting. It was a watercolor, a Czech Christmas market with a snow-covered castle and tiny people dotting the streets below it. She said she wanted to go with me." I'd barely spared it a second glance; I'd been eighteen, too absorbed in my own life to worry about hurting her feelings. I'd joined Les Gardiens a month earlier, and training took all of my time. I'd given the painting to the servants and told them to pack it up with the rest of the Christmas decorations Lucy had strewn across the house. The first of many mistakes I'd made with my sister.

"Then I think we have to assume it's them." He patted the bed next to him. "Yes?"

My face twisted in contemplation as I considered. I took a seat next to him and tucked my feet up under me. "You're probably right. But I'm sure they've moved on by now."

"Not necessarily. They spent weeks in Amsterdam, and they probably only left Rome because they caught wind of us"

I suppressed a cringe. He didn't know how right he was. Their discretion these past few weeks was because of Bluebeard; he'd seen my intentions, and he was protecting Lucy from me. I could almost admire him for it.

"We have a week, maybe two, before they leave Prague," El went on, oblivious to the turn of my thoughts. "If we leave immediately, we might still catch them."

I reached for my bag. "I'm ready now. Do you think you can manage to pack all your chaos into a bag for the next train?" As soon as we reached a new place, his belongings were scattered everywhere. It was like the man was incapable of cleanliness. One of the many reasons I was glad not to share a room with him anymore.

*And what about the reasons you wish you* were *sharing a room?* I heard Henri's voice in my head again—an occurrence that was becoming rarer, though it hadn't stopped completely.

El's eyes twinkled. "I'm already packed. And the ship to France doesn't leave until tomorrow afternoon. I've already got our tickets."

"For separate rooms, I hope." Even if there were multiple rooms available on the overnight ship into France, I wouldn't have been surprised if he'd booked a single room just to irritate me.

"And deprive you of access to my body?" he asked, leaning in. The smell of coffee and gunpowder surrounded me, warm and invigorating. "How cruel do you think I am, Legs?"

I leaned closer, wetting my lips. His gaze dropped to them. It had become a game, the flirting. Seeing which of us would give in first. It was a daily temptation to pick up where we'd left off in Rome, the night we went to the fang club, but I wouldn't lose this battle. He'd been the one to walk away. He had to be the one to come back.

"Crueler by the minute." I didn't mean to say it—didn't mean to imply that I cared. But it was too late now. I saw in his eyes the moment he made the connection. Heat burned there. Dangerous.

"How long do you plan on dancing around this?" His voice was husky.

"I don't know what you're talking about," I lied. As though I didn't know exactly where his mind had gone.

"I thought we agreed not to lie to each other."

Was I so obvious? I swallowed, not daring to move. The game suddenly felt far more real than I'd planned.

"I was trying to give you space," he said. "You said you were afraid, so I didn't want to push you."

"I wasn't the one to walk away." I meant the words to be a reprimand, but they came out breathy.

His fingers skimmed down my back. "A mistake I'll regret for the rest of my life. Do you have any idea how much I wanted you? How much I still want you?"

I shivered at the phantom touch. "And yet you haven't touched me since."

"I've wanted to trace every one of those beautiful spots on your skin for months now." He outlined a vitiligo patch on my cheek. "I didn't think I could stop a second time."

The more he touched me, the longer he talked, the harder it was to remember why I'd been resisting these feelings. I ached for him, and the fact that we'd been interrupted last time only added fuel to my fire.

"Tell me you don't want me," he whispered. His lips brushed my neck, breath caressing my skin. I tilted my head back to give him better access. "One word, and I'll pretend none of this ever happened. We'll go back to being partners—completely platonic. You'll never hear another word on the topic."

That was what I *should* have wanted. There were plenty of reasons to keep us apart, but right now, I couldn't think of any.

"Or tell me you do," he said, his hands threading into my loose hair, "and I'll lay you down and pleasure you until our ship leaves."

Blessed Virgin, the temptation was insurmountable. I could almost taste his kiss, coffee and whiskey on my tongue.

He looked into my face, and the dying light from the window showed flecks of silver in his dark eyes. "Which will it be, *ma guerrière?*"

"If you wanted to make the question fair," I breathed, "you'd stop touching me so I can think." Not that I wanted to think. I wanted to give in.

His mouth lifted up at the corner. "I'm tired of playing fair." He tilted my head, leaning closer to press his lips to mine.

I expected a gentle kiss, something tentative, but he hadn't lied. He was done playing fair.

His kiss was rough and demanding, weeks of pent-up desire finally released. He pulled me onto his lap, tightening his grip on my hair as he plundered my mouth. He gave me no leverage, but I took it anyway, clinging to him like he was the only thing holding me to earth. A low moan rose in my chest as he drove his hips into mine.

"Say it," he demanded. "Say you don't want me. Make me walk away." It was the last thing he wanted. I could feel the evidence of his arousal, hot and hard against my center.

"Stop torturing me." I kissed along his jaw, tasting the salt on his skin.

"Stop what?" His hand found its way beneath my shirt, palming my breast. "Stop that?"

"You don't know what you're asking for."

"I think I do, *ma belle guerrière.* I'm asking for you to give me what we both want."

Bad idea or not, I couldn't take this anymore. I shoved him onto his back. A grin lit up his face, and when I climbed on top of him, he put his hands behind his head.

"Good girl," he crooned.

*Good girl.* He'd pay for that comment. "Careful," I said. "You might not like the results."

"If it involves you on top of me, I'll take it. Whatever you give me."

Knees on either side of his hips, I sat upright and stripped my shirt off, revealing the black jumps I wore beneath.

El trailed his gaze down my torso, taking in the curve of my breasts and the simple ribbons keeping them hidden. "Divine."

My skin heated at the unabashed lust on his face. I wanted him bared for me, laid out on the bed for me to consume at my leisure.

But not until he begged for it.

Leaning down, I kissed his lips, then peppered kisses down his chest over his shirt. He didn't touch me, content to watch with his mouth quirked in that infuriating smirk and his eyes blazing with desire.

When I reached his waist, his breath caught, just enough to let me know that I affected him as much as he affected me.

I met his eyes as I hooked my fingers into his waistband and dragged his pants down with his underwear.

His cock sprang free, and I grabbed it. It was thick, and the way his eyes fluttered closed when I ran my thumb over the slit filled me with an electrifying sense of power.

"I want your mouth," he said.

I wasn't inclined to give him what he wanted. With a smirk of my own, I licked it base to tip, then blew cool air over the trail my tongue left. He groaned.

"You're trying to kill me, aren't you?"

"It's crossed my mind a time or two." Not at the moment, though. I needed him alive tonight.

I took my time exploring him with gentle licks and touches. He moved his hands from behind his head and buried them in the blankets, knuckles white with the effort of restraining himself.

"Have I done something to upset you?" he asked finally, voice tight.

I took his cock in one hand and his balls in the other. "Why would you ask that?"

"I did, didn't I?" His hips jerked upward as I wrapped my mouth around the tip of his cock, but I didn't allow him to go deeper. "Is this because I called you a good girl? I won't do it again, I swear." He sounded almost pained.

If he wanted to, he could have turned it back on me. He could have flipped me over and been inside me in a moment. He was stronger than me. But he was enjoying being at my mercy, even if he wouldn't admit it.

"No," I agreed. "You won't." I took him fully into my mouth, and he let out a moan so loud I was sure the other occupants of the hotel would complain.

"Enough!"

He shoved me off. I landed next to him on the bed, looking up into his face. His ever-present grin was gone, and his eyes held a half-feral look.

Had I pushed him too far?

"No more." He dragged my pants down in one swift move, trapping my ankles together. Then he reached into his pocket and pulled out a rubber condom. Slipping it on, he pinned my wrists above my head with one hand and guided himself to my center with the other. "I'm done playing."

Our gazes locked, but he didn't go further. He trembled with the effort of holding back, a fine sheet of sweat on his forehead.

I could hardly breathe. "What are you waiting for?"

"You're in control," he said, dragging his head through the wetness at my center. "If you want this to stop, it does."

"I don't." I'd never wanted anything more than this. "Please."

He slid into me, eliciting a gasp.

"You're so wet for me," he said, moving out and back in. The fabric keeping my legs from moving made everything tighter, more intense. "So perfect."

"El..." I closed my eyes, arching against him.

"Anything you need, *mon amour*. Just tell me."

I tugged my hands free, wrapping them around his neck and pulling his face to mine. "Kiss me?"

He thrust into me, swallowing the sound I made with his kiss. "You're beautiful," he whispered when we pulled back for air. *"Tu me rends fou."*

*You drive me crazy.* The knowledge drove me higher, and I ground against him. My fingers dug into the hard muscles of his back. The sound of our breathing filled the room, punctuated by moans.

"Say my name," I begged, moments from release.

"Anne." His hooded eyes locked on mine, and he kept his thrusts steady, even. *"Ma belle* Anne. *Tu es parfaite."*

*You are perfect.* The words send me over the edge. My core exploded in a wave of pleasure that threatened to drag me under, and I called out his name as I climaxed.

Before the stars behind my eyes faded, he stiffened, finding his own release.

As he pulled out and collapsed on the bed next to me, I rolled toward him. His smile, for once, was genuine, and simple joy crinkled the corners of his eyes.

"I hope you're pleased with yourself," I said after a minute.

"I'm certainly pleased." He traced the top of my jumps, causing my chest to pebble. "More with you than with myself, though."

I rolled my eyes, as though the words didn't affect me. "You've managed to thoroughly disrupt all my plans for the night."

"Oh, I'm just getting started." Lifting himself up onto an elbow, he pressed his lips to mine. "I'm going to go clean up, and when I come back, I'm stripping you naked and worshiping every inch of this beautiful body."

"Where did you get your tattoos?"

As the sky turned gray outside the window, I traced the outline of the cross on El's back. After spending all night tangled up in his arms, every muscle in my body ached, but I was thoroughly sated.

"Hm?" He was half-asleep, turned away from me with his face buried in the pillow.

"Your tattoos." I kissed his shoulder. "Do they mean anything?"

He groaned, shifting to look at me. "Some of them."

"Where did the cross come from?"

"Dublin. I knew my mother wouldn't like it, and I was trying to distance myself from her."

He'd never spoken about his parents. "Do you talk to her now? Or did she disown you for it?"

"She's dead."

"I'm sorry. I didn't realize."

"Don't be." He kissed me, fingers playing in my hair. "We were never close."

I sensed some reticence around the topic of his parents. "What about the phoenix?" I asked, changing topics. I ran my hand down the bird adorning his arm, feeling the strength of the muscles beneath.

"I got that one in Venice as a reminder that no matter how bad my past was, I could rise from the ashes." He caressed my cheek. "I never expected to rise quite this high, though."

Despite everything we'd done over the past few hours, my face flushed at the gesture. "What about the lion on your chest?"

He grinned. "That one...is a reminder not to get drunk in Rome."

I laughed. "Does Detective Bianchi have one as well?"

"Bianchi would never!" He clutched his chest with a look of mock horror.

I sat up in bed and stretched. "We should get dressed before we miss our train."

"Must we?" He grabbed me by the waist and pulled me back down to him. "I'd much rather stay here with you for the rest of our lives."

I rolled my eyes as I reached for my jumps. "I'm going to need days to recover from this, El. I'm not sleeping with you again until we get to Prague." With St. Joan's blessing, we'd get there on time and finally end this. "Come on. We're going to be late."

We didn't miss the train to the harbor, but it wasn't for lack of effort on El's part. He did his best to distract me, even going so far as to run me a bath and wash me thoroughly. When we boarded the ship, a man showed us to our room.

"What?" El shrugged when I turned an accusatory glare on him.

"I thought you said you got us separate rooms." The ship was far from booked; if he'd asked for adjoining rooms, he would have gotten them.

"I said nothing of the sort."

"But you assumed I'd be okay with this." I took a step toward the sturdy oak bed that was bolted into the floor, but the ship rocked, making me stumble.

El tried to catch me. His foot slipped, and we tumbled onto the bed. "I'm an eternal optimist," he said, brushing a kiss to my jaw. "I knew I'd get you into bed one way or another."

"No. Don't even think about it." I shoved him off of me. "I'm still sore from earlier." I knew my limits. Right now the ache was a pleasant reminder of last night; if I pushed myself any further, I'd run the risk of injury. "Don't you have anything better to do?"

"Than you? Not a chance." He sat up on his elbows, watching as I reached for my bag. I had an actual trunk now—El insisted on buying me one in Rome to hold my new dresses—but I still kept my weapons on my belt or in the leather bag I carried with me everywhere.

I drew my Saint-Étienne from the holster at my hip and laughed at the hint of apprehension on El's face. "I wasn't planning on shooting you." I sat at the vanity across from him. Like the bed, it was made from oak and bolted into the ground to keep it from moving with the ship.

"And yet it wouldn't be the first time the thought has crossed your mind." He sat upright, holding his hands up in surrender. "Point taken, *ma guerrière*. I'll keep my hands to myself for the time being."

"Why do you call me that?" I set my gun and cleaning tools down on the vanity. It had been too long since I'd had the opportunity to shoot anything. Maybe while we were in Prague I could find somewhere for target practice. *"Ma guerrière."*

"What better name for a Gardien? You're a warrior, are you not?"

"I haven't been a Gardien for months." A fact which he knew well.

"Ah, but I've experienced those fighting skills in the bedroom, Legs. Gardien or not, you're still a warrior."

On second thought, I wouldn't need to find someplace to shoot targets. El's face would do nicely.

He must have seen the threat on my face, because he coughed. "I'll just, um, go stretch my legs."

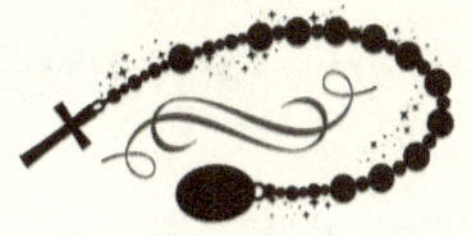

The ship took off without incident, but on the open sea we discovered that I had a severe aversion to ocean travel.

"You don't have to stay in here with me," I told El in between bouts of retching. It was humiliating enough to be stuck in the cabin with my head over a bucket. It was even worse knowing he was sitting next to me, holding back my braid so I didn't soil it.

"Nice try, Legs. I'm not going anywhere." He didn't even flinch as I leaned over and spewed more yellow bile into the bucket. When I sat back up, he held out a clean handkerchief for me to wipe my mouth. "But I can ring for some tea."

"Please don't," I gasped. Just the thought of trying to drink something made me gag.

"At least try to drink some water."

Despite the waves that seemed to be tossing the ship through the air, the glass on the bedside table was still full. El handed it to me, and I gulped down the water. How he was able to stand, I didn't know. Once we landed safely at Calais, I was never setting foot on another ship.

I clutched my rosary and retched into the bucket again.

"Only a few more hours," El said, wiping sweat from my forehead. "We'll be there soon."

Not soon enough. "I'm sorry I'm keeping you up." It was late, and he should be sleeping. At least one of us could be well-rested when we landed.

"It's not the first time you've kept me up all night."

He'd been the one to keep me awake, actually, but I didn't bother to correct him.

"Hold on." Leaving me seated on the bed, El walked over to his trunk. He rifled through the contents, and a pile of papers scattered across the ground, dislodged by his search. "Here it is!" He held up a tiny brown bottle.

"That's poison, I hope." Death was the only possible escape from this torment.

"And risk depriving mankind of the most beautiful creature to ever have walked the earth?" He tutted. "It's only peppermint extract."

Before I could ask why, exactly, he was traveling with a bottle of peppermint extract, he opened it and wafted it beneath my nose.

The relief, though mild, was instantaneous. Without the stench of vomit filling my nose, I could take a full breath.

"Better?"

"A little." I set the bucket down and took the peppermint from him. I held it close to my nose, breathing the sweet scent in.

"Do you think you could drink something? Or eat some biscuits?"

I shook my head, but the movement caused my stomach to churn again. "No. Definitely not."

"Hm." He frowned but didn't argue. "Maybe some lemon water?"

My only answer was a groan. El laughed.

"I guess not." He picked up the bucket and took it to the door, where he rang a bell on the wall. "At least we can get you a fresh bucket. Maybe you'll be able to get some rest."

With the way the boat was rocking, I doubted it, but I curled up on the bed, the peppermint still clutched in my hand.

"Sleep, *ma belle guerrière*. We'll be docked before you wake."

16

Despite my doubts, I did sleep, and when I woke, the ship had slowed to a gentle rocking. The view from the tiny round window showed the welcome sight of Calais port. My bout of seasickness left my throat raw, and my mouth tasted like something died in it. Thankfully, El was absent, and I had time to brush my teeth, rebraid my hair, and slip into my clean shirt and pants before he returned.

I'd just finished when he walked back into the room. "I was coming to wake you. We'll be able to disembark soon. Are you ready?"

"I think so." My belongings, as always, were packed in an orderly fashion, but knowing the way El lived—or at least lived while traveling—I wanted to check the rest of the room for any clothes or weapons he might have dropped during the single night we were on the ship.

"I was in the middle of a conversation with some of the men up on deck. You can find your way up without me, right?"

I rolled my eyes at him. "Believe it or not, El, I've managed to live twenty-seven years without you. I think I can handle getting from the room to the deck by myself."

"Ah, but now that you've met me, you'll never be able to live without me again." He ducked back out the door. I shook my head after him. Arrogant man.

*Is he wrong, though?* Henri's voice sounded in my head.

I scowled. I cherished my independence, and the thought of being dependent on anyone, even someone like El DuMont, chafed.

Though it had been nice to have someone taking care of me last night. I hadn't had someone cater to my needs like that since Maman died. Probably longer.

Brushing away the thought, I scanned the room. Our trunks were already gone, probably carried up to the deck while I was sleeping. El knew I didn't like to let others handle my leather bag, so it waited on the chair before the vanity.

I opened the few drawers in the room and found El's comb and a pair of gloves. At the foot of the bed, the blanket half-covered a small pile of letters. I gathered it all up and put it into my bag. How the man managed to create such chaos in such a short time was beyond me.

Belongings gathered, I scanned the room one more time, then headed out the door in search of solid ground.

On deck, the clean, salty breeze washed away my lingering nausea. I took a deep breath, relishing the warm sun on my skin. Hopefully I'd be able to stomach some food once we were back on land.

Passengers crowded the rail of the ship, waving and shouting at loved ones down on the dock. Crew members dodged between them, carrying trunks and barrels. I ignored a glare from a sour-faced governess as she spotted my unconventional attire, and I smiled at the young girl in her care. The girl tugged at a long ribbon on her hat and smiled back at me before her governess rushed her away.

"Corrupting the youth of France, Legs?" El's voice came from behind me.

"Apparently."

He wrapped his arms around my waist and pulled me to him. "Well, I'm no youth, but you can corrupt me whenever you want."

"One can't corrupt what was never pure to begin with, DuMont."

"Oh, it's 'DuMont' now, is it?" he whispered in my ear. "It wasn't 'DuMont' yesterday morning when you were moaning my name."

I searched the heavens for some sort of relief. "If I didn't know better, *El,* I'd say you were trying to distract me from the hunt."

"Never." He brushed his lips against my ear, sending a shiver through me. "Just trying to make it more enjoyable."

"Maybe you should be more focused on getting us off this godforsaken ship."

"As you wish, my lady." He released me, only to offer a mocking bow and extend his hand.

When we reached the bottom of the gangplank, I could have kissed the ground. Sweet, solid land beneath my feet. The beautiful streets of France.

"You look like you just entered Paradise," El teased.

"Close enough." I closed my eyes, drinking in the sounds and smells of my homeland. I was home. "If I had food, it would be heaven."

He looked at his pocketwatch. "We have time for breakfast before our train leaves."

*Thank the Virgin.* My stomach rumbled, emptied from last night's seasickness.

We found a little cafe near the train station, and I took a seat outside in the sun as El went to get our food. He returned with two *chaussons aux pommes* and two steaming mugs.

"Coffee!" I exclaimed, reaching for one of the mugs. "You're a saint."

He grinned. "Not quite." The drink was thicker than coffee, though no less dark. "You like chocolate, don't you?"

I narrowed my eyes at him. "Why chocolate?"

"I thought you needed some extra sweetness in your life." He sat down and took a bite from one of the pastries. "It's just chocolate, Legs. Not everything has some ulterior motive."

"Hm." I considered him for a moment. "In the future, coffee is fine."

"I'll make a note that you're planning a future with me."

My scowl deepend, but I lifted the drink to my lips. The rich flavors called me back to my childhood. Before I was old enough for coffee, Maman had the servants bring me chocolate in the morning, and we would sit at the table and read together. Her favorite author was Alexandre Dumas. We'd read all his works together over our morning drinks.

I'd stopped drinking chocolate the same time I'd stopped reading: when Maman and Papa died. I'd been nearly grown by then, but that had been the day my childhood ended.

"Is it good?" El prompted.

"It's okay. A little sweet." I set the mug down, pushing the memories away. I couldn't think about Maman. *If she saw me now...*

Reaching for my *chausson,* I pinched off a bit of the pastry to reveal the bits of apple inside. I popped it into my mouth, focusing on the sweet treat rather than the disappointment Maman would have had at the way my life turned out.

"You seem distracted." He nudged my foot with his. "What's on your mind?"

"Nothing," I said quickly. Too quickly. He raised a questioning brow, but I shook my head. "I'm just tired."

"That's a shame. I was hoping you might have some energy for me once we're alone."

"You know, most adults are capable of having a conversation that doesn't mention sex." I took another bite. "Such a shame you're not one of them."

"Anyone capable of talking to you without thinking of sex has obviously never seen you naked, Legs. I'll be lucky if I can think of anything else ever again."

The compliment, insincere as it was, made me flush. "Has anyone ever told you you're an incorrigible flirt?"

"Only for you." He winked and finished off his *chausson*. "Finish you breakfast, *ma guerrière*. I'm eager to have you alone again."

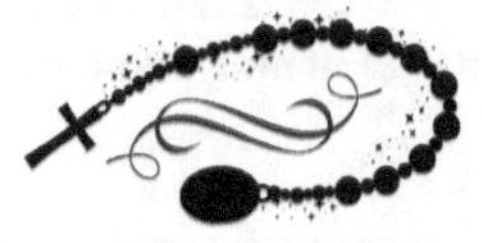

To El's chagrin, our room wasn't ready when we boarded the train.

"I'm sorry, *monsieur*," the conductor said as he punched our tickets. "We'll have a free room this afternoon, but all the rooms are occupied until we reach Paris."

"Shame," El muttered as we headed to the dining car. "I had plans for you."

"You say that like you expect me to repeat the same mistake twice." It hadn't been a mistake, but I couldn't help teasing him.

He took a seat at a booth, looking up at me with a grin. "I might be offended by that if you hadn't made that 'mistake' half a dozen times the other night."

I scoffed as I sat down. "Half a dozen? It wasn't more than three. Probably two."

He leaned in and lowered his voice. "I may have only filled you twice, Legs, but that wasn't what I was referring to. I'm certain you had at least six *petites morts, ma jolie.*"

Heat rushed through me as I thought back on the night. He wasn't wrong. "You think rather highly of yourself."

"It's not arrogance if it's true."

"Yes, well..." I had no defense against him. I crossed my arms and huffed. "It's probably for the best, then, that we don't have a room. We need to make a plan for Prague. Without distractions."

"If you insist." He dug through his bag and pulled out a folded paper.

I leaned in, peering at it as he spread it out. "A map?"

"Prague. See? I can focus when necessary." Pointing to three marks on the page, he said, "This is where each of the bodies was found. If I had to guess, I'd say they're staying somewhere in this circle. Maybe near the clock tower."

The marks grouped near the bend in the river, in what was marked as the *Old Town.* Frowning, I studied it. "That's the wrong side of the river."

"What?" El considered the map. "It's the dead center of the culture. Where else would they be?"

"Lucy likes to paint before she goes to bed. She'll want someplace with a picturesque view. The river to the east, so she can catch the sunrise on it." She might have been barred from stepping in direct sunlight, but she wouldn't give up her painting. She'd always said natural light was best, and she'd want to do whatever she could to preserve that.

"What about here?" He pointed to a spot on the west side of the river. "She'd be able to see the sun rising over the Old Town, and they'd be near enough to Charles Bridge to walk into the city once night falls."

"Yes, exactly. I doubt they're staying at a hotel; if they know we were closing in, they'll want someplace more defensible."

"He has centuries worth of wealth. I'm sure he has more than enough to buy a house on the river."

His grin was contagious. I felt my own cheeks split as a plan began to take form. "So if we find a list of homes purchased in that area over the past few months, we find Bluebeard!" My pulse quickened with excitement. This was it. I knew it was. This was where we would find them and put an end to this chase.

An end. My excitement faded, dampened by reality. If this hunt was over, what next? I couldn't go back to Les Gardiens. Not after letting my own sister be taken by fangs. Not after leaving them. And what about El? He'd have his own life to return to. I could go home, but Emile wouldn't be around forever. Without my family and my purpose, what would I do with my life?

*One step at a time,* I reminded myself. I could get trapped in a spiral of thoughts about the future, but until the hunt was over, there was nothing I could do about it. *Find Lucy. End this. Then you can worry about what to do next.*

"We make a good team," El said.

Right. Because I wasn't completely useless to him. "You do most of the work," I reminded him.

"Even if that was true, I wouldn't mind. I believe I told you once that I needed a pretty face to look at while I hunted."

"Besides your own?"

He pressed a hand to his heart. "You think I'm pretty, Legs?"

I hadn't had nearly enough coffee to verbally spar with him. Actually, I hadn't had any coffee. And I desperately needed some. I stood, grabbing my bag. "I'm going to find myself a drink. Something a little less sweet than chocolate."

"And here I thought you were just trying to get away from me."

"If only."

His laughter followed me through the train car toward the counter where a bored-looking man polished a glass.

*"Un café, s'il vous plaît,"* I said, reaching into my bag for my purse.

*"Le sucre?"*

I'd had more than enough sugar for today. *"Non, merci."*

As I tucked my purse back into my satchel, a paper fluttered out. I picked it up to tuck it back in the bag, reminding myself to return the abandoned papers to El, but something on the page caught my eye. I stopped short.

It was a letter from Lucy.

I read through it quickly. The words were familiar, though it wasn't in her hand. It was the letter she'd written me before Amsterdam, the one that hinted at her destination.

*Why would El have this?*

There was only one explanation. His appearance in Lisbon hadn't been a coincidence. He'd been following me. Reading my letters. Copying them. That was how he'd known where I was and why I needed to go to Amsterdam.

Rage burned through me. But who held the greater blame—him, for betraying me, or me, for trusting him?

*Was it really a betrayal?* a voice inside me asked. *He barely knew you. He was hunting Bluebeard, and you had a connection. You would have done the same.*

No. I wouldn't have done the same. If he'd just followed me, that would have been violation enough, but to open my letters? To make copies and keep them for months?

How many had he read? I pulled the other papers from the bag. Two from Captain Rodin, three from Emile... Each one added fuel to the fire of my anger. The man set my coffee down on the counter in front of me, but I hardly noticed. Letters clutched tight in my hand, I walked back to the table where El waited.

He glanced up at me from the map and grinned. "You forgot your coffee, Legs."

"How did you know?"

The tone of my voice warned him that this wasn't a joke. He sat upright. "How did I know what?"

"How did you know I'd need a room on the train?"

Understanding dawned on his face. "I didn't want to lie to you, Anne."

"No, you just kept secrets." *I think we can leave some space for secrets between us.* That's what he'd told me in Rome. But secrets could be just as damaging as lies. "You were watching me, weren't you? That's why you were in Lisbon. Those letters you sent me while I was traveling—you were nearby the whole time."

He didn't meet my eyes. "It wasn't personal. You had a direct connection to Peller. A connection I needed. I would have done the same to anyone."

It shouldn't have hurt. Shouldn't have felt like he stabbed me through the chest. But it did. Stupid, really, to assume there was anything between us but pure physical attraction. I'd never made that mistake before. I'd always managed to keep my emotions tightly in check. If I hadn't been so absorbed in my lust, I would have seen that he'd been using me from the start.

"We'll finish this in Prague," I said, my voice tight. It was too late to give up now. "If, by some chance, we don't catch them there, this is over."

"Anne, I—"

"Whether we find them or not, after Prague, I never want to see you again. Find someone else to manipulate." I tossed the letter onto the table and headed for the door. He called after me, but I didn't turn around.

I found an empty seat far from the dining car, and I spent the next few hours in prayer. I held my rosary tight enough to draw blood as I begged St. Joan for guidance in the upcoming battle. I refused to think about El. When my prayers were exhausted, I took out my knife and began sharpening my stake, earning apprehensive looks from the people around me. I ignored them all. At the stops, as passengers disembarked and new ones boarded, I remained on the train, my posture stiff and eyes fixed on the horizon out the window.

Around sunset, a conductor approached. "Your room is ready, *madame.*"

I was so tired. Tired of being stared at. Tired of running. Tired of it all. I didn't want to see El, but the exhaustion of the past few months had all crashed down on me at once. I'd have to risk running into him in the room.

I gathered my bag and followed the conductor. The room was empty. I locked the door behind me; El was capable of unlocking it if he wished, but at least I'd have a moment of warning before he came in. Unlike the room we'd shared on the train to Amsterdam, this one had a bed rather than bunks. It was small but luxurious, the type of travel one might expect for a newly married couple on their honeymoon.

Just another way he'd been manipulating me. Trying to make me believe we were in love.

I sat down at the desk that folded into the wall and went through the unnecessary process of disassembling, cleaning, and reassembling my gun. Hours passed, the sky outside the curtained window growing darker, but still El didn't appear. I didn't wonder where he was. I didn't care.

When I laid down in bed after midnight, I still wore my day clothes, not wishing to be caught unawares if El decided to slip into the room while I slept, but the next morning, I woke alone. The door was still locked, the room untouched, and the familiar smell of gunpowder and coffee was absent.

El wasn't in the dining car, either, when I found my way there in search of something to eat. I hadn't eaten since the *chausson* yesterday morning, but despite my grumbling stomach, I wasn't hungry.

I wouldn't be able to hunt on an empty stomach, so I forced myself to eat a simple lunch of chicken and potatoes. As I finished it off, the train pulled into the station at Prague, and I saw sharp spired towers and tiny cream buildings with rust-colored roofs. It was a beautiful city. Romantic, even.

I brushed the thought of romance away. I had no time for, nor interest in, romance.

"Are you ready to go?"

I turned from the view outside the window to see El standing by my table. He didn't meet my eyes, and his face remained carefully blank. Apparently he wanted to pretend there had never been anything between us. Fine. I could do that. It had all been imagined, anyway.

His eyes flashed to my face and away.

I picked up my bag. "Let's go."

As we walked through the city, tension coiled in the air between us, punctuated by the bustle and chatter of the people around us. The language was incomprehensible to me, but it was a comforting sound, almost familiar, like the half-remembered conversations of childhood. The smell of burning coal followed us from the train station toward the river.

In the square, vendors hawked their wares, from fresh-caught fish to sweet pastries. An involuntary smile spread across my face at the life and excitement filling the city.

"We can stop, if you like," El said.

My smile stopped in an instant. I'd almost forgotten myself. "No," I said, jaw tight. "We have a job to do."

He didn't speak, just nodded, and we left the crowd behind. "If you want to find us a hotel, I can look into the property sales, get a start on finding where they're at."

"No. We do that together." I wouldn't give him a chance to lie to me again.

We dropped off our luggage at a small hotel in Old Town. By the time we'd found the land register and El had convinced them to give us the records we needed, it was late. We stopped at a small pub for dinner and pored over the lists in the low lamplight. For a few minutes, I almost forgot the betrayal I'd been feeling all day, as we sat side by side and traded thoughts.

"What about this?" El pointed to an address. I searched for it on the map.

It was the right type of house, but the wrong location. "Too far from the city center."

A few minutes later, I gasped. "Here! Bought two months ago by Lucien Chauveau. It has to be them." Scanning the map, I found the address next to the river, directly across from the Old Town.

"It's the right area, but why are you so sure?" El frowned at the page.

"Papa's name was Lucien, and Chauveau was Maman's maiden name." Monster though he was, Peller cared for my sister. He'd bought this house for her.

"So we found them. Now what?"

"We can check it out tonight." It was late enough, Lucy and Blue-beard would be out enjoying the sights of the city. "Once they're asleep tomorrow morning, we'll come back."

His lips formed a line, a sort of morose look behind his eyes. "And then we finish it."

"Yes." I didn't feel any remorse over that. Over any of it—killing my sister, leaving El, ending this. I couldn't. "We should go."

The silence between us returned as we walked toward Charles Bridge. From what El had told me before we left Ireland, it was a medieval bridge, the most famous in the city, and statues of saints guarded each side.

The bridge itself wasn't holy ground, but I'd be glad to have the saints watching over me as I went to this grisly undertaking.

She wasn't my sister anymore. This was a demon I was hunting. No matter what pretty words it had spoken, no matter how familiar it had felt, this wasn't the Lucy I had loved. She was dead, and this beast killed her.

I reached for my rosary, rubbing the wooden beads. Some of the statues on the bridge were familiar images; I stopped before the Pieta, the Virgin holding Christ's lifeless body, and crossed myself. El walked to the other side of the bridge to give me space.

We didn't have time for me to say the full rosary, but I took a moment to silently pray the Hail, Mary, and beseech her for direction. I'd need all the guidance I could get tonight.

"Anne." Almost as soon as I finished praying, El called out to me. He stood beneath a statue of a woman with two children, an infant and a young girl. "Your namesake."

I looked closer. The statue was St. Anne, the mother of the Virgin. The full moon above us illuminated a small smile on her downturned face. I'd always felt more of a connection to Joan d'Arc than St. Anne, but something swelled in my chest to see this woman I'd been named for smiling down at me in blessing.

"It's a beautiful statue," El said.

It was. The details were exquisite, flowing fabric carved from solid stone. The saint's face was lifelike in its expression.

But we had a job to do. I could admire the saints later. "Come on," I said, turning away.

A woman stood across the bridge. Her long black hair, curled over her shoulders, danced in the breeze off the river. She hadn't noticed us yet, but the sight of her chilled my blood.

It was the fang responsible for Henri's death.

El noticed me tense and followed my gaze. "What is it?"

I reached for my Saint-Étienne, not daring to remove my eyes from the fang. I couldn't kill her yet, not until I knew if she was alone. That mistake had cost me Henri; I wouldn't repeat it.

She saw us, and recognition flared in her eyes. Her red lips stretched in a mockery of a smile as she approached us, but she didn't speak to me.

"Hello, Azazel."

El sucked in a breath. "Mother."

Mother? My attention slipped from the monster before us, and I glanced at him. His face was a mask of shock, eyes trained on hers. This demon, the one who lured Henri to his death, was his mother? And if so, where did his loyalties lie? He'd told me he wanted to avenge someone Bluebeard stole from him. Was that a lie, too?

"I thought someone finally did the world a favor and ended you," he said, his voice remarkably steady considering how pale he was.

I took a tiny step back, into the shadow of St. Anne. With a fang before me and an unknown at my side, I didn't dare leave myself unguarded.

"Alas, not yet." Her gaze slipped to me. "But you brought such *interesting* company! A disgraced Gardien, so far from her beloved Notre Dame. What brings you here, *Mademoiselle* Allard?"

"I go where the demons are." My pistol was a comforting weight in my hand as I watched her. "What is this, DuMont?"

He hesitated. "It's...complicated."

The fang laughed. "Not so complicated as all that, Azazel."

Azazel. He hadn't even told me his real name. How many lies had he told in the months since he met? Too many.

"Are you a fang?" I demanded, not removing my eyes from his mother. He'd done things that were impossible for vampires. He'd walked in daylight, drank holy water, held my crucifix... He'd even prayed in St. Peter's Basilica.

"No! No, of course not."

"Not completely," his mother added, her grin growing wider. "His father is. I died not long after he was conceived."

My brain whirled, trying to understand it. "That's not possible. When you died, he would have died, too."

"Only if I was human."

His mother hadn't been human before she became a fang. Which meant that El wasn't human at all. I swallowed down revulsion. What sort of monster had I invited into my bed? "What are you?"

"My father was a vampire, and my mother was a witch."

A witch. Not a creature of evil, but a creator. And I let him—

Nausea rose in my throat as memories of our time together filled my head.

"For someone whose sister is a vampire, you seem quite distressed to find Azazel's parents are also." The fang leaned against the side of the bridge, propping a hand on her hip. "That's a touch hypocritical, isn't it? But then, Les Gardiens were founded on hypocrisy."

"Mother, you need to leave," El said, a warning note in his voice. "Anne is off limits."

I wanted to scream at him not to protect me, but the words stuck in my mouth.

She ignored him. "What demon could draw a Gardien so far from home? Are you chasing me? Or your sister? I'm amazed she was able to coax Jakob into transforming her."

"Don't talk about my sister."

"Such a weak-minded thing she is. She won't last a decade as an undead. The only question is what will be her doom—Jakob's caprice or your morals?"

"Don't talk about my sister!" I snapped again. My blood boiled. It was bad enough to have lost Lucy, to have to kill her, but to be forced to listen to these taunts? I glanced at El, but he wasn't looking at me. His fingers were white-knuckled around the handle of his dagger.

"Why are you here, Mother?"

"Can't a mother want to visit her son?"

"You never have before. And you didn't know I was here." He took a step toward her, putting himself between us. Who was he protecting? Me, or her?

"Maybe I've changed, Azazel."

"I wish I could believe that," he said.

"You've certainly changed. Traveling with a Gardien? I thought you knew better. She's going to kill you, you know."

My whole body revolted against her matter-of-fact statement. But wasn't that what I had to do? I was a hunter of the supernatural, and he was half-fang, half-witch. It was my job to kill him.

"You wouldn't care if she did," he told her. He didn't bother to deny her claim. Maybe he expected me to try to kill him.

Why did that thought hurt so much?

The fang pouted. "I'm ashamed that you think so little of me."

"Stop dancing around it, Mother." El's tone turned sharp, and he raised his knife. "Why are you here?"

She laughed, the sound like breaking glass. "Merely visiting an old friend."

"Leave."

He planned to let her go. She was the reason Henri was dead, and he wanted to let her walk free.

As though he'd heard my thoughts, he looked at me. "You might think I'm a monster, Anne, but even monsters draw the line at matricide."

"I'm not letting her go," I hissed. "Fight with me or against me. I don't care. But she's not leaving here alive."

"I won't fight you." His brow furrowed, pain etched onto his face. "Don't make me choose."

"As touching as this is, *mon fils,* I have a prior engagement." She took a step forward. *"Mademoiselle* Allard, perhaps we will meet again soon."

"We won't." I raised my pistol and aimed for her heart.

As I fired, she spun away, and my shot barely scraped her arm. The bullet crashed into the stone wall behind her, and she clutched her arm. A howl of pain twined with the echo of the gun's blast.

Before the echoes faded, she ran off toward the Old Town. I moved to chase after her, but El grabbed me.

"Please, Anne," he said, barely audible over the ringing in my ears. "Don't."

I shook him off. "She killed my partner. I have to."

My feet pounded against the pavement as I left him behind. She'd gotten a head start, but she wouldn't get away.

Up ahead was a synagogue. She skirted the building, leapt up onto the wall behind it, and disappeared. I followed just as quickly and found myself in a densely packed cemetery. Trees blocked most of the moonlight, leaving me half blind. I moved slowly between the gravestones tilted and worn by age. The smell of moss and decay filled my nose.

Holding my breath for silence, I listened for any disturbances. Behind me, El clambered over the cemetery wall.

"Come out and end this," I called, trading my pistol for my stake. It was too tight in here, the stones and trees too close to risk shooting.

"You don't want that, little Gardien." The wind carried her lilting whisper to me. "You're all alone. No partner to protect you."

"Good. It will be a fair fight."

The rush of air was my only warning as her fist flew toward my head.

I dodged, letting the momentum carry her past me, and swung around to aim my stake at her heart.

El was yelling something, but I couldn't focus on him. His mother crashed into me and knocked us into a tall gravestone. The grit of the stone dug into my shoulder. I channeled the pain, pushing back. She gnashed her teeth, seeking purchase on my skin, but I kept just out of reach. A single bite would end this, and I had no intention of becoming her meal.

My hand caught her by the jaw, and I drove her head into the gravestone, again and again until her leg swept out and knocked me off my feet.

We rolled on the ground. Sticks and rocks caught our skin and clothing. She hissed as the tip of my stake scraped her bare arm, but I couldn't get enough space to drive it into her body.

"Stop!" The rush of blood in my ears gave the illusion of distance to El's voice. "Don't hurt her!"

How could he defend her? She and her sire had killed the only man I'd been able to trust since Papa had died.

A vicious snarl burst from my lips, and I grabbed the loose fabric of her dress, twisting it until she couldn't move her legs. "This is for Henri."

I drove the stake toward her heart, but she grabbed my arm and sank her teeth into the skin.

"No!" El cried.

The venom coursed through me, and I went slack.

I was going to die.

I tried to muster up the appropriate terror, but the venom was strong. Even with the faint sting of her fangs still embedded in my arm, I couldn't bring myself to move.

Then she was ripped away. Cold air hit the wound on my arm, and I laid gasping for air, my eyes fixed on the skeletal branches above me.

"I said, 'don't hurt her.'" El's voice was a barely recognizable growl. I rolled over to see him holding his mother in the air by her neck.

"You should know better than to get attached to a Gardien, *mon fils.*" She kicked. Her leg connected with his shin, and he dropped her to the ground.

She landed on her feet, turning to me, but before I could move, El grabbed her again. "Leave, Mother. Now."

She shoved him off her, then turned him around and drove him chest first onto the sharp point of a gravestone. His head smacked against another stone with a sickening crunch, and he didn't move.

"El!" I crawled to him. Henri's face flashed before my eyes, the summer ground icy beneath me as I knelt next to his body and felt for a pulse.

It was there. And he was breathing, albeit raggedly. Blood streamed from his nose and chest, leaving his black coat warm and sticky.

"Wake up." I hardly recognized my own voice, the desperate, pleading tone.

His eyes fluttered open. "Is she gone?" he rasped.

I'd forgotten about his mother. I looked around, but she was nowhere in sight. "Yes."

He closed his eyes again.

"Stay awake," I ordered, pulling up his shirt to get a look at the wound. It was a testament to the severity of his injury that he didn't make a joke about me undressing him. "Don't you dare die while I'm still mad at you."

"Ngh." His reply was a half-conscious groan.

Faint moonlight streamed through the trees, too dim to see the wound properly. I could tell the point of the stone had pierced below his ribcage. There was blood everywhere. So much blood. I swallowed, my mouth cottony. How much blood had he lost? How much blood *could* he lose? He wasn't human, so there was no telling how his body would react to this kind of injury. It wouldn't have killed a fang, but he wasn't fully fang.

Where could I take him? I didn't know where the nearest hospital was.

*Not a hospital.* Henri's voice, clear as day, rang in my ears. *They'll realize he's not human. They'll lock him up to study him.*

"Then where?" I begged aloud. "I have no one."

*You have your sister.*

Lucy was nearby. I'd been trying to kill her, but I couldn't think about the morals of the situation right now. If I didn't get El to someone, he'd die. I wouldn't let that happen. Not with so many things left unsaid between us.

His breath grew fainter. I smacked his face. "Wake up." I couldn't carry him to Lucy's house. He was too heavy. "I need you to help me get you out of here."

"Later, *ma guerrière,*" he slurred.

"Not later. Now." I wrapped my arms around his chest and struggled to pull him to his feet. "Please, El." Biting back a gasping sob, I begged him to move. "Just out of the cemetery."

Eyes unfocused, he tried to look at my face. "Don't cry, *ma jolie.*"

"Then *help me.*"

He took some of his weight, though he still leaned heavily on me. Together, we hobbled toward the gate.

Outside the cemetery, he collapsed again. "Help!" I shouted for someone. Anyone.

A gentleman in a tailcoat came running, drawn by my cries. Seeing me and El, he dropped to a knee next to us. He asked a question, but I shook my head.

"English? *Italiano? Français?" Please, let us have a language in common,* I prayed to any saint that was listening.

"English, *ano.* Little." He nodded encouragingly. "He is hurt?"

"I need a cab." I stripped off my coat and pressed it to El's wound, trying to staunch the bleeding. "A carriage?"

The man frowned. "Carriage. *Kočár?*"

"Carriage." With one hand, I mimed cracking reins. "Horses."

"Horses. *Koně.* Carriage." He nodded again. "I find."

"Yes." I held my breath as he went to the corner and waved down the connecting street. A few moments later, the clop of horse hooves neared.

Together, the man and I managed to get El into the carriage. I thrust the map into the driver's hand and pointed to Lucy's address. *Please, God, let us be right about this.* If they weren't home, if we had the address wrong, I didn't know what I'd do.

The man who helped me put his hand on my arm. "Hospital?"

"No." I shook my head, stepping up into the carriage. "Friend."

He frowned, confused, but nodded. "Hurry," he said. He paid the driver for me, then spoke to him in Czech.

I closed the carriage door and took a seat next to El on the bench, holding my ruined coat hard on the wound and praying to all the saints and angels that I wasn't too late.

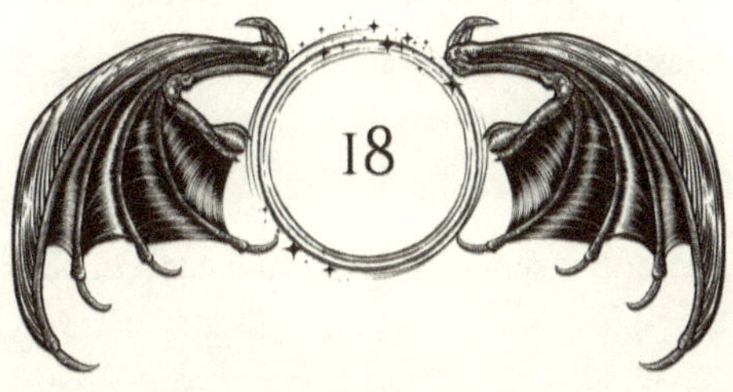

I hardly noticed anything about the huge white house as I bounded up the stairs, leaving El unconscious in the carriage. I grabbed the brass knocker and banged on it until someone answered.

The uniformed servant's eyes widened when he answered the door, but I didn't give him a moment to speak. "Lucille. Get Lucille."

As if summoned by my words, Lucy appeared behind him. Her mouth formed an 'o' as she looked me over, taking in my disheveled appearance and the blood staining my hands. "Are you hurt?"

"Not me. El." I waved frantically at the carriage behind me. "Please, Lucy."

She didn't ask anything else. "Get the blue room ready," she commanded the servant, and he ran off.

She carried El out of the carriage and into the house with supernatural ease. I followed, heart pounding and breath coming hard. Had I made the right choice?

If they could save him, it was worth the risk. I wouldn't think about the alternative.

"Find the baron," Lucy called as she glided past another servant. "And bring towels and boiled water." To me she said, "What happened?"

"A f—a vampire attacked him."

She looked over her shoulder, shock and concern written on her face. "Bitten?"

"No, he—he was tossed onto a gravestone. The point stabbed his chest." The moment flashed before my eyes, and I clenched my fists. Another partner dying in front of me. Just like Henri.

No. It wouldn't be like Henri. He would be fine. He had to be.

We reached a bedroom, and she deposited him on the bed, heedless of the fine blue quilt. He'd stopped bleeding, but I shuddered at the red stains that formed on the fabric beneath him. So much blood...

Bluebeard was only a moment behind us, followed by a crowd of servants carrying clean white towels and bowls of water. He took one look at the scene.

"Get out."

For a moment, I thought he was talking to me, but all the servants rushed out, leaving me alone with my sister and her husband.

Peller ignored me and walked to the bed. Taking a pair of scissors from the bedside table, he began cutting off the ruined layers of El's clothes. My stomach churned as he revealed the clotted wound. It angled beneath his ribs, several inches wide with jagged edges. Had it hit anything vital?

*He's not dead yet,* Henri's voice whispered in my ear.

I kept my eyes locked on El's face, so focused that I almost missed it when Peller dragged his finger through the blood on El's chest and lifted it to his mouth.

My stake pressed against the fang's throat before he could swallow.

"I brought him to you for your *help,*" I hissed. "Not for you to *eat.*"

Lucy put a hand on my arm, trying to soothe me. "We'll do everything we can. Trust me."

"It's not you I'm worried about."

Peller sneered at me. "If I wanted to make a meal of him, you'd know it. I don't drink the blood of my own kind. Even if it is diluted."

I glared back, holding the stake so tight I could almost hear the wood cracking. "Then what are you doing?"

"I needed to know what he was. He's not human, or you would have taken him to a hospital."

"You can tell that from the taste?" My eyes darted to the blood staining his finger and back up to his face.

"To an extent." He pushed the stake away, and I didn't fight him as he turned back to El. "I don't make a habit of tasting every being I come across, so I can't tell what he's mixed with."

"He's a vampire?" Lucy looked between me and her husband.

"Half." I reached for El's cool, sweat-dampened hand. "His mother was a witch."

"More than half," Peller said.

I shuddered, seeing her face in my mind. "She was transformed while she was pregnant."

"The transformation must have affected him as well. He's not a full vampire, but he's close to it." He poked gingerly around El's stomach and chest. "I've never heard of it happening, but I'm not surprised that it could."

It should have appalled me, but I couldn't be upset about the secrets El had been keeping. Not when he was bleeding out before my eyes.

"I don't see any signs of internal bleeding, but it looks like he has a couple broken ribs. And this wound needs to be cleaned before I can stitch it." He took a towel and dipped it in the bowl of water. "Lucille, could you send the servants for some sturdy thread and a large needle? And..." He considered for a moment. "A knife and drinking glass."

She took my hand and squeezed it. "I'll be right back."

When the doors closed, I realized I was alone with the demon I'd spent months chasing. The one who'd killed my sister. *I might not get a chance like this again. I should kill him now.*

But I couldn't bring myself to raise my stake again. Not when El's life hung in the balance.

"I can save his life," Peller said. "But not without collateral."

My eyes widened, and I swallowed down my panic. "What do you need?" Right now, with El's ragged breathing, I would promise almost anything.

"Your word that once he's recovered, you'll leave me and my bride alone. Both of you. No hunting." His voice took on a dangerous tone. "If you harm Lucille, I'll kill you both."

Was I ready to give up this chase? To let them walk away unpunished for the crimes they committed? Was El's life worth such a price?

Looking at El's pale face, I knew it was worth all that and more.

"You have my word." I shoved my stake back into its holster and held up my empty hands. "Just help him."

When Lucy returned with the needle and thread, I watched, heart in my throat, as Peller stitched the wound closed.

Finally he clipped off the end of the thread and set the scissors to the side. "Sit him up."

As I struggled to lift El into a sitting position, Lucy moved to the other side of the bed. She reached around his back to help me, but when she touched him, she let out a yelp of pain.

Peller was holding her before I could move. "What is wrong?"

"His back—" She clutched her arm, staring at the unconscious El. "It burned me."

The tattoo. I remembered it just as Peller turned him over.

"What is this?" he snarled at me. "Is this some sort of trick?"

"He got it to keep his mother away from him." I laid across El's chest, guarding him with my body. "It's got nothing to do with you."

"I'm fine, Jakob." Lucy showed him her arm. "See? It's already healed. I'll just be careful to avoid it."

Peller considered me with narrowed eyes. "No. No, I will do it."

He lifted El easily, and together, we wrapped a long linen bandage around his torso several times before laying him back down. Then Peller grabbed El's nose and jerked it back into place with a small crunch.

"There's not much more I can do for him right now," he said. His dark gray eyes took on a sadistic glint. "I can give him something for the pain and blood loss, but I don't think you'll like it."

"What is it?" I wouldn't refuse anything that would help him recover.

"Vampire blood and venom."

Revulsion turned my stomach, but I looked down at El. "It will help him heal?"

"It will."

"Do it."

He took the knife and slashed it across his wrist. Once the cup was half full of thick, gelatinous blood, he wrapped a spare length of linen around the wound. Picking up the cup, he spat into it. I turned away, unable to stomach the sight of blood and venom mixing together.

Glass clinked against wood as he set the cup onto the bedside table. "The venom should keep that from coagulating further throughout the day. Have him drink it when he wakes. I will have the servants bring up some ice for the swelling." He glanced out the window at the pink streaks appearing in the east. "It is late now, but in the evening I will send for one of my local contacts. A witch. He might be able to assist further."

Lucy rubbed my back. "If you want me to stay here until he wakes, I can."

Peller's eyes narrowed, but he went to her side without speaking. I met his gaze, seeing the resolve there. If Lucy was going to stay, so was he. Vow or no vow, he wouldn't leave his wife alone with a Gardien.

"We'll be fine," I murmured. "Thank you."

"If you're sure." She wrapped me in a hug, and I stiffened. Letting go almost immediately, she stepped back to stand by her husband. "The servants can bring you anything you need."

I nodded and sank into the chair Peller vacated.

"And Anne?" Her face wrinkled with sympathy. "Thank you for trusting us."

Before I could answer, Peller pulled her out the door and closed it behind them.

The rasp of El's breathing filled the air, too loud in the silence left behind. I took his hand and used my other to brush sweat-soaked curls from his forehead.

For the rest of the day, I didn't dare to move from his side. I sponged the blood from his face and chest, iced his face to limit the swelling, and counted every breath. Blue and purple bruises decorated his face, mottling it like a stormy sky. The servants brought me a bowl of dumplings and a cup of coffee around midday, but I couldn't stomach more than a few sips.

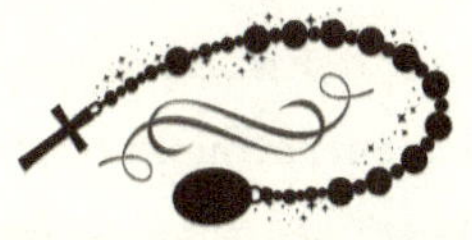

"Anne?"

I bolted upright in my seat. At some point in the afternoon, I'd fallen asleep in the chair next to his bed, resting my head on the quilt.

The orange sunset illuminated El's open eyes. My throat swelled with emotion. I reached for the glass of blood and venom and held it to his lips. "Drink this."

He took a sip and gagged. "What is that? IT's vile."

"Don't ask." I helped him take a few more drinks, then set it to the side and took his hand. "How do you feel?"

"Like I have a hole in my chest." He looked down at his torso, bare but for the bandages. "If you wanted to see me shirtless, Legs, you didn't have to go to all this trouble. You could have just asked."

"I have seen you shirtless. And more." I'd spent all day out of my mind with worry, and the first thing he did when he woke up was start joking.

"I'm afraid I'm not feeling up to 'more' right now, but if you give me a few hours, I might be able to manage it. You'll have to be on top, though." He winked at me, the effect somewhat hampered by his swollen nose and the dark bruises beneath his eyes.

I made a choking sound that was almost a laugh. It was definitely not a sob. I wasn't crying about this. "You almost died last night. I'm not sleeping with you."

"Who said anything about sleep?"

I shook my head, trying to shake away the stinging in my eyes as I did. "Do you ever think about anything but your cock?"

"Of course I do." He grinned, his eyes slightly glazed. From the venom? "I think about your—"

A knock on the door interrupted whatever crude statement he'd been about to make.

"Oh, good! You're awake!" Lucy said as she glided into the room. "How are you feeling?"

I've been better, but it's nothing a tender touch won't fix."

She flushed—I hadn't even realized she *could* flush—at the suggestive look he gave me. "I would recommend rest instead. Jakob just sent someone to fetch his healer friend."

At the name Jakob, El jerked upright, wincing at the pain. "Anne," he said, his voice thick but deceptively moderate, "where are we?"

I adjusted the pillows around him, avoiding his gaze. What if he was upset with me for the choice I made? He'd been seeking revenge against Bluebeard for saints only knew how long, and I'd thrown that chance away in a single night.

I swallowed hard. "I'm sorry I should have introduced you. This is my sister. Lucille Allard."

"Lucille von Peller," Lucy interjected. "Formerly Allard."

Right. She'd gotten a new name with her immortality. I gave her a tight smile. "Lucy, this is El DuMont. We've been traveling together for a few months now."

"It's nice to meet you, *Monsieur* DuMont. I was just bringing an extra cup of your—umm, tonic." She held out a fresh glass of blood and venom. "You two obviously have a lot to talk about. I'll bring the healer up when he gets here."

She left the room, and El frowned at me. "You brought me to Bluebeard?"

"I couldn't exactly take you to a hospital," I said, defensive. "You're not human."

"And what about the hunt?"

I couldn't read his tone. Was he angry with me?

"It was your life or his. You were unconscious, bleeding everywhere. I couldn't—" My voice cracked. "I couldn't watch you die."

He didn't speak. I stared at my hands, twined in my lap. "I had to swear we wouldn't hunt them anymore. He wouldn't save you without my word."

He took my hand in both of his. "I'm not angry."

"I'd understand if you were." I didn't regret what I'd done, but I'd made a decision that he might regret.

Tugging my hand, he indicated the spot on the bed next to him. "Come here."

"I don't want to hurt you."

"Please. We need to talk, and I'd rather have my arms around you when we do."

His words cracked the wall between us. Swallowing the lump in my throat, I crawled into bed, careful not to jostle him as I did.

He adjusted me so my head rested on his shoulder. We sat in silence for a few minutes, his hand tracing a path up and down my arm.

"I shouldn't have read your letters," he said finally. "I'm sorry."

"You were hunting, and I had answers you needed. I might have done the same."

"Still, I invaded your privacy, and then I hid it from you."

I sighed. "I've kept my own secrets."

"I've kept more."

He had, but the questions that had been burning my insides were silent now. "You had good reasons for that," I muttered. If he'd told me when we first met that his father was a vampire and his mother a witch, I would have killed him on sight. Nothing would have convinced me he was anything but evil. Nothing but time and familiarity.

"I'm sure you've got a lot of questions," he said.

"They can wait." He needed rest, not an interrogation.

He waved a hand. "I'm not going anywhere. Hit me. I can take it."

"Much as I appreciate the offer, I don't think it would be good for your wound," I said dryly.

He was silent for a moment. Then he let out a shocked bark of laughter, followed by a groan. "Was that a joke, Legs? I must be rubbing off on you."

"You've certainly been trying to."

His body shook as he tried not to laugh. "Of all the times—" he gasped, clutching his wound. "Of all the times for you to develop a sense of humor, it had to be while I have a hole in my chest."

"It serves you right for nearly getting yourself killed. If you'd died—" I couldn't even finish the thought. I closed my eyes, trying to drive away the image of his motionless body in the middle of the cemetery.

"Hey," he said, his voice uncharacteristically gentle. He cupped my face, turning me to look at him. "I have no intention of dying."

Leaning into his touch, I took a deep breath and counted to ten. He was safe. It was over. "I would call you arrogant for making a claim like that, but I suppose with both your parents being fangs, it's not an unattainable goal."

He winced. "That's not what I meant."

"It doesn't matter." It did matter, but I could only focus on one thing at a time. His potential immortality wasn't on the list right now. "So...you don't drink blood, do you?"

The sound he made in response was a cross between a snort of laughter and a grunt of pain. "No!"

I shrugged, trying not to show my relief. "It's a reasonable assumption. You obviously have some vampire characteristics." Like, presumably, the aforementioned immortality that we weren't talking about. "But you're still..."

"Warm?" he offered.

"That wasn't what I was going to say, but yes. What's human and what's not?"

He thought for a moment, absently stroking my arm. "No blood cravings. No aversion to silver, sacred spaces, or being uninvited. I don't particularly care for garlic, but I can tolerate it. I have all the same problems as humans—hunger, thirst, hot and cold, sickness, susceptibility to injury, and so on. I did inherit the vampire healing ability, though. My body heals from injury or illness in half the time a normal human would."

That explained how, just a few hours after he'd almost died, he was sitting up and talking. "And the witch side?"

He stiffened. "I may have inherited a few special skills."

Narrowing my eyes, I looked up at him, instantly suspicious. "Like what?"

"I can read minds."

*Oh. Oh no.* How many of my thoughts had he heard?

"Please don't make me laugh," he groaned. "My body can't take anymore."

I scowled, trying to pull away. "Excuse me if my thoughts are too amusing. I didn't realize I was supposed to be guarding them."

El pulled me back to him. "Don't be angry with me, *ma guerrière.* I only listen to the really tantalizing ones."

Yesterday, that revelation would have horrified me, but today, my overwhelming feeling was relief. What did it matter that he'd read my thoughts? At least he was alive to read them. I settled into his touch. "You exist solely to torment me, don't you?"

"Only as much as you torment me with desire."

My gaze snagged on the orange and gold phoenix on his arm. "Your tattoos. Do they mean what you said they do?"

"More or less." He extended his arm, rotating it so I could see all the feathers. "When I found out who my mother was, I got the cross to drive her away. At the time, it seemed like a good way to keep her from ever coming near me again.

"The phoenix I got later. I was in a dark place, wishing I'd never been born. The son of a vampire and a witch—who would want me?" Guilt flashed through me at his words, but he went on. "Then I read about the myth of the phoenix, a mythical bird that died in flames and was reborn from the ashes, and it spoke to something in me. I got the tattoo to remind me that I was more than the ashes my parents left me with."

"What about the lion?" I asked. The tip of its mane peeked over the top of the bandages; I traced it with my finger. "Does that have a meaning you didn't tell me about?"

"No." Laughter tinged his voice. "I had one too many glasses of wine when I started working with Bianchi. I woke up the next morning with this on my chest."

"And what did he wake up with?"

He chuckled. "I'll never tell."

A knock at the door announced Lucy's return, this time accompanied by Bluebeard and a third person, a slight young man with glasses. He looked between me and El, and his cheeks colored.

"Anne, *Monsieur* DuMont, this is Evžen Berčík. Evžen, my sister Anne Allard and her partner, El DuMont."

El squeezed my waist as I slipped off the bed to give the healer space to work. "Thank you for coming, *Monsieur* Berčík," I said.

"Evžen, please." His accent was slight, voice soft. He approached the bed, coming to stand opposite me. "Jakob informs me you have a laceration to your torso. Might I observe the wound?"

An intellectual, or a snob? I couldn't decide.

El's gaze was locked on Bluebeard's face, his expression unreadable. He didn't respond to the healer's question.

"El?" I prompted.

He shook himself. "Whatever you need."

As the healer began his examination, he asked El about his ancestry, the nature of his injuries, and how he'd been injured. El answered everything, leaving out only the detail that his mother had been the one to attack him.

"Your judgment was correct, Jakob," the healer said at last. "There are some contusions on the lungs. The nose is broken, as are three ribs. The ribs will need to be bound and the laceration kept clean, but with adequate rest, I predict you will make a full recovery. You are taking something for the pain?"

"Blood and venom," Jakob answered for him. "My own."

El blanched. "I took *what?!*"

"Yes, consuming the blood of a fellow vampire can be beneficial for hastening the healing process." The healer pulled several bottles from the bag on the floor next to him. "However, I have some potions that will be more effective."

The relief on El's face was palpable as Evžen went on. "Consume this one orally as needed. This one may be applied topically to bruises to limit swelling. This bottle must be applied to the stitches before bed each day to prevent infection." He pulled out a final bottle, a small green one. "If the pain becomes unbearable and you have difficulty sleeping, this will help, but it should not be consumed often. It renders even full vampires unconscious for several hours. Take no more than a small spoonful."

"And how long until I can resume...vigorous activities?" El asked, glancing at me.

*Vigorous activities.* I could melt into the floor. Was he really asking about sex in front of my sister and her husband?

The healer's face turned pink. "Physical activity such as exercise, fighting, and...anything else you might wish to do," he coughed awkwardly, "should be avoided at least until the stitches come out next week."

El frowned, obviously disappointed in the answer. Behind the healer, Lucy stared at the ground, her face a brilliant shade of red. Jakob quirked his brow, an amused smile playing on his lips.

*If you ever want to have sex with me again,* I thought at El, *you will stop this conversation right now. Or I will kill you myself.*

"Yes, umm, thank you again," El said quickly.

Evžen picked up his bag. "If you require anything else, Jakob knows where to locate me."

Lucy and Jakob followed him out, and I turned to El, my face heated.

"Really? Vigorous activities?"

"Just making sure everything works properly for you, *ma jolie.* I know how devastated you would be to lose access to my body."

Despite the lopsided grin he gave me, I could see the signs of exhaustion in his face. I shook my head. "You need rest."

He stifled a yawn. "I'm fine."

"That wasn't a request. You need to get out of those filthy pants, and then you need to sleep." He'd need a bath soon, but right now, sleep was the priority.

"If you'd told me you wanted me out of my pants, I would have been happy to oblige."

"Nevermind." I rolled my eyes. "Sleep in them, for all I care."

He laughed, then groaned. "Fine. I'll stop."

Together, we managed to get him out of the bloodied pair of pants. I filled a bowl with warm water and sat down next to him to sponge the worst of the blood off his naked body. He laid back and closed his eyes, too tired even to make a suggestive comment, and I was too focused on avoiding his injuries to admire his firm physique.

As I patted his skin dry with a soft towel, one question buzzed at the back of my mind. I needed an answer before he fell asleep. "Azazel?"

"Hm?"

"That's your real name? You never told me."

"Oh." He cracked his eyes open to look at me before closing them again. "I stopped using it ages ago. It means 'scape-goat,' and I was tired of being that for my mother." He sighed. "It was the only thing she ever gave me. She didn't even bother to give me a surname. The nuns called me DuMont because my mother came from the mountains."

It was no wonder he'd chosen to distance himself from his mother. She'd abandoned him, left him an almost nameless child to be raised by nuns, and now she'd tried to kill him. I wished I'd killed her for him.

I cupped his face with my hand, and he pulled me in for a kiss. I melted into it, wrapping my arms around his neck. He was gentle, his injuries demanding caution, but his touch still sparked a fire in my chest. I'd come so close to losing him. So close to never feeling this again.

"I'm here," he whispered when we finally broke apart. "I'm not going anywhere."

I nodded, swallowing down the lump in my throat. "You need sleep."

This time, he didn't fight me. He leaned back into the pillows. "Stay with me, *ma guerrière?*"

As if I could leave him. I crawled into the bed and pulled the covers over us both. We drifted off to sleep in each other's arms.

# THE HEALER

The young man holds his bag tight, hurrying along the street. He hates being out at night. Evil creatures lurk in the darkness.

Many people would classify him as one of those wicked creatures, but his birth isn't his fault. Yes, he's a witch, but that's almost a technicality. Really, he's a healer. If his potions are a bit more effective than modern medicine, how is that an act of wickedness? And if some of his customers use his potions for sinful purposes, that's not his fault. He can't limit who he sells to; he'd go bankrupt. He has no other way to provide for himself in this world.

Which is why he's out tonight. When a vampire calls for him, he can't very well ignore the summons. Jakob von Peller pays enough to make the disruption to his schedule well worth it—and ignoring Peller would be a death sentence. There might be vampires in the world who have a shred of compassion, but Peller isn't one of them.

A shadow seems to move to his right. He walks faster, clutching his bag tighter. He's a small man, easy prey for anyone with ill intentions. He shouldn't be out this late. But he's far richer now than he was this morning. The money was worth the risk.

As he turns a corner, someone steps in his path. He crashes into him, then stumbles back.

"Pardon!" he gasps, though the large man was in *his* way.

The man wears ragged clothing and reeks of sweat and grime. Greasy blond hair clings to his head. A beggar, most likely. The healer recoils. *Disgusting.*

"Are you the witch?" the man demands.

What does he want from him? "I—I—" He searches for the correct response.

"Evžen Berčík." A second man steps up behind him. "Are you him?"

"I—"

"It's him," the first man says, grabbing the healer's bag and rifling through it. "The bag's full of potions."

Trembling, Evžen reaches for his bag. "I would b-be obliged if you would return m-my belongings."

The man tosses it to the ground, and the bottles crash together. From the sound, at least one breaks. Evžen lets out a strangled sound.

"Don't need your belongings," the man behind him says. "Just answers. Where's the blood-sucker?"

He backs toward the river. "I—what? I'm sure I—"

The blond one waves an impatient hand. "The vampire. *Upír.* Whatever you want to call it. We know you went to see him tonight."

They're hunters looking for Peller. They're not after him.

Panic quickly follows his relief. If he leads them to Peller's home, the vampire will kill them, and then he'll kill him for the betrayal of leading them there.

When he doesn't respond, the man in front of him grabs his shirt. "Take us to him, or we'll have you burned."

They can't burn him. Witch burnings don't happen anymore. They haven't happened in centuries.

At least not official, government-sanctioned burnings. He sees the truth of the threat in the man's eyes.

Tears distort the scene before him, and his lip quivers. "Please," he whispers. "Please don't kill me." He clutches at the man's sleeve. "I've never hurt anyone."

The man's lip curls in disgust. His partner spits on the ground. "Pathetic."

The grip on his collar loosens, and Evžen sees his chance. He jerks free, running full speed for home. The contents of his bag—money and potions—are a loss. Better his belongings than his life.

Something slams into him from behind, knocking him flat to the ground. His glasses crunch against the street, and he tastes blood.

Nothing is broken, he notes in the back of his mind as the men pull him to his feet. If he survives til morning, he'll be bruised and bloody, but at least his nose and cheekbone are intact from where he hit the stone.

*If* he survives until morning.

He blinks his one open eye at the hunters. The cool spring air numbs the sting of his face. His throat hurts from the force of holding back tears.

"Nice try, witch," the lighter-haired man snarls. "But you'll take us to the blood-sucker if you want your death to be painless."

A painless death. Tears drip from his eyes, mingling with blood and snot. Is that all he can hope for?

Peller's household contains two vampires, and the woman in man's clothing wore weapons. Surely they can handle two hunters. If Evžen leads the hunters to them and they manage to win, he can explain the situation. Beg for mercy. Peller's bride is gentle enough. She'll save his life. Or the violent woman, the one with the weapons, will save him out of gratitude for helping her lover.

"I'll do it," he says, sniffling. He wipes the fluids from his face. "I'll take you to him." And may God have mercy on his soul.

19

I t was midnight when Lucy finally coaxed me to leave El's side.

"You need to eat something," she insisted. "He'll be fine for a half hour."

I lingered in the doorway, watching his chest rise and fall, until she took my hand and pulled me away.

The house, now that I could observe it properly, was far cozier than Peller's castle in Alsace, though no less extravagant. A gold and crystal chandelier hung above the dining room table, the walls papered with white and cream. Rich green curtains, tightly closed, protected the inhabitants from the dangers of the sun. Carved cherubs, painted white, decorated the off-white ceiling, and the wooden floor was polished to gleaming.

The table was set for three, candles in golden candlesticks casting a warm glow over the sage tablecloth. Lucy sat, indicating that I should take the seat next to her, and poured us each a glass of wine.

"Tell me everything," she said. Her eyes twinkled as she took a sip of her drink.

"About El?"

"Of course!" Setting her cup down, she folded her hands in her lap. "Where did you meet him? Is he your mysterious partner from Les Gardiens?"

Pain clenched my heart. After all Henri had meant to me, she'd never even known his name. It wasn't her fault; she wasn't even supposed to know about the existence of Les Gardiens, let alone who worked for them. But Henri had been my other half.

"No," I murmured, toying with the rim of my glass. "No, El isn't a Gardien. I left them."

"What? Why?"

Surely she wasn't still so naive. "I couldn't exactly continue working for them after allowing my sister to be turned, could I?"

"I suppose not." She had the good grace to look abashed. "I'm sorry, Anne. I didn't mean to cost you your job."

"You didn't. Not really." It was my own fault. My fault for being so wrapped up in my work that I hadn't noticed what was happening in my own home.

"Well, it seems like the change has been good for you. Or at least he has. You're different, Anne."

I took a sip of wine. I felt different, but only time would tell if that difference was good or bad. Who was I when I wasn't a Gardien? Wasn't even a hunter?

"Where did you meet him?" Lucy asked.

"Alsace," a voice behind me answered.

Lucy's face lit up at the sound of her husband's voice, but the hairs on my neck rose. He might have saved El's life, but I still hadn't ruled out the possibility that he'd been murdering people all across Europe.

I couldn't kill him for it, but I wouldn't allow it to go on, either.

"He was on the police force in Blaubart, was he not?" Peller asked, coming to sit next to me. The table was small, his seat at the head too near me. I didn't give any indication that his presence disturbed me, though. The worst thing one could do around a predator was show fear. "I presume you met the night Lucille was transformed."

"We met the next morning, yes," I said, feigning nonchalance.

"And you've been traveling together ever since."

"More or less."

"So where have you gone?" Lucy asked, eager for word of my travels. As though she didn't understand that I'd been following her. Hunting her.

Trying to kill her.

"Everywhere we have been, my Lucille." Jakob said as the servants came into the room and filled the table with plates of rich beef stew and fresh-baked bread. "Isn't that right, sister? You've been following us."

"Really?" Lucy turned a wide-eyed stare on me. "I thought you'd stopped following us after Rome."

"Of course I was still following you."

Jakob snorted, dipping his spoon into the thick stew on his plate. "Following? Or hunting?"

The question hung in the air between us, thick and heavy.

"Anne?" Lucy prompted after a moment.

"Yes. I was hunting you."

"Oh. I thought...I thought when we met in Rome, you'd realized that was a mistake." She reached for her glass, hand trembling almost imperceptibly. "I thought you came to me because you trusted me now."

Did I trust her now? I'd come to her for help because I had no other choice. But did that mean we could pretend the last few months had never happened?

"Do you?" Her voice was flat. Emotionless.

"Lucy, I—" I stopped myself. What could I say? I'd sworn not to kill her, but I'd devoted my life to hunting down vampires. To ending the beasts that had killed Maman and Papa. Killed Henri. Killed my sister.

So why did the betrayal on her face hurt so much?

I pushed my plate back untouched. I didn't deserve to be here. "I should go."

Neither stopped me as I rushed out of the room. The yellow walls of the hallway around me blurred, but I blinked back the tears. I didn't deserve to cry. Not when this was all my fault.

When I entered the room where I'd left El, my heart stopped. The bed was empty. He'd been asleep when I left. He wouldn't have gone anywhere. Maybe Bluebeard had used the excuse of dinner to get me out of the room so he could get rid of El without my interference.

*Think rationally, Allard,* Henri chastised me in my head. *Where would he have gone?*

The sound of running water gave me the answer as it came from the door on the opposite end of the room. The water stopped, and a moment later, El appeared.

The washroom. He'd been in the washroom.

"What's wrong, *ma guerrière?*" he asked, seeing the distress on my face.

I crashed into him, heedless of his wounds. "I couldn't find you," I whispered.

"I'm okay. I'm fine." He held me tight. "I just needed to use the toilet."

"You shouldn't be out of bed." Even knowing he was safe, I couldn't help the moisture that blurred my sight. I bit the inside of my cheek, trying to force my body to cooperate. There was no need for tears. Crying was a waste of energy.

"What happened?"

"I'm a monster."

"You're anything but." He climbed on the bed and pulled me to him.

The steady thump of his heart calmed me as I rested my head on his chest. "I've spent months trying to kill my sister. What sort of normal person does that?"

"You've spent months trying to protect the world from what you thought was a demon."

She wasn't, though. She was still Lucy. And I'd wanted to kill her.

"But you didn't kill her. When you finally had the chance to, you didn't do it."

"I did kill her, though. It's my fault she's a vampire." All of it was my fault. Henri's death, Lucy's transformation, El's injury.

"This isn't the first time I've been injured, and it won't be the last." He kissed the top of my head. "And as for your sister, she jumped in front of the stake. She chose death of her own free will, and it seems to me that she's happier for it."

He was right about Lucy. In all of our lives, I'd never seen her so happy. It was like she got a new life, filled with everything she'd ever dreamed of.

"But she's damned," I whispered into his skin. "How can I be happy for her when I know she's damned?"

"Is she really? Or is that just what you've been taught?"

A spark of hope fluttered in my chest. I didn't dare to trust it. "If vampires aren't damned, why can't they enter holy ground? Why does holy water burn them? Why do crosses drive them away?"

"Why don't the same things apply to the living damned?" he countered. "Maybe the aversion to sacred objects has something to do with their genetic makeup. Or maybe it's got to do with the beliefs of the wielder. Have you ever seen a vampire enter a mosque or synagogue or temple?"

"No," I admitted after a moment of silence.

"They're barred from those places just as firmly as they are from churches. I spent some time in the Ottoman Empire, and the few vampires I met there reacted the same way to a mosque as they would to a church."

Islam and Catholicism couldn't both be true. Their teachings opposed each other. Scripture warned believers not to be taken in by false gospels like the Muslim teachings. If what El was saying was right, if holy symbols of both true and false religions affected vampires, then maybe it wasn't a result of their damnation.

It was too much to take in all at once, the idea that everything I'd learned since my parents died was a lie. I'd process it later, when I had more time. When I had a priest or someone to guide me through it. Maybe Captain Rodin would have some wisdom to share with me on the topic.

I shifted on the bed to look at him. "That still doesn't absolve me of guilt. It was my hand that stabbed Lucy. I was the one who started the fight with your mother." I hadn't noticed the fang approaching the night that Henri had died. "I'm a liability."

He flipped me over so I was lying beneath him, caged by his arms.

I gasped at the sudden change in position. "Don't do that!" He was going to reinjure himself.

"I'd rather tear my stitches than let you believe lies like that. You are *not* a liability." His words were a growl. "You are strong, and intelligent, and infuriatingly stubborn, but you are not a liability. I got hurt because *I* made a mistake. Not you."

His gaze bored into mine, and the heat I found there told me that our conversation was at an end. He was done arguing with me.

I wasn't done talking, though. I had no intention of allowing him to hurt himself just because he was too busy thinking with his cock to be rational.

"Fine," I said, trying to wriggle free. "Then it's your fault, and my presence drove you to it." He'd been defending me, after all.

He bit me, teeth digging into my neck. I jerked back, but he held me firm.

"I thought you didn't crave blood." He hadn't pierced the skin, but pain radiated from the bite. It was the kind of sting that verged on pleasure, and my core throbbed.

"I don't. I crave you."

"Stop." I pushed his shoulder, trying to dislodge him.

He gave me a little room, confusion wrinkling his brow. "You don't want me?"

Saints. Why did he have to ask such difficult questions?

"It doesn't have to be difficult." He wrapped his lips around the lobe of my ear, sending a shiver through me.

I groaned. "I want you. And I don't want to hurt you."

"Then don't leave me. Because if you do, I swear by Saint Columba, I will hunt you down using all the skills I've learned in my centuries on this earth. And then I will kiss and taste and fuck you until you never think about leaving me again."

Centuries. I froze. How old was he?

He sat back on his heels. "Does it matter?"

"Yes. No." I still cared for him, even knowing what his parents were. Did his age really make a difference? "I don't know."

He shifted to lie on the bed next to me, our bodies barely touching. Pain lurked behind his eyes; he tried to hide it, but I could see what he didn't want to show. He was afraid of my reaction. "About four hundred, give or take a few years. I stopped keeping track somewhere after my hundredth birthday."

Four hundred years old. He was ten, maybe fifteen times my age. And presumably immortal, if not invincible.

It was just another barrier between us. How could he care for me when my life was just a flash compared to his?

"My lifespan has no impact on how I feel about you, *ma guerrière,*" he murmured. "I've searched the world for hundreds of years and never found someone like you."

"And when I grow old and die, you'll live for centuries after that. What's the point?"

"What's the point in anything?" He placed his hand on my cheek, leaning in for a gentle kiss. "What happened centuries ago and what will happen centuries from now have no bearing on the present. I love you. Right here, right now. That's what matters."

Time stopped. I searched his eyes, hardly daring to breathe. "You love me?"

"Since the moment you walked into that brothel in Amsterdam and nearly got us both killed.

It was hardly the most romantic proclamation of love, but a smile spread over my face. "You fell in love with me because I nearly got you killed?"

"I fell in love with you, little warrior, because you came in ready to kill me yourself." He kissed the tip of my nose. "And when you realized the mistake you'd made, you played your role perfectly."

I ran my hand over the stubble on his jaw, unable to wipe away my smile. "I was so angry with you."

Mischief danced in his eyes. "Until you felt my cock. I distinctly remember you thinking something along the lines of, 'what would it feel like inside me?'"

"A fair question." I bit my lip, looking up at him through my lashes. "It felt better than I imagined."

He groaned. "Don't tempt me, Legs. My stitches are already killing me, but if you keep looking at me like that, I can't promise I won't pounce on you again."

I brushed my lips against his once, twice, three times. "Another time." I ached for him, but I wouldn't risk hurting him while he recovered.

"Tomorrow, maybe."

"Or maybe, like the healer said, you can wait until your stitches come out."

He pouted. "Fine. But only if you tell me when you fell in love with me."

My cheeks heated, but I scowled at him. "Who says I did?"

"I can read minds. Did you really think you could keep secrets from me?"

"Then you must already know. Since you know everything."

"Ah, yes, of course." He stroked his chin, pretending to consider it. "I remember now. It was the moment I opened the carriage door, and you saw my smiling face for the first time. Love at first sight."

"Which is why I spent so much time plotting different ways to end you," I deadpanned. "Because I was so desperately in love."

"Exactly."

I rolled my eyes. "You're impossible."

"Tell me the truth, and I won't have to guess."

"Fine." Sighing, I pretended to think about it. As though I hadn't known since Rome. "It was Mass at St. Peter's Basilica." My voice dropped to just above a whisper. "No one's ever done anything like that before."

"Taken you to church? If I'd known the standards were so low, I wouldn't have tried so hard."

I swatted him on the arm. "You know what I mean."

"I do." He took my hand, pressing a kiss to the knuckles. "Watching tears stream down your face as you listened to the service was the second most beautiful thing I've ever seen in my life."

I raised a brow. "What was the first?"

"You, writhing naked beneath me."

I smacked his arm again, less gentle this time. He rubbed at the spot. "*Ma guerrière violente.* Violent little warrior."

"You need to rest," I said, sitting up. "And before you say it, I know. You'd rather I keep you awake in other ways. I don't care."

He laughed. "I thought I was the mindreader."

"I need to go talk to Lucy." I owed her a thousand apologies. For everything I'd done over the past few months. No, for years. Ever since Maman and Papa died.

"I'll be here," he said, squeezing my hand.

One last kiss, one I never wanted to end. When we released each other, I headed reluctantly toward the door, then stopped in the doorway to look back at him. Exhaustion lined his bruised features, but he smiled at me.

"Thank you," I said. "For everything."

20

I went in search of Lucy, but she wasn't who I found.

The library, with its vaulted ceilings painted in a scene from an ancient battle, was brightly lit. Jakob sat in a high-backed chair, a book in his lap. He looked up at my entrance.

"Excuse me," I said, taking a step back toward the door. "I was looking for Lucy."

"She's not here."

My lips tightened. It was clear he had no intention of directing me to her. "I'll look for her elsewhere.

He closed his book and set it down. In a blink, he stood a step away from me, and air from his sudden movement rushed past me.

"You don't like me, do you, Anne?"

"You murdered my sister." I injected all the venom I'd been carrying for months into my voice. "Why shouldn't I hate you?"

His lips twitched in what might have been a smile. "As I recall, you were the one who struck the killing blow. I was merely the one who saved her."

A mistake I'd regret for the rest of my life. But I didn't let him distract me. "Your hands may not have driven the stake through her heart, but you're still responsible for her death. You manipulated her into falling in love with you." His storm-colored eyes remained fixed on my face, but he didn't respond to my accusation. "Do you deny it?"

"Of course not." His smile was real this time. Real and vicious. "From the moment we met I was driving her to me. I went out that night with the express purpose of finding a meal, and I was blessed to find so much more."

A blessing for him. A curse for her. Disgust turned my stomach.

"Would you like to hear how I ensnared her?"

I shrugged as if it didn't matter. As if his words wouldn't echo through my mind, tormenting me. As though I wouldn't pore over every move, wondering how I could have changed the outcome.

"The night I met Lucille, I'd gone to see the play *Axël*. I had a private box, the ideal position to view the rest of the audience. That was where I saw her. Her golden hair glittered in the lamplight, and the rapture on her face as she watched the play... I was bewitched."

Bewitched. An ironic choice of words, considering he'd been the one doing the bewitching.

He circled me slowly, like he'd done the night Lucy died, and just like that night, I turned to keep him in sight. "I knew I had to have her as my bride. Even if she proved as fickle as all the other women I'd taken through history, I would still make her mine, if only for a brief time.

"But I couldn't just take her. I had to make her want me as much as I wanted her. So I hunted her."

When he stopped moving, I stopped as well, swallowing. He'd hunted her. Like his prey.

"I terrified her, made her believe she was being followed, and drove her right into my arms."

Every word he said only made me hate him more. "You sound so proud of that fact."

"Why shouldn't I be? I set my sights on something, and I obtained it."

"My sister isn't *something,*" I snarled. I wouldn't reach for my weapon—I'd given my word, and unless he attacked me, I wouldn't break it—but there was no need to hide my loathing. Not when he knew already. "She isn't some prize for you to win."

"And yet I won her anyway. Even knowing my true nature, she loves me. She chose me over you." He leaned in close; I could smell his fetid breath, the stench of cold death. "Doesn't that just kill you?"

It clawed my insides apart. No matter what El had said, I held the blame for my sister's choices. "Even if I could forgive you for what you did to my sister, I would still hate you."

He laughed, the sound low and throaty. "Because I am a demon, and you are a demon slayer?"

"Because you murdered dozens of women before Lucy." The scene flashed to the forefront of my mind. "You kept their bodies like grisly trophies. You denied them a proper burial, and you denied their families peace and closure. Just because you've stopped killing doesn't absolve you of the sins of the past."

A predatory grin spread across his face, revealing the monster beneath. "Oh, my dear sister," he said, and the tone of his voice sent a shiver down my spine. "Who told you I stopped killing?"

I tensed. Lucy had seemed so sure that they weren't murderers. Was she mistaken about Peller? Had he been hiding his kills from her?

"I may not end the lives of those who bring Lucille and me pleasure and sustenance, but I am still a killer. And if I sense a threat to my beloved, I won't hesitate to destroy it."

I barely breathed as he leaned in, lips inches from my ear, and whispered, "Are you a threat to my beloved?"

"No." The word came out weak. I shook my head and answered again, louder this time. "I have no intention of harming my sister." She was innocent, despite what I'd been taught. Her husband might be a threat to mankind, but she wasn't.

He straightened. "Then there is no reason for contention between us." The spark in his eyes warned that he would be watching me, though.

As I would be watching him. This was a temporary ceasefire, not a true peace. If I harmed his wife, he would kill me; if he harmed my sister or any other innocent, I'd kill him.

Soft footsteps entered the room, and by the sudden gentling of Jakob's face, I knew it was Lucy.

"Is something wrong?" she asked, coming to wrap an arm around his waist.

"Not at all, my sweet Lucille." He smiled down at her, no trace of the predator remaining in his expression. "I was merely getting to know my new sister."

She beamed up at him, and guilt twisted once more inside my chest. I'd almost lost her twice, first when I'd driven her to leave me, and then when I'd killed her. I wouldn't lose her a third time.

"Can we talk?" I asked, drawing her attention from her husband.

Misgivings filled her face when she looked at me, and I cringed internally. I'd hurt her in so many ways, so many times. I had to fix things between us.

Jakob took her hand and pressed a tender kiss to the knuckles. "I'll be nearby if you need me, Lucille." With a final warning look at me, he left us alone in the library.

Tension radiated in the air between us. I racked my brain for something innocuous to say and came up short.

Lucy floated over to the globe on the table in the center of the room, turning it with a gossamer tongue. "There's so many places I've never been."

"I wish I'd taken you."

"Do you?" She gave me a sad smile. "We both have regrets, don't we?"

I bit my tongue. My hands hung awkwardly at my sides. *Just say it.* "You know—"

"I'm sorry, Lucy." The words bubbled out of me, cutting her off. "For everything. I should have been there for you after Maman and Papa died. I shouldn't have thrown myself into Les Gardiens. I should have taken you to see the world. I should have let you into my life and learned about yours." I closed my eyes so I didn't have to see the hurt on her face. "I'm sorry I killed you."

Silence lingered in the air. Then cool hands took mine. I opened my eyes to see understanding written across her features.

"I forgive you, Anne. For everything."

My breath caught in my throat. "How?" I choked out.

"You're my sister. How could I not?"

Her forgiveness was a gift I never deserved, and when she wrapped her arms around me and folded her smaller body into mine, the dam broke. I cried into her neck, sobs shuddering through my frame. Lucy's own tears wet my shoulder.

When we'd cried ourselves dry, we pulled back and looked into each other's faces. Tearstains marred her cheeks, and my nose ran. I patted my pockets in search of a handkerchief. She laughed, wiping her face with her hand.

"I haven't cried like that in weeks," she said.

It had been far longer than that for me. I didn't usually allow myself the luxury of crying. "I haven't since Maman and Papa died."

A watery smile crossed her features. She took my hand again and led me to a soft green couch on a windowless alcove. She pulled the chain on the lamp next to the couch, and yellow electric light filled the space.

"Tell me about everything," she said, holding my hand as if she was afraid to let me go.

So I did. I told her about Henri and what he'd meant to me, about how he'd died and she'd gone missing in the same week. I shared how afraid I'd been for her. How relieved I'd been to find her still alive and the guilt that had plagued me when they'd flown away.

"I thought I'd lost you forever," I whispered.

She wrapped me in a hug, squeezing me just a little too tight. "You didn't."

But I very nearly had. I held her a little tighter, breathing in the scent of chrysanthemums and paint. Familiar smells, mixed with something new, the hint of expensive musk.

"Lucille." Peller's voice, cold as death, broke us apart. He held a paper in his left hand, violent eyes locked on mine. "Step away from her."

Lucy rushed to him. "What's wrong?"

He angled his body between us as I stood. Protecting my sister, as though our conversation earlier had meant nothing. "You have one chance to answer me," he said. "Where is Evžen?"

I couldn't have been more confused. "The healer?"

He relaxed visibly. Lucy's hand rested on his arm; he raised it, pressing a kiss to her knuckles. "I received a letter from the woman he lives with. His niece. He didn't make it home last night, and when she went looking, she found his bag down by the river. She suspects hunters."

"It wasn't me!" Even if I hadn't been by El's side all night, I wouldn't have harmed the eccentric man. He'd seemed harmless, and more importantly, he'd helped El.

"It's probably just a coincidence," Lucy said, ever the optimist. "Maybe he went to see another patient and lost his bag on the way."

"Perhaps." From the look on Peller's face, he didn't share her optimism.

"I can help you look for him, if you want." I didn't want to leave El, but if someone here was hunting witches, it was better if I found them now. Before they could hurt him.

Peller considered me for a moment, as if judging whether I could be trusted. Then he nodded. "We leave in ten minutes."

It felt odd, strapping on my belt and weapons for this hunt. My target, for once, wasn't fangs—it was humans. Hunters. They would have been my comrades, if they hadn't been a potential threat to the man I loved.

El watched me from the bed, worry knitting a line across his forehead. "You don't have to go, you know."

I gave him a dry look. "It's not the first hunt I've been on."

"It's the first time you've had to hunt humans, though." He shifted, wincing as the movement pulled his stitches. "And can you trust Peller?"

Sitting down on the bed next to him, I pulled on my boots. "He...cares about Lucy, in his own way." Unhealthy as it was. "He won't hurt me unless I'm a threat to her. And he saved your life."

"You don't owe him anything." El took my hand, pressing a kiss to the palm and closing it.

"I have to do this, El." I traced the outline of a bruise on his chest. "I'll be fine."

He didn't say anything else to stop me, even though I could see in his eyes that it was killing him to watch me leave without him. So I didn't object when he twined his fingers into my braid and pulled me tight against him. He kissed me, our tongues tangling until I was breathless and almost ready to lock the door and forget the world outside. I wanted to lose myself in him, to remind us both that we were alive and well.

"Later," I whispered as I pulled away. He groaned and nipped at my bottom lip one last time.

"I'll hold you to that." Squeezing my hand, he added, "Be careful, *ma guerrière.*"

Peller waited for me by the front door. He was unarmed—his body was weapon enough—and dressed casually. He tucked his hands into his pockets.

"You are ready?"

I rested my hand on the gun at my side. "I am."

"Then let us go."

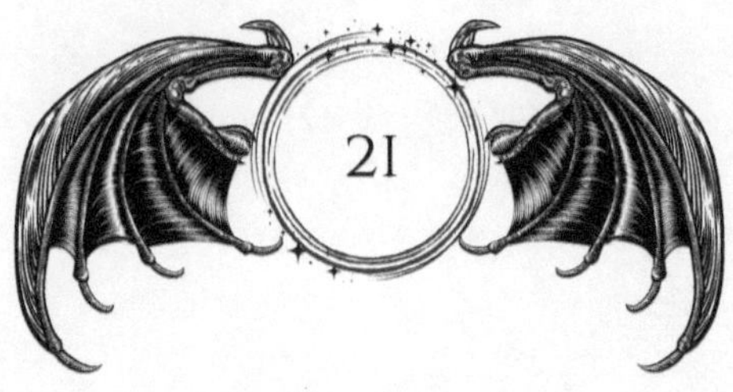

21

Near dawn, we returned to the house empty-handed. Wherever Evžen was, he'd left no trace behind. Tension left both me and Peller quiet. It seemed El's mother wasn't the only danger in Prague.

Lucy met us at the door, biting her lip. "Did you find him?"

"No, my sweet Lucille." Peller kissed her softly, and I turned my face away. "Not tonight."

"Oh." She smoothed her dress, trying and failing to hide her disappointment. "Well, I'm sure he'll turn up."

I stifled a yawn. The sun was rising in the east, lighting up the rust-and-cream buildings of the city. We all needed to find our beds.

I tried to squeeze past them, but Lucy put a hand on my arm to stop me. "Thank you for going with Jakob," she said. "I'm glad he had someone to trust out there. Protecting him."

Protecting a fang. Hunting Hunters. My life had been completely turned upside down overnight.

"It was nothing." I gave her a halfhearted smile.

"Now that he's able to move a bit, I had *Monsieur* DuMont moved to the room across the hall to a fresh bed."

My smile was more genuine this time. "Thanks, Lucy." Clean sheets. I couldn't wait to fall into them. I headed up to the room.

El slept soundly, his color better than before. I washed up quickly, slipped into a long shirt, and laid down next to him. The sound of his breathing lulled me to sleep.

The sound of shouting woke me a few hours later. Sun streamed in through the window, and the clock on the wall told me it was almost eleven.

Another shout rang out, and El jerked upright. "What is it?" he asked.

I recognized Jakob's furious voice, but not the others. "I don't know. They're speaking Czech." I reached for my pants.

He closed his eyes, listening closely. "I can't make out everything," he said. "It sounds like Peller's saying something like, 'Let him go.' The other two—three?—are refusing." He blanched. "They called him an *upír*. A vampire."

*Hunters.*

I bolted out of bed before he finished speaking, buckling on my belt. I didn't know who they were here for, but they couldn't be allowed to endanger Lucy or El.

El stood, reaching for his own clothes. I glared at him as I loaded my pistol. "Where are you going?"

"With you, obviously." He tried to hide the wince of pain as he bent over to put on his pants.

"You're a liability." Harsh words, but ones he needed to hear. "Stay here. I'll be back soon." There was no time to say more before I slipped out into the hall.

I crept toward the voices on silent feet. I didn't have far to go; they were in the entryway, two grizzled-looking men in patched clothing. One of them had a tight grip on Evžen's arm. The healer's eye was bruised, dried blood painting the skin beneath his nose.

"I didn't want to," he whimpered, sniffling miserably.

Peller, standing between them and the rest of the house, gave him a withering look. He said something to the healer; I didn't understand the words, but the sentiment was clear enough. He blamed Evžen for bringing violence to his home.

Evžen wailed out a response.

The second intruder, a blond middle-aged man, barked out an order in Czech and drew out a knife. The healer fell silent, quailing before the weapon.

I tapped gently on the wall, just loud enough that Peller, with his supernatural hearing, was aware of my presence

"What do you want of me?" he asked the intruders, switching to English. "I will not allow you to threaten those in my household."

The first one, the one holding Evžen's arm, laughed. "Nothing but your death, *upír.*"

"Then what are you waiting for?" He moved slowly toward them, drawing their attention from me. "I have harmed no one in Prague, but if you wish to challenge me, I will not balk."

Now that they were distracted, I could inch forward to get a clearer view of the room. They stood between us and the door, but in order to enter the house, they would have to fight their way past both me and Peller.

They wouldn't succeed.

The fair-haired man scoffed. "You've 'harmed no one,' eh?" He spit on the floor. "Keep your forked tongue behind your teeth, demon. Your lies won't save you."

"I pose no threat to anyone in Prague who does not threaten me and mine."

"The merchant from England would disagree."

Genuine confusion crossed Peller's face, quickly smoothed away. "I know nothing of English merchants."

"Stop talking to it," the darker one ordered. "We need to finish this before its demon bride comes to help it. Then we can end her, too."

Fury roared through me. My sister would not be their prey.

Jakob and I locked eyes. For once, our purpose was united.

We all moved at once. The two men lunged for Peller. Evžen fell forward, landing on his face. I grabbed the first man by the back of his shirt. The fabric ripped in my hand, and he twisted out of my grasp.

"Demon bitch," he growled at me.

He thought I was Lucy. I cocked a grin at him. "Not quite." I bashed my revolver into the side of his head.

He staggered back. Recovering, he aimed his stake at my stomach. I dodged the blow, backing against the wall.

"Nowhere to go now, blood-sucker." He sneered, stepping closer. He raised his stake, aiming it for my heart.

I held my gun up to his chin and pulled the trigger. Blood and brain matter rained down over me, and he dropped to the floor.

"I'm not the demon you're looking for," I told his lifeless body.

The light-haired man, locked in hand-to-hand struggle, let out a roar of rage at his partner's death. Taking advantage of his distraction, Peller grabbed him by the neck and raised him into the air. The hunter kicked and thrashed, but Peller squeezed tighter. The man's face turned purple. He clawed at Peller's hands, gasping for air.

One final squeeze, and the light in his eyes went out.

The body slumped to the ground at the vampire's feet. Breathing hard, I walked over to him and fired a bullet directly into the hunter's heart.

Peller considered the wound. "Silver?"

"Lead. No need to waste silver on humans."

"Anne."

I whipped around to see El in the doorway. Relief painted his face, though he leaned heavily against the wall, breathing hard.

"I told you to stay put."

"I heard gunshots." He folded me into his arms and kissed my forehead. "I had to make sure you were okay."

His voice was distant beneath the ringing in my ears, and I was surprised to find myself shaking in his hold. It had been ages since I'd last fired my Saint-Étienne in combat.

"I'm fine," I told him. He was unhurt. So was Lucy. Nothing else mattered.

A moment later, Lucy ran into the room, a wide-eyed stare on her white face. She spotted a bloodstain on Jakob's shirt and shrieked.

"You're hurt!"

"No," he said, gathering her to him. "I am unharmed."

"It's not yours." She traced his face with her hands, as if assuring herself it was true.

Peller held her close, breathing her in with his eyes closed. "You are safe, my sweet Lucille."

The healer, who had been hiding in the corner, crawled toward the doorway. Peller's head snapped up.

"A moment, Lucille." Jakob gently removed her arms from around him. He walked across the room toward the shivering Evžen.

"I warned you not to betray me." His words were cold as ice.

"Jakob." Lucy put a placating hand on her husband's arm. "Don't you think he's been punished enough?"

"Not remotely." Jakob reached down and grabbed the small man by the neck. He twisted his wrist, and Evžen's head snapped unnaturally to the side.

Lucy screamed. All the blood drained from my face. El's grip on me tightened.

"I'm here," he whispered in my ear, as though he knew the sound had sent me back to the night Henri died. But he did know. He could hear my thoughts. I turned and buried my face in his shoulder.

*I can't look,* I thought to him.

He stroked my back. "You don't have to."

"How could you?" Lucy shrieked at her husband. "He was your friend!"

"He was a danger to you." Jakob remained calm despite the dead body in his hand. "I warned you from the moment we met, Lucille. I am not a good man."

It took everything in me to force myself to turn back around, to face the room where Peller had just broken someone's neck, but I did. For Lucy. El squeezed me once and released me so I could go to my sister.

She didn't seem to notice when I took her hand. Tears streaked her face, but they weren't tears of sadness. Rage twisted her features. "You didn't have to kill him."

"And yet I did." He dropped Evžen's corpse to the floor. "You knew what I was when you chose to join me in this life, Lucille. I've killed hundreds. Even those closest to me, from my first wife to your immediate predecessor."

El flinched, and my stomach turned at the reminder of the room where Lucy had died. Peller was our tentative ally, but that didn't stop him from being a monster.

The anger in Lucy's face gave way to melancholy resignation. She slipped her hand from mine. "I don't need you to kill for me, Jakob. Just to care for me."

He put a finger beneath her chin, drawing her gaze up to meet his. "I will care for you from now until the stars fall, my sweet Lucille." Then his dark eyes turned hard as steel. "And I will stop the hearts of anyone who tries to get in my way."

Pulling her in for a hungry kiss, he lifted her up into his arms. Her legs wrapped around his waist, and it was as though El and I didn't exist anymore. Peller stepped over the bodies on the floor, carrying Lucy toward their bedroom. In the hall beyond the entryway, he murmured something in Czech, and as his footsteps faded, a few servants came into the room and began cleaning up the scene.

Nausea filled my throat. It had been one thing to know what he was, to have seen his victims, but to actually see him kill? I wanted to be glad Lucy had a protector who wouldn't back down, no matter what. But was he a protector? Or was he just another monster, staking a claim that wasn't his to make?

El took my hand. "He can be both. It doesn't change how you feel about your sister."

It didn't. And I wouldn't abandon her here with him now.

I turned from the grisly scene before us. "You need rest."

He led me back to the room, but when I closed the door, he took my face in both his hands and kissed me. I melted into it, twining my hands around his neck and letting him back me into the wall.

"*Ma guerrière,*" he groaned, moving his lips to my neck. I tilted my head back to give him space.

"No vigorous activity, remember?" The reprimand came out too breathy to have any weight. "You'll hurt yourself."

"Then you'll have to be on top, because stitches or no, I need you." He kissed me again, until I was breathless. "Please."

I melted at his words, at the pleading look on his face. "If it hurts, we stop."

"Anything." His eyes were hooded, pure animal desperation on his face. "Drive away the darkness with me."

I needed that. Needed something to replace the horror of the day. "Yes."

He let out a sigh of relief. "Thank the saints."

Light streamed into the room through the gauzy curtains, the only room in the house not completely shrouded in darkness. I said a silent prayer of thanks for the illumination when El stripped off his shirt and stretched out on the bed before me.

"I thought you'd want to take off the rest yourself."

I couldn't roll my eyes at him. I was too busy drinking in the sight. Even bruised and battered, with a bandage wrapped tight around his middle, he was breathtaking.

"No need to keep your hands to yourself, Legs," he said, folding his hands behind his head. "If you like it so much, take it."

Blood rushed to my face and my center at the same time. I'd forgotten he could read my thoughts.

"Only the really tantalizing ones. But with that look on your face, I don't need to." I scowled at him, and he just laughed. "Even when you're angry, you're beautiful."

No one had ever said that to me, at least not seriously. Henri had teased me about my beauty marks, and my limited bedfellows had whispered sweet nothings on occasion, but no one had ever truly seen me. Lucy had always been the beauty of the family. My patchwork skin was a curiosity, like something from a circus. It didn't bother me—I'd never wanted to be the center of anyone's attention. But the way El was looking at me right now, I could understand the appeal of being thought beautiful. The heady sensation drew me further into his orbit.

"Take off your shirt," he said, eyes trailing down my still-clad body.

I could have refused. Could have tortured him. But I wasn't interested in self-denial, so I stripped off the shirt and left it in a pile on the ground, leaving myself bare.

"Get the condom from the side pocket in my bag, and come here."

My body moved of its own accord. He sat up and took the condom from me, setting it on the bedside table.

"I would love to find every single person who ever made you feel less than exquisite, *mon amour*. I want to show them just how wrong they are." He ducked his head, pressing a kiss to a patch of lightened skin just beneath my breast. "Lie on your back."

"You'll hurt yourself," I started, but he nipped at my skin, cutting me off.

"I said, 'lie down.' I want to taste you."

Heat throbbed between my legs, but I clenched them together. I wouldn't risk his well-being just because he was too busy thinking with his cock to see reason.

"I promise, I won't hurt myself." He captured my nipple between his lips and sucked on it, arching my back off the bed. "Let me do this."

I'd lost the capacity for speech, and apparently reason as well. My eyes fluttered shut when he climbed between my legs.

"Eyes open. I want you to see every moment of this."

My eyes flew open, and he grinned. He took my pants, sliding them down my legs, and threw them somewhere behind him on the floor. I couldn't look away from his face, the laughter and desire mingling in his brown eyes.

He trailed his finger over the crease in my legs, next to my core. "You have a lighter spot here, like the ones on your face and your arms. Did you know that?"

I shook my head, too breathless to speak. It wasn't a place on my body that I'd spent a lot of time examining.

"Someday I'm going to lay you down and taste every one of those marks," he said, and the promise sent a shiver through me. "But right now, I'm more interested in tasting something else." He lowered his face and licked my center.

Something shattered inside me, and only the press of his hands on my legs kept me in one piece. He kissed and licked and nipped until I begged for release, my hands buried in his hair.

When I was moments away from climax, he pulled back.

I sagged into the bed. "You're soulless."

"Maybe." He grinned, licking my arousal from his lips. "But when you come, it's going to be with me deep inside you."

"Then *hurry up,*" I snarled, lunging for him.

He met me with a fierce kiss, hands all over my body as I rolled him underneath me and dragged off his pants. His groan into my mouth spurned me on, and I pumped him with my hand.

He grabbed my throat, just enough to catch my attention. "No more playing."

"Finally." I took the condom and slid it over his cock before guiding him into me.

It was like being whole again. I couldn't even move, too full to do anything but relish the moment.

"Beautiful," he whispered. I looked down to see him watching me, eyes hooded. He held me by the hips.

The urge to move was overwhelming now. I ground against him, our gazes locked together.

He moved with me. "That's it. Take what you need. *Ma belle guerrière.*"

Words were impossible. I leaned down to kiss him, his two-day beard rasping against my skin. He flicked his tongue against mine. The movement echoed the joining of our bodies, and I moaned.

*"Ma jolie."* He kissed down my chin, my neck, everything he could reach. *"Mon bel amour. Vens pour moi.* Come for me."

The words sent me over the edge. I spiraled into oblivion, calling out his name. He continued plunging into me through it all, and as my tremors faded, he thrust in deep, his own release finding him.

I tried to roll off of him, but he wouldn't let me go.

"Not yet." Despite his tight grip, his eyes were heavy. He nuzzled my neck. "Stay with me."

"I wasn't trying to go anywhere." But I settled atop him, twining our legs together, and rested my head on his shoulder.

When he spoke a moment later, he was half asleep. "The gunshots... I didn't know who was shooting. I know you're a warrior—I know you can handle yourself, but I was so afraid for you."

Affection flowed through me. I reached up to brush his bristled cheek. "I'm not hurt."

"Tell me you love me," he said, his words half-slurred from exhaustion.

Amusement quirked my mouth. He was demanding, often infuriating...but I couldn't deny him. "I love you." I rolled off of him, taking his face in my hands, and kissed him. *"Je t'adore."*

Cool air blew across our bodies, making me shiver. Something sticky had dampened my stomach. I glanced down, expecting to see some mark of our joining, and tensed.

Blood.

I sat up, shaking El awake. "You're bleeding." We'd torn some of his stitches, and he'd bled through the wrappings around his chest.

"I'm fine." He tried to tug me back down next to him, but I refused to be distracted.

"I told you this was a bad idea," I scolded as I lifted the bandage to examine the wound. The bleeding had already stopped. My immediate panic faded.

"You weren't complaining a few minutes ago," he murmured.

When I climbed off the bed, he groaned and reached for me, but I slipped into the bathroom. I came back a moment later with a wet towel and fresh bandages.

He jerked away when the towel touched his skin. "That's cold!"

"Don't be a child." I had no sympathy for him. His lack of self-preservation had brought this on himself.

His head sank back into the pillows. "If I died inside you, it would have been worth it."

"You weren't going to die from sex." Though he might one day kill me from worry.

"Not from worry. Only from pleasure."

"Arrogant man," I said affectionately.

22

Near sunset, I snuck out of the room in search of coffee. El slept peacefully, potions and clean bandages applied to his chest.

In the kitchen, I found a young fair-haired girl taking a loaf of bread from the oven.

"Could I get a cup of coffee?" I asked.

She frowned at me, saying something I didn't understand in Czech.

"Coffee." I mimed taking a drink. *"Cafe?"*

"Ah!" She pointed to the coffee grinder that stood on the counter. *"Káva?"*

"Please!" I hadn't had a cup in days, and I felt the beginnings of a headache.

She reached for a ceramic jar, taking a scoop of coffee beans and pouring it into the grinder. "You go," she said, gesturing toward the parlor. "I bring."

The parlor wasn't empty. Orange and pink streaks of sunset light filtered in through the open window, and Lucy sat in a shadowy corner. A canvas leaned against the easel before her, paints strewn across the coffee table.

"Oh!" She nearly dropped her brush when she saw me. "You startled me."

"Sorry." I took a seat on the couch, in the midst of the fading light. "What are you working on?"

She turned the easel to face me, and I saw circles of black and gold, surrounded by tiny figures. "Prague Orloj. The astronomical clock in the Old Town. I've only seen it at night. I came in here hoping the sunlight would help me picture it in a daylight setting."

A knot formed low in my throat at the reminder. She'd never feel the warmth of the sun on her face again. Never enjoy an afternoon stroll in the late spring, or a morning ride through the park.

"There's no need to pity me, Anne," she said, picking up her brush and dipping it in the gold paint. "I see the look on your face. I'm perfectly content with my life now."

"Are you?" Her reaction when Jakob killed the healer made me think her marriage wasn't everything she'd dreamed it would be.

"Of course."

Silence stretched out between us. Then she let out a heavy sigh and set her brush down. "I don't know. I love Jakob. I truly believe he's my destiny. But…"

"But?" I prompted when she paused. I didn't dare to hope that she was seeing the flaws in her husband.

"He treats me like a child!" She stood, crossed her arms, and began pacing the room, carefully avoiding the dying patches of sunlight. "I know he's stronger than me, and he has centuries more life experience. And he respects me on matters of opinion and intellect. But the instant there's any perceived danger, I'm relegated to hiding in my bedroom, waiting for news. It's just like—" She glanced at me and cut off sharply, shaking her head. "Nevermind."

Just like the years after Maman and Papa died. Guilt tugged at my chest.

"I just..." She stopped, looking out the windows to where the streetlamps were being lit. "I just wish he would see me as an equal, rather than someone who needs protection."

But she did need protection. If she didn't, she wouldn't have been susceptible to his manipulation. She wouldn't have married him.

I didn't say that out loud. No matter how I felt about her husband, I wouldn't allow him to be the wedge between us.

The girl came in with a tray of coffee, saving me from having to respond. She set it on the low table before me. Tiny blue flowers decorated the white porcelain coffee pot, from which the girl dispensed thick black coffee into matching cups. She cut slices from a round brown-and-white cake dusted with sugar and put them on plates for us.

"*Děkuji*, Běla," Lucy said. The girl bowed to her before leaving us alone.

I raised a brow at my sister. "When did you learn Czech?"

She laughed. "I didn't, but I make a point to at least know how to thank the servants wherever we are."

Another thing that hadn't changed about her. She'd always had a caring spirit. When I'd been too busy worrying about keeping us safe,

Lucy left her generous heart open to the world. She never forgot to express her gratitude or affection. Death hadn't killed her kindness.

She stirred several cubes of sugar into her coffee before taking a sip. It seemed death hadn't affected her sweet tooth, either.

"I tried to talk to Jakob about this, but he won't listen. He just keeps telling me I'm too precious to risk." She pursed her lips. "It's not as though I don't understand the dangers. My sister was a *Gardien*, for heaven's sake! But with the right training, I could learn to defend myself."

I made a noncommittal noise, taking a drink of my own coffee. It was rich and dark, an instant cure to my impending headache. Lucy's frustration was reasonable, even if it reminded me of everything I'd done wrong in the past few years. I'd coddled her too much. Henri had warned me against it—it had been one of the few topics we'd argued about. He'd thought Lucy deserved the same opportunities as me, the chance to learn to defend herself and fight against the beasts that had killed our parents. I'd always told him he didn't understand how naive Lucy was, how much she still needed protection.

"You could teach me."

I looked up from my drink, wary. "Teach you what?"

"To defend myself. If you show me how to fight, I can prove to Jakob that I'm not completely useless. That he can trust me."

Stalling for time, I took a bite of cake and chewed it slowly. It was light and fluffy, tasting of chocolate and vanilla.

Teaching a fang to fight hunters... It went against everything in me. But keeping Lucy in the dark had gotten her killed. I had a chance to rectify that mistake now.

*Do it,* Henri's voice urged. *If her husband ever turns against her, at least she'll have a fighting chance.*

"Yes," I said finally. "I'll teach you."

Her face lit up in a brilliant smile. If possible, death had made her even more beautiful. She was ethereal. "Thank you!"

Infectious as her enthusiasm was, even my mouth turned up at the corners. "Later." I'd have to find someplace we could work, somewhere with plenty of space, and decide how to start her training.

"Oh, of course. I need to tell Jakob first. And I'm sure you want to check in on *Monsieur* DuMont." Her cheeks pinkened. "Jakob and I usually eat dinner around nine. If *Monsieur* DuMont is feeling better, the two of you are welcome to join us."

Oh, saints. Of course she knew he was feeling better. She'd probably heard us having sex this afternoon. Now *I* was the one flushing. "That would be nice." I set my cup down, avoiding her gaze. "I should go see if he's awake."

I didn't wait for her response before rushing out of the room, cheeks hot enough to ignite. I could almost hear Henri's laughter chasing me down the hall.

Stupid sensitive vampire hearing.

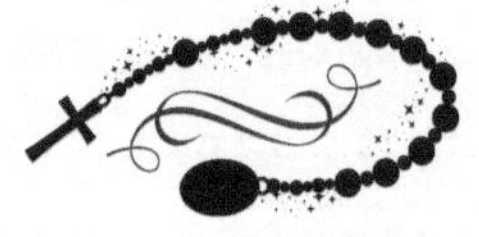

As I helped El into his jacket for dinner, he looked as nervous as I felt. "Dinner with the in-laws," he muttered. "What are we thinking?"

"I'm not sure they count as 'in-laws.' We're not married."

He laughed. "Not yet."

His jokes only seemed to get worse when he was uncomfortable. "I suggest you stop toying with my emotions, DuMont. You almost died a couple days ago, I killed a man in the foyer a few hours ago, and we're about to have dinner with my vampire sister and her husband. I can't handle anything else right now."

"Who says I'm toying, Allard?" Grabbing me by the waist, he pulled me into a breathtaking kiss. "Now that I have you, *ma jolie,* I have no intention of ever giving you up."

The color rose in my cheeks. I'd never pictured myself getting married. I'd been too focused on Les Gardiens and my sister to ever consider it. But now I could almost see it: a simple white lace dress, a bouquet of violets, El standing at the altar with the priest...

I swallowed hard, shaking away the image. We needed to make it through the night first. We had to decide what would happen when he was healed. Any other decisions would have to wait.

El pressed his lips to my forehead. "I'm not asking yet. You don't have to make a decision now. I just wanted you to know my intentions."

I didn't know what to say. I brushed invisible dust from his jacket. "You're sure this isn't too much? We can eat up here instead."

"I'm fine, *mon amour.* I'd like to have a chance to meet them without venom or worry clouding my mind."

It was just dinner. I could do this. There was nothing unusual about having dinner with my sister, my sister's vampire husband, and my half-vampire lover. Nothing strange about it at all.

El stopped, his hand on the door, and put his lips to my ear. "Stop stalling before I have to take you back to bed and tear that beautiful dress off of you."

I was wearing the dress he'd bought me for Easter Mass, the only clothing I owned that was appropriate for any sort of dinner. Why I'd taken the extra time on my appearance tonight, I didn't know. I'd coiled my usual braid on top of my head and pinned it there. El had swiped a sprig of lilac from the vase on the bedside table—Lucy's touch, I was sure, since Peller didn't seem the type to decorate with flowers—and added it to my hair. It matched the silk of my dress perfectly, and when I glanced in the mirror, I looked sufficiently presentable.

"That would be counterproductive," I said in response to his suggestion. I wished he would take me back to bed. It would be far more pleasant than facing the evening.

He laughed. "Later, *ma guerrière.* I promise."

Right. Dinner first.

In the dining room, the brightly lit chandelier revealed a table set for four. The pewter dishes had been polished brightly enough to pass for silver. Lucy and Peller were already waiting for us; when we entered, Peller rose from his chair at the head of the table.

"*Monsieur* DuMont." He inclined his head. "I am pleased to see you so well recovered."

El bowed as well. "Thank you. Anne tells me I owe you my life."

I frowned at that. I'd never said those words, nor would I have. El was more generous than I was.

Peller waved a hand, indicating that we should sit. "There is no debt between us. You are practically family, no?"

I nearly choked. Was everyone in this house conspiring to marry me off to him? Lucy, at the foot of the table, seemed to be hiding a laugh. A strange look crossed El's face, as though he was trying to parse out some hidden meaning in the words.

"I hope to have the honor one day," El said smoothly, expression gone as soon as it had appeared.

A glass of red wine waited behind my plate. I picked it up and took a healthy swallow. I was going to need something stronger than wine if I wanted to make it through the evening.

Conversation, thankfully, remained light as the servants brought in dishes of braised beef, creamy gravy, and dumplings. Lucy asked about El's time working for the police near Jakob's estate—"After all, Blaubart is my home now. I should know about it."—and he entertained us with stories of the inhabitants of the small town.

When the food was gone, the servants returned, this time with cups of coffee and a crumbly cake that tasted of honey.

"Now that everyone is sated," Jakob said as we dug into the dessert, "I believe we have some matters to discuss." He looked at me. "My wife trusts you. You swore not to hurt her or me. And you rendered us assistance this afternoon when hunters came to my door. I assume this means they were not allies of yours?"

I bristled at the suggestion. "Of course not!"

El reached across the table to take my hand. "It's a fair question, *ma guerrière*. We were hunting them ourselves just a few days ago."

I glanced over at Lucy and found her staring fixedly at her plate, as uncomfortable with the discussion as I was.

"We were working alone." I met Peller's storm-colored eyes, narrowed at me in suspicion. "Following the trail of bodies behind you. I assume they were doing the same."

Lucy looked up at that, distress painting her face. "We haven't left any bodies!"

"You haven't, but someone has. There have been violent murders in every city you've visited. In Amsterdam, someone killed a curator at the Rijksmuseum the night you were there. A vampire killed a young boy in Rome just before Easter. And then the deaths here in Prague the past few weeks. You can't say that's a coincidence."

Horror widened her eyes. "You know we didn't—I would never—"

"We're not accusing you," El said. "But someone arranged the bodies to look like famous art pieces. They're going to a lot of trouble to make it seem like you're killing people. I have a feeling you," he nodded at Peller, "would be more circumspect if you were involved."

A faintly amused smile crossed Peller's face, but he nodded. "I know how to keep my kills from being noticed."

"Can you think of anyone who might want to draw hunters to you?"

"When you live as long as I have, you're bound to make enemies." Lucy blanched at her husband's words, but he seemed untroubled by the prospect. "No one specific comes to mind."

"We encountered someone from your nest the other night," I said.

El gave me a sharp look.

*What?*

He widened his eyes, shaking his head almost imperceptibly.

*Do you not want them to know she's your mother?*

He shook his head again.

*I won't mention it.*

Oblivious to our silent exchange, Peller raised a brow. "I assume you mean my sire? I left his nest centuries ago."

"Your sire is dead." I said it without thinking.

Lucy gasped. El set his cup down with a loud clink. Even Peller looked shaken.

"Oh." His voice was steady despite the shock. "How?"

"He was caught by Les Gardiens the week you left with Lucy." I didn't mention my involvement. I didn't need to. I saw by the glint in his eyes that he understood. But I didn't know what that glint signified—was it just recognition, or did he plan to avenge his sire?

El cleared his throat. "He knew the dangers of going to Paris. Anyone who steps into Les Gardiens' territory has to know the risks." He stared at Peller, the warning evident on his face. Injured or not, he wouldn't allow me to be threatened.

"Yes, he made his choice and faced the consequences for it." Peller turned back to his cake. "Do not fear. I have no intention of pursuing retribution, so long as no one threatens me or my bride."

His constant refrain was becoming tiresome. I turned to Lucy, eager to change the subject. "If we clear out the furniture, the dining room would be a good space to begin our training. We could start after we eat, if you like."

She cast a nervous glance at Jakob and bit her lip. "I, umm..."

"Training?" Peller's eyes narrowed as he looked between us. "Training for what?"

"I offered to teach Lucy how to defend herself. Didn't she tell you?" I feigned surprise, as though she should have told him as soon as I'd left the room.

The look of irritation on his face was worth the prickling sense of fear I felt as he rose to his feet. El pushed his chair back, his hand on his dinner knife.

"Sit down, Jakob." Lucy glared at me, her expression uncharacteristically stern. "You said you were sorry about what happened between us, Anne. If you really want to make things right, you won't antagonize my husband."

"I wasn't—"

"Yes, you were. You're not Maman, Anne, and I'm a grown woman. If you don't like the way I'm living my life, you're welcome to leave." Her voice softened a little. "I want you to stay. But I won't stand for this contention between you." She narrowed her eyes at Jakob. "From either of you."

Jakob took a seat, wiping his face to hide his smile at her words. "Forgive me, dear sister," he said to me. "I did not mean to offend."

I muttered an equally insincere reply.

El stood, cognizant of my discomfort. "My stitches are beginning to ache. Would you help me with my medication, *ma jolie?*"

He didn't need my help, but I seized on the opportunity. "Yes, of course." *Anything to get out of here.*

His mouth twitched with mirth while he bowed to Jakob and Lucy, one hand on his wound. "Thank you for dinner, *madame. Monsieur.*"

Back in the room, I collapsed on the bed and groaned. "It's harder than I thought, having a monster for a brother-in-law."

El made a noncommittal noise.

I sat up, frowning at him. "Is something wrong?" Maybe he objected to my use of the word *monster.*

"That's not it." He shed his jacket, sinking into a chair.

"Is it your stitches? I thought you were just giving me an excuse to escape." I reached for the bottles of potions on the bedside table, but he shook his head.

"No, it's…" He sighed. "I don't want you to feel like I'm keeping things from you."

Tension settled low in my stomach. I crossed the room and perched on the edge of his chair. "So don't." We'd had enough secrets between us.

"But I don't know how you'll react."

My anxiety grew the longer he waited. "Neither do I, unless you tell me."

He laughed humorlessly. "No, I suppose not." Taking my hand, he squeezed it. "I think Bluebeard is my father."

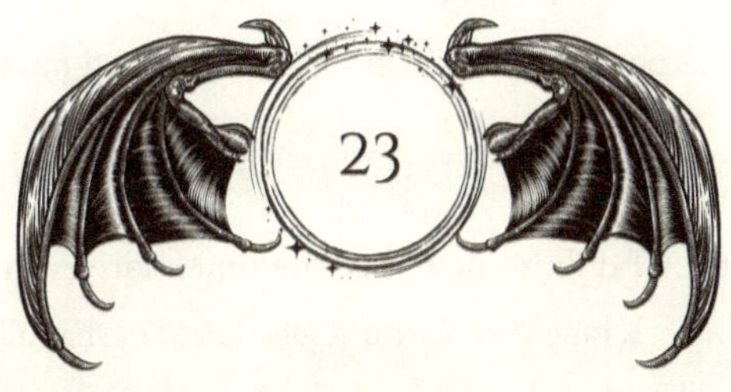

I stared at him, unable to think of a response.

After a moment of silence, he shifted uncomfortably. "Are you angry?"

"I'm...not sure." I wasn't sure of anything. It was a lot to process. His father was married to my sister. "Not angry, exactly. Confused. How did it happen? How did you know?"

He pulled me onto his lap. "They didn't know she was pregnant when he killed my mother. I don't think he meant to transform her, but he did. She realized a few weeks later that she was pregnant with me.

"She didn't know how the transformation would affect her pregnancy—being both a vampire and a witch, there were too many unknowns. So she went back to her hometown of Sens. There's an abbey there dedicated to St. Columba."

I'd heard of St. Columba. Patron saint of witches. She was a controversial figure, adored by some, rejected by others. Les Gardiens taught that her followers were all evil. There had even been talk about sending a team to Sens to wipe them out.

"Once I was born, she left me in their keeping and ran off to find my father."

"Peller."

He nodded. "I didn't know it at the time, but yes. It took me decades to find her, long after the nuns who raised me had all died. She was half-crazed by then, living as a cat on the streets of London—"

"I'm sorry, what? As a *cat?*"

He swallowed, averting his gaze. "Ah. Umm, yes. She can shapeshift."

Oh, that was much worse than the identity of his father. "You don't...do that, too, do you?" If he did, then I couldn't trust anything I knew about him. Not even his appearance.

He took my hand and pressed it to his cheek. "Look at me, *mon amour.*" I looked into the deep brown eyes I'd come to love. Faint flecks of gold danced in them. I didn't want to give them up. "I'm exactly what you see. No more secrets."

"You can't turn into anything else?"

"No." He quirked his mouth in a crooked grin. "And even if I could, I wouldn't. I know how attached you are to my body."

My breath rushed out of me with a sound that wasn't quite a laugh. I didn't know what I would have done if he'd said he could shapeshift as well. There had to be a maximum limit to how much stress a single person could take.

"Anyway, I found her in London and coaxed her to return to her normal body, but she refused to tell me anything about my father. I was convinced that he'd driven her mad when he killed her. I hated him."

I couldn't imagine what it had been like for him. The women who raised him, dead. His mother, insane. His father, a monster. I settled my head on his shoulder and wrapped my arms around him as I listened.

"I resigned myself that I would probably never know the name of the man who fathered me. I traveled around a lot in the centuries that followed, spending some time in a long-forgotten kingdom in what's now the German Empire. I navigated the courts of Suleiman the Magnificent, saw the birth of America, fought against Napoleon, watched the conquest of the Dahomey Kingdom.

"And then, just a few years ago, my mother reached out to me. She apologized for abandoning me and for how she treated me after I found her again. She offered to tell me about my father, and I came back to France.

"She met me in Sens and told me about a cruel man who beat her and drank her blood nightly. When she finally found the courage to tell someone about him, he accused her of being a witch. The townspeople tried to burn her."

I gasped. Even Les Gardiens, who staunchly opposed witchcraft, had stopped burning witches centuries ago.

"She saved herself from the burning and crawled back to my father, who, according to her, drained her of all her blood and left her for dead. When she awoke, she was a vampire. She said she hadn't seen him since."

Doubtful, but I didn't interrupt El's story to express my opinion.

"She told me his name, but it took me two years to find where he lived. He wasn't in the little town of Blaubart. He was off, presumably finding a new bride. I ingratiated myself into the town, joined the police force, and established a reputation as a completely average bachelor. Once he returned, I planned to observe him, to see if my mother's stories were true, before approaching him."

"And then I happened," I said softly.

"And then you happened," he agreed. "The best thing to appear in my long life."

I pressed a kiss to his cheek. "I'm glad you went looking for him." Without that, we would never have met.

He smiled. "Me, too."

We sat there for a minute. I listened to the sound of his breathing, steady and even, until my eyelids fluttered closed.

"I don't know if I'm ready to tell Peller yet," he said, his voice a low rumble in my ear. "I don't know how he'll take it. But it's possible that my mother is the one following them."

Following them and murdering innocents. Trying to draw hunters down on them. I sat up, no longer tired. "Does she hate him that much?"

"Maybe." He lifted one shoulder in a shrug. "I barely know her, and what I do know isn't good. She may have spent some time living as a harmless stray cat, but not all her years were so innocent. There's a trail of blood in her wake. If she wanted to get revenge on my father, she wouldn't worry about the morals of it."

"We need to warn them." Lucy was innocent in all of this. I couldn't let her be caught up in the midst of their feud. "We don't have to tell them everything, but they need to know she's coming after them. I don't want Lucy to get hurt."

"She won't be." He squeezed me. "You're going to train her, remember?"

I groaned. "It was her idea. I only went along with it to irritate Peller."

"You can't lie to someone who can read your mind, *ma guerrière.*" He kissed my neck. "You agreed because she's your sister, and you want to protect her."

"Your insight is infuriating sometimes."

He laughed. "That's okay. I don't mind if you only love me for my body."

"Ugh." I dragged myself from his lap. "I should go find Lucy."

"To help her, or to antagonize her husband?"

"Why not both?" I pulled my dress over my head, revealing my petticoats and corset.

El's eyes darkened as I removed my petticoats, then loosened the strings of my corset and dropped it to the ground. I preferred the comfort of my jumps, but I had to admit the corset had benefits as well. It created the illusion of curves that my lithe figure lacked. Left only in my chemise and stockings, I should feel self-conscious about my lean muscles and patchwork skin, but it was impossible to feel anything but beautiful with the way he devoured me with his gaze.

"I've changed my mind," he said, his voice hoarse with desire. "You need to stay here with me. Your sister can wait."

I put my hands on both sides of his chair and leaned down to brush my lips against his. He tried to deepen the kiss, but I pulled back and smirked at him. "Later."

"Cruel woman." He swatted at my rear.

Blowing him a kiss, I dodged the blow and escaped to the bathroom, where my familiar shirt and trousers waited.

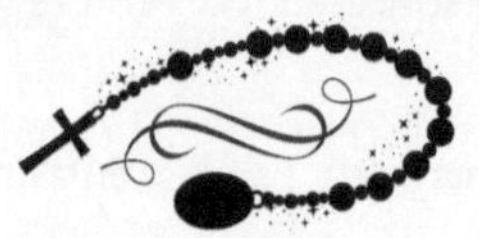

In the parlor, Lucy sat before her easel, hard at work on her painting in the electric light. She'd changed out of her mint-green dinner gown into a simple blue wrapper with black paisley print. When I entered the room, she looked up, and her lips formed a line.

"I'm sorry," I said, the words foreign to my mouth. "I should have waited for you to tell him yourself."

She nodded graciously in response. "Thank you." Making a final swipe on the canvas, she set her brush in the cup of dirty paint water waiting on the table. "The servants just finished clearing out the dining room, if you want to start now."

"Will Jakob be joining us?" I hadn't expected him to leave her alone with me for this. He'd want to watch her training, whether to ensure she was learning to protect herself or to make sure she couldn't stand against him.

"He was hoping to watch, yes." She stood, trying to wipe a spot of yellow paint from her cheek but only managing to smear it. "He had the table moved to the corner so he could work on some business paperwork while you teach me."

"Hm." At least he hadn't outright refused. Maybe he wasn't completely unreasonable. Or maybe he was so arrogant that he didn't believe she could ever fight back against him.

"Will this dress do, or should I find something else to wear?" She spun, showing off her wrapper.

"It should be fine. Tonight, I just want to test your balance and what you can do. Unless you intend to start dressing in trousers all the time, you'll need to learn to fight in whatever you normally wear. Even if trousers are more convenient."

"More convenient?" she asked as we headed toward the dining room. "I don't understand how you wear them. They're so restrictive."

*Thus begins the lesson, I suppose.* "The more fabric you're wearing, the more your enemy can grab onto. And when you're moving a lot, your legs can get tangled up in the skirts." I'd never minded wearing dresses as a girl, but when I'd started Captain Rodin's training course to join Les Gardiens, I'd learned quickly that trousers could be the difference between life and death. Now I rarely wore anything else, even at home. Maman and Papa had been safe inside the house when they were killed; I didn't often make the mistake of letting down my guard anywhere but in the safety of a church.

That, and when I was with El.

Lucy shook her head. "I would feel like I was half-naked."

"Yes, and why do something halfway?" Peller said. He leaned against the wall of the dining room and gave my sister a wicked smile. She flushed crimson at the implication.

Ah, there was the family resemblance I hadn't noticed. Presumably, El had gotten most of his looks from his mother—his brown eyes and soft curls had no similarity to Jakob's gray eyes and blue-black hair—but there was a familiar curl to Peller's lips when he was amused, and it seemed both father and son had the same penchant for making sexual remarks at inappropriate times.

It was more than a little unsettling. I coughed to hide my discomfort, stretching my arms. "Lucy said you wanted to watch her lesson."

"I assume you have no objection?" He raised a brow at me. "I will not be in the way."

"Not at all." I gave him a forced smile.

Lucy seemed pleased at our civility, despite how disingenuous it was. She leaned up to press a kiss to Jakob's cheek.

"We'll start with stretches," I said, moving to the center of the room as he took a seat in the corner.

An hour later, Lucy was dripping with sweat, another feature I hadn't been aware vampires had, and breathing hard. Death had strengthened her body, but she had no skill to discipline it.

"You did well," I lied, and she beamed at me.

"You'll need to practice your exercises daily." El had just entered the room, and he leaned against the doorframe, crossing his arms. "I've known some vampires that neglected to train their bodies, and a child could have defeated them in combat."

She looked to Jakob as if for confirmation, and he nodded. "Minds and bodies, even immortal ones, need exercise. If you gave up painting for a century, your skill would suffer, no?"

"Of course."

"And it is the same with any skill."

"Oh." She frowned, taking it all in. "I'll practice. But you'll be here to teach me, right, Anne?" Her expression turned hopeful.

"I—" I glanced at El. We hadn't talked about what would happen after he was healed. And there were other factors at play. Like his mother.

"That's what I came to talk about," he said, rescuing me from having to answer. "I don't think it's safe for you to stay here now that hunters have found you."

Worry wrinkled her brow, and she moved to stand next to Jakob. "You think there are more?"

Still so naive. "There are always more hunters, Lucy."

"I am already making plans to leave." Peller took her hand in both of his. "We have not left yet because I know Lucille has missed her sister, but we will not remain in a house that has been compromised." He looked into her eyes. "Forgive me, my sweet Lucille. I planned to tell you this morning."

"Must we?" She looked to me and El, hoping to find an ally. "Surely it was a mistake that they were hunting us. We haven't done anything wrong."

"You haven't, but someone is trying very hard to make it look like you have. Someone, perhaps, with a grudge against your husband." El nodded at Peller—at his father.

Jakob shook his head, stroking Lucy's hand absently with his thumb. "I can think of no one who would wish to see me hunted down like an animal. Perhaps it is a coincidence."

"Yes!" Lucy latched onto that thought like a lifeline. "You said you saw his sister. Maybe someone's targeting Leda instead of us."

I flattened my lips into a line. She wasn't exactly right.

"I believe she may be the one causing it," El said.

The look on Peller's face was genuine bafflement. "Leda? Why would she do that?"

El shrugged, and I didn't answer. Lucy bit her lip.

"I...don't think she likes me."

"Why would she not?" Jakob's frown deepened. "She did not have much time to know you, but she was more than civil. And even if she did not like you, she would not want us both killed by hunters."

"'Like' was perhaps the wrong word. Jakob, your sister hates me."

El and I shared a wide-eyed look. I'd expected this conversation to be more difficult, having to explain that Jakob's first wife was hunting him down without explaining who she was and how we knew. But it seemed Lucy had her own reasoning.

"You must be wrong," Peller insisted.

"I'm not. You didn't see the way she looked at me the night of our wedding. You were talking to Aeron, but the look on her face, it was pure hatred. I don't know what I did to anger her, but she would gladly see me dead."

I swallowed back the acidic taste of fear rising in my throat. She was right. The fang wanted her dead. Wanted both of them dead.

"You do not know Leda as I do, Lucille. You do not understand the vampire culture—"

She pulled away from his grapes and stomped her foot like a child. "No, *you* don't understand, Jakob. She hates me. She wants to kill me. I saw it in her eyes. If someone is trying to bring hunters down on us, it's her."

"There may be a simple way to find out," El said gently. "We can draw whoever it is into the open. Lay a trap for them."

Jakob narrowed his eyes. "My bride is not bait."

"But you might be." El met his gaze, unflinching.

They stared at each other for a long moment. Then Jakob nodded infinitesimally. "If you have a plan to discover who is following us, I am willing to hear it."

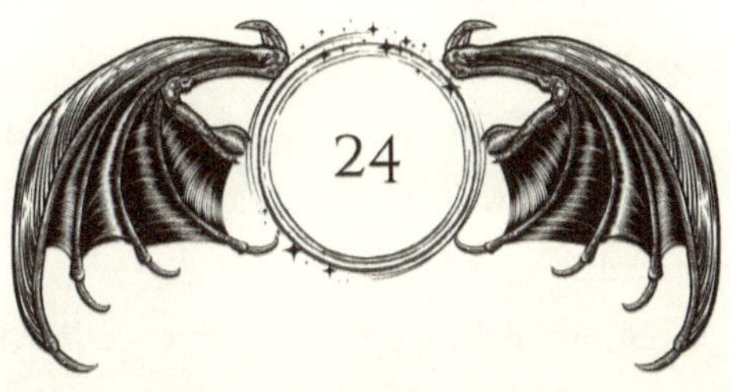

24

The next day, I watched out the window as we pulled out of the train station at Prague. Hot sun beat down on the city, and beautiful though it was, I breathed a sigh of relief to see it fade into the distance, taking the memories of the past few days with it.

I turned to look at the room Jakob had booked for us. It was more luxurious than any we'd had on our journeys. El sprawled among red and gold pillows across the enormous bed. Red curtains lined the walls, and the matching furniture was plump and soft.

"No," I said to the mischief dancing in El's eyes. "We *just* got here."

"I didn't ask."

I flopped onto the couch and took off my boots, setting them neatly next to the door. "No, but you were going to."

"Can you blame me?" He grinned. "You're irresistible, *mon amour.*"

I rolled my eyes, then groaned and ran a hand over my face. "I'm just so…"

"Tired?" He moved from the bed to the couch and began massaging my shoulders.

"I could sleep for days."

"You can rest all you want until we get to Athens." He found a knot, digging into it with his thumbs until I moaned. "Unless you keep making noises like that."

I wanted to rest, but the danger wasn't over yet. We still had to face his mother again. In Athens, the next intended stop on Lucy and Jakob's grand tour of the continent, we would lay our trap.

"She'll be fine," El said. "She has Bluebeard protecting her."

And Peller wouldn't allow anyone to get close to Lucy. But my sister wasn't the only person I was worried about.

"I'll be fine, too, *ma guerrière.* Things are different this time."

"Are they?" He'd nearly died the last time we saw his mother. I couldn't handle that again.

He stopped rubbing my shoulders and moved to kneel in front of me. "I've searched for this—what's between us—for centuries. I want a life with you, Anne. Marriage. Children. All of it, whenever you're ready. And I'm not letting anyone get in the way of that. Not my mother, not my father, not your sister."

Marriage I had considered, albeit abstractly. Children I hadn't. I stared at him, unsure what to say.

His expression turned blank. "You've never wanted children?"

"I never thought about it as a possibility. I was too busy raising Lucy to think about starting a family of my own." And who would want someone like me? I was an oddity, dressed in men's clothing and out at all hours of the night. The bulk of my romantic encounters had been adrenaline-induced flings with other Gardiens. No emotional entanglement.

"What about before that?"

I shrugged. "I was a child." No matter that I'd been almost grown when Maman and Papa died. I'd known nothing of the real world. "Marriage was an abstract concept. I didn't have any suitors. I wasn't looking for them."

"And then you had to grow up overnight."

I shifted. "But what about you? Four hundred years and you've never been in love?"

He knew I was avoiding the subject, but he didn't stop me. "I've had romances before. A few years here and there. There was someone in the sixteenth century that I thought about settling down with, but she left the continent."

"I'm sorry," I murmured.

"It's been almost three hundred years, *mon amour*. Any pain I once felt is long forgotten."

And that was the crux of what I couldn't say. Even if we solved everything with his mother and Lucy, even if we got married and had children, then what? I was human, and he wasn't. How could he still love me when I was old and wrinkled, when he was still young and beautiful? And after I died, he'd forget about everything we shared, just like he'd moved on from his long-ago love.

His eyes narrowed, and he stood. "Don't even think such lies."

"Are they lies?" I scooted back on the couch and hugged my knees to my chest. "I'm sure you told her something similar." I wasn't jealous of her. It would be ridiculous to be jealous of someone who'd been dead for centuries. But I was afraid of ending up like her. Marriage was meant to be lifelong for both parties, barring any unforeseen tragedy. Knowing that my life was just a fleeting fraction of his...

"Stop." He jerked me to my feet, eliciting a gasp. "In over four hundred years, I've never felt this strongly about anyone. I cared for her, yes, and for many people that I've known in my life. But I've never known someone whose death would break me like yours would." He pressed his forehead to mine and closed his eyes. "If you don't want marriage and children, I understand. But I don't think I would survive losing you."

The panic I'd felt the other night when he almost died came rushing back. "I don't want to lose you, either," I admitted, my voice shaky. I couldn't bear it. But it was inevitable.

"I don't care if it's inevitable. I'll turn the world upside down if it means I can keep you." He pushed me back onto the couch and climbed on top of me.

"You can't change the laws of nature. We're never going to work." It killed me to think about that future, the future where I died and left him alone, or where he grew bored with me and left for something better.

He drove himself into my center, our clothing the only barrier between us, and I cried out at the friction.

"Think about leaving me again," he growled into my ear, "and I'll chain you to my bed."

"We can't—" I moaned as he captured the lobe of my ear in his teeth.

"We most certainly can. Whatever it takes, I'm yours for the rest of my life." He ground against me. "I'll find a way to bind my life to yours, to make myself age. Someone has to know how to end the curse of immortality."

A lump formed in my throat. "You would do that?"

"Anything."

I pulled his mouth to mine. I could see the future he was promising. A small wedding with a few close friends watching as we pledged our lives to each other. A son with his eyes and wild dark curls clambering onto his lap and begging for a story while I rocked the baby to sleep. Walking along the Seine as the children threw snowballs at each other. Growing old together and seeing our children and grandchildren grow.

"Yes," he groaned against my lips. "I want all of that and more."

I pulled at his shirt, needing to feel his skin against mine.

"Say you want it, too."

"I do." More than I'd ever wanted anything in my life.

He sat up and yanked his shirt over his head, and I barely had time to notice the quickly-healing wound across his abdomen before he was tugging at the hem of my own shirt.

He tossed it haphazardly into a corner and pulled my jumps down to bare my breasts to him. He captured my nipple in his mouth and swirled his tongue around.

"El..." My back bowed beneath his ministrations.

He nipped at my breast, then released it. "You don't leave me," he demanded. "Ever."

"Never," I swore, hips rising up to meet him. We were both still wearing too many clothes, and he ignored where I needed him most, moving to the other breast to give it the same treatment.

"I'm going to make sure the thought never crosses your mind again."

"It won't." I wanted to see him, to taste him, but when I reached for his pants, he grabbed my hands.

"No." He pulled me to my feet, removing my pants and undergarments and dropping them to the floor. He did the same to his own, but I didn't have time to enjoy the view. He turned me around and traced the outline of my body with his hands.

"On your knees, *ma petite guerrière,*" he whispered in my ear.

I hurried to obey, and he rewarded me with the soft caress of his hand on my back.

"So beautiful," he said. "On your knees, your whole body pink with arousal. I could watch you for hours like this."

He stepped away for a moment, and I heard the rustling of a bag. I craned my neck to see what he was doing.

"The condom, *mon amour,*" he answered my silent question. He returned to the couch, lining himself up with my entrance. "I may want children, but I think we can both agree the timing isn't ideal."

It wasn't, but I'd been too caught up in the moment to think about it. "I didn't realize you were—"

My words cut off with a gasp as he thrust into me.

"You were saying?"

I tossed him a glare over my shoulder, though the effect was lost in my lust-heavy eyes. "If you were done talking, you could have just said that." I'd been more than ready for him. I thrust back against him, relishing the feeling of fullness.

He reached around, seeking the bud between my legs, and rubbed it slowly. "Tell me what you like."

"Harder," I urged. I took his hand and showed him how to touch me, guiding his fingers to the right movement.

"I can feel you tightening around me," he said a few minutes later, his voice strained.

"Just like that," I moaned. "Don't stop."

"I'm not going to last much longer, *mon amour.*"

Molten liquid rushed to my center at the desperation in his voice. I ground against him, moaning a wordless plea for more. He gave it to me, fingers and body moving in tandem, as I spiraled toward a heady climax.

He didn't stop moving, even as we tumbled over the edge together. The sound of the train whistle drowned out my cry of pleasure, and the train chugged down the track.

El caught me as my knees gave out. Maneuvering us both onto the couch, he wrapped his arms around my waist and pressed a kiss to my bare shoulder.

The after-effects of our love-making and the steady rocking of the train lulled me into a contented torpor. I closed my eyes, listening to the steady rhythm of his breath.

"Have you ever been to Athens?" I asked, only half awake.

He took the ribbon from my hair and began combing the braid out with his fingers. "A while ago. St. Paul was there; I went to hear him preach."

I kicked out blindly, and he groaned when my foot connected with his shin.

"I surrender!" He laughed. "Vicious woman."

"Maybe you should learn to answer questions properly the first time they're asked." St. Paul had died over a thousand years before El's birth. He was old, but he wasn't *that* old.

He nuzzled my neck. "I apologize for my ill manners, *ma jolie*. No, I've never been to Athens."

"Not once in four hundred years?" He'd had enough time to see the entire world twice over.

"I haven't seen the whole world."

"No. Just most of it."

He laughed again. "What about you? If you had eternity to travel the world, where would you go first?"

It was hard to focus on the question with the soothing motion of his hands along my scalp, but I considered it. "I'd like to see Jerusalem. To visit Christ's tomb."

"When this is done, I'll take you there."

I wriggled closer to him, enjoying the warmth of his skin despite the heat of the day outside. "I need to go home after this. Emile will already be furious with me for neglecting my duties for so long." I couldn't go back to Les Gardiens, much as I wished, but I still had obligations in Paris.

"You deserve more than obligation." He disentangled his hands from my hair, wrapping his arms around me again. "When was the last time you did something that wasn't for duty?"

"About two minutes ago," I deadpanned.

"Point taken." He tweaked my nipple. "I'm glad you don't consider me a duty, but I want to give you more than that. I want to take you to see the world."

"And then take me home?" My consciousness was fading fast. I barely heard his reply.

"You are my home, *ma guerrière.*"

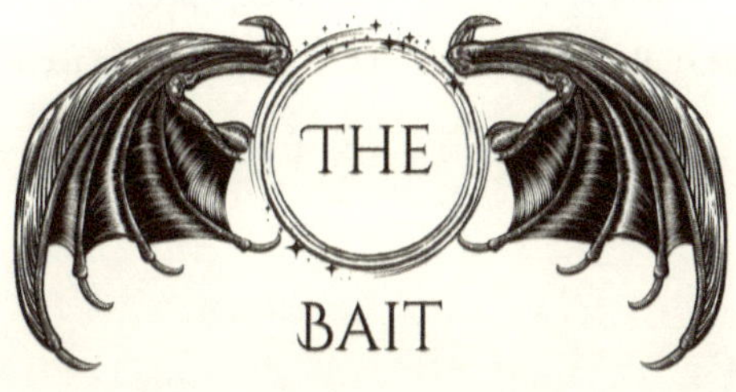


The woman's dress glitters in the light. As she passes through the crowd, hanging tight to the arm of the man at her side, no one can turn their eyes from her. The sapphires and emeralds sewn into the fabric complement the peacock feathers in her hair perfectly, and the white silk of her dress is so fine it could have been spun by spiders. Her eyes glisten, following her partner's every move as if she can't bear to be away from him.

The man she's with is no less impressive. His clothing, though not so ostentatious as hers, was designed with equal care. A blue-dyed chrysanthemum adorns his pocket, and the black of his suit makes his hair look almost blue.

They cling to each other in a way that's almost indecent for a public setting, and the smile on the man's face when he looks down at the shimmering young woman seems to say he's going to devour her.

Neither of them glance at the sable-haired woman in the black dress. She stands at the top of the stairs, gloves in hand, and her eyes follow them down the hall like a hunter tracking its prey. When they enter their box, she smiles a secretive smile, revealing sharp teeth. Her trap is laid.

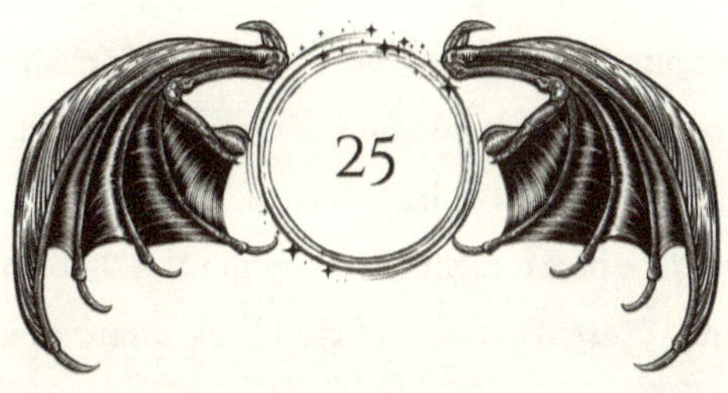

25

A thens was hot.

Even after dark, with the intoxicating scent of night-blooming jasmine floating in a cloud around us, and the moon gleaming off the white stone of the buildings, the heat of the summer sun still lingered. I waved my fan in front of my face, wishing I didn't have to wear the emerald evening gown over my trousers. Light as it was, it still had far too many layers to be comfortable.

"We could always go back to the room and get you out of those layers," El murmured. He was dressed formally as well, a white bow tie around his neck and a black silk top hat under his arm. Like me, he had a veritable arsenal hidden in his eveningwear. He'd tucked a small pistol, already loaded with silver bullets, into his breast pocket. His boots concealed two small daggers, and a small silver chain hid beneath his stiff shirt collar, perfect for detaining our quarry. We'd been here for a week without sign of El's mother, but we weren't letting our guard down.

"After all the trouble it took to get me looking like this," I replied, "I'm not taking the dress off until the night is over." It was, thankfully, large enough to hide my belt full of weapons beneath the skirts. A vial of holy water hung between my breasts on a silver chain, one light enough to pass as jewelry but strong enough to immobilize the fang until we could get her back to Jakob's house.

I prayed she'd be here tonight. This interminable limbo had to end.

Despite the apparent poverty of the Greek countryside that our train had passed through, the upper class of Athens still maintained a culture equal to that of the rest of the continent. Jakob had secured tickets this evening for a Russian ballet. Not my ideal choice of entertainment, but El and I weren't going to watch. The ballet, at least. Our box was opposite Lucy's, and we'd be scanning the crowd for any sign of El's evasive mother.

I kept a wary eye out as we walked through the city, and not just for supernatural threats. Dressed as we were, we were prime targets for theft, and the dimly lit streets provide countless places for predators, both human and inhuman, to hide.

The crowded block around the theater was a welcome solace. I spotted Lucy's golden hair pinned up high and decorated with a peacock feather, her white gown shimmering with blue and green gemstones. She'd dressed as ostentatiously as possible, and she and Jakob were too wrapped up in each other's presence to even notice the mass of people around them. They were the perfect bait—undefended and completely oblivious.

Peller had wanted to lock Lucy up until we found the person targeting them was found. After hours of debate, he'd finally agreed to allow her to play the part of bait—as long as she never left his sight.

We saw no sign of El's mother as we made our way to our seats. We kept to the corners as much as possible, blending into the crowd when we couldn't hide. Lucy and Jakob were the bait, taking the spotlight; our place was in the shadows, where she wouldn't notice us.

Once we were alone in the box, El poured us each a glass of wine we wouldn't drink. I toasted him, playing the part in case an enemy was watching. "To an entertaining evening," I said aloud. *To ending this hunt* were the words in my head.

He clinked his glass against mine. "And to a long night after."

I didn't have to force my laugh. "You'll have to wait for that, *monsieur.*" Our role was that of a lovestruck couple enjoying the ballet, but our banter was real.

"Pity." He raised his glass to his lips, feigning a drink.

I took a pair of opera glasses from my large pocket and looked through them, scanning first the stage—the curtain still down—and then the crowd below.

At first I thought our planning had been in vain. I didn't see the familiar face of his mother among the hundreds of audience members awaiting the rise of the curtain.

*Maybe she took another identity.*

My heart sank at the thought. She'd be harder to find if she was wearing another skin. El might be able to recognize some of her identities, but even he didn't know everything about her. If she attacked, we'd still catch her, but we might be too late for whatever victim she'd chosen for tonight.

Then I spotted the black hair and sharp nose I so despised. She'd dressed to blend in, black elbow-length gloves and a shimmery dress that matched her hair. Her seat was only a few rows from the stage, dead center, and while she was pretending to observe the room at large, her gaze kept coming back to Lucy and Jakob's box.

When the two of them came together in a kiss altogether too intimate for a public setting, her eyes narrowed, locked onto them. Her beautiful face contorted in a disgusted scowl.

The lights went down as the orchestra began its opening strains. El came up behind me, wrapping his arms around my waist and resting his chin on my shoulder. The curtain rose, revealing a lone dancer. I turned my opera glasses to the stage, but my attention remained on the fang obscured in the midst of the audience.

If she moved, we'd see her.

She feigned interest in the show, but like me, her attention was elsewhere. She couldn't help but glance upward at Jakob and Lucy every few minutes. Lucy, for her part, was completely oblivious to any danger. She was too enraptured with the show to notice anything amiss.

Jakob, on the other hand, had spotted the fang almost as soon as I had. Our eyes locked across the dark theater, and I dipped my head in a nod. We had her.

He pulled Lucy closer, and she melted into his embrace as the music swelled.

The fang remained unmoving during the show, and when the curtain fell and the lights came up, Jakob and Lucy slipped out of their box. Their next plan had been to tour the Parthenon, but now that we had sights on our quarry, they would remain close by.

As the theater emptied, El gathered me into his arms. "Did you enjoy the show?" he asked, backing me against the balcony ledge and nuzzling my neck.

I hadn't watched a moment of it. "It was wonderful," I said.

He lowered his voice. "She's heading toward the exit. Shall we?"

I shimmied out of my dress and petticoats, leaving on the corset and trousers I wore beneath. Slipping the chain from around my neck, I nodded. "I'm ready."

We lost sight of the fang for a moment as we left the box, but we reached the main stairs at the same time she did. Ignorant of our presence, she headed up the steps and toward the boxes opposite us.

We kept to the shadows and followed her at a distance. She didn't seem concerned that anyone would follow her or that she might appear suspicious. And why should she? Her body was a weapon. Anyone who approached her, she could kill.

As we turned down the hall after her, she stepped through a door. *Is that Jakob and Lucy's box?* I thought at El.

He nodded, bending to draw a dagger from his boot. We crept closer.

"Oh, excuse me." Her voice floated through the air, twisting around me and tying my stomach in knots. "I think I forgot my fan."

A low voice said something I couldn't quite hear.

"No, I'm sure it's here somewhere." A pause, then her voice turned lilting. "Have you worked here for long?"

"A few months." The man—her intended prey, I assumed—sounded young. "I don't see your fan, *kyría.* Perhaps you dropped it in the lobby?"

The hairs on my neck stood up. El and I locked eyes and took position on either side of the door. The next few moments were crucial. If we burst in too soon, we'd risk appearing violent and unhinged, easy for Leda to spin a story against us to the local authorities. If we waited too long, we could cost the man his life.

I risked a peek into the room. They both had their backs to the door. His head was bowed, neck exposed as he searched the floor for her nonexistent fan. Leda followed him with her eyes and twisted a black curl around her finger.

"I'm sorry. I don't see it," he said. "But you can—"

His words cut off with a sharp gasp as she yanked him toward her and sank her teeth into his neck.

El's dagger flew into the room, slicing through her upper arm and landing on the ground behind her. We both followed it as she turned to us with a snarl.

When she saw El, her face smoothed, and a wicked smile spread across her features. The man she held—he couldn't be older than nineteen, more a boy than a man—slumped in her grasp, groaning. She dropped him to the ground.

"Azazel! What a lovely surprise. I was so worried for you after that incident in the cemetery. How are you feeling?"

My stomach turned at the reminder of the last time we'd met, and I stepped closer to El.

"I'm healed," he said. "No thanks to you."

She tsked. "I didn't intend for you to get hurt, *mon fils*. You got in the way."

"I told you Anne was off limits."

Everything in me screamed to stop the conversation, to kill her now, but that was the old me. The Gardien. El needed the closure this conversation would provide.

"And yet *she* attacked *me*. You can't blame me for defending my-self." She stepped over the stunned boy lying on the floor. "Tell me, will you let her kill me?"

We hadn't discussed what would happen if we had to kill his moth-er, but we both knew that was more than a possibility. She'd been killing indiscriminately for months now. Centuries, probably. She was a danger to human and supernatural beings alike.

"I don't want to have to kill you," he said.

That wasn't the goal right now. Capture and contain. That was all we had to do, to show Lucy and Jakob what she was. The rest of it could wait.

"Not even if—" She lunged for me without warning.

I was almost unprepared for it, focused on her next words, but I dodged just in time and landed on the ground next to the boy. Letting my momentum carry me, I rolled over and sprung back up on my feet. I uncorked the vial in my hand.

The water splashed into her face, and she hissed. El took his second dagger and drove it through the long black fabric of her skirt, pinning it to the floor, as I wrapped the silver chain around her neck and pulled it tight. The metal burned her skin, leaving angry red marks in its wake.

She clawed at me and gouged bits of skin from my bare arms. I didn't let go. El grabbed her hands, struggling to bring them together behind her back. She jerked her head into his nose, and it made a sickening *crunch.*

He stumbled backward, a hand to his face. "You *hint!*" Blood dripped onto the carpet.

I saw red. Bringing my knee into her stomach, I twisted the chain around her neck at the same time. She doubled over, and El took the chance to grab her arms and bind them behind her back with his own silver chain.

We forced her to the ground and chained her legs together as well. She thrashed at our feet as El looked at me, hands on his knees and breathing hard.

"You're not hurt?"

I shook my head. "I'm fine. You?" He looked awful, blood soaking the front of his suit, but I forced myself to keep breathing. It wasn't the same as last time. He was still moving.

He pulled me into his arms, ignoring the vile curses his mother spat at us.

"I'm okay, *mon amour,*" he said, his voice congested. He rubbed my back in soothing circles. "It's just a broken nose."

I let out a frantic half-laugh. "Twice this month. You're going to have brain damage if this keeps happening."

He didn't answer, just continued to rub my back. I closed my eyes and counted silently to ten to ease my racing heart.

"What's a *hint?*" I asked after a minute, opening my eyes. "When she hit you, you said, 'You *hint.*'"

"Oh." He gave me a sheepish grin, the effect muted by the blood. "It's an...unflattering Yiddish term for a woman."

"Fitting." I cast a glare at his mother. "One of us should go find Peller."

"No need." Jakob appeared in the doorway, Lucy at his side. He surveyed the scene, one dark eyebrow raised. "You could have been neater. The poor boy will have to clean your blood from the carpet."

"We wouldn't have that problem if you'd helped, rather than waiting outside the door," I retorted. Now that the fight was past, nervous energy ran through my body, slipping out as anger.

"We weren't waiting outside the door. We left and came back." Lucy skirted around Leda and knelt next to the theater boy. "Are you hurt?" she asked him, her voice gentle.

The venom, little though he must have gotten, still had its hold on him. The black of his pupils swallowed up any color in his eyes, and his face was pale. He looked up at her, dazed, and shook his head.

"It's going to be okay." She placed a hand on his arm. "No one is going to hurt you."

He looked down at where she touched him, then back up into her face. He didn't seem to understand whether what he was seeing was real or not.

"I want you to forget what you saw here tonight." Lucy's voice took on a strange tone. Hypnotic, almost. "Can you do that for me? Just go home and forget everything that happened after the show ended."

He blinked slowly, eyes glazing over. Without a word, he rose to his feet and walked with a single-minded intent to the door. He didn't look back as he closed the box behind him.

Lucy rose and dusted off her glittering skirts. "Now, then."

Peller took her hand. "It would have been better to kill him, my sweet Lucille."

She turned a scowl on him, the expression foreign to her sweet face. "He did nothing wrong. I won't continue this discussion." She pointed with her foot at the vampire on the ground. "But what do we do with her?"

Leda was no longer flailing about. She watched Lucy, hatred burning in her eyes.

Jakob crouched next to her. "What are you doing here, Leda? Are you trying to bring the hunters down on us?"

A joyless smile spread across her face. "I'm sure I don't know what you mean."

The sound that escaped him was something like a snarl, but Lucy put a hand on his shoulder. "Have I done something to offend you, Leda?"

Her smile grew crueler. "Why would you think that?"

"Do not be coy." Peller's voice was a threatening rumble. "You have been following us, leaving a bloody trail wherever we go. You have drawn the attention of the hunters—and not just Lucille's sister.

What is your goal? If you are trying to get my bride killed, I will end you."

El took a seat and pulled a handkerchief from his pocket, using it to wipe the blood from his face. "Tell them the truth. Tell them who you are."

She stuck out her lower lip in a pout. "Must you always ruin the fun, *mon fils*?"

"Show them," he said again, unmoved.

She sighed. "If you insist."

I took his hand, squeezing it tight as a cracking sound filled the air. It was loud, the sound of dozens of bones breaking at once. She thrashed against the chains and moaned. Her hair shrank, lightening and receding back into her head. My stomach churned at the grotesque sight of her body contorting into a new shape. The crackling sound of her bones adjusting finally faded, and Lucy's face looked up at us, smirking.

Lucy—the real Lucy—gasped. Peller grabbed the bound fang by the throat. "What is this?"

"Show them the truth," El said, "or he can kill you and see the truth in your corpse."

The cracking began again, setting my teeth on edge. When it stopped, a small, pink-cheeked woman with golden curls lay on the ground at our feet.

Peller sucked in a breath. "Marie?"

Lucy's eyes widened, and she looked between him and the vampire on the floor. "*The* Marie?"

He clenched his jaw and nodded. "My first wife."

"I thought she was one of the bodies," Lucy said, her voice small. "I thought you killed her."

"I thought I did, too."

El's mother—Marie—laughed, the sound sharp and grating. "I wasn't such a fool. As soon as I found out what you were, I knew you might be planning to kill me. I took precautions."

"You mean you stole his blood," El said.

Jakob looked at El, eyes wide. "She called you *mon fils*. 'My son.'" He turned back to Marie. "You didn't have a child before I killed you."

Her smile grew impossibly sharper. "Congratulations. It's a boy."

Silence fell. El and his father stared at each other. I couldn't read Jakob's face, but El's... He was terrified of what the response would be. Afraid his father would reject him. Hate him.

I wanted to take that fear away, but I was waiting with bated breath, too. Were they going to say anything? Do anything?

Lucy was the first to break the silence. She cleared her throat. "Well. This is a surprise," she said tactfully. "But I don't think a theater is the ideal place for this conversation. We can continue once we're safe at home."

Jakob blinked, as if coming back to himself. "Yes. I do not wish to drag her through the streets. We will fly her back."

"We'll meet you there." I squeezed El's hand. He still hadn't said anything. *Are you okay?*

He nodded once but didn't look at me. His gaze was now fixed on his mother, who, despite her bindings, looked incredibly pleased with herself.

Jakob grabbed Marie by the waist and hoisted her over his shoulder, hissing when the silver of her chains brushed his skin. "Come, Lucille."

She glanced back at me with an apologetic smile as she followed him out the door.

Alone with El, I opened my mouth to say something, then closed it again. What could I say?

He sighed and tucked his hands into his pockets. "It's not exactly the reunion I dreamed of as a boy. But then, he's not exactly the father I dreamed of, either."

"He just needs some time to process it," I said. "You'd be surprised, too, if you found out you had a son after four hundred years." Then I froze. It would be difficult to keep track of all of one's sexual encounters for over four hundred years. It was possible that El *did* have a child. Or more than one. Did—

"No. I don't." He cut off my thoughts. The words weren't quite bitter, but they had a hard edge to them. "I've been careful. Kept track of the women. Followed through. I wasn't going to make the same mistakes my father did. If I had a child, I would be there for him."

The way Jakob hadn't been there for him. I felt a sudden rush of pity for the boy who'd been abandoned by his mother, who hadn't known who his father was.

He shrugged. "Don't pity me too much. I had plenty of affection from the nuns who raised me."

Nuns who were now long dead. He'd been virtually alone for centuries. My throat swelled with sadness for the life he must have led, and when our eyes met, I saw the loneliness of hundreds of years reflected there. I put a hand on his cheek and leaned in to kiss him.

As soon as our lips touched, he deepened the kiss. All the emotion and energy of the night poured out between us as he held me tight, twining his hands into my hair. Our tongues tangled together. I breathed him in, the sharp smell of coffee and gunpowder, and slid my hands beneath his shirt. He groaned as I ran my hands over the hard muscles of his back.

I was on the verge of begging him to back me into the wall and take me when he pulled back, breathing hard. He rested his head on my shoulder. "They'll be wondering where we are."

I wanted to say, "Let them wonder," but we couldn't. Decisions had to be made about his mother. And he needed to speak to his father.

The loneliness and worry still lingered in his eyes when he straightened, but they were smaller now. I brushed a chaste kiss to his lips. "Then let's go."

26

W hen we finally reached the house, high on a hill overlooking the rest of Athens, they'd packed Marie into a dark room. The door was locked, and a servant had chained it with silver to prevent her from escaping.

El and I joined Lucy and Jakob in the parlor, where a large pot of coffee waited. Lucy sat stiff and straight, a cup in her hands. Jakob's face was blank as he watched us take our seats.

"I am your father." His voice, usually so expressive, came out flat.

"I don't expect anything of you," El said quickly. "I'm not a child."

He laughed without humor. "No, I suppose you are not. You are four hundred years old? Within a few decades."

"Something like that."

Lucy set her cup down and poured coffee for each of us, her hands steady. "How long have you known?"

He accepted his cup of coffee and dropped a sugar cube into it. "She told me my father's name a few years ago, but it took me a while to find him."

"You were in Blaubart for me, then," Jakob said.

It wasn't a question, but El nodded anyway. "She told you beat her every night of your marriage. I wanted to know if you were the monster she said you were."

"And if I was, you planned to kill me."

Lucy's knuckles went white on her cup, and the china cracked in her hands. Before she could drop the glass, Jakob took it from her.

"Are you hurt?" he asked in a soft voice, all concern for her well-being. As though something as small as a china cup could harm her undead body.

"I'm fine." But her hands were shaking as she mopped up the coffee that had spilled. "*Monsieur* DuMont?"

I twined my fingers with El's. There was a note in Lucy's voice that I didn't recognize, and it made the hairs on my neck rise.

"Yes?"

"Do you believe my husband is a monster?"

He considered his father. Lucy's eyes narrowed, a dangerous glint in them. No one in the room was breathing. My heart pounded out of my chest; everyone in the room could hear it, I was certain, but no one looked at me.

I'd never thought of my sister as violent, but her eyes held a promise of death. My hand went to my rosary, tucked in my pocket. If it came to a fight between the man I loved and my sister, who would I choose? I said a silent prayer to whichever saint was listening, asking for this to be resolved without violence.

"My mother has been a liar my whole life," El said at last. "You may not be a saint, Jakob von Peller, but you're not the monster she told me you were."

My breath rushed out of me as the tension left Lucy's shoulders.

"I never beat her. I fed from her, yes, but she enjoyed it. Even when she didn't know it was happening."

Lucy's face turned red, and it took me a moment to understand why. Then I realized what Peller meant. The potency of vampire venom could be easily misidentified by someone unfamiliar with sexual pleasures. His relationship with Lucy must have started similarly, with him feeding from her during intercourse.

My own face burned, and I drained my cup. There were some things I didn't need to know about my sister's life; that was one of them.

"Marie was a jealous woman," Jakob said as I poured myself another cup and stared into its black depths. "I was newly undead, and my hunger was intense. When she discovered me feeding from another woman, she tried to turn the townspeople against me."

"Which is when you had her burned." El said it as casually as if he was commenting on the weather.

"I did." Jakob's voice held no remorse. "It was her or me. She accused me of being a vampire; I accused her of being a witch. They believed me over her."

I glanced at El, wishing I could read his mind as easily as he could read mine. A slight wrinkle had formed between his brows, but he didn't look angry. Just...confused.

I could understand that. It had been a confusing night.

Lucy leaned forward, resting her chin in her hands. "What now? Do we kill her?"

It seemed wrong, hearing my sweet younger sister discuss murder in such a casual tone. But how innocent was she? She wasn't the meek and mild girl I'd tried to raise her to be after Maman and Papa died. And killing a murderer wasn't murder. It was justice.

"She's my mother." El looked down at his hands. "If that's the only choice we have, I won't stop you, but..."

But he didn't want to kill her, no matter what she'd done. I squeezed his hand, offering silent support. He gave me a small smile and squeezed back.

"I want answers first," Jakob said.

El grimaced. "You're not the only one."

"It's been a long night." Lucy rose to her feet. "I don't think I can manage any more revelations, and she's not going anywhere. Anne and I can do some training in the courtyard while you two...get to know each other."

I wasn't sure who looked more uncomfortable at the thought, El or Jakob, but I leapt at the opportunity to escape. Nervous energy from our earlier fight had left me desperate for an outlet. Teaching Lucy to defend herself was hardly the ideal chance to work the energy out of my body, but I preferred that to sitting awkwardly around the table trying to think of something to say.

El scowled at me as I stood. I gave him an apologetic look—but not too apologetic—and thought *I'll make it up to you later* before hurrying out the door.

The night was still too warm when we stepped out into the courtyard. Laurel trees shaded us from the moonlight, and in the center was a marble fountain. Water flowed into the basin from the eyes of a weeping woman, her naked body bent with sadness. It was a beautiful, disturbing image, and I didn't want to stare at it for too long.

Thankfully Lucy didn't seem interested in the scenery.

"What are we going to work on?" she asked, practically vibrating with excitement.

While on the train, I'd had plenty of time to consider what she needed to learn next. "Stunning."

Her brows raised. "Stunning?"

"Knocking your opponent out for a moment or two can give you the time you need to get away or subdue them." I wasn't concerned about her learning to fight regular humans—with her strength, she could easily take on anyone who wasn't a trained hunter. But if she had to fight vampires or, God forbid, hunters, she'd need to know how to stop them in their tracks. "It doesn't take much force. Just speed." Speed was something she'd be able to achieve without difficulty. The problem would be targeting her movements.

I walked her through the steps. *Distract them, get them to leave their neck open to attack, and strike just below the ear.* I practiced on her, pulling my blow back before it hit her neck so I didn't actually stun her.

"Now you try." I adopted a defensive stance, raising my fists to block my face and neck.

She was clumsy, unsure of her movements, but she made up for it with enthusiasm. When I knocked her to the ground, she jumped back up with a grin. At one point, she landed an accidental blow to my ear. I doubled over, head ringing

"Are you okay?" Worry tinged her voice.

"I'm fine." A flash of pain went through my neck. The next moment found me flat on my back, staring up at the stars through the branches of laurel trees.

"Sorry! I'm sorry. I didn't mean to hit that hard." She leaned over me, excitement dancing in her eyes even as she bit her lip to hide it.

"I'm fine," I said again. "But maybe don't do that outside of an actual fight." I stood, rubbing at the spot she'd struck. "That was good. Do it again—*without* hitting me this time."

An hour later, we were both breathing hard. Lucy had plenty of energy and raw strength, if not fighting discipline. It wouldn't be enough to protect her from a serious threat, but it was a start. If she kept practicing, she might even be able to hold her own against Jakob one day.

All she needed was the wisdom to see him for what he really was, and the will to leave him. I said a silent prayer that she'd find both one day.

We headed back inside. In the parlor, El was alone, going through his own series of exercises. His shirt was off, and his muscles rippled with the movements as he stretched his arms above his head.

Lucy coughed and averted her eyes. "I'll, umm, go see if the servants have dinner ready." She hurried out of the room.

I didn't say anything to stop her. We'd eaten a light meal before the opera, but with the strain and exertion of the evening, I was looking forward to a full dinner.

After I finished admiring El.

His movements stopped as Lucy fled, and he looked over at me with a grin. "I didn't mean to scare her."

"I don't think she expected to see a half-naked man in her parlor."

He laughed at that. "I would have done my exercises in the court-yard, but it was already in use."

"Mm." I trailed my gaze down his torso, too distracted to pay attention to his words. He glistened with sweat. Though he'd gained a couple pounds in the past fortnight, they only served to enhance his physique, adding a touchable softness to the well-defined muscles. His bruises were long gone, and the wound on his abdomen was a puckered pink scar now.

"Legs?"

My eyes slipped back to his face. "Hm?"

"You're drooling."

I scowled at him. It wasn't my fault he was so beautiful and shirtless. And we were alone.

"Do you want something?"

*Where to begin?*

"I can give you guidance if you need it." He prowled closer, hunger in his eyes. "You can drop to your knees and taste me. Or you can lie on your back while I worship every inch of that beautiful body." My breath hitched, but he wasn't finished. "You can ride me until we're both too exhausted to move, or I can wrap that braid around my fist and use it as reins while I ride you."

I wanted it all, but not in the middle of the parlor. It was bad enough knowing they could hear us; I wouldn't survive the humiliation if Jakob or Lucy walked in on us.

"Then you'd better find your way to our bedroom, *mon amour*, because I intend to be inside you in about thirty seconds."

"Lucy just went to check on dinner," I said, taking a step back. The heat on my skin had nothing to do with the exercises I'd just finished, and everything to do with his proximity. His very sweaty, very bare proximity. "She'll wonder where we went."

"Our door has a lock. And she won't look for us until Bluebeard gets back."

"Oh? Where is he?" I didn't care, but it served as a distraction from his movements as he drew closer, backing me toward the staircase in the hall.

"He went to clear his head with some fresh air."

My heels hit the steps, and I stumbled. El caught me before I could fall, swooping me up into his arms. Before I could speak, we were in our room, and his lips were on mine.

"El," I began, pulling back, but he silenced me with another kiss.

"No more talking." He settled me on the bed and pulled off first my boots, then my pants. "I've had enough talking tonight."

"I can do that." I stroked his cheek, and he leaned into the touch.

We didn't need words as we crashed into each other. His lips moved against my skin, and I moaned as he ground into my bare center. The fabric of his pants, now wet with my essence, felt deliciously erotic, but I wanted him naked.

He gave me exactly what I wanted, stripping off his clothes. I leaned back against the pillows, drinking in the sight before he pulled me to my feet and removed my shirt and jumps.

Finally bare against me, he cupped my face in both his hands, kissing me with exquisite care. *"Ma petite guerrière,"* he whispered. "Thank you."

I didn't know what he was thanking me for—this moment? Being his?—but a moment later, it didn't matter. He slipped his hand between my legs and sank a finger inside. I arched toward him, trying to get him deeper, closer. With his thumb, he rubbed circles around my clit while he kissed my neck.

"I love this." He leaned back to look at me, movements unceasing. "So desperate for me. Barely able to keep your eyes open. You're beautiful."

"I thought," I panted, "you said no more talking."

He tweaked my breast. "Such a smart mouth. I should give it something to do."

*Oh yes. Very much yes.*

He laughed. "Not yet, *mon amour.*" He kissed me, soft and slow, as he quickened the movement of his fingers. "I can feel you tightening around me. You want to come for me, don't you?"

I whimpered, bucking into his touch. "Please," I begged. I needed just a little more...

He added a second finger, and stars burst to life behind my eyes. He continued massaging until the pleasure turned almost painful.

"Stop," I gasped, unable to handle another moment of delightful torture.

He stopped at once, moving to sit next to me. He kissed the top of my head and held me tight.

"I hope you don't think you're finished," I said, trailing my hand down his chest. I could feel the proof of his arousal pressing into me, but he made no move to address it.

His eyes danced as he grinned down at me. "Not at all. I was giving you a moment to recover."

"Good." I disentangled myself from his touch. Sinking onto the carpet in front of him, I licked my lips. "Because I'm far from done." I took him in my mouth, eliciting a desperate moan.

His hands sank into my hair, not taking control, just holding me. He was sweet and salty, and the sound of his groans sent moisture flooding to my center again.

It didn't take long before he was trembling with the force of holding himself back. "I'm close, *mon amour.*" He tugged at my hair. "I want to finish inside you."

A wild spark of mischief took me, and I hummed, taking him deeper.

"Anne!" he gasped. He stiffened and spilled inside my mouth. I swallowed it all, relishing my victory.

"Cruel woman," he scolded, pulling me to him. "Didn't you hear what I said?"

"You told me I was always in charge."

"A mistake I won't soon repeat." He laughed and kissed me deeply.

The smell of the ocean wafted in through the window on a warm evening breeze. We laid there together breathing it in.

"Is it really almost over, El?" After months of hunting, we'd finally found the person responsible for so much destruction across the continent.

His hand stilled where it was tracing circles on my back. "I hope so."

"But?"

"I don't trust my mother." He sighed, his chest rising beneath me. "It doesn't matter what promises she makes. If we want peace, I'm afraid we'll have to kill her."

"And you don't want to."

He was silent for a moment. "I do. Is that wrong?"

"Of course not." I shifted to look into his face. "She abandoned you, lied to you, manipulated you, and nearly killed you. No one could blame you for that."

He quirked his mouth in a smile that didn't meet his eyes. "I doubt Les Gardiens would look kindly on a son killing his mother."

"Fuck the Gardiens." His eyes widened in surprise, but I caressed his cheek, letting some of the anger out of my voice. "They'd condemn you for what you are without even considering your actions. I don't want any part of that."

He took my hand and pressed a kiss to the palm. "I don't deserve you, *ma guerrière.*"

"No, you don't," I agreed, and he raised a brow, grinning. "You deserve better. But it's far too late for that. I'm not going anywhere."

"I wouldn't let you even if you tried."

I settled back into his touch. It didn't matter what was coming next. We were together. That was all that mattered.

# 27

I woke to a sun high in the sky, too early in the afternoon for anyone to be awake. A faint commotion came from the floor below me. I knew it wasn't from my sister; Lucy and Jakob's room was on the other side of the house, a floor above ours.

My heart pounded in my chest. Hunters.

No, there was no sound of violence. I listened closely, trying to make out voices. I heard Greek, the words tense, but no one was fighting. El spoke, saying something I didn't understand.

I threw on clean clothes, pinned my hair up, and hurried downstairs toward the disturbance.

Several servants stood around the room where El's mother was being kept. Their argument cut off sharply when I approached, and they scattered.

The door was open, the silver chains missing. I peered inside and found El pacing the room, arms crossed and worry wrinkling his brow.

"What happened?" I asked. "Did you move her?"

He shook his head. "She's gone."

"What do you mean, 'gone?'" I looked around, as though she was going to magically appear. "She can't have gotten out by herself." The silver on the door would have prevented her. There were no other windows in the room. No other exits.

"No. She had to have an accomplice."

"Do Lucy and Peller know?"

He let out a long breath. "Not unless the servants woke them."

Judging by their conspicuous absence, I assumed they were still asleep. "Should we wake them?"

"We'll have to," he said. Not that there was anything we could do about her escape now. She had to have disappeared before sunrise, or she would have been caught outside in the daylight.

We sent a maid for them, though I pitied the poor girl as she climbed on trembling legs up to Lucy and Jakob's room. A few minutes later she returned, teary-eyed, with my sister and her husband following behind her.

"How did this happen?" Jakob demanded. The servants had all disappeared, leaving the four of us alone in the empty room.

"I got up to use the toilet and heard a couple of your men down here arguing," El said. "When I came down, she was gone."

Jakob's mouth formed a line, eyes narrowed as he considered his son.

El straightened. "I didn't let her go."

"No one's accusing you of that, *Monsieur* DuMont," Lucy said, laying a placating hand on Jakob's arm.

"He didn't have to say anything. I saw what he was thinking. It was written on his face."

It didn't take a mind reader to tell that Peller blamed El for it. El was Marie's child, after all. And while I knew he wouldn't have helped his mother escape, Peller didn't have the same insight.

"None of us would have let her go," I cut in. "So let's stop casting blame and try to figure out where she went."

"No." Jakob's voice, though quiet, demanded attention. "Someone in my household helped my prisoner to escape. I will not allow this to be overlooked."

"I'm sure no one did it on purpose," Lucy said. "I told them not to go anywhere near the door."

"Told them?" I stared at her, incredulous. "Or stopped them?" She or Jakob could have hypnotized them to stay away from the room entirely, like he'd done with the tower room in his castle in Blaubart. Lucy had shown in the theater that she was capable of doing such a thing. If they hadn't done that...

She didn't meet my eye. "I gave them an order."

"It is not a matter of orders, Lucille." A hint of irritation crept into Jakob's voice. "Marie's powers can be used against them, just as ours can be. When you said you would keep the servants away from the room, I assumed you understood that."

"Maybe it wasn't the servants. Maybe she found another way out."

Jakob raised a brow. "That is doubtful."

"But not impossible," she challenged, her hands on her hips.

El interrupted. "We'll need to question them either way."

I had no doubts about what we'd find. If Lucy had told the servants to avoid the room, rather than compelling them, then doubtless Marie had lured one of them closer and used them to unchain the door.

"We will question them," Peller agreed, "and we will find whoever betrayed us."

Lucy's eyes narrowed as he turned away. "You won't punish them."

"I will punish whoever needs punishment," he said without looking back.

"Even me?"

His shoulders tensed, and he turned back to her. I dropped my hand to my stake, ready to intervene if things turned violent. I didn't *think* he'd hurt her, but I wouldn't take that chance.

She stared him down. "If you punish them for letting her escape, then you have to do the same to me. I was the one who didn't compel them."

He didn't respond.

"What are you going to do, Jakob?" She took a step toward him. "Are you going to punish me? It's only fair, after all."

His gray eyes turned steely. "I will not lay a hand on you, my sweet Lucille. But your actions have consequences."

She faltered. "What are you going to do?"

I glanced at El. His eyes were wide with shock as he watched his father. Whatever he heard in Jakob's mind wasn't good.

"As I said, I will not lay a hand on you." Without another word, Jakob strode down the hall toward the kitchen.

El swallowed hard, exchanging a worried look with me, as Lucy followed her husband.

The kitchen was bustling, men and women hurrying to and fro. The savory aroma of spinach pie and the clatter of dishes filled the air, but when we entered the room, it all fell silent. My neck prickled with foreboding.

Jakob said a few words in Greek, and the crowd of people parted. A young woman, no older than Lucy, stepped forward, her dark head bowed.

"You let my prisoner escape?"

The girl replied in Greek and dropped to her knees, hands folded in supplication.

"Jakob, please." Lucy grabbed his arm. "It's not her fault."

"No. It is not." But he barked out an order in Greek, and a moment later a man appeared with a long leather strap. The girl trembled as two older women helped strip her top half bare.

My stomach churned. He planned to whip the poor girl. I wanted to say something, to stop him, but when I opened my mouth, El shook his head. He took me by the hand and pulled me close.

"Don't interfere," he breathed.

There wasn't time to ask why. Peller shook Lucy off and stepped behind the girl. He raised his arm and brought the strap down on the girl's back with a resounding *crack*.

Lucy screamed with the girl. She dropped to her knees, begging Peller to stop.

He didn't.

The room was silent but for the snap of the whip, the girl's pained shrieks, and Lucy's sobs. I couldn't breathe, too horrified even to look away.

After ten agonizing strikes, Jakob dropped the strap to the ground. He said something in Greek to another servant, who helped the girl to her feet.

As they shuffled out of the room, Jakob crouched next to Lucy. "It is over now, my Lucille."

Her shoulders shook, and she didn't look up at him. He lifted her into his arms, carrying her like a child.

"Hush," he said gently. "Her injuries will not last long."

"Why would you do that?" she sobbed against his chest. "It was my fault! Not hers."

He cradled her to him. "You had to learn the impact of your actions. I will never lay a hand on you, my bride, but you will not soon forget this lesson. Will you?"

She shook her head, and my gut twisted. How dare he manipulate her like this? I didn't know what to do to stop him. *Do I intervene? Wait until I can get her alone?*

I doubted she'd listen to me even now. He'd beaten a girl to punish her, and still she clung to him for comfort. It was demented. Their whole relationship was demented.

He carried her out of the room, muttering soothing words as though he wasn't the cause of her distress. Once they were gone, the bustle of the kitchen resumed, though somewhat muted now.

"We should go," El said.

"Pardon, *kyríos.*" A gray-haired woman with a dusting of flour on her apron approached us. "You will be eating in the dining room this evening?"

She addressed both of us, but it was El who answered. "We'll eat in our room."

She nodded, turning back to her work.

"I assume you have no objections?" El asked, leading me up the stairs. "I don't particularly feel like spending time with my father just now."

I hated to leave Lucy alone with him, but I didn't want to be around Peller either. He was every bit the demon I'd believed him to be. His affection for my sister, twisted as it was, didn't excuse the rest of his iniquities.

"They won't be coming out for some hours, if his thoughts were any indication." El's face twisted in disgust. "Lucille needs rest."

"Why didn't you let me stop him?"

"I didn't want to see you under the strap instead." He squeezed my hand and gave me an apologetic look. "I'm sorry, *ma guerrière*. I know that was selfish."

"He wouldn't have dared."

"That was his intention if we got in the way."

All the blood drained from my face. Any hint of respect I might have felt for Peller had completely disappeared. "We can't leave her with him." I wouldn't let him continue to hurt my sister. Not when it was my fault she was with him in the first place.

El closed the bedroom door behind us. "We've talked about this, Anne. It's not your fault. She made her own choices."

"Choices I drove her to."

"And ones she's not ready to give up." He shook his head. "Until she sees him for what he is, all you can do is be a steady presence in her life. Let her know you don't blame her and that you'll be there for her if she ever chooses to leave him."

"And what if she never leaves him?" I couldn't imagine how centuries with that monster would change her.

"Then she'll still know you care for her." He kissed me gently. "These things take time. Just keep trying."

Trying to save her. To protect her from her own husband. To set her free. "I will," I vowed. *No matter how long it takes.*

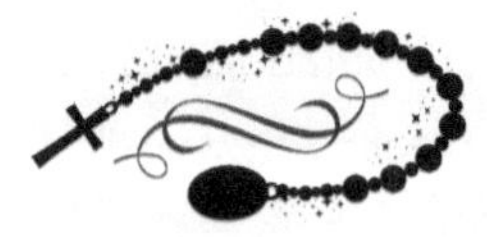

"We have to go after her."

I looked up at Lucy's pronouncement. The four of us sat in the parlor. Lucy was next to Jakob, their hands twined together but her face drawn. The fiasco of that afternoon hadn't drawn her away from him, but it had affected her nonetheless.

"She knows we're onto her now," El said. "She won't fall for a trap like we did before."

Lucy shook her head. "I'm not talking about that. I'm talking about hunting. Like you used to do in Paris." She addressed the last remark to me.

"That was different. It wasn't personal." When Les Gardiens hunted, we hadn't been chasing a fang with a grudge against us. "She's probably already gone into hiding."

"No." Jakob tossed down the newspaper he was reading and nodded at the page. "She fed last night after she escaped." Lucy flinched at the word *escape,* but he went on. "Her victim was in the obituaries. She didn't have time to leave the city."

"She wouldn't want to, anyway," El said. "We didn't end her vendetta, we just brought it out into the open."

Lucy looked between me and Peller. "See? She's still here. We need to take the fight to her. To finish this."

El shrugged. "It wouldn't hurt to try."

I wanted to end this almost as much as Lucy. Whether we'd find anything, I didn't know, but I nodded. "We might as well look."

Jakob moved directly into planning. "I will circle the sky tonight. If the two of you wish to patrol the ground and search for signs of her—"

"What about me?" Lucy cut in.

He raised a brow. "There is no need for you to leave the house, my sweet Lucille. What would you do?"

A storm crossed her face. "I may not have as much experience as you, but that doesn't make me useless."

"Of course not," he soothed. "I only meant that—"

She crossed her arms and glared at him. "You *only meant* to exclude me. I won't have it."

"You will accompany me, my bride." He said it as though there had never been any doubt.

"No. I'll go with Anne. You and *Monsieur* DuMont can search together."

I expected him to refuse, but he caught my eye. I let him see the loathing I felt for him, and the promise that I would do whatever was best for Lucy. Even if that meant ending him.

"Whatever you wish, my Lucille."

An hour later, Lucy and I made an odd pair strolling down the street together. I wore my black shirt and trousers, dressed for hunting with my belt of weapons around my waist. She wore a white evening gown, the back cut scandalously low to provide space for her wings, should she need them. A shawl provided the modesty and warmth she didn't need.

I kept my eyes wide, watching every corner and shadow, but Lucy didn't seem to notice anything. Just another way I'd failed her; she'd been so sheltered, she didn't think about potential threats. It would have been safer to leave her at home, but after the events of the afternoon, she needed the escape. And I was capable of protecting her should we face any attack.

"Have you seen the girl from earlier?" I asked. She stiffened, guilt crossing her face, and I immediately regretted bringing it up.

"No. I didn't think she'd want to see me."

"Why not? You weren't the one who beat her."

"But it was my fault Jakob did it," she said. Her voice was small, defeated.

"No." I stopped and took her by the shoulders. "This was no one's fault but Jakob's. He made his choices. You don't have to feel guilty for what he did."

"He only did it because he needed to show me the consequences of the choice I made. I didn't protect our household. What if, instead of escaping, Marie had killed someone?" She pulled away, shaking her head. "He was right. I need to understand what's at stake."

"You made a choice. That doesn't give him the right to abuse someone to punish you." I sighed and scanned our surroundings. Still no sign of our quarry. "He's manipulating you, Lucy. You deserve better."

"He's protecting me."

She couldn't be that foolish. "No, he's not. He's controlling you."

"You mean like you used to?"

I jerked back as though she'd struck me. "I—"

"No." She crossed her arms. "You're jealous because you're not the one in charge of my life anymore. I'm sorry you don't like my husband, Anne, but I spent too long with you controlling my every move. I've made my own decision, and I won't allow you to keep criticizing him."

"You're being ridiculous." She was as naive as ever—maybe even more than she had been as a child. "I'm not trying to control you. I'm trying to help you see that he doesn't have your best interests at heart."

Wings unfurled from her back, and she gathered her skirt in her hands. "I'm done listening to this. I need to clear my head. I'll meet you at the Parthenon in an hour."

"Lucy, don't." But she lifted into the air. The wind from her wings tugged at my braid and blew dust up into my face.

Fine. If she refused to see reason, there was nothing I could do to help her. I scowled at her silhouette shrinking away in the sky. Eventually she'd realize I was right.

I continued down the street. Lucy might not be interested in catching this fang, but I was. Hopefully El and Jakob were having better luck than us.

A man stepped out of the shadows, hands in his pockets. He was tall and gangly, with a hooked nose. I settled my hand on my gun. A human out for a night of debauchery, or a vampire out for the same?

By the wicked gleam in his eyes when he spotted me, I assumed the latter.

"Stay back," I said, drawing my weapon."

"And lose the chance to face down a Gardien?" He grinned wide enough to show the sharp tips of his fangs. "Why would I do that?"

He knew I was a Gardien. Acrid fear burned my throat, and I wished desperately that I had someone at my back. I could handle a long fang, but if his nest was nearby, or if Marie had sent him, my odds of escaping this encounter weren't good.

"What's a Gardien?"

He laughed, the sound bouncing off the tight walls of the street around us. "You're a terrible liar, little huntress."

"Terrible." An echo of laughter, lower and more gravelly, came from behind me. I swallowed hard, backing into the wall so I could still see the first fang as I glanced at the newcomer, a short, stocky fang. "But delicious, isn't she?"

I fired a round at the first fang's heart, but not fast enough. He dodged, and the bullet lodged into the wall behind him.

"And here I thought Les Gardiens were the greatest hunters in the world," he taunted. "I'm disappointed."

I ignored him and fired again. This one grazed past his shoulder, putting a hole through the fine black jacket he wore.

He grinned. "Closer this time."

His companion, taking advantage of my distraction, came up behind me and tried to grab me by the waist. I twisted, shooting again—three bullets left—but the shot went wide.

The chain around my neck held a fresh vial of holy water. I pulled it off with one hand and splashed it in the fang's face.

He wiped frantically at it, hissing as it burned his eyes and left pink burn marks on his pale skin. I kicked him to the ground and aimed my gun toward his chest. Two bullets left.

As I pulled the trigger, hands closed around my neck. I didn't have time to see if I hit my mark. I lunged forward, leveraging my weight against him.

It almost worked, but something smashed into my knee. I dropped to the ground. The fang grabbed my arms, twisting them behind my back. My gun fell from my hand and clattered onto the street.

"Gardien bitch." Something wet landed on my cheek, and I looked up to see the second fang, the one I'd hit with holy water, glaring down at me. One eye was closed, his whole face swollen from the touch of something sacred.

I remained still, breathing hard as I met his gaze. Letting them think they'd beaten me.

"I'd like to kill you now." He leaned closer until I could smell his half-rotten breath.

"She's not the only one here," his partner said. "Stick to the plan. We'll kill the other hunter when he comes looking for her."

They were after El. My heart stuttered in fear. They were right; he would come looking for me as soon as he realized I was missing. I knew he could handle himself in a fight, but I couldn't watch him be hurt again. Especially not if his mother was involved in this. I had to get away.

"Get up," the injured one ordered. He grabbed me by the shoulder and jerked me to my feet, holding me tight enough to bruise. My knee throbbed, but I didn't resist as they positioned me between them. They each took an arm, and the tall one glanced behind us.

That's when I made my move.

I broke free from their grip and grabbed the stake at my waist. Before they could move, I drove it into the first one's back, straight into his heart. He dropped to the ground, a small gasp the only sound he made as he died.

Jerking the stake free, I turned to the second fang. He wasn't there.

Something struck me over the top of the head, and the world went dark.

28

I awoke in the sky. Wind whipped my face, and rough hands held me tight by the arms. Looking down, I saw the land at a dizzying distance below me, and my stomach rose into my throat. I shouldn't have looked.

The fang's wings beat against the sky, carrying us to an unknown destination. I didn't know where he was taking me, but I had a feeling I'd be better off if he dropped me right now and let my body shatter against the stones below.

His grip was unwavering. I closed my eyes, trying to keep the contents of my stomach from expelling all over the unsuspecting seaside.

After what seemed like forever, he descended, and a fresh wave of nausea went through me as the ground rose up to meet us.

We angled toward a rock face, but instead of slowing, he picked up speed. I closed my eyes, waiting for the inevitable crash.

It never came. When I opened my eyes, darkness surrounded us. I blinked, trying and failing to adjust to the loss of moonlight. Cool, damp air brushed against my skin. We were in some kind of cave.

The fang landed and dropped me onto the stone floor. I searched my surroundings with my hands, feeling damp rock. Definitely a seaside cave.

"You should have let me kill her," the fang said. "She killed Martin."

"You both knew the risks when you joined me."

The voice coming through the gloom turned my blood cold. Marie.

I heard the hiss of a match being struck, and the warm glow of a lamp filled the cave, revealing El's mother among dripping stalactites. She wore her natural body, the small figure and golden hair of Jakob's first wife. "There," she said. "I'm sure you were struggling to see."

I didn't bother to respond. I was too busy scanning the cave for escape routes. The sound of crashing waves came from behind us, through the narrow entrance. The ceiling was low, the room small. Someone had set up a table and three chairs. The fang tossed my belt to Marie, and she snatched it out of the air. I made a quick inventory of the weapons I had as she dropped it on the table. My empty vial of holy water, my stake, my crossbow pistol and bolts...everything but my revolver.

"Is it to your liking?" she asked. Without waiting for my reply, she turned to the fang next to me. "Tie her to a chair, then go back and collect the body before sunrise. We don't need anyone sniffing around."

He dragged me to a chair, disgust evident on his face. With a long coil of rope produced from his pocket, he bound my wrists together behind my back. The legs of the chair dug into my legs as he wrapped the rope tight around them.

When he finished, I tried to shift. There was no chance of sliding free; he'd tied his knots well. He gave me a look of loathing.

"Toss the body into the ocean and come back here," Marie ordered. "You can stay here during the day to guard her in case her partner comes looking."

That was a valuable bit of information: Marie wasn't staying in the cave. Daylight would be my best chance for escape, when I only had one opponent rather than two. If he fell asleep and I managed to get the dagger from my boot, I could free myself and make it to safety before they realized I was missing.

The nameless fang's expression showed his displeasure at the arrangement, but he didn't argue. He stepped back toward the entrance to the cave, and his wings flared. With a rush of wind, he flew away.

Marie tsked. "No manners." Then she turned to me. "But at least we have some time to get to know each other. We haven't been formally introduced. I'm Marie von Peller. You must be Anne."

I kept silent. She could talk all she wanted. The more she said, the more she might let slip.

"I ought to ask you how you ended up with my son, but I really don't care." She hopped onto the table and let her legs dangle over the edge. "I gave up on Azazel long ago. Though I am curious how the two of you found yourselves working with my husband and his whore."

"My sister's not a whore," I snapped. Once the words were out, I immediately regretted them. Everything I said was potential ammunition for her.

"I'll call her what I like." She laughed. "Anyway, we'll be seeing her soon."

My heart stopped. Did she have Lucy?

"We'll be seeing Azazel soon, as well, though that's inconvenient. I'll have to send them proof I have you, and I expect he'll come rushing to your rescue. Pity. It would be easier to have Lucille alone."

The tension in my chest eased. She didn't have Lucy, and Jakob wouldn't let my sister risk herself on some foolish attempt to rescue me.

She tilted her head, considering me. "What shall we send them? An ear is a bit cliche. But hair just doesn't send the right message. It's not threatening enough."

"Why not just send them my head?"

Her laughter filled the room. "And kill my leverage? The point is to draw her here, *ma fille,* not merely to hurt her."

"Jakob won't let you touch her. He'd tear the world apart to protect Lucy."

"The creature who killed his wives and displayed their bodies in a tower? I think you overestimate his affection. Lucille is hardly the first woman he's been obsessed with."

That gave me pause. Was I really putting my faith in a man who'd killed dozens of women, perhaps more?

No, I'd seen the possessive look in his eyes. He was a threat to her—emotionally if not physically—but he wouldn't allow anyone else to be. The fang was trying to mess with my mind, and I couldn't let her. I wouldn't be a weapon for her to use against my sister.

"Lucy won't come alone, and you can't take on the three of them."

"Of course I can." She picked up my stake and touched the point to her finger. "You've already seen I'm not working alone. Your sister is new to this life, untrained and unskilled. She won't pose any danger. I think we can take on Jakob and Azazel without too much difficulty, if need be. But I intend to tell your sister to come alone."

"Jakob won't let her." Of that, I was certain. He'd be happy to never let her out of his sight again.

"Which is why I brought Leonard. It would have been easier had you not killed his brother, but the two of us can manage alone." She grinned, teeth glinting orange in the lamplight. "Look at this cave. A perfect bottleneck, a trap ready to spring shut around them. And you're the bait."

I shuddered at the image that flashed before my eyes. Lucy, Jakob, and El charging blindly into the cave. Marie and her crony ambushing them. The bloodbath that would ensue, leaving the only two people I cared about dead at my feet. I'd be powerless to stop it.

"Ah, yes. I know what to send them." She dropped the stake onto the table and stood. Moving behind me, she dropped to her knees. I could feel her cold breath against my bound hands. "Now. Hold still."

# THE SISTER

"A delivery for you, *kyria*." The girl who brings her the black velvet box doesn't meet her eyes, and her stomach churns. It's the girl Jakob whipped, the one who suffered for her mistake.

"Thank you," Lucille murmurs, taking the box. The girl hurries out of the room.

*Monsieur* DuMont looks up sharply as the girl leaves. His face is drawn, dark bags of worry beneath his eyes. He hasn't slept since she returned without Anne. He went out searching for her missing sister, but all he came back with was Anne's revolver and a scraping of blood. Vampire blood, thank the saints. She doesn't know if the saints listen to the prayers of a vampire, but she thanks them anyway.

"Who is it from?" *Monsieur* DuMont demands.

She turns it over, searching for an address, but it's bare, tied with a simple red ribbon. "I don't know." She unties it and pulls the lid off. A scream tears from her throat.

It's a finger.

Her stomach roils, and she stumbles backward. Jakob catches her, his strong arms a steady comfort.

*Monsieur* DuMont pulls a handkerchief from his pocket and uses it to pick up the disembodied finger. "It's Anne's," he announces, his face pale. "See this patch of white just below the nail? And those look like teeth marks at the bottom. It was bitten off."

Lucille doubles over, gagging. Someone bit off Anne's finger and sent it to her in a box. Who would do such a thing?

"There's a letter." A slight tremor shakes his voice as he reads it. "'Come alone, or the next piece of your sister I send will be larger.' There's a map on the back."

"I have to go," Lucille says, wringing her hands. "I have to help her."

Jakob's grip tightens around her waist. "You will not risk yourself for a *Gardien*."

Heat rises in her cheeks, and she twists to look at him. "She's not a *Gardien*. She's my sister, and I won't let her be hurt just because *your* wife wants revenge on us."

When the words leave her lips, she freezes. He hates when she's disobedient. He whipped a woman for her last offense. What will he do for this?

He gives her a condescending look, one brow raised. "I do not know what you think you can do for her. You cannot fight, and anyone who assists you in going against my wishes, I will kill." He flicks his glance at her sister's lover, the merest suggestion of a warning.

"That's not fair, and you know it." She stomps her foot. "Anne is in danger because of *you.*"

"And if you disobey me, I will kill her myself."

She sets her jaw, meeting his gaze. She loves her husband, but she won't allow him to be the cause of Anne's death. Not when she can stop it.

Dropping her chin, she sighs, pretending defeat. "I can't lose my sister, Jakob."

"I will think on it, my sweet Lucille." He pulls her into his embrace. "If there is a way to rescue her without putting you in danger, I will do it. For you."

She sniffs but doesn't reply. She wishes she could believe him, but by the time he comes up with a solution, Anne could be dead. They have to act now.

Pulling herself from Jakob's touch, she stares at the ground. "I'm going to rest before dinner."

Jakob kisses her cheek. "I will come wake you soon."

As she turns to go, she catches *Monsieur* DuMont's gaze. His eyes hold suspicion, as though he can see what she's planning.

The thought unnerves her, and she hurries out of the room before he can speak to her.

The empty vial burns in her pocket as she takes her seat across from Jakob at dinner. She tries not to stare at him or his glass of wine. *It renders even full vampires unconscious for several hours.* That's what the healer said. One drink, that's all she needs him to take. She just needs him incapacitated long enough for her to rescue her sister.

When the servants dish out roasted leg of lamb, potatoes, and vegetables, she picks at her food. The image of Anne's severed finger is fresh in her mind, and the rich food holds no appeal. Even the thought of fresh blood turns her stomach.

Jakob lifts his cup, and Lucille stops breathing. He takes a drink, swallows, and frowns at the glass. He waves a servant over.

"This wine does not taste right," he says to the man. "Bring a new one."

*Monsieur* DuMont sniffs at his own wine. Lucille does the same, though she knows there's nothing wrong with it.

*Whatever gods or saints might be listening, please let it work.*

As the servant hurries off with the bottle, Jakob wipes his face with the napkin. "Once we have finished eating, we can discuss how best to trap Marie. Now that we know she is looking for you, Lucille, you will not leave my sight."

She pinches her mouth together at that, but she doesn't contradict him. She watches him closely. Is it her imagination, or are his eyes glassy?

"*Monsieur* DuMont—"

"Surely you can call me El." Irritation tinges *Monsieur* DuMont's voice. "You're my father, after all."

"El, then," Jakob concedes. "I assume you intend to remain with us?"

"I *intend* to save Anne. If you can help me do that, I will. But I won't be waiting until my mother sends the rest of her to us in pieces. I'm only here now because I'm waiting until sunrise."

Lucille blanches. Across the table, even Jakob looks pale—though that could be the effects of the potion.

"I do not…" His words come out thick, almost slurred. He frowns down at his plate. "Forgive me."

"Is something wrong, Jakob?" Lucille's voice is a bit too high to be natural, but that can't be helped.

"I feel as though…" He shakes his head and reaches for his water. "The wine…" His hand knocks the glass, spilling water across the table. He slumps forward, and his head lands in the puddle.

Lucille breathes a sigh of relief. She rings for a servant. "Please take the baron to his room. He seems to have overindulged in the wine this evening."

As three young men struggle to carry her husband from the room, Lucille rises to her feet.

"What's wrong with him?" *Monsieur* DuMont asks when they're alone. "And don't tell me it's the wine. He only took one drink."

She crosses her arms. "I'm not waiting around until Marie kills my sister."

"You know it's a trap, right? If you do what she says, my mother will be waiting for you."

Lucille sets her jaw. "I know. That's why you're coming with me."

29

Sweat clung to my back. The stifling heat and humidity of the cave parched my and the stifling heat and humidity of the cave left me parched. The stub of my ring finger stopped bleeding around the time the venom wore off, leaving me with a throbbing pain. The ropes had rubbed my wrists and ankles raw, and my hands were sticky with drying blood.

The fang, Leonard, slept on a cot in the corner of the cave all day. He didn't bother to bring me even so much as a sip of water. Not that I was surprised. I'd killed his brother, after all. He was probably hoping I'd die of thirst.

At the moment, death by dehydration sounded like the least pleasant way to go. Though bleeding out as Marie chopped me to pieces to send to my sister was probably worse.

The sound of waves outside echoed through the cave. Nearby, a steady drip of water counted out each passing second. I tried to ignore the incessant noises, but the pulsing ache in my head and missing finger pounded a drumbeat of insanity into my skull.

I'd watched Marie pack my severed finger into a black velvet box and tie it with a ribbon. Had they received it yet? I could picture Lucy's horror on opening the box. She'd blame herself for letting me get captured, though the blame rested solely on my shoulders.

The longer I waited in the darkness, the more my mistakes plagued me. I should have shot the first fang as soon as he'd mentioned Les Gardiens. I shouldn't have allowed myself to be distracted by my argument with Lucy. I shouldn't have gone hunting without a competent partner.

I knew El would be blaming himself, as well. What was he doing now? Searching for me? He'd probably found the spot I was taken from. Had he seen the bloodstain from where I'd shot the fang? Did he think it was my blood painting the street?

A shuffling sound interrupted my spiraling thoughts. Leonard was awake.

His footsteps neared. "Still alive, Gardien bitch? Enjoy it while you can. It won't last long." He spat a glob of venom at me, and it streaked down my cheek. "I'll be back soon. Don't go anywhere."

He was leaving. My heart picked up speed. I didn't have much time, but this was my chance. Possibly my only chance.

I couldn't see anything, but I didn't need light to know what I was doing. I'd seen enough when we arrived to know where everything was. As soon as I was sure the fang was gone, I began jerking my chair in the direction of the table.

Progress was slow. Every minute or two, I stopped to listen for the return of Marie or Leonard. The movement of my chair jarred my aching head, and I was fairly certain I'd reopened the stump of my missing finger, but I had to keep trying. Marie was trying to use me against the ones I loved; I couldn't sit here as bait in her trap. I had to escape for Lucy and El.

I jerked my body again. The chair lifted up onto two legs, wobbled, and crashed to the ground. My head bounced off the stone floor with a sickening thunk that rattled my teeth and sent pain shooting behind my eyes.

I laid there with my eyes closed, gritting my teeth against the ache. If I survived this, it was going to take weeks to recover.

*If.*

I couldn't stop the tear that slipped out at the thought. What if I never saw El and Lucy again? How long would it take before they forgot me? They were immortal; no matter how much they loved me, they'd forget me eventually.

"No," I said out loud. I couldn't think like that. If I gave up now, I'd never survive. "I can do this."

I'd lost my bearings in the fall. Was the table behind me? To my left?

A faint sound near the entrance of the cave made me freeze. Marie was back, ready to torment me some more. Or Leonard had returned to kill me.

A whisper came through the darkness. "Anne?"

"Lucy?" Cold fear ran down my spine. What was she doing here? Jakob should have stopped her. We agreed on this one thing—that Lucy was to be protected at all costs. What was he thinking, allowing her to come find me? And where was he?

I heard the hiss of a match, and my sister's face appeared in dancing orange light. She lit the lamp on the table to my left and shook out the match.

From my position on the ground, it was hard to make sense of what I was seeing. She wore trousers that were several sizes too big for her, only kept up by the belt. Her white shirt was better suited to a parlor than a filthy cave. She carried a dagger in one hand, and my Saint-Étienne was tucked into her waistband.

"What are you doing here?" I whispered furiously as she set my chair back upright. The movement set my head spinning, and bile rose in my throat. I swallowed it back down, trying to ignore the pain threatening to blind me. "You have to leave!"

"Not without you," she whispered back. She sliced through the bindings around my legs.

"You're late."

My stomach flipped over as Marie stepped out of the shadows in the back of the cave. When had she come back? How long had she been there?

"I was beginning to think you'd abandoned poor Anne," Marie said.

Lucy straightened, mouth twisting in a scowl as she considered the fang. "Never."

"I'm glad you finally came. We have a lot to discuss." Marie took a seat at the table. "Please. Sit."

"I'm not inclined to socialize with someone who wants to kill me," Lucy said. "If you don't mind, I'll take my sister and go home before Jakob realizes I'm missing."

*No. No no no.* My blood turned to ice in my veins. She'd come here alone. What was she thinking? Why hadn't Jakob been watching her? And where was El?

Marie's grin spread across her face. "How delightful. You actually followed my instructions."

She shrugged, pretending nonchalance, though I could see the tension in the set of her jaw. "It was the least I could do, since I came here to kill you."

"You're welcome to try." Marie held her arms out wide.

I saw the hesitation on Lucy's face. *Don't do it.* She couldn't win this. Marie had centuries of experience using her body as a weapon, and Lucy had only had a few short lessons.

Lucy dove across the table with a shriek.

They tumbled to the ground. I jerked at my bindings, pain forgotten in my desperation to get free.

"Anne, thank God." Out of nowhere, El was at my side, and hope fluttered in my chest. He could help Lucy.

He ignored the two vampires and knelt behind me. "Are you hurt?" he asked as he sawed at the rope around my wrists.

"I'm fine." I craned my neck to see Lucy. Marie kicked, and Lucy flew backward, crashing into an enormous stalagmite. She landed in a heap at its base but immediately jumped to her feet. "She's not working alone, El. You have to—"

He soared over my head, landing on the table with a splintering crack.

"El!" I thrashed against my weakened bindings and finally broke free. As I struggled to stand, Leonard came into my view.

"You're mine now, Gardien." He grabbed me by the hair, forcing me to my knees before him. "I'm going to tear your pretty little head off."

My hands shook, but I grabbed the dagger concealed in my boot and drove it upward between his legs.

He released me and stumbled backward, howling in pain.

I staggered toward the ruined table as El climbed to his feet. A bit of blood trickled down his forehead. His eyes held the promise of death, and he clutched my stake in one hand.

"Get out of here, Anne," he said. "We'll be right behind you."

I wasn't going anywhere without him and Lucy, but I didn't have time to say so. He charged at Leonard as I grabbed my belt.

The stump of my finger left a trail of blood on the leather. Drawing my crossbow pistol, I kept one eye on Lucy. She struck at Marie's neck, almost too fast for me to see. A stun, perfectly executed—but Marie anticipated the move. She dodged, grabbing Lucy's arm and twisting it. It snapped, and Lucy let out an ear-piercing scream.

My stomach turned watery at the sound of her agony. My hands shook as I tried to load my crossbow pistol. Too weak. I was too weak to load the bolt. Glancing up, I saw Marie standing over Lucy, a triumphant grin on her face. She was going to kill my sister.

I dropped everything and lurched toward Lucy. I tripped, and the ground rose up to meet me. I flung out my hands before me.

My uninjured hand hit cool metal. My Saint-Étienne. *Please, St. Joan, let it be loaded.* I opened the cylinder, heart in my throat. Only two bullets. *Let it be enough. Guide my bullet.*

Lucy lay on the ground, cradling her injured arm. Marie grabbed her by the collar and lifted her into the air.

"You stole my husband, you little *putain.*" She dragged the nails of her free hand down Lucy's face, and vicious red wounds streaked the skin.

I stood, trembling as I chambered a round. "Marie!" I raised my gun.

She turned toward me, still holding Lucy tight. Her mouth curled in a sneer when she saw me. "You wouldn't dare."

Lucy's one eye—the one not marred by claw marks—widened. She dipped her head in the merest suggestion of a nod.

"I would." I pulled the trigger as Lucy collapsed.

Marie's mouth opened in a wide 'o,' but she didn't have time to react before the bullet struck her in the stomach. She toppled to the ground.

"She's not dead," I warned Lucy as she scrambled to her feet. My sister stopped, turning to the vampire lying on the ground.

Marie wasn't dead, but the silver was doing its work, burning her from the inside out. She held both hands tight over her wound, unable to move as she fixed Lucy with a look of loathing.

I swayed, but El caught me before I could fall. "I have you," he murmured.

"My stake." I leaned into him. "I need my stake." We had to kill the fang before she hurt anyone else. This had to be done. Tonight.

"I know." He pressed the stake into my uninjured hand. The wood was smooth in my hand, worn by the familiarity of touch. I ran my finger along its edge.

Then I held it out to Lucy.

She held her broken arm. Confusion wrinkled her brow. "What?"

"You do it." I'd spent too long trying to protect her. She'd earned the right to defend herself. She'd proven tonight that she was more than capable. "She came after you. You should be the one to kill her."

She stared at me for a moment before her good hand closed around the stake. A steely glint came into her eyes—an executioner's resolve.

Marie snarled when Lucy approached. She tried to scramble back, but with the silver poisoning her blood, she only got as far as the wall. Lucy knelt on top of her, pinning her in place.

"He's my husband now," Lucy hissed, and she drove the stake into Marie's heart.

The fang let out a piercing scream that echoed through the cave. Her face contorted in pain and rage. The light faded from her eyes, but the horrific expression remained. Her body slumped over.

She was gone.

The adrenaline holding me up gave out, and I swayed. El caught me, lifting me up into his arms.

"You're safe, *ma guerrière*. It's over."

*It's over.* We'd all survived it. Not without injuries, but we would heal. I snuggled into El's chest. *It's all over.*

His lips pressed against my forehead as oblivion took me.

"Anne. Anne, we need to go." El shook me awake.

I looked around the unfamiliar room. A hotel? Lamplight revealed rose-colored bedding. It was still night, the open curtains showing a starry sky.

"What's wrong?" I sat up. My head pounded, my missing finger ached, and my stomach churned. Someone had cleaned and wrapped my injured hand while I slept. "Why aren't we at Lucy's house?"

He went to the window, peered out, and snapped the curtains shut. "I thought we had more time. She said she could stall him. Maybe talk him out of it."

"Talk him out of what?" I pushed the blankets off of me. Everything hurt. I'd thought the danger was past. What more was there? "Who are you talking about?"

"Peller. He's coming to kill us."

Fear dragged me from the bed. "Is Lucy okay?"

El grabbed his bag from the chair. "She's fine. A broken arm and some scratches, but she'll be healed in a week." Swinging the bag over his shoulder, he took my face in both his hands. "I'm sorry, Anne. I wish we could stay, but he's coming."

"What—how do you know?"

He nodded at a paper on the bedside table. It bore one word: *Run.*

There wasn't time to talk about it. If Bluebeard was coming after us, we had to go now. I took El's hand, and we raced for the door.

I couldn't breathe as we burst out of the hotel and into the stifling Athens night. I kept one eye on the sky, watching for wings. "Where are we going?" I gasped.

"Anywhere." He pulled me down the street. I was slowing him down with my injuries, but I didn't dare ask him to stop. We couldn't.

A shadow blocked out the moonlight, and a strong hand wrapped around my throat, tearing me from El's grasp.

Peller.

"Let her go, Jakob!" El's voice came from far away. I clawed at Peller's hands, gasping for air. We ascended toward the heavens.

"You've been a thorn in my side since the moment I met your sister," Jakob hissed. His wings beat steadily against the air, holding us high above the street. "Now your foolishness nearly got my bride killed."

"Didn't—" I choked out, but he squeezed tighter.

"I should drag this out. Make you feel the same pain Lucille did." He held out his arm, letting me dangle over the city. I clung to his arm, though I couldn't breathe. If he dropped me, I'd be dead in moments. "But she's alive, so I'll give you the mercy of a quick death." His grip on my throat tightened.

"Jakob!"

Lucy's voice, carried on the wind. The stars around me were fading into shadows.

"Stop this, Jakob." Her words carried an edge I'd never heard before.

The grip on my throat eased. I turned my head and saw Lucy hovering nearby. The wounds where Marie had clawed her face were scabbed over, brutal but healing quickly. Her broken arm had been set and wrapped in a sling. That wasn't what had stopped Jakob, though.

With her good hand, Lucy held a stake to her heart.

"If you kill my sister, you lose me forever."

No one moved. The only sounds were the beating of their wings and the thunder of my heartbeat.

Peller wouldn't let Lucy kill herself. He cared too much for her. He'd let me go.

Wouldn't he?

"Give this up," El called. "Let Anne go, and you'll never have to see us again. But if you kill her, I promise you, it will be the last thing you ever do."

Fury burned in Jakob's eyes as he considered me. Then air rushed past me as he flew toward the ground. A few feet above the street, he dropped me.

El helped me to my feet. "You're okay, *mon amour*. You're okay." He sounded like he was trying to convince himself more than me.

"I want the two of you out of here by the time the sun sets tonight," Peller said as Lucy alighted on the street. He walked toward her with single-minded intent, eyes locked on hers. He grabbed the stake from her and dropped it to the ground, where it landed with a clatter that was too loud in the sudden silence. "If I see either of you again, no one will be able to save you."

"Likewise," El responded as I rubbed my throat, gulping in air.

Lucy took a step toward me, reaching out her hand, but Jakob grabbed her. His fingers dug into her arm. She gave me a sad smile. "Be safe, Anne. I'll write as soon as I can."

"Come with us," I rasped. I couldn't leave her with this monster.

"I can't." Their twisted form of love shone in her eyes as she looked up at her husband. "He's my destiny." She turned her gaze back to me. "But someday—we'll fix this someday."

"Someday," I echoed, though I could feel Jakob's gaze boring into me. As long as he walked the earth, he would always stand between me and Lucy.

His wings flared. "Come," he told Lucy.

"Be careful." Tears stung my eyes as they lifted into the air. "I love you, Lucy."

Her own eyes glistened. "I love you, too."

They soared off into the night, and I sagged against El. He kissed the top of my head as tears streamed down my face.

"I'm sorry, *ma guerrière*. I hoped this would end better."

"I'm fine." I wiped my face with my sleeve, sniffing. "There really wasn't another way things could go." Until Lucy was ready to leave him, he'd always come between us.

"Just keep trying," he said. "One day she'll see him for what he is."

"I hope so."

We stood there holding each other until the stars faded.

"What happens next?" El asked finally.

What next? It was an impossible question. We couldn't stay. I wasn't ready to go back to Paris and face everything I'd left behind. But the whole world lay before us. "I don't suppose I can spend the rest of my life hunting vampires, can I?"

"You could. They're not all as conscientious as your sister." He shrugged. "But a little variety might be nice."

I frowned. "Variety?"

"Oh, Legs." He grinned at me. "You didn't think vampires and witches were all there were, did you? Les Gardiens kept you too sheltered."

The thought sent a thrill of anticipation through me. A whole world of excitement, and there was nothing to stop me from facing it. I could spend the rest of my life hunting it down.

"Maybe I'll let you show me what the underworld is like, then." I pressed my lips to his.

"Or maybe I'll let you tag along," he murmured into my kiss.

I melted into his touch. The past few days had been hell, but we were safe. The danger wasn't over, but whatever came next, we would face it.

Together.

# ACKNOWLEDGEMENTS

Mom: I planned on writing this book for you long before you started complaining that I'd never dedicated a book to you. I know you don't like vampires. Or smut. Or violence. Or darkness. But after thirty years of being my mother, you knew there really wasn't another way this could go, and I chose the settings in this book because I knew you would love them. So…I'm sorry, and you're welcome?

Harmony, thank you for taking my little goblin trash and turning it into marketable treasure. I'd be floundering in the sea of self-publishing if it weren't for you. This book, like everything I write, only exists because of your love and support.

Courtney, thank you for your patience with all my questions about Europe. Your descriptions gave life to Anne and El's travels.

Amelia Cognet, thank you for answering all my un-Google-able questions about the French language. El's dirty talk and sweet nothings are all dedicated to you.

To my beta readers, Sarah, Curtis, and Kelly: You polished up this story until it shone. I loved reading your notes, and I'm so grateful for all your help.

To my family: Andrew, you went above and beyond to give me time and support to write. I couldn't have done it without you. Delanie, I swear I didn't write this book about trying to kill you, and Keaghn, I like you much better than Anne likes her brother-in-law. Aunt Ammy, thank you for caring and encouraging—and for pestering me for more vampire smut. Dad, Dyami, and Dalton, I still don't believe you're going to read this, so you get nothing! You lose! Good day, sir!

Finally, to my readers: You are the reason I write. May you find strength like Anne, love like El, and conviction like Lucy.

# ABOUT THE AUTHOR

Dakotah Gumm is a fantasy romance author living in the beautiful Missouri Ozarks. *Hunting Lucille,* follows her debut novella, *Lucille: a Bluebeard Retelling.* When she's not busy writing or homeschooling her two kids, she's usually found curled up with a cup of coffee and a good book or dancing to showtunes in her kitchen. She also writes children's books under the penname Dakotah Pike to use as a decoy when her kids ask her what she's writing.

To find out more about Dakotah, check out her website at dakot ahgumm.com.